RAYNA'S SACRIFICE

The Katori Chronicles
Book 3

A. D. Lombardo

BOOKS BY A. D. LOMBARDO

The Katori Chronicles:

The Half-Light

Mariana's Secret

Rayna's Sacrifice

Rayna's Sacrifice

The Katori Chronicles Book 3
A. D. Lombardo

Published by Nichols INK

ISBN (Paperback): 978-1-7333376-4-9

Cover design by A. D. Lombardo
First Edition 2020

www.ADLombardo.com

I dedicate this book to my son Connor,
his joy of reading and enthusiasm for my work,
changed my life.

ACKNOWLEDGMENTS

There were so many people instrumental in creating book three. Each of you, and you know who you are, gave me a little bit of yourselves when I needed it most. You encouraged me to keep going through significant changes that broke this book in half.

I remember being thrilled with my original manuscript and eagerly awaited news from my editor, Keith. I was sure it would only need a few adjustments here and there before it would be perfect. When I received my first round of edits, I can honestly say I was speechless.

His comments were positive, glowing even, then I reached the third chapter of the book. From there, the typical suggestions began—enhance this and cut that. When I neared the middle of the book, I sank in my seat. Let me sum up the rest of his edits with this idea.

Imagine asking a professional landscaper to tidy your yard with pruning shears and a weed-whacker. Only to come home and find he took a machete and a backhoe to everything.

My husband's response. "Hey, the guy is putting in a pool. Go with it!"

Once I took a two-day breather, I eased into his suggestions, and I began again. With a new purpose for the story, I changed the name and resubmitted it. Because of Keith, this story became something new—something better. Thank you.

As always, I must thank my son, Connor, for his encouragement and willingness to read and reread at a moment's notice. A big thank you to my devoted husband; I don't know where I would be without you. We have juggled so much over the past six months. I am happy I was holding your hand through it all.

Special thanks to my family and friends for your continued support. And last but not least, thank you, Buddy, for keeping me company at four in the morning.

CONTENTS

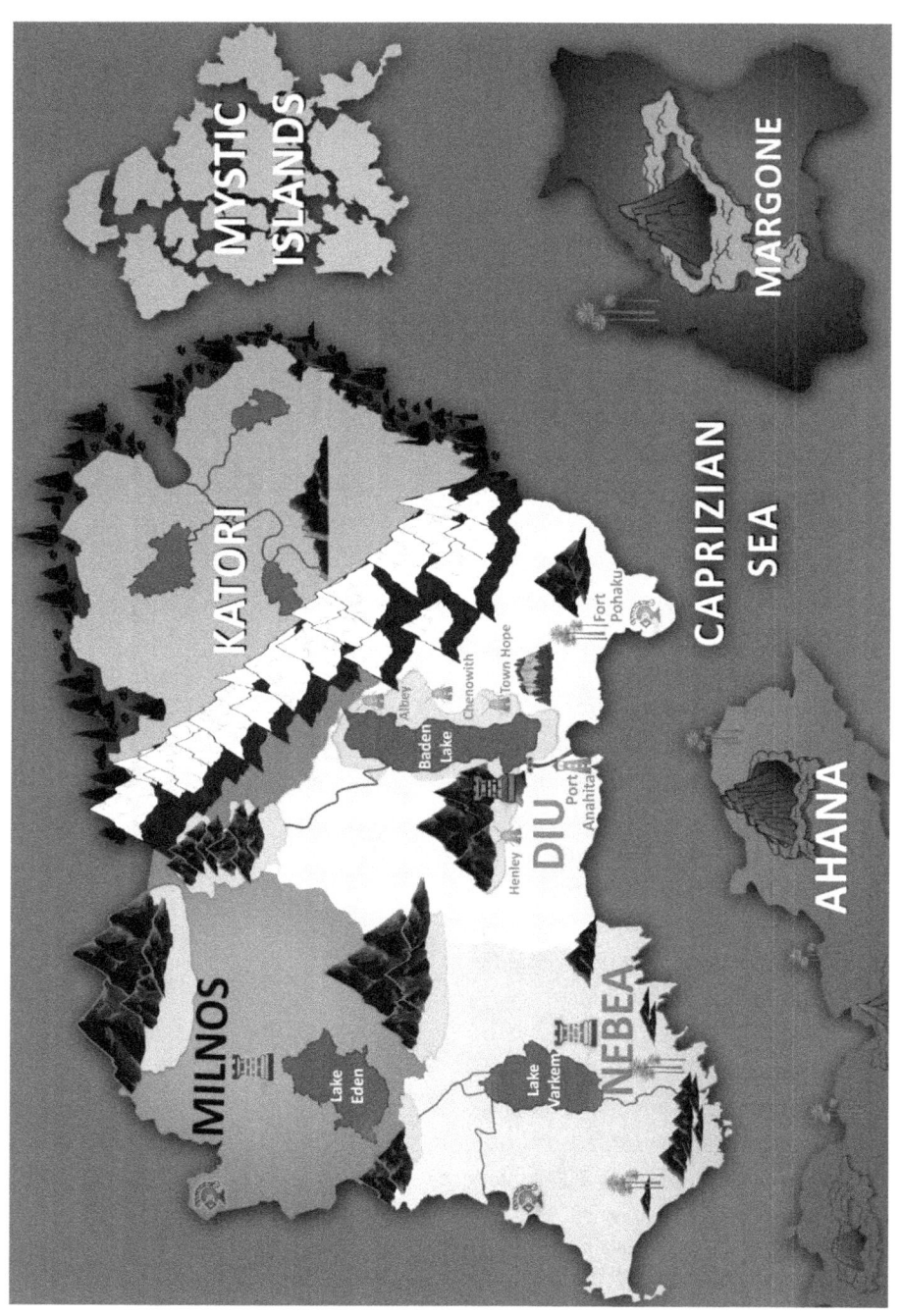

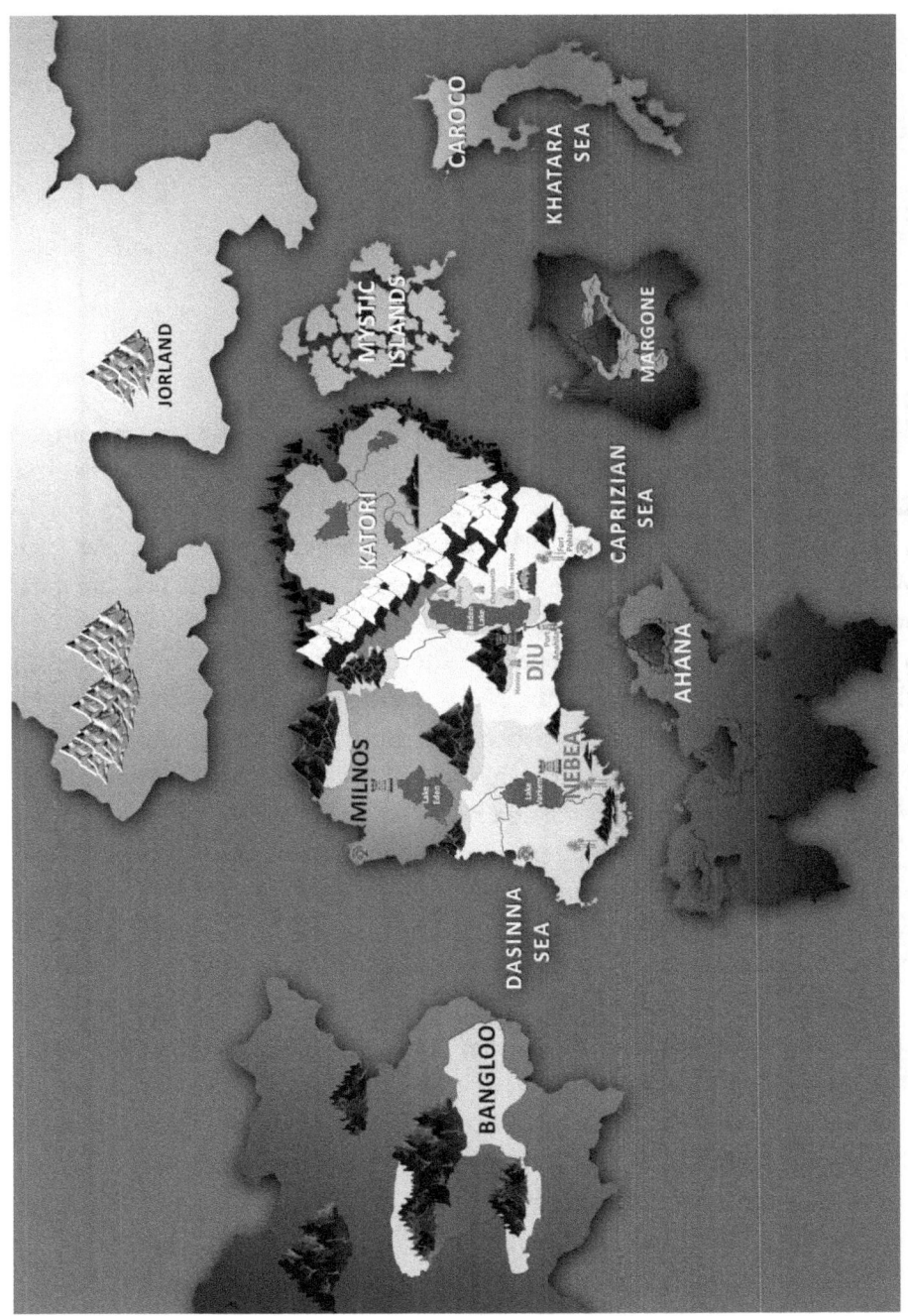

PROLGUE

Keegan's reflection danced upon the waves as he cast an angry glance across the sea. His gaze narrowed on the horizon behind his ship. The plumes of smoke from Port Anahita were barely visible in the fading light. The evening breeze and his crew, the Weathervanes, set a quick pace. The wake of his vessel churned the dark waves of the Caprizian Sea.

"You anger me, boy," Keegan seethed under his breath. "Defending those weaklings is beneath us. Mere average humans with no magic. They are nothing but vermin beneath my boot. I could have crushed Iver's heart with the death of his sister. He will pay for the loss of Mariana. Don't get in my way again."

Arjun, a young Beastmaster, approached. "We are down to one ship, Keegan." He stated, interrupting his leader's contemplation. "Attacking Iver seems a waste of time as is chasing this boy. Do we limp home to Caroco?" He looked to the others for support.

The nearby Caroco sailors glanced around, nervous in the presence of all these powerful Katori. The other Katori warriors held their breath. Rage brewed in Keegan's eyes. "How dare you imply we were defeated!" In a flash, he was on Arjun. His grasp held the man's life in the balance. Every part of him wanted to kill this man for his implications, yet Katori warriors were in limited supply. "That *boy*—is my son. Prince Kai. One always knows their own flesh and blood."

"What use is a boy without his powers?" Padar, a nearby Weathervane, asked. "It is plain to see. If we take the prince now, he will never be allowed to collect a crystal or gain access to Alenga's sacred pool. He will have no magic."

Like it or not, Padar was right. Without magic, Kai would be useless. Keegan closed his fist around his own crystal; it was black as night and filled with hate. He knew that since the dawn of time, the Katori needed the crystals to control the power written into their design. Without them, the Katori's powers were greatly limited. "We must be patient," Keegan mumbled, his stone pressed against his lips.

"I say we need more men, disposable Caroco men," Padar suggested. "Should we not attack again? We did hurt them."

A Kodama man clutched his green crystal and elbowed the woman beside him. "Should we Katori not join in the fight? They would be no match for us."

The Kodama woman at his side swept her long brown hair over one shoulder and nodded in agreement. "It is time the world felt our might."

Contempt tightened the corner of Keegan's lips. "I underestimated Iver's people. Killing his sister would have been a mighty blow to the Diu king, but this substance they used to destroy our ships thwarted my plans—to say nothing of what Kai has done. Make no mistake, my son is worth our pursuit."

"So, do we venture home for reinforcements?" the Kodama woman asked.

"No!" Keegan barked. "Do you not see it? The boy—his age. He is ripe. I can feel it. The Conhaspriga is upon him, Alenga will call him soon. If he has the power to light up the world before his blessing, imagine how powerful he will become." A flush of electricity rolled down Keegan's spine at the memory. His son had sent his mind around the world in a wave of Katori magic. Kai was more powerful than he knew, and the possibility of controlling this boy elated Keegan. Was it possible Kai had even more power than Mariana?

The more Keegan thought about what Kai had done, the more he believed that his son was the key to his reign. "It won't even matter what discipline he develops—Beastmaster, Kodama, Stoneking, it makes no difference. The depth of his magic, once he acquires his full power, will make us unstoppable. With him by my side, I will easily convert other young Katori to our cause. Our numbers will grow. Mariana was meant to stand at my side, but our son will serve the same purpose. Once we have him, I will take control of Katori, and Alenga's crystal mountain will be ours. The sacred pools will empower our soldiers and bless our noble cause. I will rule this world."

Bowing slightly, another Beastmaster stepped into the conversation. "No disrespect, sir, but what about Lucca and his elders? You challenged them once, but the Lumens are unbeatable."

The very mention of Kai's grandfather's name twisted Keegan's face. "Mariana was capable of stopping them. She saved my life in the Agora when the Lumens tried to kill me. Her love of all life saved me and our cause. The very idea that this boy could have her power means we must acquire him quickly before they fill his head with their peaceful ideals. We need access to Alenga's mountain, and we must control who has access to the Agora. Obtaining my son is our priority. I cannot rule this world without his powers."

The group nodded in agreement. Meanwhile, Keegan searched the skies for his next move, all but his Weathervanes left the upper deck. If he was to capture his son, he would need to be swift. He could not risk letting Kai understand how to use his magic against him before he could turn his son to his side.

With a decision made, he turned to his men. "Sail to Margone. It is out of our way, but we need men and supplies. Caroco ships are working on the far side. Then when we sail around the Mystic Islands to our forgotten Katori brethren on the mainland."

The Weathervanes nodded with understanding and set to change the ship's direction.

Alone with his thoughts, Keegan once again watched the wake of his ship churn the dark waves of the Caprizian Sea. Years of anger boiled in his veins. His white-knuckle grip held fast to the railing. He hated the elders and their rules.

"My dear boy, your mother should not have run from me. She would be alive today if she'd stayed by my side. How cruel the Katori elders were to have killed her and abandoned you. They must think you a Half-Light, but I know the truth. And if I cannot have Mariana—you will be my weapon. I will use her death to turn you against them. They must see reason—we do not belong in hiding. Magic makes us superior."

CHAPTER 1

Stormy Weather

Dawn's golden light burned across the clear sky. Baden Lake gleamed with promise. Prince Kai held Rayna's hand; her feverish skin matched his own. While everyone on board believed they sailed to find a cure for their prince and his mysterious fever, he knew this trip was so much more. Their Katori blood beckoned them home. This birthright would seal their gifts and expand their magic.

The *Dragaron* sailed swiftly, its white canvas sails angled to catch the morning breeze. Grand Duke Dante's cutter was known for its incredible speed. Her bow cut decisively across the water, leaving shattered waves in its wake.

Behind them, Diu city was a soft white blur on the fading landscape. Ahead, as far as the eye could see, dark blue ripples playfully bounced up at the sky. Squinting, Kai noticed a few gray-green specs forming on the horizon. Islands. Three of them.

The captain and his crew eagerly scurried about—each offered Kai a silent nod, mutual respect passing between them. Kai had earned their admiration. Dante's precious vessel was not for joyriding. Given they were practically stealing the ship without permission, he was thankful they were willing to come to his aid without question. He could only hope Dante would forgive him, and the captain, once the ship returned safe and sound. After all, the captain was helping the prince of Diu—how could Dante be angry?

His heart panged at the thought of home. Diu was becoming a distant memory, lost behind in the waves. He stopped looking back. Focused on his future, he resolved himself to face his destiny in Katori. The sadness left Kai as he watched Rayna lean her head towards Yulia. He was fortunate that Yulia traveled with them. Even the captain looked pleased that she was on board. He heard the captain say it was good luck to have a Katori sail with you.

Yulia gently rubbed Rayna's arm and whispered in her ear. Once again, Yulia's youthful appearance puzzled him. She did not look old enough to be the mother of Riome. How did she maintain her beauty? She bore no gray hairs, no wrinkles. Not one sign of age dotted her skin.

Overhead a shadow rippled across the sky. High above a massive eagle flew, and Kai knew by its size it was a Katori Beastmaster. Whom, he did not know. But its trajectory meant it had come from Diu City. Moments later, another great eagle passed overhead. Based on its course and the golden tipped wings, Kai knew it was Sabastian, his friend and ally. The second bird flew on an intercept course after the first.

Sabastian swooped higher. In midair, the lower bird rolled, and Sabastian collided, locking talons with the first bird. The pair spiraled downward. Kai feared for Sabastian. Neither bird let go. Nervous, Kai tightened his grip on Rayna's hand.

"What's happening?" Rayna asked, squeezing Kai's hand in concern.

"The golden tipped eagle is Sabastian," Kai said heavily, watching the aerial battle unfold. "Kendra's husband."

Locked together, the eagles plummeted. Then, perilously close to the water, they broke free. Each bird struggled to regain height over the other. Sabastian, the larger of the two, pulled a few feet higher and dove. His sharp talons latched onto the other bird's wings. Screeches echoed on the wind.

Everyone on the *Dragaron* eagerly watched the fight unfold. The crew insisted it was a territory dispute—Kai knew differently. Still, the men cheered. It wasn't every day they saw such a spectacle. The first bird flipped its claws upward, desperate to grab Sabastian. Kai kept a keen eye on Sabastian's wingtips—it was the only way to tell friend from foe.

Golden feathers ripped from Sabastian's outstretched wing, and Rayna gasped. Sabastian struggled to fly. The pair dropped. Sabastian pecked at the other bird's head. His talons ripped out feathers, and he let go of the other bird. In a blur of blood and feathers, it crashed into the distant waves. Helpless, it flapped and sunk beneath the whitecaps of Baden Lake.

Kai almost felt bad—then he saw two more eagles pass overhead. Sabastian flew after them in pursuit, and all three disappeared into the bright sky.

Yulia whispered into his ear. "If those two make it, they would surely warn the elders you're coming. They aim to stop you." Her fierce look reminded Kai of Riome.

The elders' desperation to keep him away was puzzling. Power and fear. One or the other. His birth father, Keegan, was said to be power-hungry and cruel. Did they judge him for his father's actions, a man Kai had never known? Mariana, his mother, was kind and loving. Would they not give him a chance to show his own nature based on her? What of his grandfather, Chief Lucca? Did he also want to keep Kai away?

Either way, Kai knew Yulia was correct. The Katori people meant to stop him from completing the Conhaspriga, his right of passage. They intended to keep him from his birthright and his power. For that alone, he would see this through. He meant to prove he was his own man—he would not be defined by their fears of Keegan.

What mattered most was saving his mother, and he believed finding her would take magic. If he did not make it to Katori in time, he would lose everything—both his power and a chance to return her to her natural form.

Around his neck, his mother's necklace reminded him that he had the one element the others never had during their search. With her crystal, he was sure to track his mother and bring her home before her mind was lost forever.

Hours of pleasant winds and smooth sailing lulled everyone into finding a comfortable corner to relax. The graceful movement from Yulia generated a low-level wind to enhance their progress. The crew remained steadfast at their stations. Smoke, his beloved wolf, sat at attention near the mast. Kempery-men Redmon and Albey leaned against the railing while Drew and Dresnor stood conversing at the stern of the vessel. Kai hated lying to his men. They believed they were on a quest for a cure for him and Rayna. He had convinced them Rayna discovered a plant that grows in the Katori Mountains that would stave off their fevers.

Yulia noticed it first—looming black clouds rolled in their direction. Thunder rumbled and lightning charged across the sky. The hair on Kai's arms and neck tingled with energy. Power rolled on the wind. The unnatural storm aimed straight for them.

Rayna's keen eyes focused on the developing thunderclouds. "Should we turn back?" she asked, gripping his arm. "Or take cover on one of the islands?"

"You know we cannot." Kai pulled her close. "We've come too far. The captain has two choices. Moor the ship against one of those islands and wait this out, or charge ahead and keep us in open waters."

The captain quickly shouted orders, and the crew rushed to change the large sails to sleek ones ideal in windy weather. Instantly, Kai knew the strategy was to survive the storm. "We will be fine. The captain is making preparations. Smaller sails will give him more control. The thicker material has less risk of tearing. Even now, he steers us into the waves. Trust the captain, he will keep the ship away from danger. He knows we are already too far out to turn around. Our only option is to sail through the storm. Dante's ship can take it."

Wind gusts stirred the waves and whipped the men changing the sails. Engorged waves surged all around, and the ominous storm charged towards them. Twenty-foot swells pounded the ship. Rain began to pour from the black clouds. Lightning ripped open the sky, a momentary flash of light. Hail bombarded the ship deck. Kai sent Smoke for cover, and

Dresnor quickly ushered everyone below. Only the captain and his crew stayed above.

Below decks, everyone grabbed timbers to secure their footing and keep from being tossed about the ship's hull. Kai ushered Rayna into the captain's cabin. He steadied her as she grabbed for the captain's desk. Her expression matched the turmoil in his own mind.

Wave after wave battered against the *Dragaron*. Lightning cracked the sky, the dark windows along the hull of the ship flashed. Kai looked out a small window and held fast as the vessel rocked and rolled. One glance at Rayna, and he could see the fear on her face. Wanting to believe everything was fine, Kai rubbed her shoulders, but a small part of him wondered if they were in trouble.

"Kai, this weather is not natural," Rayna called over the storm. "I have lived through hurricanes at the beach. This storm is too intense, too sudden. How is this possible?" Her eyes wrapped around an idea. "Weathervanes. They stand against us. Why?"

With a finger to his lips, he acknowledged her concern. Why indeed? If only he knew the answer, but she was right. This was no natural storm.

Kai searched his group; Yulia was not below. "Yulia must still be on deck. I have to help her!" he yelled over the thunder cracking the sky. "Stay here!" He crossed the cabin and reached for the doorknob.

The cabin's door opened, and Dresnor entered, soaking wet. "Kai, where are you going? Stay below."

"I can help Yulia. Trust me, Philip. She needs my help." He gave his Kempery-man a glare.

Dresnor grabbed Kai. "Either we both go, or I must insist you stay here."

There was no time to argue. "Fine, see if you can get the rest of the crew to come below. You can operate the helm. The fewer people above, the better." With a nod, they plunged into the rain.

Kai and Dresnor climbed the stairs as rain pelted their faces. Halfway, Rayna's hand locked with Kai's. "I want to help," she insisted, stepping to his side.

"Go back below, where it's safe," he yelled over the howling winds.

Rayna charged ahead of him into the storm. Fearful, Kai chased after her. "Rayna," he called, but she did not stop.

Dresnor made for the captain and his crew, but each man refused to go below. He approached the captain, but the captain's white-knuckle grip held fast to the helm. Dresnor grabbed the captain by his coat and pulled their faces together. The storm swallowed the sound of his voice. Shocked, Kai stepped in their direction. Dresnor released the captain, pointed, and took the helm. The captain and his crew scampered below.

Kai turned his attention to Rayna. He reached for her, but before he could protest, Yulia motioned to him. Yulia stood near the center of the vessel, water dripping from her face. Her movements were familiar. He had seen her perform them once before. He did not need to glean to know she was collecting energy, folding and shaping it with her hands, directing it upward against the storm. He surmised that she was forming a weak windbreak around the mast.

Whipped by the ferocious storm, the foresails tore from the rigging and flapped violently in the wind. The *Dragaron* sat dead in the water. Lightning pierced the sky, and thunder pounded.

Yulia yelled to Kai, "You know these movements. Riome taught them to you. Repeat them. Work one sequence behind my moves." While she spoke, she continued the movements. "See the energy within the storm. Collect the energy, pull it from the storm, and push it to me."

In their hesitation, Yulia called out again. "I cannot stop this storm, but we can use it. See the energy in the storm. Feel it. Draw it out of the sky. Use their power. Trust me. Each of us draws on the same essence. Magic surrounds us—you need only to take it from this storm. Weaken the storm. I will convert it and feed the windbreak around us."

Kai took a deep breath and connected to his sight. He could see the energy Yulia collected from the black cloud. A small waterfall of light fell from the storm and splashed around her. In her hands, she converted the raw power. Magic she could control to protect the ship.

Kai pulled Rayna's face to his. "Do as I do," he instructed.

He took his stance. Rain, wind, and waves threatened his footing. Yulia's small windbreak barely protected the mainmast and the remaining sails. He stepped closer to Yulia and felt the wind and rain slacken. The small protective sphere extended to Rayna and himself.

Focused on the dark mass thundering above, Kai reached out with his mind. The pulse within the storm rolled against him. He called out to Rayna. "Glean, connect to the energy within the storm. Feel its power. Draw it to you."

Kai thought of the many lessons with Riome. How energizing the room often felt when they trained. As he pulled at the storm, he felt the power wash over him; then, he pushed the energy to Yulia. The loss felt hollow. The empty void drained him. Again he cycled through the movements. His movements recharged by a waterfall of magic pouring down from the storm.

Rayna copied his movements. After a few repeated moves, he noticed Rayna had grasped the pattern. Her body flowed in unison with his. Her precision behind each action impressed him. She was a natural. He looked to the storm—while neither of them could convert the energy, he saw they were affecting the intensity of the squall. The clouds above them began to thin and lighten.

Yulia used the increased power that Kai and Rayna sent her to create a more substantial windbreak around the ship. Struck with the occasional gust and pricked by rain, Kai felt hope that the boat would survive—they would survive.

But surviving wasn't good enough. "Yulia," Kai shouted over the pounding thunder and lightning crackle. "We cannot stay here! You must find a way to feed the sails and get us to land. If you give out, we are doomed."

Wave after wave continued to pound the hull. Dresnor looked on in awe at the change in weather around the ship. Still, Dresnor held them steady. Yulia slid back behind the mast. Her movements changed slightly. The windbreak around the vessel shrank, but the sails swelled, and the *Dragaron* lurched forward. They were moving again.

Kai and Rayna continued to weaken the storm above them. Their energy supported Yulia's efforts. Wind and rain clawed at each of them. At the stern of the ship, Kai saw Dresnor was unprotected from the storm. The rage-fueled storm pelted his Kempery-man, and yet, Dresnor held fast. He kept one hand on the tiller and used the other to protect his body from the hail with his heavy shield.

Waves continued to ravage the ship. Yulia's decision to focus her power on the sails reduced their protection. Waves slapped the deck, and Rayna lost her footing. The surge washed her towards the railing. Kai dove after her, but a second wave knocked him to his knees. Water splashed over him as he scrambled to grab Rayna.

He watched helplessly as she tried to stand. The next wave slammed her to the deck and washed her out of reach. He called to her, but she was unconscious—her limp form pressed against the railing. Blood trickled down her cheek. Frantic, he ran to her side. He felt the ship reduce speed. The wind around him lulled, and Kai rolled Rayna to her side. She coughed. Water spewed from her mouth. She was alive.

He tenderly wiped the blood from the cut on her cheek. "Let me take you below."

She shook her head. "No, we need to help Yulia. I will be alright."

Suddenly aware of the calm around them, Kai looked to the sky. Once again, the storm rolled black over them. Yulia kept the weather at bay, but they were again motionless in the water. Ripped in two, another sail flapped in the wind. Yulia's movements barely protected the mainmast. Her focus had shifted to protect Rayna.

Kai pulled Rayna to her feet, and they rejoined Yulia. Once again, the ship lurched into motion. They were not streaking across the waves as before, but the windbreak Yulia created protected them from the surge. The storm clouds continued to dump heavy rain. The howling wind pushed against the *Dragaron*. Hail again pelted the ship. Lightning cracked the sky.

Hours passed, and there was no sign of the shore or the weather easing. Kai wondered how much longer they could hold out. They were exhausted. He felt his strength wane. Rayna's movements were sluggish; tears welled in her eyes. Even Dresnor was slumped by the tiller. Everyone was exhausted. The push-and-pull of magic made Kai very weary.

Yulia's focus, however, was unyielding. She pulled, folded, and pushed the energy, ever resilient as she worked. Rain poured from above, the wind stirred the waves and whipped against them. Thunder and lightning pierced the black sky. Renewed by Yulia's commitment, Kai continued to pull the energy from the storm. Their only chance was to push onward.

Off the port side, far in the distance, Kai saw a shaft of light break through the storm. Unsure what to make of the weather change, he dared not stop. He continued to draw power from the storm looming above the ship. Then another ray of sunshine burned through the clouds, and more and more light poured through. The wild weather shifted in a wave across the sky. The black clouds crumbled away and slowly dispersed altogether.

Relieved, Rayna dropped her arms. Kai stepped to hold her upright. Yulia refocused all of her energy at the remaining sails. The *Dragaron* surged forward with astounding speed. Dresnor stood tall and cleared the water from his face and beard. He dropped his shield at his feet.

The waves started to recede, and the ship cut through the water of Baden Lake once more. Kai and Rayna stepped forward. The early evening sun kissed their faces and the wind blew against their soaked clothing. They were saved. He wrapped an arm around Rayna's waist and pulled her close. A thin dark line cut into the horizon. They were close to land.

"Yulia, you can stop. Look, I can see land." Kai gestured.

Yulia did not stop. She worked harder. Their speed increased. The prow of the ship rose out of the water. Rayna stumbled. Kai caught her elbow and steadied her. Concerned, Kai looked to Dresnor.

"Make her stop," Dresnor called. "We are close enough. Quick before she crashes the ship or the crew comes up." He gestured at the hatch.

It was enough that Dresnor witnessed everything. The ship's incredible speed. Yulia controlling the wind. No one knew that Yulia was a Weathervane. While the crew may be thankful for her help, they would also whisper that she was a witch or some other fanciful creature.

"Yulia," Kai pleaded, "you must stop. The crew, they will see you. The storm is gone."

In front of them, the horizon began to take shape. The thin line became lumpy and green. Out of the corner of one eye, Kai saw the hatch door rise. There was no time to wait for Yulia to comply. Kai grabbed her hands. "Yulia!" He startled himself with the violence of his tone.

Alarmed, Yulia stared half-crazy into Kai's eyes. "Sorry, I...I couldn't. If the storm returned, we needed to be closer to shore. Why did they stop?" she whispered, mostly to herself.

The sails sagged, and the ship sloshed down into the tiny waves. Only the faintest breeze remained. Grunts echoed from the hatch as men spilled out into the fresh air. The captain eyed Dresnor. "I see my ship is still in one piece." He glanced across to Kai and his group. "I won't ask what you did, nor tell what I believe. Now, Your Highness, let's see if I can deliver you safely north of Albey." The captain gave them a slight nod and took the helm.

Dresnor nodded to the captain. Kai escorted Rayna and Yulia below, leaving his men behind. Satisfied they were in good hands, Kai took them to the captain's quarters.

Yulia wasted no time stating the obvious. "Well, it is pretty obvious to me that the elders don't want you to make it to Katori, Kai. To create a storm so intense, the Katori must have a dozen Weathervanes, maybe more."

"I agree. But if that is true, why did the storm stop?" Kai rubbed his sore shoulders, each one in turn.

Before Yulia could answer, Dresnor entered the cabin. He slumped down into one of the chairs secured against the wall. "You mind explaining what in Alenga's name just happened?"

No logical explanation would satisfy his friend. Kai knew they were not permitted to tell Dresnor the truth. Plus, if he knew the Katori people fought against them, Dresnor would not let them continue. His friend had no idea what was at stake. Kai and Rayna had little time left before their fever consumed their power. They needed to complete their journey.

Yulia leaned against the desk and eyed Dresnor. "We prayed to Alenga for her mercy. Our steadfast faith saved us."

Dresnor scoffed. "You don't honestly expect me to believe that was Katori luck and prayer?"

Yulia turned away to gaze out the window. Dresnor looked to Kai, who only offered a shrug before slumping into a chair by Rayna to rest for the remainder of their journey.

CHAPTER 2

Old Friends

Their ship made landfall on the eastern shore north of Albey. Pale gray clouds dotted the dusky sky. Light rain danced on their shoulders—a natural shower, peaceful and calm. Soaked once again to the bone, Kai helped Rayna into a small rowboat. Dresnor, Drew, Redmond, and Albey climbed in beside him, and the two crewmen rowed deep into the secluded cove. Near the mouth of the Conha River, Kai pointed. "We should get out there. Find a clearing to make a suitable campsite."

Once on shore, Kai thanked the crewmen, and they returned to the ship with the rowboat. Each Kempery-man hefted a bag of supplies. When they finally sat around a warm fire, everyone was silent. They were merely relieved to be safe on dry land.

Exhausted and caught in thought, Kai's focus was not on point. He barely noticed the man approach them through the thicket before Smoke growled. Drew and Redmon circled the fire. Their eyes focused into the woods, swords at the ready. Kai searched the trees. The corner of his mouth curled; he knew the man that waited obscured by the darkness.

Kai stepped in front of his men. "Davi. You may approach," he called into the early evening shadows.

Davi stepped out from the gloom. "Kai, I'm pleased to see you. May we speak, in private?" He nodded and disappeared back the way he came.

Before Dresnor could protest, Kai faced the group. "Davi is a good man. He is Katori and a friend of Haygan's. I met him last summer. I trust him with my life. Rayna, Yulia, please come with me. Please, Philip. I need to speak to him alone. He may be able to help us find the herb Rayna needs for our cure—or know who can. Mountain Katori people are not fond of strangers. We will be back at dawn." Kai tapped his leg, and Smoke followed.

Dresnor opened his mouth, but no words came out. He relented with a nod and stepped backward. The other men began to protest, but Dresnor held up his hand. Mouth pursed in a thin line, he approached the newly built fire that Drew stoked.

Guilt about the lie stuck in Kai's throat as he ventured into the woods after Davi. Rayna held his hand, and Yulia brought up the rear. Behind them, he could hear voices. His Kempery-men commiserated about the storm and their seasickness, but Dresnor spoke no words. Kai felt bad excluding him, but he could not possibly explain where they were going or whom they would meet. Dresnor had already seen more than he should.

Deep into the forest, Davi waited. Gabe and Hale, two of the other Katori outcasts that Kai had met last year, stood with him. "It has been too long, Kai," Davi extended his hand. "Good to see you and yours survived the storm." Davi tucked a section of gray hair behind his ear. "Yulia, I am glad you were with him."

Stunned, Kai looked over his shoulder. "You know each other?"

Yulia chuckled. "Kai, like my daughter, I know everyone. I go everywhere. Where do you think Riome gets her wanderlust?" She smiled and stepped around Kai. "Where are the others?"

"Safe," Davi announced. "We have a makeshift camp a few miles from here. It was good you sent word. Sabastian is with us."

Silently they tramped through the woods. Kai's mind filled with questions. He pushed a query at Davi's back. "Last summer, when I came to your camp, did you know who I was?"

"You mean, did I know you were a Half-Light? That you were the Prince of Diu? Or did I know you were Mariana's son? Possibly Keegan's son?" Davi chuckled to himself.

The details Davi knew astonished Kai.

"No, Kai," Davi stepped over a felled tree. "Yulia came after you. She thinks the world of you, in case you didn't know. She came with news of the Caroco ships spotted around the Mystic Islands. We all speculated Keegan had returned. I knew Keegan briefly. Sabastian said Keegan is your birth father. No offense to King Iver, but you are no Half-Light. I see you have the fever. I've been through it. The pain will only get worse."

It wasn't hard to believe the pain could get worse. The agony pounding in his chest and head left Kai feeling on edge. Every part of him hurt, but he had to keep going. His mother's life depended on him coming into his powers. He touched Yulia's arm. "Why are you helping us? Did Riome ask you to help us?"

A solemn wave washed over Yulia. "I— know Benmar, Keegan's father. He is a dear friend. Riome did not ask, but she did not have to. I am here because it is the right thing to help you."

Kai touched her arm. "Thank you, Yulia."

Davi ducked under a limb. "The storm confirmed the elders aim to keep you out. With rumors of Keegan's return flooding Katori, I can understand you being lumped in with his arrival. These two events don't seem coincidental. Not to our obsessive, controlling chiefs. They fear you, while others believe in what you might represent."

"What exactly do I represent? They don't know me." Kai stomped closer to Davi to gauge his reaction.

"Change. You are either Keegan's son, power-hungry and planning to rise against them. Or, you are the legend, meant to change the Katori way of life. I told you this before. The legend speaks of a story depicted on the walls of Alenga's lost Agora. Two warriors fight against the man with a black soul. Nobody wants a war, Katori fighting Katori."

The burden of carrying the future of the Katori pressed on Kai's heart. He never asked for this. All he wanted was his mother back.

Rayna stepped between Kai and Davi. "So how did you come to our aid in the storm?"

Davi's kind eyes smiled at her. "Sabastian came to us, asked for our help. Another came to your aid, a young man named Shane. He has returned to his wife for the night, but promises to join you at dawn."

The mention of Shane made Kai's heart leap into his throat. It was not his wish to pull Shane into a battle. Guilt clawed at his insides. Kai dipped to avoid banging his head against a low branch. Shane had only just started his new life with Julia. *This is not Shane's fight.*

Ahead of them, Kai could see the light from the campfire. It would be nice to rest, eat, and visit with old friends.

Davi crossed a small stream and offered a hand to Rayna. "Your friend, Shane, is a good man. He hunts with us, and we have met his young wife. The storm was already pounding the sky when Shane reached our homestead. Together we found a long line of Weathervanes along a ridge, south of Albey. We were lucky they had no Beastmasters with them, besides the two eagles. They outflew Sabastian to warn of your arrival. Sabastian is quite the Beastmaster. He took on both birds. You know, I can honestly say I have never seen anyone fight the way he did. Changing into a man and back again midflight. The other Weathervanes were no match for us. With their focus on the storm, we took advantage of their distraction. Shane is mighty quick with his arrows. Almost as fast as me. We wounded them, and they fled into the Zabranen Forest, lost in a white fog."

Davi stepped into the campsite, and Naia rushed to hug Kai. Everyone was there, Kalia and Jada and her new baby. After introductions were made, Naia offered them shelter, clothes, and food. It felt good to be dry. They were safe for the moment, but Kai knew they could not stay here long. Time was running out, and his pounding head ticked like a clock announcing his approaching time limit. He feared his and Rayna's magic would burn out with the fever before they could complete the Conhaspriga. Not that he fully understood how it worked—he only knew they needed to hurry.

Gabe poked at the fire. Davi dropped two more logs into the blaze. "Kai, what do you know about the Conhaspriga?"

"I know it is a rite of passage performed by all Katori when they come of age. It is a Calling. I know some choose to spend the year or two prior exploring the world before making their choice. They must either choose to return to live in Katori, or live out here, giving up their gifts."

Hale interrupted, "A rare few choose to venture out into the unprotected world. Not worth the risk, I guess. Very few are curious about what lies beyond the Katori Mountains. Those that choose to skip all this adventure have a simple ceremony after a year of silent meditation. They still select a crystal from Alenga's mountain, and dip into the sacred spirit pool within the Agora."

"I know about the crystal stones, the Weathervanes, Beastmasters, Kodama, Stonekings, and Lumens," Kai continued. "I even know my journey starts at the Three Sisters—three oak trees at the base of the first waterfall. They mark the entrance into the Zabranen Forest and the passage back to the Katori Lands."

Gabe laughed. "Boy, your test started the moment you left Diu. The elders know you have the fever. Lucca may have never visited you, but he knows your age and that you are being called. The chiefs have no intention of letting you complete the Conhaspriga. Is nobody else thinking about it?" He paused to survey the group. "Kai is the legend." Gabe rolled his eyes. "He will be a Beastmaster, and no ordinary Katori man who walks among beast. He will talk with them. He will become them. He was born to lead us to a new age."

Kai pulled his feet back from the fire, feeling the heat. "I have heard this legend. Kendra spoke of two warriors who stand against one man whose soul is black as night. Davi and I already discussed this. But I don't care to lead a revolution. Kendra said this story is carved in stone, but I will not let it define me or my future."

Naia nodded in agreement. "Nobody has seen the lost Agora in centuries."

This was new. Kai knit his brow together. "A lost agora. As anyone seen this place?"

"As far as I know, nobody alive today has laid eyes on the stone carvings. They are twisted stories passed down by each generation. Alenga holds your future, do not worry about what has yet to happen. When you get to Katori, you must seek out the invisible man. He will teach you if you are meant to become his equal."

Bewildered, Kai looked at the others. "How exactly do I find an invisible man?"

Naia laughed. "He is a legend. I have no idea, but I have a feeling he will find you."

Davi calmed his wife's enthusiasm. "Enough talk of legends. Nothing matters if Kai can't make it past his journey through the forest and through the mountains and back into Katori. Most youths have weeks to complete the test. You have only a matter of days before your fever consumes you." Davi leaned towards Kai. "Listen to me, Kai. The tests are intended to confuse you, draw you away from your goal. The Guardians are meant to test your resolve. We Katori are warriors through and through. Everyone believes the Katori retreated to study spirituality as the world negotiated peace. We spread the rumor that Katori had had enough of war. Partly true. We did want peace. That does not mean we became soft." Davi's face became serious. "They will fight you. This is no game of hide-and-seek."

Kai nodded gravely. "Up until now, I would have thought they would welcome us. Now I see I was wrong." He placed his hand on Rayna's knee. "I fear we have no idea just how hard this climb will be."

Kaia leaned into the fire. She kicked a shifted log back into the yellow and white flames. "You must climb the Katori mountain's three central waterfalls. Ice melts from its snowy peaks, which feed the Conha River. Each level is steeper than the previous one. They are surrounded by an unclimbable sheer rock face."

Concerned, Rayna asked. "Sounds impossible. If I understand you correctly, we must leave the river. Travel south, deep into the Zabranen Forest. All to climb up to the next level."

"My father told me—stay near the river. It takes longer to hop from stone to stone, but you have no chance of getting lost," Kaia reassured her.

Gabe continued. "Walk the river to the falls. Venture south into the woods. Find the first available route back northeast. After each climb, it is imperative you return to the river. Stay close to the water. Keep the sound close. Always listen. The Guardians will pray on your fear. They want you to give up. That is the purpose of the test. Control your fears."

Davi chimed in with his own words of wisdom. "In a typical test, only two or three, from each discipline, would challenge you. The Lumens will take your sight. Don't bother trying to glean. Weathervanes can raise fog, rain, and wind against you."

Kai huffed. "I've seen their power. I am tired of being wet."

Hale scoffed. "I don't believe they mean to make this a fair fight. I doubt they aim to kill you, just keep you from finding the cave, before your fever breaks."

Davi tamped the air with his hand to quiet the group. "The Beastmasters, they will come for you. I believe you will need to fight like no other before you. The Guardians know who you are, who you could become, and they fear you. Do what you must, but try not to kill anyone. That would be unnecessary. Their true job will be to delay you or make you flee. You will need to stand your ground. Never give up."

Don't kill. Kai could live with not killing, but could the Guardians who were waiting for him?

It was clear that Kai and Rayna were headed into a trap, but he had made up his mind. They both had. Rayna deserved to find her parents, and he wanted—no, needed—to search for his mother. Her time was running out, if it was not already too late to change her back. She was out there, lost in the world. And, he was going to make it his mission to find her. His powers were a necessary gift he dare not lose. Yes, he had made up his mind. He wanted this.

◆ ◆ ◆

Dawn came too early. Kai's heart ached with worry. With Rayna's hand clasped in his, they headed to the Kempery-man's camp. As much as Kai wanted to leave without an argument, he owed his men an explanation. Over the years, they had spent months traveling the countryside and fought battles. Drew was his oldest friend, and he was the first to tell Kai he could be more than a prince. Drew deserved the opportunity to say goodbye.

And then there was Philip Dresnor, his lead Kempery-man. For three years, Kai had spent nearly every day with Dresnor; they were like brothers. It would be no easy task to tell this man he must return to Diu without him. There would be an argument.

Through the trees, Kai sensed another person. Smoke barreled through the woods. A man in shadow leaned against a tall tree. "Shane waits for us there," Kai pointed.

They changed their course. Kai was excited to see his friend. Shane stepped out from a large copse of trees, bow in hand and a battle-ax strapped to his back. "Morning, you two. Good to see you made it through the storm."

"Shane." Kai pulled his friend into a welcoming hug. "How did you know to come yesterday?"

Skepticism washed over Shane's face. "I want to say you wouldn't believe me if I told you. But then I've learned there is much I do not know about the world around me. We all keep secrets. For one reason or another. You have yours. The Katori seem to be nothing but secrets." He gave Kai a severe look before he continued. "My mother...talks to me." Shane paused for acceptance. "At least I believe it is her voice I hear on the wind. When all is quiet, I often feel her presence. She died giving birth to my sibling, and it was a boyhood fantasy to talk with her in my mind. Now I believe it was real. Yesterday morning, I heard your name, and Davi's, echo through the trees. When I walked into Davi's camp, the storm was raging, and they were all set to leave with Sabastian. I had to believe I was meant to help."

Concerned for his friend, Kai apologized. "Shane, I am sorry you were brought into this. It is not your fight. I know how you feel about fighting. Killing."

"True, I moved here for a quiet, easy life. But what happened all those years ago in Hamrin no longer haunts me. I have made peace with my choice. Besides, I am an excellent shot with a bow. I can maim a person without killing them. The four I dropped yesterday will all live. I can't speak for them doing much running, but they will live."

The three friends continued through the woods towards the Kempery-man's camp. "Thank you, Shane. Today Rayna and I must enter the Zabranen Forest. I will not lie to you, but I cannot tell you everything. We are both sick with a fever. There are Katori in the mountains that wish to help us, and those who wish to stop us. Neither group will take kindly to you or my men entering the forest. You're correct. We all keep secrets."

Shane nodded. "I understand."

They continued in silence. Although Kai knew the heart of his men, he had to try to send them home. When they entered the camp, Drew stood off to one side, brooding silently. Kai had known Drew the longest. It would not be easy for Drew to leave Kai to the dangers for the Zabranen Forest. Dresnor's posture was resolute, Redmon's looked defensive. Albey was the only one who seemed relaxed. This would be difficult for all of them. They were all too close to recklessly leave one another's life to fate.

Hands tucked into his pockets, Kai faced his friends. "I have spoken with Davi, and he assures me there are healers high on the mountain willing to help us, but only if we come alone. If we build trust with them, they may help us find Rayna's parents. She is the reason they are even considering helping us. To them, she is Katori. She is one of them. They believe they know who her parents are."

Their stern faces said enough. They were not interested in staying behind. Frustrated, Kai stepped back to take a moment. Maybe he should have left without saying goodbye. No, the guilt would have been too much, not to mention they would have hunted him down.

The smell of pine surrounded their little clearing. Smoke and wet ash filled his nostrils. Guilt welled in Kai's stomach. What he needed to do was like kicking a loyal dog. Where he needed to go, they could not follow, and he needed to be sure they left.

"Dresnor, it would be best if you all returned to Diu. The captain of the *Dragaron* will wait until mid-morning. I have paid him well for his silence. He assures me that he can convince Dante that Rayna and I were his only passengers."

Dresnor scoffed. "We came as your friends. Not as guards. I will not return without you."

"I am not here to argue, Philip. I am ordering you home." Kai took a breath. "We must go alone. When I do not return at the end of summer, my father will want an explanation. Once he learns you left me alone in the Zabranen Forest, he will be angry."

"I for one will not go back without you," Drew insisted.

"Davi believes we will be gone six months, maybe longer. The treatment must be administered daily over several months. As payment, once we are well enough, they request we work the land. I hope we can return to Diu by the Winter Festival. Please, I beg you to return on the ship. John, you have a family. Think of them. They need you. Surely you will see sense."

His men were unwavering. Their steadfast loyalty did not surprise him. Still, Kai held his ground. Rayna stood back from the group, her head low; she did not make eye contact. Perspiration gathered on her forehead, and she sank to the ground. Shane offered her water to drink.

Kai rushed to her side. Heat coursed through his veins. Sweat dripped from his brow. Dresnor knelt next to them both. "Rayna, are you sure you can make it?"

Drew joined them. "Let us help you both. Please," he begged.

"I wish you could, my friend." Kai placed a hand on Drew's arm, then he glanced around the group. His eyes pleaded silently with his men.

Kempery-man Redmon broke first. He offered a hand to Kai. "You are my friend, always. I want to stay, but I must obey my Prince. I will wait for your instructions in Diu. Get well, both of you." He nodded to Rayna, and she smiled back.

Kempery-man Albey and Drew stepped forward next. Heads bowed, they offered a hand and said their goodbyes. With each man, Kai felt the prick of loyalty stab his heart. It was hard to lie to his friends, but it was for the best.

Kai reached for his pack and collected a stack of prewritten letters. "I wrote these letters. Shane, take one to Albey every month. Ask Kinnon to see them delivered to Diu. Shane, if any letters come for me, hold onto them until I can return. If I can send word through Davi, I will."

Drew finally spoke up. "You give us little choice. I owe you my life. Are you sure I cannot stay, take my chances here? If I can be of service, I want to be close."

Knowing the heart of each man, made being dishonest difficult. "Thank you, Drew. I appreciate your sacrifice. But this really is the only way. If you follow, they will not help us cure our fevers."

"How far *can* we go?" Dresnor challenged.

Dresnor would not bend. He would push to go farther and farther each step of the way. Still, Kai and Rayna were out of time, they needed to get moving. "I was told you must turn back at the first waterfall."

"Fair enough." Dresnor motioned to the river. "I will travel with you to the first waterfall. We go due east. I will catch up with the rest of you in Diu. I can take a ship tomorrow from Albey."

Drew angled around the group. "I see no reason why I cannot join you as well."

Everything settled, they collected their gear and parted ways. Redmon and Albey headed to the ship, and Kai, Rayna, Drew, Dresnor, and Shane went into the forest.

CHAPTER 3

Waterfall Hunting

The sun crested the Katori Mountains, spilling warmth and light through the trees. Birds chirped, and animals scurried. It should have been a pleasant walk in the woods, but instead, Kai could feel the tension in his Kempery-man. Stress pulled at Dresnor's shoulders and neck. There was little Kai could say to ease his mind, so he let the man ponder.

Drew, however, reminisced about old times, going on about Kai's younger years. It took Kai back to simpler days. How he longed for the times when he ran through the palace courtyard or first learned to ride a horse. Back before responsibility and choices overwhelmed his everyday life, he laughed and played without a care.

The light conversation brought laughter to Rayna's eyes. It was good to see her happy, given the stress and pain they were both under. Along the way, she plucked flowers and herbs, often waving them at Kai before tucking them into her leather pack.

As the area around them started to look familiar, some of the landmarks brought back memories. Kai had traveled this area last summer. A small glade of dogwoods and a trickling brook reminded him of the afternoon with Smoke and the alpha's pack. Later they passed a fallen hollow oak. Vines wormed up and over the massive trunk. The tree must have been hundreds of years old; now it lay decaying on the forest floor.

One lone redwood towered over all the other trees. Its massive trunk had to be twelve feet wide. This was one of the last remaining markers Kai could remember; from here he listed for the sounds of the first waterfall. The thunderous rush of water began to drown out the burbling river.

They were close. With each step, the pounding waterfalls grew louder. Kai anxiously though about how to convince Drew and Dresnor to return to Diu. He knew his friend would not turn back without a challenge.

Out of nowhere, he heard a rumble. Constant and steady, the mountain seemed to grumble at their approach. Kai looked to the others; they seemed unaware of the noise. The crashing waterfall thundered up ahead. He continued, not wanting to draw attention to something he could not explain.

The trees began to thin. Hot sunshine hit Kai's scalp as the group stepped into the clearing. He wiped the sweat from his forehead and marveled at the tower of water rolling over the rocks. Before them was a curtain of water cascading down into a crystal-clear plunge pool. Mist splashed off the rocks, creating a delicate rainbow.

Observing their surroundings, Kai realized the moss-covered rock walls on either side were unclimbable. Kai craned his neck to look up. "That has to be at least thirty feet high."

"Maybe higher," Rayna added.

While the others enjoyed the beautiful view, Kai tilted his head east. He strained his ears, searching for the grumble within the mountain. Either he had imagined the sound or the roaring rapids slamming down on the rocks made it impossible to hear.

Thirsty, each of them went to the water's edge for a drink. Kai splashed his face with the cold water, stood and wiped his mouth. "Dresnor, Drew, and Shane, this is where you must leave us. We must cross the river here alone."

Dresnor scoffed. "Nah, I think I will continue. Kempery-man Albey tells me the Zabranen Forest starts at the second waterfall. It is another hour or two around and up. I will turn back there—not a step before. If you'll remember, Albey grew up in these parts. He knows the rules well. I will not leave you or Rayna alone in the forest."

Shane smirked at Dresnor. "Well, if he stays, so do I."

Drew nodded and raised an eyebrow in agreement.

There was no arguing. Kai dropped his pack and sat on a nearby rock. "We should stop for food. Refill our canteens. We have a long way to go, and mine is empty."

He knew Dresnor was only avoiding the inevitable, but for now, he let him have his way. They kept the conversation simple. Fun, happy adventures around Baden Lake. Rayna tossed Smoke a few scraps and tucked the rest of the dried meat and cheese into her pack.

Ever mindful of the time, Kai hurried the group together, and they crossed the river using a downed tree wedged between the large rocks. Although he wished the others had turned back, he was happy for the company. He figured Shane tagged along out of curiosity, while Dresnor did so out of pure stubbornness. The man was utterly unreasonable. Kai laughed inside his head at the resolve of his friends.

Once on the other side, Kai felt a sudden uneasiness. The path into the trees looked well-worn. Dresnor wanted to follow the trail farther into the forest, but Kai was skeptical. He knew better. Everyone had warned him to stay near the water.

They walked into the trees about fifty feet, and Kai pointed. "We climb." He pointed out the various ledges and boulders along the slop. Thick vines climbed upward. "Davi instructed me to stay near the water. He cautioned that the trails can be misleading and send you hours out of your way."

Kai looked at the climb above. Smoke would not be able to climb with them. They would have to separate. His faithful companion stood beside Rayna. Her hand sank into Smoke's thick fur. Sending Smoke off alone did not worry him. Kai knew the Katori would not harm a wolf; however, the loss of the second pair of eyes and keen senses did cause him some concern.

Confident his wolf would not bother with the path, but sniff out the route to find his own way, Kai sent him into the woods, instructing him through their connection to reach the next waterfall. Smoke bolted from the clearing, disappearing into the dark underbrush.

The climb was steep and arduous. The vines gave them a handhold, but the moss-covered rocks made their ascent slippery and dangerous. Several times Kai pulled Rayna up to the next level. The narrow ledges were barely wide enough to stand on. Drew and Shane seemed to enjoy the challenge, while Dresnor mumbled to himself the entire climb.

Both Kai and Rayna were soaked with sweat. Each time before hoisting her up, Kai thoroughly wiped his hands dry on his pants. When they reached the top, they walked back to the falls. Kai looked down. Beautiful, he thought. "Too bad we can't spend the day here." He nudged Rayna.

Feverish, Rayna wiped the sweat beads off her forehead. She begged for a break with her weary expression. Kai offered her his canteen, and she sipped eagerly. It may have been a challenging climb up, but Davi's advice to stay near the falls saved them hours of walking.

Between the sun, the climb, and his fever, Kai felt like he was on fire. Sweating profusely, he wiped his brow. He wasn't sure how much more he could take. They were all tired, but they needed to keep going. A survey of the riverbank was not good. The trees were dense, and the rocks were jagged. They offered no easy path for walking.

Challenging by design, Kai thought. *We're not meant to stay near the river. The Guardians want us to leave the water, travel into the forest.* Kai crossed his arms, frustrated. If he'd been alone and had more time, he might have hopped from rock to rock. Alone, he could slowly work his way along the water's edge. His friends would never understand the risks of such a path when the forest was easier.

Deeper into the forest, Kai sensed a presence. The hair on the back of his neck tingled. Magic filled the air. Reasonably sure the Katori Guardians were already watching them, he reached out with his mind. He gleaned the forest.

Nothing. Odd. How can there be nothing? No light, no magic emanated from his surroundings. He could not glean. Rayna tapped the corner of her eye and shook her head. She, too, was unable to glean the path ahead.

Fear crept around the edges of his mind as he remembered Haygan's words: *"You can't be afraid. Out here, it is survival of the fittest. Choose to survive or choose to surrender. Your life will be determined by your strength of spirit, and you have a strong spirit—trust it."*

His uncle was right. Kai had to have faith in himself and in Rayna. They could do this. Although the trail angled into the woods, Kai continued to cut through the underbrush. Shane's battle-ax came in quite handy, and both he and Shane took turns clearing the path. It was exhausting work, hacking away at the vines and bushes.

Drew took the lead and their weapon. His forceful strike against the clinging vines made a clear path. Dresnor guarded the rear and kept a sharp eye on their surroundings, his sword at the ready. "You sure we cannot follow the path? This seems like a lot of effort to shave off an hour or two of walking." Dresnor scanned around, searching for hidden threats.

"Stay near the water, that's all Davi said," Kai responded. "I will not chance getting lost for an easier route."

Ever vigilant, Kai kept them near water. At times the water was barely moving while other times it dashed around and over large rocks. They worked methodically—climbing over rocks and between dense tree saplings. Their hours of persistence finally paid off when they hacked through the last thicket and stepped into a clearing.

Smoke darted up the path behind them. Rayna ran her fingers through the wolf's fur and smiled at his arrival. "We are all back together," she beamed.

They had reached the base of the second waterfall. Twice as massive as the first, the water thundered over the towering falls and crashed onto the rocks below. An enormous plume of billowing mist lingered around the base of the falls. Kai could feel the change in the air. The snow-capped Katori Mountains fed the Conha River, making the water especially icy as it collected into pools.

But Kai did not feel cold—the heat from within was more than he could tolerate. Clothes and all, Kai waded into the large pool and sank below the surface. The water instantly chilled his inflamed skin. It was refreshing. He stood up in the waist-deep water to see Rayna removing her boots. "You could have removed your boots first," she chided.

"I don't care," he laughed, falling back under the water again.

Dresnor and Drew conversed from the nearby rocks. Shane cleaned his ax, and Smoke drank from the water's edge.

Relief from the heat relaxed Kai's mind. As he tramped out of the water, steam rose from his shoulders. Rayna stood waist-deep and attempted to wring out her wet clothes and hair. They were a sight.

Kai ran his hands through his sandy-blond hair and glanced at his friends. "Time to go back. From here, you will need to return to Albey. I appreciate you escorting us this far, but Davi warned if you go any farther, our word would mean little to the mountain people. They do not like outsiders. They will not help us if you continue. Don't make me beg. Please, go back."

Kai prepared himself for an argument.

Dresnor crossed his arms. "I know I promised to turn back, but I do not understand why I cannot meet these people. See them for myself, know the truth of their worth. I will not trust your safety to the mysteries of the Zabranen Forest."

"Philip Dresnor, are you not a man of your word? Don't push me on this!" Kai thundered.

Wide-eyed, Shane chimed in. "It is not my place, but Kai is not questioning your loyalty, Dresnor. We all know you would die for him, as would we all, but I have lived in the area. The Katori are hesitant to trust outsiders. Before Julia and I moved here, I hunted the area to learn the terrain. Davi and his group stalked me in the shadows. I learned through Kinnon, Kempery-man Albey's brother, that Davi had spoken with him about who I was. I had to be patient and earn their trust."

"But these people are not Davi," Dresnor countered. "He is not even facilitating the introduction. How can I trust any of them?"

Kai had not considered asking Davi to join them, but in retrospect, it would have helped convince Dresnor to return. This was not supposed to be this difficult. "One tribe to the next," Kai began to spin a tale, "they keep to themselves. I am sure if Davi felt I needed an escort, he would have come, but it is time for you to turn back."

Rayna let her hand touch Dresnor's shoulder. "We will be fine. They promised Davi they could help us, but we need to be true to our word and not lead others to their camp. Please, all of you, go back."

Dresnor was doubtful at first, but then he reluctantly offered his hand. "Good luck—both of you. I suppose we will leave you here, then."

Kai took the offered hand and pulled Dresnor in close. "I can do this, you trained me well."

"I did train you well." Dresnor let Kai go. "Be safe."

Drew sighed heavily. "Rayna, you're a strong woman. Look after Kai, and we will see you in a few months." He hugged her and pulled Kai into their moment. "Take care, little brother. I will be waiting for your return."

This would be the first time Kai had gone anywhere without one of them for more than a few hours. This was not like dodging their watchful eye for a run or an afternoon sailing on the lake. He knew full well this could be goodbye for much longer.

Shane extended a hand. "Be safe. I will speak with Davi. Maybe he can visit and bring back word."

Even though Kai knew better, he nodded to give them a sense of hope. He took in a deep breath of fresh, pine-scented air and took Rayna's hand.

Everyone parted ways. Kai watched his friends fade back into the forest through the trail they had created. He listened to the occasional whack of Shane's battle-ax strike underbrush and small saplings that evidently blocked their chosen direction.

Unable to glean their path, Kai hoped they would continue to follow the same route and keep close to the Conha River. The forest was dense and unwelcoming, but Dresnor and Shane were expert trackers, and they would have no trouble getting back to Albey as long as they followed the same course.

CHAPTER 4

Shifting Landscape

Rayna laced up her boots, studying the cliffs and various trees around the clearing. "So, what next?" she asked. "What are we looking for next?

Kai thought of Kendra's reminder—three oak trees near the base of the second waterfall. Those trees marked the entrance to the Zabranen Forest. But as they looked around, they didn't see anything remarkable. Every tree looked the same, and certainly, none of them looked like an entrance. He resigned himself once again that they would have to venture away from the water's edge to find a way up to the third level. His brow knit together with concern.

Could the Guardians have hidden the entrance to the forest somehow? Was it possible to change the landscape?

The lack of challenge so far made Kai wonder if the Guardians stayed away because of his friends, or because they were willing to let them begin their test proper and fair inside the Zabranen Forest. But deep down, he knew. The guardians were never about to make it easy...

What were they missing? There was no way to climb the immense waterfall. Kai thought harder on his dreams. His vision came back to him. There would be no path marked by signs of man. The giant oaks were here, but which ones? An eerie, fog-shrouded forest loomed in front of them. The thundering water crashed down beside him. He stepped toward the falls; the sound was louder. But there was nothing but dense forest in front of them. No clue they were in the right place.

Again, focusing on the dream, he touched his face, thinking about what he felt. "That's it. The mist. We are not close enough to the falls," he said, taking Rayna by the hand. "We need to stand in the mist."

Together, Kai and Rayna ventured around the edge of the plunge pool. Kai turned his head to the right, searching. The raging water roared beside them, and cold mist speckled their faces. Smoke waited nearby. Kai reached out his hand and touched the sheer cliff wall. They were practically under the falls before he saw the arch in the trees, the entrance revealed by the angle they now had.

Vines and thick underbrush distorted the arch, but it was there: three tall oak trees set at an angle. Large arm-like branches, originally meant to be open and welcoming, were now covered by dangling moss and ivy. Gray mist hung in the damp air, further hiding their way. Still, their new path became visible.

Sunlit rays danced over the vine-covered ground. A feeling pulled at Kai's soul, and he felt a longing in his heart. Rayna looked up at him, as if she felt the magic too. Something guided them into the Zabranen Forest. Was it Alenga calling them home? Kai did not know, but he felt compelled to follow the feeling. Hand in hand, they walked under the moss-covered oaks. They stepped under arched branches covered with bright green new growth. Acorns crunched under their feet. Squirrels dodged for safety within the trees. The fog swirled around the tree trunks.

The fresh, crisp scent of the waterfall morphed into damp earth, decaying leaves, and pine. The overgrown ivy gave way to pine needles. As they made their way, the trail twisted and turned, this way and that. Deeper into the forest, the trees changed. Towering pine trees blocked out the sun. Birds chirped in the canopy above.

Wanting to reassure Rayna, Kai tried again to glean the area—but he saw nothing. No light beaming from the foliage, animals, or earth. There was absolutely nothing. He thought of the skillset of the Katori. The only one that fit was the Lumens—Haygan had said they could manipulate the energy that flowed within all life. Davi had also told him to expect to lose his magical sight.

Kai felt blind. Everyone was right—gleaning would provide him no benefits. They would need to navigate another way. The only landmark he trusted was the river, and they were leaving it behind. What other tricks could they expect along the way?

Each step took them away from the only indicator that they were on the right trail. Over rotten hollow logs and around dense foliage, they pressed on. Thicker leaves and thorny brambles closed in around the fading path. Creaky trees swayed in the breeze. Kai felt uneasy. Dark foreboding sounds echoed through the hillside. Low overhanging branches grew closer, and their trail was gone.

If he didn't know better, he'd swear he heard whispers on the wind. Voices that warned them to go back. Rayna squeezed his hand. "We've lost the path. Should we go back to the falls and start again?" she questioned, stepping in close.

Kai pointed to a felled tree near some large boulders. "We should stop, eat, and get our bearings before we continue. We have been walking for over an hour. I can't tell which way we are headed—" he pointed at the clouded sky above "—but something feels wrong. At every turn, more obstacles block our path. We take more steps down the mountain than we do up. It seems to me that the path is forcing us southwest. Down the mountain."

"You're right," Rayna agreed. "They have us outmatched. The Katori have skills we do not understand, and they've had a lifetime to perfect their gifts, not to mention design this trial."

Rayna handed Kai a bundle of food. The dried meat, cheese, and bread helped lift Kai's spirits. He drank some of the cold mountain water they had collected at the falls before passing it back to her.

"We need to..." Kai let his voice fade.

He had no idea what to do. They were lost and basically blind. The landscape seemed to be designed to push them off course. He felt infuriated. His pulse quickened. Were the Guardians this difficult on others who tried to complete their Conhaspriga? He let out a heavy sigh and clenched his fists. He felt his insides boil with fury. Then he felt Rayna's hand touch his knee. His breathing steadied, and he relaxed, softened by her reassuring smile.

She lowered her head next to Smoke's ear. She gazed at the delicate ferns and holly bushes. "We must change our perspective," she said quietly. "We are thinking too small. When I practice gleaning at home, I am limited to the palace and a small portion of the city. But Kai, when you focus, you can reach well outside the city."

He thought about her words and nodded in agreement. "You're right, I have been thinking small. The Lumens cannot blot out the whole world. Nor do they need to. They only need to hide the way east, closer to Katori. Back at the second waterfall, I sensed Shane and Philip's departure. But they were going west. Down the mountain. We need to be more strategic." He paused. "The Katori use their gifts against us, effecting our surroundings, but they cannot change *us*. Nor can they change the nature of everything around us."

Kai closed his eyes and took a deep breath. The world around him fell silent as he sank deep into his inner self. Strength bubbled within his core. Raw power. Quietly focused within, he felt the threads of energy, the fabric of life that connected him to the world—and, more importantly, to the things around him.

He reached out with his mind. Nothing. Blackness surrounded everything. Concentrating on the emptiness, he felt a drain on the energy. Rayna's light seemed to be muted, pushed deep inside of her. In his mind, he ventured further west from their present location. He reached out, searching for life. A white light bloomed and assaulted his senses. It was as if all the light from this area had been shoveled away like snow from a path. He pushed farther, and the energy subsided of its own accord. Iridescent light emanated within the plant life, animals, and river.

The Lumens had not stolen the light—merely pushed it away, and hidden some deeper within itself. Kai followed the border of light and dark. An empty void surrounded them. It was as if a thick blanket covered their location, enveloping the river and the surrounding landscape. High in the hills, he found the third waterfall free and clear of the blackout. Mentally he drew a line between the river he could sense on his level behind them and traced it east upriver to the third set of falls.

He knew where they were and where they needed to go. They needed to head back north. Back toward the river. They had made no progress. On the boat, Yulia showed them how to pull at the energy from the storm. Weaken it. There was no storm from which to draw power. There had to be another answer.

Could he pull at the magic around the blackout? He wanted to try, but the idea of revealing his new-found clarity held him back. If he weakened the border, the Guardians might know he had discovered their illusion. No, he could not risk giving them any information.

Focused on Smoke, Kai pushed his energy specifically at his wolf. A faint white glow emanated through the blackness. He saw Smoke's outline. He felt their connection. Thrilled, he opened his eyes. "We need to continue east, but slowly move north. Let's go, I'll explain along the way."

After securing his supply pack, he pushed his thoughts to Smoke. Obediently his wolf darted off between the trees. Concerned, Rayna tilted her head. "Where is Smoke going?" she twisted her neck to watch for Smoke.

"All this time, we foolishly relied on the trail to guide us, relying on our eyes. We both tried to glean, but it was a futile attempt to survey our surroundings. As you said, they've had time to prepare this place."

Rayna nodded. "I see your point, but how does this help us?"

Kai smiled. He knew even the Katori had limits. "You said it earlier, we need to change our perspective. Smoke can hear the waterfall, even though we are several miles away."

"So he could lead us back to the falls." Rayna stroked Smoke's back.

"Well, yes, but that is not what I had in mind. There is a wolf pack that lives north of Albey and they hunt the land between here and Chenowith. Each summer, they find me. If they are near, Smoke can find them."

Rayna squinted her eyes. "I suppose it is worth a try. I can only imagine the Beastmasters will attack us at some point. It would be good to have reinforcements."

A howl echoed through the hills. No return call. "We need to climb. In my mind, I can see the third waterfall. The Guardians do not hide it yet. We must walk that way. It means we must climb those rocks. I must simply hold tight in my mind the angle of the river to each waterfall."

Thankful for the bond between him and his wolf, Kai hopped up onto the rocks and pulled Rayna along. He leaped to the next spot and offered her a hand. They climbed up two more boulders and found a small crevasse, a deep open crack in the rocks. From their view, the crack widened and led into a narrow passage between two rock walls.

"This looks like an easy way to get back on track." Kai pointed along the route ahead.

"How will Smoke be able to follow us?" Rayna questioned.

"He knows we are going to the third waterfall. Animals have a much better sense of direction. Our scent is not only on the ground but in the air—that is how they hunt. He will find us," he assured her.

"See there, the stone begins to open up wider and wider." Rayna pointed the way. "The ground down there is even and smooth. Plus, that is northeast."

Pleased with the new course selected, Rayna insisted on going first. Twisted sideways, they squeezed between the rocks and climbed down. The confined space was barely large enough for Kai's muscular chest. When he slid through the opening, he took in a deep breath. They were out and headed in the right direction.

Ahead on the path, Rayna pointed; sunlight streaked through the trees above. Kai was happy to see the blue sky again. It was the first opening in the trees they had seen in a while. The opening above continued to expand as they walked, as did the space around them. The rock walls rose up on either side and eventually widened enough for them to walk side by side. Kai took stock of the area.

The air had a metallic earthy smell. Dim, filtered sunlight hardly reached down into the canyon. Even though the area where they walked was nearly fifteen feet wide, the rising cliffs kept the sun from reaching the soil.

The more Kai looked, the more it seemed like the dirt was freshly brushed. Bewildered, he also noticed there were no pine needles, no acorns, even though pine and oak trees towered above them. There were no decaying leaves, except for those close to the wall's edge. Upon further study, he noticed that no moss covered the rocky walls around them. They had not walked downhill, but the walls were getting taller.

He wasn't sure if this should worry him. Interrupting his thought, off in the distance he heard a wolf howl. It was barely auditable. With bated breath, he paused and waited for a return call. Still, nothing.

With Smoke running in the opposite direction, Kai felt divided trying to keep them on track. He let go of the connection to Smoke's location. Finding the alpha and his pack was a long shot, but they could make all the difference when the Beastmasters came to challenge them.

Kai heard a faint rustling in the trees, followed by a high-pitch whistle. He knew that sound, an eagle's call. Again the trees rustled. A large looming shadow streaked across the tree canopy into the open sky above, confirming his assumption. The eagle circled twice, then flew off. "We are being watched," Kai whispered.

"Well, that's not creepy at all. Are you sure this is the way we should be going?" She glanced left and right at the rock walls.

To be honest, he wasn't sure. What if there was another way? Without being able to glean the forest, he had no idea about anything. "We are going in the right direction, though I cannot say if this is the easiest path."

Kai felt the hollowness in his response. It was his responsibility to protect them and get them through this, but he did not feel confident at all right now.

Monitoring the edge of the blackout, he noticed a shift in the border. The circle now encompassed the third waterfall. "They are on the move. The Lumens have shifted their locations. The circle they create has now encompassed our destination. " Gutted, he tossed up his hands. "I should have foreseen this and been prepared."

Rayna arched her neck. "Don't worry, I know in general where we are going." She pointed up into the trees. "Do you see those dark purplish leaves? They grow on a Poni-euca tree, known for its dark foliage and rainbow bark. I noticed them before we climbed down. All we need to do is keep them in front of us."

"Well done, Rayna," he felt relieved she'd thought to observe their current surroundings while he focused on the distance. "Seems your study of plants has more uses than we knew." Kai took her by the hand and charged forward, the purple leaves guiding their way.

One step later, a rumble started to build beneath their feet. Kai grabbed for Rayna. Earlier in the day, the mountain had grumbled. This time Rayna heard it too, her eyes filled with fear. Then they felt the ground shake. Small rocks tumbled down from above. Tiny dust particles plumed into the sun's rays above them. The sound grew louder, and the falling stones became larger until they were as large as his fist. Afraid he took Rayna's hand. "Run." He yelled, pulling her along.

They dodged falling rocks, and the ground in front of them began to shake and shift. Rayna stumbled and let go of Kai's hand. He stopped to help her to her feet. "The walls. They are closing in on us!" he shouted through the din. "We must find a way up."

Rayna turned to go back the way they'd come but stopped. "We have come too far to go back. There is no end in sight either way." She froze and looked to him.

Kai grasped her arm, but he didn't know what to do next. "Wait." He let his eyes trail the walls from top to bottom. "Wait," he repeated, swatting away a few falling rocks.

She pulled at her wrist, trying to break free of his grasp. "Let me go. We have to run back, or we'll be crushed!" she shouted.

Kai reached around her waist and pulled her close. Their eyes locked together. "Do you trust me?" he asked, pushing a feeling of calm to her.

Frozen in fear, tears ran down her soft cheeks. Rayna's brown eyes locked on Kai's. She watched them turn from their usual deep blue to green. Her breathing slowed. "I trust you. What do we do?" She wiped the tears from her face.

If he had been thinking ahead, maybe he would have seen this coming. Doubt clouded his mind. The pressure to find a way out hung around his neck. The metallic, earthy smell intensified with the shifting rocks. That is what he'd smelled earlier. Stones scraping over damp earth had created this smell. He would need to remember the smell.

Kai watched the various levels closing inward. Staggered interlocking tiers of stone jutted out from each side. They looked like stone teeth, ready to devour them. Slow and steady, they moved. He studied the ground. She was right, the canyon was going to clamp shut around them. He thought again about how the Guardians had had time to prepare this place. The test was about fear and control. Everything in his gut told him the Katori people were warriors, yes—but, killers no. "This is the work of Stonekings. They are moving the stone walls around us. They must be close by."

Above them, the trees were closing the gap. The sunlight was fading. "Could we climb up the sides?" Rayna's finger bounced up the jutted rock formation.

He contemplated her idea. "Yes, I think we can." He pulled her along. "Step where I step."

Kai leaped onto a low protruding rock and pulled Rayna with him. The ground continued to shift and grumble. He pointed to the next jump. She hopped the gap and fell to her knees. Taking a step back, Kai ran and jumped, landing safely on the next tier. He pulled Rayna to her feet. The other side was getting closer, and they still had a long climb to get out.

The next level was above their heads. Kai hoisted Rayna onto his shoulder, and she climbed up. With another step back, he stood on the far edge of his current level. He ran diagonally at the wall, pushed off, and reached up with his hands. His hands locked onto the stone ledge, and Kai pulled himself up, joining Rayna.

He looked for the next level. "That ledge is too high," she insisted, pointing across to the other side. "There, that is the next jump, but it is ten feet across. There is no way we can make that!"

Above them, the walls were closing in. Did they risk waiting for the other side to get closer? Or climb up the wall on this side. Kai wasn't sure. Beside them, the steep wall was filled with tiny cracks and crevasses. "We can't wait, too risky. We climb here." He pointed. "Get on my back, I will carry you. It's not that far to the next level." He crouched down.

Without hesitation, she wrapped her arms around his neck and her legs clamped tight to his sides. He stood and reached one hand up. He jammed his foot into a crack and began to climb. Above he felt another crag in the stone; he pulled them higher. Dust fell from above and caught him in the face. He shook his head. Oh, how he wished he could use his sight to climb.

Rayna dusted debris from her eyes. Kai reached for the next crack in the wall. On his left, there was a small ledge; he reached his leg over and stepped up and grabbed a thick root jutting out between the stones. Again, he found another spot for his foot and pushed up. Finally, Rayna tapped his shoulder. "I can make it from here."

Kai held fast, and Rayna climbed up his back, tugging the exposed roots. Once she reached the next level, he jumped up beside her. The ground shook harder, and the stones closed in. Now the gap was only five feet apart, but they had another twelve feet to climb. Rayna did not hesitate—she hopped across the gap to the next level, then up one and over again. Kai quickly followed suit. Back and forth, they leaped, up and over and back. Around them, the ground rumbled and shook.

When they reached the top, Rayna ran from the edge with Kai hot on her heels. He took her by the hand, and they ran through the trees. Twigs and pine needles crunched beneath their feet. When she slipped on the damp leaves, Kai dropped down beside her. "We made it through the Weathervanes storm and now the Stonekings rock obstacle course, and the Lumens test of our dependency on gleaning."

Rayna dusted off her hands. "So, that leaves the Beastmasters and the Kodama. I get how the Beastmasters might fight us, but how could the Kodama use plants and healing to test us?"

"I'd say they have been shifting more than rocks around. There is new growth everywhere."

She touched the bright green ivy beneath her knees. "I suppose we are not meant to run these tests in one day. If you had weeks to be lost in the forest, this would be almost easier."

They were exhausted. Sweat rolled down his back. He didn't want to think about what might have happened. While they lay there, he heard stone grinding against one another, and then the ground fell silent. He opened his mouth to comment about their insane climb, but a wolf's howl interrupted him. They listened in silence. A return howl echoed through the trees, followed by multiple wolf calls. Smoke was returning with the alpha.

"What a relief," Kai sighed, placing a hand on Rayna's shoulder.

He stopped to meditate and focus his own internal power. It was something the Lumens could not take from him. He needed to search for Smoke. He caught his wolf and the wild pack moments before they were consumed by the blackout. Still, Kai meditated on gathering his strength while thinking of Smoke. Focused on the memory of his companion, he channeled his energy in the direction he'd heard the howls.

Miles away, he felt the connection and saw an iridescent glow wash over Smoke. For a few seconds, he saw their approach. They were closing in fast and would reach them within moments. Now that the ground had stopped shaking, he could hear the rush of the waterfall. They were close.

Back on their feet, they walked in the direction of the river. The sound grew louder, and the trees thinned. To their delight, they were now well above the second set of falls. *Thank goodness*, Kai thought. He did not want to have to re-climb any more today. At least they had made some progress.

As the ground ahead slanted upward, rays of indirect sunlight filtered through the trees. The think foliage made walking a challenge, but it was good to know they were going the right way.

Smoke and the alpha bounded through the underbrush behind them. Relieved, Kai knelt with pleasure to welcome his old friends. Smoke leaned into Rayna. "How are the wolves meant to help us? I am not sure I understand..." She lowered her hand to the alpha, and he sniffed her fingers.

"My strategy is to use Smoke and the wolves in a way I hope the Katori Guardians will not anticipate."

"Wait," she interrupted him. "Can't all Beastmasters connect with animals? They will know you are using Smoke."

"True, they might think I was communicating with him, so I will keep him close to us. But I share my mother's rare gift of focusing on someone and bouncing light off them to find their location. If I can ricochet my magic off the pack, I could use them as beacons. Each wolf could be set along a route pointing to the third waterfall. They can find us a clear path."

Rayna raised an eyebrow. "Sounds complicated…"

"Good to see you, old friend." Kai counted the other wolves. "Two new pups. Your pack has grown since last summer."

The alpha licked Kai's face before he set off into the woods. Through their connection, Kai sent Smoke and the pack ahead. They needed to find a path to the third set of falls. Kai did his best to stay connected to Smoke while he kept the river within earshot. Unfortunately, it didn't take long before dense foliage and thorny underbrush pushed Kai and Rayna back into the forest.

CHAPTER 5

Dragon's Breath

This time, Kai refused to go too deep into the woods. They took any chance they had to climb a rock or traverse a small stream. There would not be a repeat of losing ground, tramping too far south. However, when they came to a large stone wall, he paused. He leaned against the rock, frustrated that it seemed to stretch on forever. His sweaty forehead rested against the cold stone.

"Are you alright, Kai?" Rayna asked.

"I chose wrong," he confessed as doubt consumed him. "I just don't know what I am doing. Maybe we should have kept the pack closer. Since I am unable to glean, I do not know how they got around this wall. Is there an easy way up? A place to jump?" He stepped back a few paces and wiped dirt from his face. The disturbed pine needles beneath his feet told him an animal had turned here. "I am not a tracker, I don't know which way they went. "He shook his head. "We cannot venture back south," he felt deflated with all his choices now.

Rayna ran her hand down his arm and took hold of his hand. "We climb up here. It seems if the wolves could have, they would have gone up here. This doesn't look any harder than the other things we've climbed today. I think we can follow that ledge all the way back to the river."

Her confidence in him quieted the doubt wrestling in his mind. "You're right, this wall can't be more than ten feet high. The ledge will get us out of the undergrowth and make for easy walking. Not sure what is farther up the wall, but the ledge will work."

Bent down, Kai interlocked his fingers. Rayna placed her foot in his hands and grabbed his shoulders. "On the count of three. 1—2—3."

He heaved her upwards. She grabbed the narrow lip and stepped with one foot, then the other. Within reach, she found a rock rim and pulled herself upward to the next ledge. Once on her feet, she called down to Kai. "Your turn."

Kai backed away from the cliff face to study the cracks and crags in the rocks. He noticed the nooks Rayna had used. Ready, he charged at the wall and jumped. One foot landed on a small lip, and his hand caught a crevice within the rock face.

He shifted his weight and reached for another handhold. After he swung his leg up to reach the next jagged rock, he was able to reach the top (for what good it did). They were now on a narrow ledge, scarcely the width of Kai's shoulders. Staring at the way forward, he took a few steps. "At least this ledge goes towards the river."

Inch by inch, they navigated the narrow lip of their route. Sounds of roaring rapids echoed through the forest. The ground evened out into a rounded knoll. Through the trees and the fading sunlight, Kai caught hints of whitewater rapids.

With head pounding, Kai stopped. Rayna offered him some water. "You alright?"

He didn't want to think about how much he needed to rest. "Let's keep going."

Again, he reached out to Smoke. His energy pinged off the wolves. They had already found another way up and were actually above them. Confident he and Rayna could discover the same route, they ventured away from the river along the rolling knoll. It was a risk, but one he was willing to make given the wolves' location.

As they went, the sounds of the river faded and were replaced with new noises echoing from the treetops—the hoots and squeaks from the unseen creatures of the night. The wind brushed past Kai's face and he wished it were colder. His body was being consumed by terrible fever. His shirt drenched in sweat, he marched along the narrowing path. Rayna was two steps ahead of him. Her pace was quick.

"Do you hear that?" Kai called to her. "It's water. There must be a small stream ahead of us. We should stop there. Get something to drink. Maybe rest."

Rayna nodded in agreement and continued. Crowded with trees and rocks, the narrowing path twisted and turned. Hopeful, they followed the curve around the rock face. The route narrowed again. They were forced to walk single file, Rayna ahead of Kai. He ducked under a low tree branch and turned to edge around another limb. The ground narrowed again, forcing them to sidestep along a small ledge.

"Our light is fading. Scaling these uneven ledges and knolls at night is probably a mistake. When we reach the stream, we should make camp."

"I could use a break," Rayna called back.

Kai studied the slope below. The ground below was starting to angle up, and the grade was leveling. He could only hope when it did level off, there would be a shift back toward the waterfall. "Tell me you can see the end? We have to be close." He asked.

"I wish I could, it is too dark to see far," she replied. "Just keep moving."

As the ground widened, an uneasy feeling swept over Kai. His muscles tensed. Behind them, he heard a noise...the deep grunt of a man, followed by a clank of metal scraping against stone. The sound startled Kai and he spun to face their pursuer.

Distracted, he lost his footing and tumbled down the rocky vine-covered embankment. A plum of dust puffed in his face. Barbs scratched his arms. He landed with a thud. Darkness clouded Kai's mind and threatened his vision. He grabbed his swirling head. Dizzy, Kai tried to open his eyes. His skin burned hotter than before. Blood dripped from various gashes on his body. He coughed hoarsely as his consciousness began to fade.

◆ ◆ ◆

Rayna saw Dresnor step around the tree limb. "What are you doing here?" she scolded him. Her exhaustion sparked a tone she always kept in check.

"I came to help you!" Dresnor shouted. "Kai, are you alright?"

Dresnor stepped towards the embankment, intent on climbing down to help the prince.

"Stop," Rayna yelled, spotting the foliage. "You cannot go that way." She pointed to the bramble vines intertwined with red fluted flowers. "Those are called dragon's breath. The flowers are poisonous. We must continue this way, find another way down."

She remembered Kai's strange request after a fitful night's rest. He had asked her to research a plant called dragon's breath, and now she knew why. He knew this moment would happen and she would be left to decide what to do.

She hurried along to a spot where the ground leveled off and merged with the gully below. When she reached Kai's side, his exposed skin was covered in large red welts. Dresnor fell in beside them and reached out to touch Kai. Rayna smacked his hand away.

"Kai. Listen to me. You are covered in poisonous sap. You have to remove your clothes before we can help you."

Rayna watched Kai's hands tremble as he removed his pack, coat, boots, shirt, and pants. When he gasped for air, she knew it was becoming difficult to breathe, and she noticed his eyes rolled back in his head, and he collapsed just as he pulled the shirt from over his shoulders.

Rayna pulled a cloth from her pack and tore it into four large strips. "Wrap these around your hands," she instructed Dresnor. "Drag him into the stream."

Dresnor wrapped his hands and grabbed Kai from behind, just under his armpits, and pulled him through the ferns. The prince's eyes fluttered open when the freezing water enveloped his legs and back. His body tensed in the rushing water. He began to wheeze. His breathing became ragged.

"Wash the oils from his skin. Keep him in the river while I make a fire." Her terse tone spoke volumes. She was angry.

In the fading light, she searched the area for branches and twigs. From her pack, she gathered burlap, oil, and flint. She cleared the ground and made a fire. With a pot of water set in the flames, she ran to Kai's side.

Kai was covered in scratches and welts. His one eye was swollen shut and he was gasping for air. Rayna lowered her ear in front of his face to listen to his breathing. She heard Kai try to speak. With her hand wrapped in cloth, she wiped cold water across his inflamed skin. She lowered her ear to his face to listen again to his labored wheezing.

"The tea will take too long," she whispered. Tears streaked down her face. What could she do? She had to help. Could she heal him?

"What tea could cure this?" Dresnor begged.

"We cannot have come this far to fail here," she pleaded, looking up into the dark trees. "Alenga, please help me. Help *him*."

She closed her eyes and delved deep within her soul. She thought of how much she loved Kai. She searched for the strength inside herself. Barehanded, she pressed on his chest and channeled her internal power into Kai. She pushed him down under the water and held him in place. White light emanated from her palms.

"What in the name of Alenga?" Dresnor gasped.

Rayna felt her magic pulse through her hands and into Kai's chest. The welts shrank and he sprang upright gasping for air—then he passed out.

"Drag him from the water," Rayna ordered. "When he wakes, I will have the tea ready."

Dresnor did as she instructed. "What are you?" he asked. "How did you heal him? That was not natural."

"You know very little about the things around you," Rayna scoffed in frustration. "The storm on the ship, did you think that was natural? You were there, you saw what we did. Can you explain that?"

"I did. Not that I believe it, but yes, I saw. And no, I cannot explain it. But it's not like I even know what to ask either of you," he shot back with a tone of frustration all his own.

"Why are you here?" Rayna demanded. "We told you to go back. This is all your fault. We were doing fine until you came along."

"I came to help!" Dresnor barked. "I didn't mean for Kai to fall. How is this my fault? Don't turn this around on me. Besides, if you can heal those welts and help his breathing, why not heal your fevers?"

Rayna gulped. She knew their fever was nothing she could cure with an herb or her touch. "Don't you think I would if I could?" she snapped bitterly.

Dresnor dropped a log on their growing fire. "Why are you yelling at me? I came to protect you both."

"How did you even find us? We have been all over this mountain."

"It wasn't easy, but I am an excellent tracker. At one point, your trail completely disappeared."

She knew all too well where they had been. Deep under the ground, their real path was now covered by stone and earth. Sealed as if the deep canyon had never been there. "Kai told you to go home."

The Kempery-man slumped near the fire. "You know I didn't mean any harm."

"And yet here we are," she continued to poke at him.

"This is not like you, Rayna. You have never addressed me with such disregard. Are you sure you're alright?"

Rayna could barely contain her emotions. She was exhausted and scared, so she took it out on Dresnor. "You should not have followed us!" Part of her wanted to go back home and forget about their magic, let the gift burn out, but then she thought of Kai's mother. She would give anything to know her birth mother—helping him save his was the least she could do.

Dresnor reared back. "I know it has been a long day, and we are all exhausted. You should get some rest. I will watch over you and Kai…"

When Kai awoke, he was wrapped in a blanket. To his surprise, he was able to open both eyes. The welts on his hands were smaller and only a little burned. Along the periphery of their small camp lay Smoke with the alpha and his pack.

Kai cleared his throat. "Can I get something to drink?" he rasped.

Rayna rushed to his side and offered him some of the tea she'd made. It tasted mellow and green, followed by a sweet clove and lemon flavor. He sipped slowly and finished the cup. "What am I drinking?" he asked, trying to sound positive.

"Stinging nettle tea mixed with honey and wild lemon vine. Lemon vine is a yellow and blue flower with a purple fluted center, it grows here in the forest. The stinging nettle and honey I brought from home. You once asked me to research the dragon's breath—good thing, too. I knew to keep you cold until I could make the tea." She winked at him.

It had been a good thing. Without Rayna's knowledge of the plant and its cure, he might have died tonight.

Refilling Kai's cup, she turned to Dresnor. "Philip, I believe I owe you an apology. I know you only wanted to help. We are fortunate Alenga heard my prayer. If I hadn't found those flowers on the way here, Kai would have died."

Dresnor nodded and stroked his beard. "Seems I owe you an apology, too. I should have trusted you both. I was sure without me you would not make it to the Katori mountain camp. I have spent years protecting the prince, but I forgot how capable he is on his own. Now I may have jeopardized your entire trip. If it is as you say, they may be watching you right now. With me here, they will never help you."

Rayna let her hands fall into her lap. "There's no use crying over it now. But you must go back come first light," she insisted.

Dresnor nodded. "Agreed. And I don't think you a witch. I will not report what I saw. We've all heard tales of healers. Who am I to question how Alenga works?"

"Witch? I have never heard this word before. What does it mean?" Rayna glanced between both men.

"It is an old forgotten term. A label given to people said to perform unexplained acts. In stories, they are usually wicked creatures. A rare few were good. Nothing for you to worry about." Dresnor closed his eyes to rest.

With the air cleared between them, they settled in for the night.

CHAPTER 6

Relentless Guardians

Come dawn, Kai awoke, stiff but feeling somewhat better. He scanned the campsite; Rayna slept to his right, Smoke and the wild wolves sat within the tree line, and Dresnor stood in the shadows. "I am surprised you're still here," Kai rose, holding his weary head.

"I was about to leave without saying goodbye." Dresnor turned to face Kai. "I made a real mess of things last night, sneaking up on you. When my blade scraped the stone, and you fell, I knew it was a mistake." Disappointment and shame warped Dresnor's face. "I just thought if I could keep my distance, I could follow you the entire way, with no one the wiser I'd know you were safe, and you'd feel you'd made it on your own."

Kai approached his friend. "After everything we've been through, you know I can take care of myself. You trained me well, Philip."

"I did, but it is my duty to protect you. I could never forgive myself if something happened."

"We will be fine. Trust me. Now go home, Dresnor. For real this time." Kai shook his friend's hand and he watched him slip out of camp with barely a sound.

Next to the faded fire sat his boots. They looked wet. Amongst the trees, he noticed a taut line with his damp clothes blowing in the morning breeze.

Sweat dripped down Kai's temple. Still consumed with fever, he knew they had little time left. He raked his knuckles across the short stubble along his chin. They had rested enough, and now they needed to get going. He got dressed and tugged at Rayna. "Time to get up."

She rolled over, her sweaty hair stuck to her face. Her clothes were drenched in sweat. She opened her weary eyes and sat up. "Good morning. Where is Dresnor?"

"He left. We are on our own now."

"I washed the oils from your clothes, boots, and the outside of your pack last night. They should be safe now," she assured him.

"Thank you, by the way, for saving my life."

She blushed. "If you had not asked me to research the plant, I would not have known what to do."

"No, not the plant and the cold water. You—you healed me. I felt your magic wash over me. My airway was closing, and you saved me."

Overwhelmed, Rayna hugged him, and Kai held her close. "We should get going." He let her step back. "I think we're getting close."

It was a pleasant morning. Birds were chirping, and golden sunlit rays trickled through the trees. Rayna collected their belongings while Kai dowsed the fire and collected water from the stream to refill their canteens. They broke camp and went up the rolling slope to the east. It wasn't long before they heard the roaring waterfall. The sound was loud and clear. Smoke and the other wolves spread out around the path.

Kai and Rayna entered the clearing of the third waterfall. A veil of water poured over the cliffs from above. From where they stood, they could not even see the top. Billowing mist floated on the air above the plunge pool. Astonished by the staggering height, Kai pointed. "Look at how tall it is. What, maybe two hundred feet? I can't even see the top through all this vapor."

Thrilled they had finally made it, Rayna giggled with delight. "We did it! Now what?"

Above them swooped three oversized eagles. Four black shuks bounded from stone to stone to cross the plunge pool, their black fur shimmering in the sunlight. Their silver eyes reflected the light. Kai and Rayna stepped away from the horse-sized creatures back towards the tree line. Smoke growled in response. The alpha and his pack surged to the front, ears angled slightly back. They bared their teeth and snarled. The shuk growled and barked in return.

"Beastmaster Guardians," Kai pulled Rayna behind him.

"How do you know?" Rayna asked, staying close to him.

"A feeling. I have communicated with Haygan and Sabastian in beast form. There is wisdom in their eyes and a strong feeling of power. It tickles my spine and pricks at my senses. Must be a Beastmaster thing, I am not sure."

Downstream came two leopards, and a black bear came bounding in their direction.

Rayna dropped her pack, then turned and ran. Kai chased after her. Her speed was intense as she dodged swaying trees, leaped rocks, and climbed a low embankment. As the ground evened out, she increased her speed. Rayna was fast for a Katori, but Kai was faster. He was right behind her and closing in fast.

"Rayna, stop, please!" He grabbed her arm and jerked.

They rolled into a heap and crashed into a cluster of ferns.

"We cannot run away," Kai heaved.

"I'm done fighting." Rayna's tears ran down her face. "Let's go home. This means more to the elders than it does to me. My parents abandoned me—why should I care who they are or why they left? I don't need the Katori powers." She sobbed louder.

Before Kai could console her, the Guardians were on top of them. They'd stalked them from the falls. Kai and Rayna were surrounded. Kai dumped his backpack and pulled his sword from his hip. Smoke and the other wolves formed a circle around the couple.

One shuk edged ahead, bumping into the others. Kai looked up into the shuk's large eyes; he had never noticed the various shades of silver around their black pupils. Some were bright and reflective, while others were muted gray. Standing this close, he could feel the heat of the animal's breath on his face. It was a massive creature, bigger than the others. Face to face with the beast, he was surprised to feel a sense of pride as the creature lowered its head.

Kai had seen these creatures before. His uncle Haygan had the ability to transform into a shuk, but this was not his uncle. Kai was unsure what to do. Remembering his uncle's words to be brave, he stood his ground and waited.

Angrily, the shuk leader growled and barked. Thunder reverberated in its voice. It snarled once more, mere inches from Kai's face.

Kai stood firm and showed no fear. The creature tilted its head and seemed to study Kai's posture, then it began to circle Kai and Rayna. Kai stood firm. The entire group fell silent, waiting to see what it would do. It made a slow circle and then came to stand next to Kai. "So, I have a friend among the Guardians?"

You do—Kai heard a familiar voice in his head. Ryker. To Kai's great relief, the shuk that was Ryker stepped forward, crouched, and snarled at the other Guardians.

"Thank you for standing with me," Kai whispered as he carefully watched the remaining Beastmasters consider the shift.

Then the eagles screeched from their perches on the nearby rocks as another eagle swooped in behind Kai. Its gold wingtips caught the sun's rays trickling through the treetops—Sabastian.

Kai dared not breathe. Ryker and Sabastian joining his ranks evened the odds a bit, but they were still outnumbered, and he did not know what to expect. He pulled Rayna to her feet, and she drew the short sword from her hip.

Delicate fog rolled around them. "Weathervanes—of course, they are here," Kai sighed.

Just as he processed the arrival of the fog, vines twisted and crept in their direction. Rayna lashed at the vines, cutting each as they reached out. "The Kodama are here too!"

The bear roared and charged. Beast against beast, the Beastmasters clashed together.

Creatures lunged. Kai slashed, kicked, and punched anything that came near. Rayna stood at his back. She slashed at vines that snaked across the ground. Several wrapped around the hind legs of the shuk on their side. Rayna hacked them away. A few pulled at her, dragging her from the group. She fought back and scurried back inside the circle of wolves.

Ryker fought in beast form and attacked another shuk. The wolf pack snapped and bit at the other animals if they came close. The alpha clamped his jaws around a leopard and shook its head violently left and right. Dazed, the leopard limped away. The other wolves grabbed at a shuk outside their circle and tore apart chunks of flesh. Rayna screamed in terror as the animal yelped in pain.

Ryker, the larger shuk, swatted his meaty paw at another shuk, sending his opponent to the ground. The black beast snapped its jaws around the neck of the bear. It pinned the raging bear to the ground, and the bear tried to scrabble for freedom with its massive claws.

An eagle flew and pecked in Kai's direction, swinging its talons around to claw at Kai's face. Kai ducked and swung his sword behind his head. The blade sliced through its wing. The poor bird slumped to the ground, screeching in pain. Right before his eyes, the eagle changed back into a man. Dumbfounded, the man clutched at his detached arm and fled into the fog.

The golden tips of Sabastian's wings glided around them. With precision, he dropped his eagle form, landed on another guardian, punched him in the skull and flew away. *Davi was right*, Kai thought, *the man has impressive control over his change.* He was glad Sabastian was on his side.

Smoke charged a leopard. Smoke was clawed across the snout and yelped in pain, but then he attacked again, biting the side of the leopard.

Kai watched this unfold and furiously ran his sword through the leopard's hind leg and kicked him. It yelped and hobbled away.

More eagles darted at their heads. Kai pulled the silver throwing stars from his belt with his free hand and flung them one after the other. Each star struck a bird: one in the shoulder and one in the lower leg. They flew away haphazardly.

Anger welled in the pit of Kai's stomach. The guardians had pushed and pushed. This was more than the usual Conhaspriga, more than the usual rite of passage. This was not fair. He yelled out, "STOP! ENOUGH."

Kai bowed his head and dropped to his knees. The lead shuk growled at the others to step away. Smoke and the alpha closed in around Kai and Rayna. "You've done enough. Do you honestly mean to kill us?" Kai spat. "I never wanted to hurt any of you. This is not what our rite of passage was meant to be—a deathmatch. It was meant to test our spirit, our determination, and test our fears. You've gone too far."

The remaining beasts growled in response. Furious, Kai dug deep and connected to the energy emanating within his spirit, but he needed more. A pressure built in his chest. He drew on the lifeforce around him, the magic blossomed. From the air, he pulled, and Kai felt the void created by the Lumens bend. Before he even knew what he was doing, he reached out to every living thing—plants and animals alike. The grass under his knees wilted. The animals in front of him shuddered and stepped back. He felt the power he collected amplify within his soul. It felt powerful.

Livid, Kai slammed both fists into the ground, and with it, he channeled all his fury. A blast of light-filled energy emanated outward, momentarily blinding everyone. The bear, shuks, leopards, and eagles fell to the ground—not as animals, but as men and women. Women fell from the trees wrapped in vines and covered in moss. The Lumen's blackout magic dissipated. The injured clutched at their bloody wounds. Dumbstruck, they stared at him in awe.

"GO!" Kai roared, he felt exhilarated by the rush of magic. "Tell your chiefs and your unie that we are coming to Katori. We will not give up. When we make it to Alenga's cave, your little tests are finished. You must let us enter. Remind them of that fact. Now go, before you make me really angry."

Confused, the Guardians shared glances between them. Momentarily defeated, they stumbled around and helped their wounded. Kai collected his silver stars and nodded apologetically. He watched them collect severed limbs. He had done this, hurt these people, and for what? The Guardians departed and disappear back into the forest, shrouded in ere-fog.

Kai surveyed his friends. Sabastian and Ryker were both bloody with a few deep gashes, but neither were critically hurt. Smoke had three gashes across his snout. The alpha had a bite mark on his hind leg. On the ground next to them lay one of the younger wolves, covered in blood. Rayna knelt beside the beast and tears ran down her face. She stroked its fur. The other young wolf was also severely wounded and sat slumped next to its sibling.

The other wolves surrounded the fallen wolf and began to howl. Kai's heart ached for the pack. The wolves had saved him, but at a steep cost. The second young wolf did not look good. Kai stooped down to run his hands over the animal. It whimpered under his touch. He rested his hand on Rayna's shoulder. "Can you help?"

She shook her head, tears falling. "This is beyond me. Saving you was different. You weren't bloody and broken, only infected with a poison that I could burn out. Even now, you still have unhealed welts. I... I am sorry." She sobbed.

Devastated, Kai looked at the welts on his hands, now covered in claw marks. His lungs still burned from the poison, which remained in his system. He felt better, but not perfect. "It will be alright, Rayna. You tried." He tried to comfort her, but his voice lacked the strength to be convincing.

Ryker whistled into the trees. Fog once again rolled into the area. Two women stepped through the ferns. If they had not been moving, they would have blended into the background. Ivy twisted around their bodies. Their skin was covered in a delicate moss. As they came close, the moss and ivy faded to reveal porcelain white skin and flowy green clothing. The hoods they wore partly obscured their faces.

Behind them, Kai spotted a tall man in black. His arms were across his chest, there was a glowing purple crystal secured to his wrist, like the one Yulia wore. This man must be a Weathervane, he thought. The man held his ground, but his clamped jaw told Kai he was still on guard.

The women came close. Smoke and the alpha growled. Kai touched his companion to calm him. Ryker stroked the alpha, soothing him. The older woman ran her hands down Ryker's wounds. Kai watched in amazement as each gash closed before his eyes. Before she could finish, Ryker stayed her hand. "I did not call you for myself, Niahm." He motioned to Rayna and the wolf.

The two women stooped beside the dead wolf. "We cannot bring life back," Niahm said. "Only Alenga can give life. We are sorry."

"Who are you?" Kai asked.

"We are Kodama. Tree spirits. Healers. We are friends of Ryker, and we came to heal him if needed. We do not interfere with how the elders wield their Guardians."

"If you are healers, help us save this wolf," Rayna begged. "Or teach me how to save him."

Niahm shook her head. "This is not our fight. Katori may be vast, but your imminent arrival has spread like fire across our country. I want no part of why Lucca blocks your entry." She turned to leave, pulling the other girl with her.

"Please," Rayna called, "this is not about sides. These animals are sacred—life without blame. Alenga gave you the gift of healing, would she not wish you to use it on an enemy if you could save a life?"

Both women stopped. Niahm spoke, "Would you give your life to save this creature?"

"I would," Rayna replied.

They turned back and approached the other wolf. Slumped on its side, its breathing was slow. Slender fingers ran tenderly through the bloodied gray fur. Niahm reached for Rayna's hand and pulled it to the surviving wolf. "I admire your sacrifice. I will help, and you can assist me. Maybe only a little, but I feel the seeds of power within you."

Rayna let the woman guide her. Their fingers intermingled. From head to hindquarters, they moved. "The most common mistake for a young Kodama is to use her own essence. But nature, Alenga, will not allow you to sacrifice your life for another. Instead, you must mend the body with its own internal lifeforce."

The younger woman lowered her hood and locked eyes with Rayna. The two women stared at one another. Kai glanced between them. The similarity was astonishing. If he didn't know better, he would swear they were sisters.

Niahm took Rayna's hands and bade her to focus. "There is life in your surroundings. Never draw life from one to save another. Borrow from the air around us or from the ground. A tiny amount from each living thing will not upset the balance." She raised her arms into the air and swept downward, while the younger woman pushed one hand into the soil and let the other hand rest on the wolf.

"Breathe in the essence of life floating around you," Niahm spoke softly. "Fill your lungs with it. Pull it into your core. Feel the pressure build within you. Hold it there, let it flourish with your own. Sense the power emanating down on you from the sun. Use the sunshine around us. Even the grasses can give a little."

Eyes closed, Rayna placed one hand in the soil and one on the wolf, as the other girl had done. Her face lifted to the sun. She breathed in deep. Her chest rose and fell slowly.

The other two women closed their eyes. "Use what you've collected and nurtured," Niahm continued. "Give it purpose. Let it flow through you into the wolf. Gently, ask the body to mend itself," she instructed.

Their arms and hands surged with light. The wolf's fur emanated with a delicate pulse. Gashes and torn flesh mended, threads of energy knit the animal back together. Kai looked on in amazement. He could hardly believe what he was witnessing.

As the light ebbed, the animal began to stir. The women pulled back their hands. Rayna opened her eyes. Tears of joy ran down her face at the sight of the young wolf stretching to stand. Grateful, it licked Rayna's face and playfully laid into her lap. Rayna hugged the animal against her chest. Tears streaked her cheeks.

The two Katori women stood and nodded to Ryker. Niahm spoke. "Our debt to you is repaid. We want no part of the Katori fight that is to come." She turned to Kai and glanced at the dead wolf. "We are sorry for your loss. May we take the animal and return it to Alenga?"

Kai's eyes welled once more. "You may," he choked, holding back his sadness.

Niahm scooped up the wolf and departed, joining the tall man in the trees. The younger woman turned to leave but stopped. Head down, she turned to Rayna. "If you need a teacher, I am willing." She let her dark brown eyes rise to meet Rayna's. "We are family, you and me. I feel it in my soul."

Their soft features were eerily similar. Without warning, she pulled Rayna into her arms and whispered, "My name is Imani. I wish I could stay, but you must finish your Conhaspriga. Find me, my little Kodama sister. I live with the Matoku Tribe, near Ryker's home."

Rayna squeezed tight her new-found connection. The two parted, a shared feeling of sisterly love swelled in their eyes. Imani nodded to Rayna, then she joined the others. The tall man's stone began to glow. He lifted his face to the sky, raised his arms over his head. In a downward wave, a white fog fell over them, and they disappeared into the forest.

Kneeling on the ground, Kai thanked the wolf pack. He owed them a lot, and they had paid an unfortunate price. The alpha nuzzled Kai's cheek. A sense of understanding passed between them, and the wolves darted into the forest, gone from view. Smoke watched them go, then came to stand between Rayna and Kai.

Kai shook Ryker's hand. "Thank you for standing with us. I am not sure what would have happened without you and Sabastian."

"You're a brave man." Ryker nodded. "It was an honor to fight with you. I will escort you back to the falls."

"I feel so relieved the fight is over." Rayna dusted off her hands to stand with Kai.

"Don't be too surprised if the Stonekings are unwilling to let you enter," Ryker countered. "They still have the final say. Whatever understanding you think you have with these Guardians here, does not apply to them."

"What do you mean?" Kai creased his brow. "Don't we go to the falls and enter Alenga's mountain?"

The doubtful expression on Ryker's face puzzled Kai, but before he could ask his question, Rayna spoke. "What can they do now? My vision showed a symbol carved in stone, the entrance to Alenga's mountain. Do we not find it and enter?"

Kai had thought the same thing: make it to the third waterfall, and you are home free. Ryker motioned for them to follow him. "The outside of the mountain belongs to them—the elders. You must get into the part Alenga controls."

This was news to Kai. His fear now was that they had come all this way, and now they would be turned away. It didn't seem right. He stepped through the forest as Ryker continued. "Your wolf, Smoke, will not be able to enter the cave with you. Leave him with me, and I will see him safely to the other side of the mountain within a day or so."

"Thank you, both of you." Kai offered a hand to Sabastian. "We are most grateful for your assistance today. I hope this will not cause you too much trouble."

Sabastian waved him off. "Being a rebel is much better than following the rules of the elders. Besides, I go where I wish, and I think their reasons are foolish. You are nothing like Keegan. I see it and I have spent very little time with you. Lucca is not even giving you a chance. By alienating you, they will only end up creating the very thing they fear most: division amongst our people. People were forced to choose Keegan or Lucca. Now they will be forced to choose you or Lucca."

"How do I create division among the Katori?" Kai twisted to face Sabastian.

"There are many who agree with Keegan, not so much about dominating the world, but about not living in fear or hiding our powers from the outside world. Our people want the freedom to come and go as they please, to travel the world and meet with other cultures. Imagine being told you could never leave Diu. That your children could never leave, or they would not receive Alenga's blessing. That is what Keegan initially wanted, to open our borders and expand our influence, but then he took it too far. Many wanted to follow him."

This news shocked Kai. Had his father merely meant to start a revolution to give the Katori more freedom? Ryker interrupted his soul-searching. "Time to go, Kai."

Together they stood below the roaring waterfall. Out of the mist, Liam approached. "Kai. It has been a long time. This must be Rayna. Welcome. I have come to open the passage." Liam stepped toward the falls.

Kai took a breath, overwhelmed by how far they'd come. Doubt welled in the pit of his stomach. Did he really want this? The elders clearly did not want him. He would rather turn back and suffer through the pain of his powers burning themselves out—that is, if it were not for the hope of saving his mother. He realized his Katori powers could help him do that. "Thank you, Liam."

"By the state of you, I would say you more than earned your rites. I have never seen anyone covered in blood."

"Have you helped others?" Rayna asked.

"No, you will be my first," Liam responded. "But when you exit on the other side, there will be people to welcome you. The Katori almost crave the magic that stirs around a blessing. My own experience left me bruised with a few scratches, but I did not look like either of you." He motioned up and down at Kai and Rayna.

"What did they do to you?" she asked.

"Took me almost a week to get here. Eagles would carry me off and drop me in a tree. The Stonekings had a canyon set up and then tried to crush me by closing it. I've never been so scared in my life."

Kai chuckled, relieved the stone experience was not personal and thankful they had survived. "So, now what?"

"Come, I will grant you access." Liam motioned toward the falls. "I will open the way into Alenga's Mountain within the Katori Mountains. The path inside will not be easy. Changes from long ago shifted her mountain, breaking the path into perilous segments. We tried repairing the tunnels, but her magic prevents our influence."

Kai couldn't help but ask. "Is there always someone here to open the way?"

"Yes, but I am sorry to say none volunteered to stand against the wishes of our leaders. The covenant between the Stonekings and the chiefs is everlasting. There are many traditionalists who fear your arrival. There are whispers everywhere about you being Keegan's son."

"Yet you stand here with us today," Kai stated.

"True. But I was never asked by our leaders. Yulia sent word of your impending arrival. My teacher, Benmar, your grandfather, and Keegan's own father, asked me to stand for you. Plus, no one told me I could not help you. Not that I asked." He grinned slyly. "So, I came for my friend."

Kai knelt to say goodbye to Smoke. Smoke nudged him and licked his face. Through their shared connection, Kai instructed Smoke to follow Ryker. Smoke complied by taking a stance beside the Beastmaster, and a feeling of strength emanated between them.

The towering waterfall surrounded by giant redwood trees thundered through his memory. His visions had brought him here many times. Water crashed down beside him, the icy mist sprayed his face. Rayna took his hand. "We're ready," she offered.

Kai looked at her and smiled. He knew if it were not for the promise he'd made himself to find his mother, he would not be standing here today. Rayna was right, their gifts were not worth this sacrifice. These people were not his people. Part of him wanted to walk away, but then he thought of his mother. To find her, he needed his magic. And time was running out. If he waited any longer, she might never be able to return to her human form ever again.

The base of the falls was thick trees and underbrush. They walked through the trees, and Kai closed his eyes to the mist. Together they walked through the heavy spray. The narrow stone ledge was barely a foot wide as it passed behind the falls.

The water pounded beside them and threatened to pull them away from the wall. Kai recalled his dream and searched the stone wall for the symbolic groves, three interlocking loops with no end. He had researched the symbol and learned it was called a triquetra. The drawing his uncle had shown him. When his hand felt the three converging lines, he smiled. "This is it. The symbol is here. How do we open a solid stone wall?"

"Allow me." Liam spread his arms apart. He placed one hand on either side of the triquetra. The ground trembled. Part of the wall receded deep into the surrounding stone. Kai watched in amazement.

Rayna looked deep into the dark passage. "Are we meant to walk through this tunnel?"

Liam held up his finger and shook his head. Placing his hands on either side of the opening. His knuckles turned white with the pressure he applied. Slowly his fingers dented the stone. He rotated his hands and pulled downward. Thundering quakes shook the ground. The rock wall gave way and slid down, out of sight.

They now stood in front of a shallow undercut portico, made from a mixture of white and gray marble. The entrance was astonishing, with twisted columns, arches, and several masterfully cut steps. At the center of the recessed wall, in the spot where one would expect a door, the original stone slab became an archway with the triquetra symbol carved repeatedly around the arch.

Astonished at Liam's ability, Kai approached the archway. With his hands, Kai touched the jagged white and gray marble. Again, he traced the symbol cut into the stone wall. Pain ached in his trembling hand as he ran his finger over the design. Rayna's hand touched his hand. His heart felt relief—they had made it.

Liam breathed heavy. Kai could see the task had taken a toll. "Does it look this way for everyone?" Kai asked, impressed.

"It does not. Each Stoneking is free to create and show off his skill. I have a lot to learn. I still have trouble mastering large-scale creations without feeling drained." Liam offered his hand. "You still have a long way to go, my friend. Good luck, and trust your gut, it got you this far. Alenga's mountain is a sacred place, you will feel very different inside."

Liam pressed his hand into the original stone slab, but then a look of frustration knit his brow. His knuckles turned white with the pressure he applied. The slab didn't budge. "Why did the Stonekings even let me reveal the entrance, only to bar the way?"

Kai stepped back, disappointed. "Ryker said the Stonekings may not let us inside. What now, are we finished?"

"I don't know." Liam scratched his head. "This is the way into Alenga's Mountain. We all go this way, from this side anyway."

Rayna looked up. "How close are the other Stonekings, do you think? I mean, if they are controlling this opening, they would need to be close. Right?"

"They would. Within a few hundred feet, even our best would need to be close. Within gleaning range to control the stones. What are you thinking?"

She closed her eyes. Kai and Liam watched her. "You are right, they are close. Over there, two hundred feet to our left."

"Where are you going with this?" Kai asked.

Rayna ran her hand over the stone arch. "If the door is locked, make a window."

The curve of Liam's mouth curled up. "Clever. I like her, Kai. You're a lucky man. Come, I have an idea. I believe I can trick them. Get you in another way. The Guardians were created to protect the Katori way of life. Nobody has the right to judge your soul. Your parentage doesn't make who you are. Legend or not, I have faith in you."

Liam stepped back to the ledge, knelt and pressed his hands into the stone ground. As quickly as it had fallen, the stone wall rose before them. With the twist of his hand, he pulled to the stone door through the void. No seam revealed Liam had ever changed the wall.

Damp from the water's spray, Liam directed them away from the falls, they stood behind the towering pine trees. Kai and Rayna found themselves facing a sheer, straight wall. "Stand close to one another—single file behind me. This will take everything I have left. Move fast."

"Liam, where are you taking us?" Kai asked. "There is nowhere to go."

"Trust me. Stay close. As I step up, you follow," Liam commanded. "We won't have long. Once the Stonekings discover my plan, they will relocate and try to block me. We are going up the falls. Normally you would have climbed up through the cavern to reach the entrance to her tunnels. Instead, I'm going to drop you in from above. You will drop into a pool, which is part of Alenga's Mountain."

Before Kai could ask questions, Liam touched the wall and raised his foot. A rumble emanated from the wall. The rock receded. Steep stone steps cut into the wall. "Hurry," Liam shouted. "We must climb the side of the waterfall."

Kai and Rayna quickly followed. Each knee-raising step took them deep into a dark, narrow tunnel. The claustrophobic space left little room for Kai's shoulders. After the first few steps, a crack of light appeared above. As they climbed, the skylight above became more prominent. Kai could feel the sunshine on his face once more. The blue sky made it easier to breathe.

Behind them, the stairwell began to close. Rayna stepped in closer behind Kai, kicking his heels. He lurched forward but caught himself before falling. Rayna called out, "Sorry!"

Liam kept a quick pace. "Hold on to each other and keep climbing," Liam instructed, his body twisted to the right. He glanced at the ground beneath Kai's feet. With his right hand behind him, angled outward, he curled his fingers into a fierce claw. Under Kai's feet, the ground began to shake. Rayna grabbed Kai's belt. She fell to one knee, pulling Kai down with her. Kai cringed as his knee struck the edge of the stone step. Concerned about the gap between him and Liam, he shouted, "Liam, wait!" Kai reached back and pulled Rayna to her feet.

"Hold on," Liam shouted over the rumble, still climbing while his arm arched upward over his head.

Kai rushed to catch Liam, dragging Rayna with a firm grip. Her shoulder bumped the sidewall, and she grimaced against the pain. "Slow down," she screamed.

The ground below their feet shuttered and rose skyward. Liam glanced over his shoulder, and with another twist of his hand, they were thrust forward. They were now moving in two directions at once. Up and forward. Alarmed, Kai put his hand against the wall as it slid backward. He dropped Rayna's hand, and she shoved him back upright. The walls around them flew past them.

"Thank you," he shouted to Rayna. "Are you alright?"

Sunshine continued to bloom around them. "I'm fine," she hollered.

He steadied himself, squatting to touch the next step. With a firm grasp on Rayna's hand, he took a few steps. His knees wobbled. They continued to move forward and higher. Within moments they were thrust to the surface. Free from the confines of the narrow space, Liam ran upriver and crouched near its rocky edge.

Liam motioned, wide-eyed. "Hurry!" He stepped into the river. "When I open the hole, jump, don't hesitate. I might not be able to keep it open very long. Once you are in, there is nothing they can do."

Liam dropped to his knees and plunged his fist into the river. The ground unfolded like a flower, forming a cone-shaped sinkhole. The sound of stone grinding against itself startled Rayna, and she grabbed Kai's wrist. Water gushed in the hole and dumped into a water-filled cavern. Liam shouted "GO!" as the hole began to shrink.

Kai leaned over the edge and glanced at Rayna. She leaped over the edge. Water sloshed around her as she slid down the steep gravel slope. Kai jumped after her. His rump struck the sloping ground harder than he wished. He slid right behind her.

CHAPTER 7

Conhaspriga

They plunged into the blue-green water below with a tremendous splash. Above them, the hole sealed shut, blocking out the sunlight. They swam to the surface. Waves bounced off the cavern walls, splashing back at them. Once they were sealed inside, Kai surveyed the cave. Liam was gone.

The cavern was not as dark as he had feared. Tiny multifaceted star-like gems were set into the rock, and these white-and-blue iridescent crystals illuminated the cavern. Each one was cut precisely and brilliantly beautiful. He could see the energy within set aglow. Magic thrummed from the walls, water, and plant life. The power inside the mountain felt energetic yet peaceful. Kai was no longer afraid. This was a safe place, he could feel the tranquility. Thirsty, he drank some of the water from the pool. The freshwater washed down his dry throat.

The room itself was perfectly round. Kai could see the outline of a dome ceiling, once open, now sealed shut. The white and gray marble of the Katori Mountains filled the space. Only the occasional drip down the walls reminded Kai that they were beneath a vast moving river. Various green plants grew in clumps around a shallow rocky beach. Vines grew up the walls.

"Let's go," Kai instructed, swimming to the shallow beach area to the open archway.

Kai stood on the pebbly underground beach. He took his time to listen and look around at their new surroundings. The sloshing of the pool echoed across the jagged dome, but the sound of the river above and the waterfall outside was blocked by the thick stone. On the opposite wall, he could see the marble archway and a set of stairs leading down, the place where they would have entered had Liam not opened the ceiling for them.

They climbed up to a dark open doorway. The iridescent crystals randomly placed along the walls gave just enough light to traverse the uneven ground safely. Rayna squeezed Kai's hand, and he gave her a nod. "Do you feel the magic in the air?"

Rayna wiped the water from her cheek. "For the first time in days, I feel a weight lifted off my soul. There is... almost a presence around us."

"I feel it, too."

Deep inside the tunnel, a small pedestal awaited with a single lit torch. Orange and yellow flames gave off a warm glow. Kai took Rayna's hand; her warm fingers interlaced with his. Their first steps echoed off the walls of the cavern. Gem lights twinkled above, and the space began to narrow. Weaving through a slender tunnel, Rayna slid her hand along the smooth glassy surface of the walls.

"I can see my reflection in the stone. I have never seen this type of rock before. It looks like black glass."

Around the next turn, Kai's boot sloshed into knee-deep water. In the ceiling, the tiny crystal stars continued to provide a faint blue light. Their torch bounced white and yellow splashes of light around the small space. As they went, the stones became less frequent. Some were placed randomly into the ceiling, walls, and even the floor.

Kai grabbed the torch and waved it around to illuminate the darkness. The way forward split into two small deviating tunnels. Rayna instinctively pointed to the right. "This way, I remember this from my dream."

Kai shook his head in agreement. "Me too."

As they walked, the water began to drain away. Relieved to be back out of the water, they squeezed down the narrowing tunnel. Kai continued to lead them through twists and turns. Each decision took them deeper into the tunnel. Their next tunnel led them downward.

After only a few steps, the stone sloped sharply, and Kai slid on his rump down into frigid water. Rayna, a few steps behind, stopped. "Are you alright?" she asked. Slowly she climbed down to his level and eased herself into the water. "Brrr, this water is cold."

They sloshed through the narrowing passage waist-deep in water, and Kai held Rayna's hand. As the water got deeper, the ceiling crept downward. He could sense her concern as she tightened her grip. "Kai, this place is exactly like my dream," she professed.

"Right. What concerns me is how accurately the dream depicted each part of the cave. That means we've yet to get to the difficult part." With very little light from their small torch, he could see scratch marks on the tunnel walls. The sight made him a bit uneasy. Each step brought the water higher and higher until Rayna was neck-deep in water.

"Rayna, you should climb on my back to keep your head above the water."

Methodically, they moved through the rising water. The jagged ceiling crept ever closer. Rayna clung to Kai's shoulders. They turned a tight corner and came upon a solid wall. Kai peered beyond the glow of his torch. "I think we've reached a dead end."

Kai took another step. To his surprise, the angle of the ground declined, and they slid under the water, extinguishing their torch.

As the pair resurfaced, they coughed. Kai scrambled back to where he stood earlier while reaching for Rayna in the darkness. Back on solid ground, they let their eyes adjust to the lack of sufficient light. Along the walls, the tiniest of lights illuminated their faces.

"Well, we knew at some point we'd have to swim," he said. "I had hoped for a little more warning. From here, we should glean our way forward. Are you ready?"

She firmly squeezed his hand, took a deep breath, and released it slowly. "I am," she responded.

"Together, now," Kai said. "Slow your breathing, relax your mind." He spoke softly, yet his words echoed around them.

As he talked her through relaxing, he felt and saw everything come alive around him. The water had a beautiful iridescent glow, and he could now see a luminescent version of Rayna's face just above the water. Had they wasted their time bringing the torch? Were they meant to take it or trust their sight to find their way? After spending the day unable to glean, he'd not even tried until now.

Gleaning, he looked around the dead end. Along the back wall several feet below the waterline, he saw a small broken archway. "There, on the back of the cave. Do you see the archway? I guess this is the damaged area."

"I do," Rayna replied. "It looks rather small. We will have to go through one at a time. No way we can swim together side by side."

"I should go first, in case there are any problems. The quakes could have loosened rocks, and the path could be blocked. Give me a minute before you follow. Focus on me in your mind. See the path I take so you can follow. In our dreams back in Diu, there was more than one path. In the dream, I was drawn to the left."

"Same here," she added. "Although, I...I don't know about swimming into the narrow hole. On the surface, you are free to come up whenever you wish. Down there, we will be trapped."

"You can do this," he insisted. "There is no other way. After hours of walking through dark tunnels, we are near the end. Don't think about the rocks above you, just keep moving. Relax. Don't panic. You will be fine."

After a few relaxing deep breaths together, Kai let go of Rayna's hand and dove beneath the water. A few star crystals were affixed to the rock, illuminating the water from beneath. As he swam, he stretched his arms out and pulled on the rocks to propel himself through the tunnel. With each kick of his legs, the place where the shaft appeared to be a dead-end came into view.

Kai gleaned the tunnel, and he could sense that Rayna was doing alright behind him. He pulled himself around the sharp angle to the left. His lungs began to beg for air. Again, he thought of Rayna. In his mind, he could see her following several feet behind. She was at the turn. Her hands touched the stones, and she maneuvered herself around the sharp corner. Concerned for his own need for air, he kicked and pulled harder.

Up ahead he could see the mouth of the old hallway expand. Light glimmered on the water's surface. His lungs begged for air near the end. With one last kick, he broke through the surface. He took in a deep breath, then another.

He swam across the pool to the stone stairs. He was in another round room. Knee-level to the ground, more star crystal illuminated the walls. Above, there was a ceiling with a decoratively carved ring with an open center. It was not completely dark, nor was it lit well enough to see the people he sensed waiting.

It was then that he began to worry about why Rayna had not come through. She should have been right behind him. Kai searched through the tunnel. She was now on the last leg and frantic for air. He desperately wanted to swim down and help her, but he knew she would want to make it on her own.

As she exited the underwater tunnel, she pushed hard for the surface and came up gasping for air. Kai offered her his hand and pulled her to the edge of the pool. "Are you alright?"

She coughed and wiped the water from her face. She clung to Kai's hands as he pulled her up beside him. "We're not alone. Do you sense them above us?" She asked.

"I do."

Together they climbed up. Kai stared up into the dimly lit ceiling. He could sense eight people above them on the round ledge that mirrored their own below. Their energy pushed on his spirit with actual physical strength. On the far side of the cave were two dimly lit tunnels leading out of the cave. He did not know what came next. The dream had ended here. The people above whispered indistinctly amongst themselves.

There were eight people, four men, and four women. And he had a sneaking suspicion who they were... "Are you the four tribal chiefs and the four unie of the Katori people? Have you come here to send us back or welcome us?" He feared their answer.

A man's voice echoed from above. "We've never had two come through together before. This is unusual."

A woman spoke. "We are indeed your tribal chiefs and your unie. We cannot send you back. Alenga bids us to welcome you. This was once her sanctuary, but it was broken centuries ago when the Katori Mountains were first raised by the Stonekings."

Another man spoke. "Welcome, Kai, whose name means ocean. Welcome, Rayna, whose name means queen. You've passed your tests of spirit. Here within Alenga's sacred mountain, we greet you. It is her will that you proceed. We do as she commands."

Something about the voice struck a chord inside Kai. He wondered, could this be his grandfather—Lucca?

A different woman spoke. "Our questions are meant to be answered by one. As such, you will need to answer in unison to avoid influencing each other."

The man Kai believed was Lucca spoke again. "Are you each willing to leave behind the ways of the modern world?"

"I am," they said in unison.

The first woman spoke. "Do you promise to protect and keep the secrets of the Katori, guard them with your life?"

"I do," they said in unison.

"Do you commit yourself to the bonding of your spirit to the protection of Alenga, the mother of all nature?" Lucca asked.

"I do," they said in unison.

"You cannot continue together. Choose your path, follow it to the end, and carve out your crystal. Your stone will help you control and withstand the force of your magic. Our spirits are not capable of manipulating such raw energy. Alenga created this crystal mountain to encapsulate part of our power. When she blesses you, she will reveal your gifts by filling your crystal with color: red means you're a Stoneking, green for a Kodama, purple for a Weathervane, blue for a Beastmaster, and yellow is for a Lumen. You will understand soon enough what Alenga has in store for you. We will see you at the end."

Separately, Rayna and Kai both walked around opposite sides of the small pool. Rayna quickly chose and walked down the path to the left. She did not look back. Kai stood before his only choice. The cave did not call to him, but something did.

From a voice high above came the command. "You must choose."

He knew they were right—his body burned, his chest seemed to get hotter. He closed his eyes and placed his hand on his chest. His gleaning revealed a third choice. He pressed his hands against the wall. It did not budge.

The voices above began to whisper and chatter. Kai pushed again—still nothing. More chatter echoed above. He knew there was an opening here, but why would it not open. Then he heard a word resonate within his mind—*strength.* The thought was a test. Kai considered what the word meant. Clearly, brute strength would not open this hidden door. The words of his uncle Haygan came to mind—*you have a strong spirit.* It would take his strength of spirit to open the door.

Kai folded his hands in prayer. "Alenga, give me strength and show me the path." In silence, he waited. Nothing happened. Then he leaned his feverish forehead onto the cold stone. A small light beamed from the remaining open path, tempting him to take the easy choice. Still he waited.

"Alenga, give me strength to take the difficult path. My faith will take me on the true path you set for me."

Light beamed along the floor at his feet, and the wall started to give way. He felt it give a little, then a little more. He pushed against the wall. Finally, there was a space large enough for him to slip through and he let go of the stone slab. It slowly slid back into place, sealing him into another room.

The chill in the room felt refreshing against his hot skin. Steam rose off his damp clothes, and tiny clouds of smoke formed on his breath. The glow of white crystals beaded around the wall. In the center of the room was a stone pedestal; it held a double-headed hammer and a large metal chisel. Kai took both and looked around the room.

Eyes closed, he gleaned the rocky wall. He could see the chisel marks from others before him. He searched for the crystal that called to him. White light emanated from one spot on the wall. Sweat dripped from his face, and his chest burned in agony. He did his best to calm his breathing and focus on his task.

He placed the sharp point of the chisel against the wall and used the hammer to carve out a chunk of rock-encased crystal. After each strike, he pulled the chisel out of the stone and moved it around the edge of his crystal, careful not to strike it. He landed several more blows on the nail head. One last hit and his stone came free.

Finished with the tools, he set them back on the pedestal. In doing so, it sank deeper and deeper into the stone floor. As the stand went into the ground, it slowly revealed a spiral staircase descending deep into the floor.

Kai followed the staircase down. Star-crystals illuminated the walls as he went. At the bottom, he smelled a hint of fresh air. Hundreds of star-crystals illuminated the corridor. As he continued, the walls began to weep, and the ground started to slope. Soon the grade became so steep that he slipped onto his side and began to slide downward. The smooth wet stone rushed him through the illuminated tunnel.

The ground dropped and twisted to the left, propelling him faster and faster. The next drop spun Kai to the right. He slid high up the curved wall. Water sloshed around him. The ride excited him, and he whooped with excitement.

The meandering ride continued for several minutes before another drop propelled him straight down. Water rushed by his face, nearly choking him. He covered his nose and mouth. A change in the slide eased him upward, reducing his speed. Another turn deposited him into a small pool. He sat up in the water. The air was warm and sweet.

Kai climbed out of the shallow pool. A warm breeze blew against his wet face. Sunlight leaked into the cave. The walls expanded and sunlight streamed down from above. Suddenly he knew that he was at the beginning of something new; all he had to do was trust Alenga to guide him. With faith in his heart, he stepped out of the tunnel.

CHAPTER 8

Alenga's Blessing

Kai walked out of the mountain and into a large glen. The sunshine was too bright for his eyes, which had become accustomed to the dark. He squinted against the grandeur. The jagged mountain ridge curled around them, creating a surreal meadow. Kai's eyes adjusted. He observed the faces of the people who had come to welcome him. Strangers everywhere. The crowd came closer.

Eagles swooped down from the sky, transforming into people. Beasts of all types changed into people. Kai was in awe. Great trees in the meadow morphed into women. Each person was dressed in flowing linen and silk clothes. They wore a variety of an assortment of colors. There were shades of red, blue, purple, and green, with only three in yellow. He noticed their clothes matched their crystals. The one thing they all had in common: no shoes. Their smiles seemed welcoming, yet Kai was unsure how to feel.

Concerned, he looked back toward the cave. Where was Rayna?

Whispers from the crowd brought his attention forefront. The crowd drew him closer. The same feeling he had felt from Diu was now intensified here. Something called to him. All this time, he'd thought it was the mountain or the magic within the crystals, but it was much more. Everything here had a thrum of power.

Compelled to move forward, he edged around more strangers. They bowed and smiled, welcoming him. One man stepped through the crowd, followed by a woman. Finally, there were faces he recognized. "Haygan. Simone." He grabbed Haygan's outstretched arm.

They greeted him with pleasant smiles and ushered him down a smooth stone path. In fact, they were nearly pushing him to another small gathering of people. "Kai, come quickly. You need to hurry."

When they parted, he saw Rayna. She had changed.

Gone were her muddy boots and wet clothing. Her wet hair was neatly brushed and swept over one shoulder. She stood in her bare feet and wore a bright white linen dress. She too was clutching a fist-sized rock-encrusted crystal. Yulia stood by her side.

"Yulia, how did you get here so fast?" Kai whispered.

Her toothy grin bubbled into laughter. "Dragons fly over the mountains, and I know a few."

Before he could ask more, Haygan and a few other men ushered Kai into a moss-covered stone gazebo. Thick green ivy covered the arched marble opening, concealing him from view. "Change into the white linen clothes on the bench," Haygan instructed from outside. "Do so quickly."

Vines or not, it was a little embarrassing to change publicly, but Kai quickly did as he was told. He struggled to remove his wet clothing. His damp things plopped on the white marble floor. A burst of wind whipped down from above through the gazebo and dried his skin. He hurried to put on the clothing provided. Like Rayna, he was now dressed in white linen pants and a white shirt. The material was soft and flowy.

In one hand, he held the stone he had carved out of Alenga's mountain. In the other, he held his mother's necklace. Unsure he should take it with him, he slipped it into his boot and stuffed his socks inside to ensure it would not be noticed.

"Ready," Kai announced, running his fingers through his hair.

Haygan again took him by the arm. "We need to hurry."

Beads of perspiration began to form on Kai's brow. Sweat ran down his back. Again, he felt an urge to move forward. The power of Alenga pulled at his core. He clutched his stone and took note of his surroundings.

Two massive weeping willows sprang up where the mountain ridge ended, protecting the entrance to the secluded garden. Their long tendril curtains nearly touched the path. Two women in purple swirled their hands, and a delicate breeze parted the vines for the crowd to pass.

Together they traveled along a white marble path that curved through a magical garden. Occasionally the path arched over an iridescent blue stream. Wildflowers and blooming trees dotted the landscape. Kai could feel the energy in the air. Magic rubbed against his soul. He felt happy.

Katori was much more than Kendra and Liam's descriptions. There were graceful stone gazebos, pergolas, and bridges, all modestly laced with flowery moss and variegated vines. There were sprawling gardens, each connected by endless blue waterways and delightful fountains and curvy white marble paths. Everywhere he looked there was harmony.

Unlike home, Katori gardens replaced the symmetry of Diu gardens with twisting pathways, mythical sculptures, and exotic flowers. There were green plants, arched stonework, sculpted cascades of stone and water. It was a delightful display of flowers, vines, and trees.

The sounds of bird song echoed on the wind. Birds of color fluttered across the deep blue sky. Wild animals slinked through the flowers. He saw three wolves and a mountain cat. Butterflies and hummingbirds buzzed from flower to flower.

Massive trees stood around the edge of the garden, beset with egglike structures made of living vines and branches, intertwined with stone spirals and connected sagging bridges. Strange-looking windmills swirled in the distance. There was so much to take in at one time. They were moving too fast. Kai wanted to gawk.

Haygan rushed Rayna and Kai towards a large structure. Through the flowering trees, Kai caught a glimpse of the Agora's white and gray marble. Kendra was right, the stone curves and twists around the edifice looked alive. It appeared to sprout out of the ground. The rotunda had eight curvy arched entrances, one for each side of the octagonal building.

The closer they came to the Agora, the more power he felt. Peace washed over him. Energy coursed through his veins. The structure, or rather an essence inside, emanated a great power. Even the trees nearby swirled with energy, and each had grown twisted. Shafts of power had curled the trees into individual sculptures.

At the entrance, an older man awaited them. Kai was speechless. He had never seen an old Katori person before. He had wondered if any of them ever aged. The man's skin was rugged, and his expression was serious yet playful. He stood straight and tall. If it were not for his long white hair blowing in the breeze and tan complexion, he could have been a statue.

"My name is Orin, Stoneking. I am the master of crystals. Hand me your stone," he said to Rayna.

She cupped her precious stone in both hands, offering it to him.

Orin placed one hand atop the stone and the other underneath Rayna's hands. He looked deep into her eyes. His toothy smile brought a giggle to Rayna's lips. With a bow, he took her stone. He rolled it over in his hands. Bits of ordinary rock fell away like dust through his fingers.

The sound of stone being crushed rumbled from Orin's cupped hands. He worked quickly to remove the unnecessary bits. More dust slipped through his fingers. The wind blew away the unwanted material, and Kai caught a glimpse of her true stone emerging.

Orin pressed the crystal between his palms. White sparks slipped through his fingers. Rayna shielded her face. The old man ran his fingers around the remaining gem, creating the final shape. Finished, Orin opened his hands. He handed Rayna a smooth white teardrop crystal. "I see many tears in your future, some of pain, and some of great joy. Let them be a testament to the bold woman you will become."

Then he extended his hand to Kai. "May I have your stone, please?" Orin asked.

Kai held out his rock-encrusted crystal. Orin's vise-like grip surrounded his; Kai felt the warmth in the man's touch. Orin's cosmic blue eyes looked deep into Kai's. It felt as if the man was searching his soul. Then the old man bowed. He took the stone and quickly began to roll his hands around it.

As before, plain rock disintegrated in his hands and blew away in the breeze. When he pressed against the stone, he shifted his hands from side to side. His fingers rubbed and pinched at the emerging crystal. Sparks blinded Kai from seeing the finer points of creation. Orin's maneuvers were slightly different this time. Finished, he opened his hand and gave Kai his crystal, now transformed into a white hexagonal shape. "The hexagon is the strongest shape known to me. You have a strong spirit, use it to protect others."

Kai thanked Orin and entered the Agora. The stunning room was spacious and grand. He wondered if the entire Diu palace could fit inside this massive space. Around the perimeter, arches and towers created smaller meeting spaces. The alcoves were already full of people, many holding round cushions. They appeared to be waiting.

In the center, there was a clear pool, shallow and roughly twenty feet across. Straight above, the roof swooped upward to a matching opening to the sky. Sunshine bathed the pool below. Kai and Rayna approached. At the bottom of the natural spring, Kai noticed the three interlocking loops with no end. The design was set into the stone and illuminated in blue crystal.

Haygan directed them both to wade into the water. "This is the celestial spirit pool. Both of you: enter together with your crystals. May Alenga restore your health, replenish your spirit, and bless your future." With a bow, he backed away and sat beside Simone.

The crowd sat, eagerly waiting, their posture angled inward towards the pool. Kai looked at the water's shimmering smooth surface. Light glistened down from the mirroring circle above. As instructed, he waded into the pool. Energy-charged water invigorated his body. Pure magic seeped into his skin. He could feel the power building around him. The water beckoned him deeper.

The crowd began to hum. Power filled the air.

One step, then another, Kai went deeper, Rayna at his side. The water temperature was refreshing against his hot skin. On the fourth step,

Rayna paused, glanced at Kai, and stepped forward. She sank below the water's surface. A bright light surrounded her. The power within the pool became intense.

Kai felt a presence call to him. Peace swelled in his heart and mind. He too stepped off the last step and plunged under the water. Light burst into every bruise, welt, scrape, and gash. The water bubbled with fury, and the temperature rose. He felt a heatwave consume him. The essence of healing poured through him. His bones felt stronger, his muscles strengthened, and his mind cleared.

The temperature cooled to a comfortable lukewarm. The heat within was gone. For the first time in weeks, Kai felt free of the heat, the ache in his bones, and the pressure in his chest. Warm white light surrounded him. The face of a woman appeared before him.

Without words, he knew who she was—the sacred mother Alenga. Her iridescent blue glow bloomed in front of his eyes. Her hair floated outward around her head. He had seen her before. She had saved him that day in Port Anahita when he'd nearly drowned.

She pressed her hand over his heart. Alenga spoke to him. "Breathe, my child. You are made of this water."

Kai took in a breath, and his lungs filled with the sacred water, yet he could still breathe. He could feel the power within the water healing his lungs. Alenga touched her fingers to his forehead. Again she spoke. "See, my child, how we came to be...what we were given."

Kai's mind exploded with images. His body convulsed with the connection to Alenga. Light pushed against the dark. Stars pricked against the black sky. Plants crept across a vast landscape in blooms of color. He saw towering trees. The ground shifted to change the rolling landscape. Rivers and oceans carved the world into segments. Creatures roamed the land and sea. The birth of nature was a powerful moment.

Alenga wrapped her hands around his fist. "Understand that everything is connected. Nothing is ever lost, only changed. Bring home your brothers and sisters."

An awakening stirred Kai's spirit. Raw energy swelled in his soul. Alenga clasped her hands around his, the crystal held tight within. His fist glowed as bright as the sun. He closed his eyes against the blinding light. Magic coursed through his crystal, raced up his arm, and washed through his body.

He could feel the building blocks of nature, the flexibility tangible within his core. Creatures large and small came to his mind. There was a visceral connection to each. He somehow understood that he would become a Beastmaster. When the light faded, he saw Alenga's face clearly once more.

She leaned in close next to his ear. "Understand and remember," she whispered, touching his forehead one final time.

Mesmerized by his experience, Kai closed his eyes and felt Alenga fade away. Slowly he floated to the surface. A delicate breeze blew across his face, and he inhaled fresh air. Barely lucid, he sensed his uncle Haygan. Still, Kai lingered between worlds. Haygan lifted Kai from the pool and laid him on a soft mat.

Kai felt the stone in his hand, yet he sensed the mountain range from whence it came—a mountain inside another mountain. He felt the air fill his lungs, and yet his mind floated on the breeze which blew over the vastness of this world. Layers of time pressed against themselves. He saw his childhood, his struggles, his pain. Faces flashed in his mind: his mother and father, his uncle Haygan, Rayna, Kendra, Davi's tribe.

Lost between the here and now, Kai's spirit drifted on the knowledge he'd been given—access to history itself. War and peace, loss and rebirth, love and hate, regret and joy, fear, and trust. Emotional awareness. And still, the soft mat against his back was ever-present.

When Kai awoke, his clothes were dry. He sat up to see Haygan perched on a large round cushion, near his feet, between him and Rayna. An intense white glow surrounded his uncle. He opened the palm of his hand. His stone remained crystal clear. Basically, unchanged. Although, if possible, maybe whiter than before.

He felt a little disappointed. He had been sure it would be blue like all the other Beastmasters he knew.

Rayna lay on the mat beside him. Her body emitted light that he could see without gleaning, and it pushed against Kai's sensitive eyes. He noticed she was also dry, but still deep within her experience. "How…" Kai struggled to make a sound at first. "How did we get out of the pool?" Kai asked. He wanted to touch Rayna's arm, but he refrained. "Why is everyone here glowing so bright?"

Haygan whispered. "After your… shall we say, experience, everyone floats to the surface. As your uncle, I asked to be the one to lift you from the pool. It is a blessing to enter the water while it teems with power. The entire building hums with magic."

"How is it that we are completely dry? I kind of remember you pulling me from the water, only, I…" Kai let his words fade, thinking back to the moment.

"You have been lying here for almost an hour." Haygan waved to the meditating crowd. "We are all here to pray over you and Rayna. Offer blessings. We wait for you to return." Haygan paused as Rayna stirred. "They are bright because you are attuned to their aura. I see it too, although not as brightly as you, because I was in the pool. They can also see a pale version of the magic you connected with in the water. It is the insight from Alenga, shared with us all on this day."

Lost between thoughts and emotions, Kai did not know what to say. He tried to speak again, but no words would come out. His nerves felt raw, near the surface, oversensitive. Without needing to focus, not only could he see everyone's aura, he sensed their emotions. Harmony emanated from the crowd. He took a deep breath to linger in the moment.

"Nephew, after our bonding, everyone feels at a loss for words. It is a compelling experience. Relax and enjoy the moment. It can be disorienting for some and euphoric for others. It will subside. Within a few hours, you won't even remember the experience. You will be left with the memory and feeling of pure peace and love. That is Alenga's way."

Brows knit together in confusion, Kai looked at the pool. He didn't want to forget. Just the opposite, he needed to remember her words. He was sure that is what Alenga told him. Before he could protest, Rayna sat up. Her beautiful long brown hair puddled around her shoulders. She opened her hand. The once white teardrop crystal was now deep emerald green.

"I..." She swallowed and looked at Kai. "I feel wonderful," Rayna announced profoundly. "Alenga was so beautiful. She told me...I...I don't remember." She looked to the others, her eyes ready to tear with joy. "Kai, you are radiant." She motioned to his aura. "I can feel your essence. Without gleaning, I see your light shining."

Yulia knelt between them. "Welcome back, my dear. Green, I see—Kodama. As if there was any doubt. You are most blessed, Rayna."

Yulia reached toward Kai. Her expression shifted to one of concern. "Close your hand, Kai," she whispered. "Don't let them see your stone is white. The elders will not like this. It is as they feared. You are most certainly Keegan's son. I don't know why I didn't notice the resemblance before."

Fear welled in the pit of Kai's stomach. "You mean my father's crystal was white?"

"Yes," she cupped her hand over his stone. "Before it turned black. Although his father, Benmar, your grandfather, his crystal is still white to this day."

Haygan waved her off. "There is no use in hiding it, Kai. Alenga has blessed you as she saw fit. Legend or no, your crystal is white. Like all of us, you will choose a teacher, and your gifts—whatever they are, will simply be. How you choose to use them is what will define you. Maybe even define us all. I do not know what this means, or if you will fight your father, but this is not the time to talk."

On his feet, Haygan pulled Kai and Rayna to his side. Hands pressed together, he bowed to each of them. "I see you, Kai, welcome to Hiowind. I see you, Rayna, welcome to Hiowind."

Unsure what else to do, Kai pressed his hands together and bowed in return, Rayna followed his lead, thanking each new person. Simone and Yulia followed Haygan. They offered them the same greeting and stepped aside.

The crowd stood. Each person, one by one, all came and extended their warm welcome to Kai and Rayna. Hands pressed together in prayer, they bowed. Eyes locked with each person, Kai felt the love they offered. Emotions welled in his chest. Overwhelmed tears rolled down his cheeks. He had never experienced anything so raw.

When a man with pitch-black hair and dark brown eyes approached Rayna. Kai felt tension tighten his neck and shoulders. Without him saying it, Kai knew who this man was to him. Like the others, he pressed his hands together and bowed graciously. "I see you, Rayna, welcome to Hiowind. I see you, Kai, welcome to Hiowind. My name is Lucca. I am your grandfather."

The apprehension swelled in Kai's chest. His heart pounded in his ears. He had nothing to say to this man. What could he say? Best he knew, Lucca did everything he could to keep Kai out of Katori. The smile his so-called grandfather offered looked real but did not truly reach his eyes. The softness in Lucca's touch as he patted Kai's arm left Kai feeling conflicted.

This was more than he expected after the fight it took to get here. Could it be that simple? Were they now welcome among the Katori? Face after face, he bowed and met new Katori people. So many eyes, smiles, and blessings. They all became a blur.

After the crowd stopped, Haygan put his arm around Kai. "I know this," Haygan waved to the now growing crowd, "is overwhelming. I would love to say it was over, but this will go on well into the night."

Kai rocked back on his heels. "Really?"

"Yes. People from all over Katori are pouring in to join the festivities. Word has spread that you are here. The moment of the bond and Alenga's presence this close to our plane of existence brings pure power and harmony. People will come to celebrate and enjoy the energy your bonding creates. This happens every time someone completes the Conhaspriga."

"After tonight, what do we do? I want to search for my mother. But— I don't know where to start. Or do I have to find a teacher? How do I pick? Can you be my teacher?"

"I would love to be your teacher, if mentoring were my gift, but I don't believe I can teach you how to reach your potential. Riding a horse, yes. Bonding with your companion, certainly, but considering your crystal is white, I don't know how to help you search your spirit for your calling—I am no shaman."

"I know my mother was a shaman, a spiritual guide, and a teacher. She helped young Katori learn to control their gifts. Kendra told me all about it months ago. Who is the Shaman now? Has my mother not been replaced?" Kai felt sad that nobody had followed in her footsteps.

"Mariana, your mother, was a wonderful teacher. She helped many find a suitable teacher. A select few she mentored herself. It is most unfortunate nobody has felt capable of replacing her. How we all miss her dearly. Times change, it is no longer our way to have one shaman. The four tribes decreed we did not need a new shaman. Now each new Katori study with many teachers."

"What are the four tribes again?"

"There are the Hiowind, the mountain tribe where we are now. There is the Matoku, the highland tribe; the Kahoma, the coastal tribe; and Gemidi, the Mystic Islands tribe."

"Which one was my mother?"

"Our family is Hiowind." Haygan motioned to Lucca, who was lingering next to a column nearby. "Lucca, my father, your grandfather, is our chief. The woman with him is Kendra's mother, Olina. She is our unie.

Haygan's eyes turned sad at the memory of his lost sister, Mariana. "I wish your mother were here to see you, Kai."

"Me too, but soon enough." Kai surveyed the room. "Are you sure you could not teach me? Time is of the essence. I must find my mother."

Haygan scratched his chin. "You do me a great honor by asking, but I am not the right person. Given your white crystal, I can think of only one man who might be willing to teach you—Benmar, your other grandfather. But since Keegan's betrayal, he does not come here much."

Yulia stepped into their conversation. "Benmar might teach you, but not here in Hiowind. He rarely leaves the dragon meadows. He is a wise teacher and a rare few have the courage to seek him out on the mountain. You will not find anyone more qualified."

Meeting his grandfather tore at Kai's heart. There was something familiar about a man from his past, his face, but Kai could not recall the complete memory. He had sent Liam to aid him in accessing Alenga's Mountain. But Benmar was Keegan's father, and if truth be told, Kai didn't want to bother with lessons. He felt in the prime of his life. His fever was gone, and, if challenged, he was sure he could move a mountain.

"We don't have time for lessons. I need to search for my mother. She may be a manta ray somewhere in the ocean, but I know I can find her. This is our last chance to save her, if it is not already too late to turn her back. Can I not use her necklace and track her?"

His uncle curled in close. "Not so loud, Kai. We don't want anyone else to know you have your mother's crystal. We will use it to track Mariana, but the manta rays don't migrate near the Mystic Islands until autumn. She could be anywhere right now. In the meantime, you better learn what your white crystal means."

Simone interjected. "It might be wise if Kai and Rayna start out working in the gardens together. It will be better if they meet people as a couple. That will strengthen their bond and soften the integration into our community."

Curious, Rayna tilted her head. "For all the Katori who don't venture out into the world for their Conhaspriga, how do they take their rite of passage?"

"The ones who choose not to venture out spend their year in silent meditation. They are provided access to the cave from this side to carve out their stone. The rest is basically the same. They go into the pool to discover if Alenga will bless them with a gift. Not everyone has magic. And most that don't are usually happy without the burden."

"Doesn't seem fair," Kai interjected.

"Fair?" Haygan tilted his head. "A rare few choose to leave. They fear the outside world. Those that do leave have a warrior spirit. They want to test their mettle against the world and our Guardians. Explorers at heart. Most of them return, but as you know, a few do not. It is unfair you did not have a choice. But I do not make the rules. Nor am I the one to change them."

Before Kai could counter, Simone stepped between them. "This is a celebration. Debate tomorrow." She wrapped her hands around Haygan s arm.

CHAPTER 9

The Agora

No sooner did Simone stop talking than a delightful melody filled the air, and the crowd burst into celebration. Kai pressed his hand on the side of his leg, tracing the weight of the crystal in his pocket. He wished he understood the power it held. Something was reassuring about feeling the shape of it against his fingers.

People with trays of food and drinks flitted between the crowds. Flute and violin players wandered about, and in one corner Kai noticed several stretched cylindrical drums being placed in a semicircle. One man rhythmically tapped them with his hands to blend with the current melody. Other instruments slowly joined to build on the tune.

Behind them, a group brought round pillows to sit around the spirit pool. They nibbled on food, sipped wine, and conversed. In another area, people set up easels and began painting the scene. Ladies meandered through the crowd passing out tiny flowers, which women placed in their hair. Kai instantly thought this reminded him of a city festival.

Rayna slipped her hand into Kai's. "I feel overwhelmed. I want to blurt out a million thoughts, yet the words are unable to capture what my mind has shown me."

Grateful he was not experiencing this alone, Kai cupped his hand over hers. "We should get something to eat, that may help." He escorted her to a low table with blue round plush cushions.

Cheeses, fruits, and vegetables covered the marble table. They sat eating food and sipping some strange brown liquid. It was smooth to the taste and warmed Kai's throat. People continued to welcome and bless them before joining in the festivities. Unsure when the string of new people would end, he was at least thankful they did not stay to chat. When they finally stopped approaching, Kai and Rayna sat quietly watching the event.

"Rayna, do you feel the thread? It pulls at my soul. We are tethered to this place." He motioned to the Agora. "But this place is not the only one, there are two others. One in the highlands and one more near the shore. Can you feel them?"

She shook her head. "I only feel this place."

"The one in the highlands pales in comparison to the one by the shore. It feels old and forgotten."

"How could you possibly know..." She let the thought go and popped a grape into her mouth.

He ran his hand over the back of her hand. "I have to remember to live for now. Let go of the past and the struggles it took to get here. I am lucky to have you in my life."

She blushed at his comment. "We are both lucky."

Tired of sitting, Rayna stood to stretch her back. Before Kai could join her a group of girls approached, all wearing various shades of green dresses. They surrounded Rayna. "We are Kodama, little sister. Come with us!" And with that, they swept her through the crowd.

Kai was pleased to see her making friends. He stood to get a better view of where they were taking her. They fawned over her like newly found treasure. Each seemed to ask her a question and pull her this way and that. Several girls placed flowers in her hair and wrapped green silk around her body. Through the crowd, he felt someone staring at him. When he locked eyes with the man, Kai instantly recognized him.

He was one of the Guardians from the morning's battle. Regret panged Kai's heart. When they met in battle, the man was an eagle; in fact, Kai had sliced off his wing, or rather the man's arm. The man approached, and a lump formed in Kai's throat.

They locked eyes, blue on black. Kai held his breath. Gingerly the Guardian raised both hands, pressed them together, and bowed. "I see you, Kai. Welcome to Hiowind."

Befuddled, Kai bowed back. "Thank you." His words tumbled out in shock. "How could this be? Only earlier today, I severed your arm. Cleaved it entirely through your bicep. Sorry for that, by the way." Kai gulped.

The man smiled and lifted the corner of his pale blue shirt sleeve. Across his upper arm, there was a pink circular scar that cut through his copper complexion.

"My name is Ari. I am proud to be a Katori Guardian. No hard feelings. Our Kodama restored my arm. It will be sore for a few days, but good as new within a week." Ari rubbed the newly earned battle wound. "Scars are good. They remind us to learn from our mistakes. It is not my first, and I doubt it will be my last."

"Pleased to meet you, Ari," Kai said with relief.

Ari nodded at Kai's clenched fist inside his pocket. "It may be rude to ask, but is it true? Your stone remained clear?" His voice was low, and he covered his mouth as if they were sharing a secret.

Talk about direct. Ari cut right to the heart of what everyone wanted to know. Kai nodded. "Yes. My crystal is completely clear." Unsure what it meant himself, he asked in return. "What does that mean to you?"

"Well, as I am sure you know by now, each person's stone is green, yellow, purple, red, or blue." He pulled the necklace from his shirt. On the chain dangled a solid blue gem, irregularly shaped with smooth edges. "The darker the color, the stronger the connection, some say. Although my father's stone, while dark blue, has a coil of white. I can't imagine a man stronger with his Beastmaster connection." Pride emanated in Ari's voice and carried through to his eyes.

"I'm not sure what white means. Our gifts are usually defined by the color Alenga fills the crystal. There have only been two other people with white crystals. There was Keegan, who is—or was, rather—a Kodama healer. And there is his father, Benmar. He is more legend than man nowadays, a Beastmaster who lives secluded high up in the Katori

Mountains. I have never met him. Dragons are not very welcoming these days. I chose not to be rejected by the dragon's discriminating nature and became an eagle. But I doubt that's what you meant. Am I right?"

Kai contemplated Ari's expression. "I was hoping for a different answer."

"The talk is you are Keegan's son. One look at you, and I can see it. Having met Keegan and knowing both he and his father are the only others with a white crystal, it is easy to jump to the conclusion. I only wonder why Mariana chose to stay away. Why hide you?"

Kai knew why. Keegan was not a nice man, and she feared him finding her and Kai. Pretending Kai was a Half-Light gave them security. "Only my mother knows the answer."

Tempted, Kai wanted to ask how old Ari really was, even though that was not considered polite. But nothing about the past few days had been polite. Time for answers. "Ari, it may be wrong to ask, but how old are you?"

Reserved, Ari folded his arms across his chest. "I am seventy-three."

Shocked, Kai shook his head. The man in front of him could hardly be a few years older than he was—twenty-three at the most. His mind spun with questions.

"How old is Orin?" Kai asked cautiously.

Ari smirked. "The old man is two hundred and fifty-two. He is among the oldest. Great man. You should spend time with him. He could teach you more than us young folk."

Kai stood stunned. What else could he ask?

Before he could learn more, a young blonde woman swept Ari away. They merged with the other dancers. Kai observed the subtle changes in the room, the changes in the people. Their magnified aura had nearly faded. Everything looked more natural. Only the tiniest light emanated from the crowd.

The evening had settled over the sky. The once bright skylight had turned a blend of purple and blue. Starlight pricked the night sky. More and more people sat on the floor. Placed in their center, irregular shaped blue crystals illuminated their conversations. A few groups surrounded musicians or storytellers.

Kai's sensitive aura sensed a growing source of energy around the room. Crystals were set into the ceiling, and the walls began to glimmer. Stones on the columns and floor slowly came to life. Their orange hue gave a warm atmosphere to the Agora. Near him he watched a woman scoop the air with her cupped hand and lift it toward the crystal. The stone bloomed yellow.

On the far side of the room, Kai spotted Lucca talking with a small group, deep in conversation. An older gentleman stepped into Lucca's space. They exchanged words, private from the group. Unhappy, Lucca stepped back from the man and cut his eyes in Kai's direction. Distress wavered in the man's eyes. The group waited for Lucca to respond; instead, he threw up his arms and walked away, lost in the crowd.

Unsure what to make of their exchange, Kai searched the room for a familiar face. Haygan's aura still bloomed as he danced with Simone. The style of Katori dance was unlike anything Kai had ever seen. Their moves were primal. They danced apart as individuals, then two lines of dancers crossed and formed a circle. One circle enclosed the other. The outer ring of men circled in the opposite direction, then narrowed in on the circling women.

Their circles collapsed in tightly. Each man took the hand of their partner and swept her outward across the floor. Together as a group, they danced. They were swirls of color drifting around the room. Palms pressed against each other when a couple met. They stared into the eyes of their partner.

Then they circled and pushed away to the next person. When the pair reunited, they danced together, then split apart to start the routine again. The more he studied their moves, the more he noticed the slight similarities to Diu dance styles.

Thirsty, Kai downed the remainder of his water. A young man glided by and took his empty glass and handed him another drink. The liquid was dark. Kai took a sip. It went down warm and smooth. Across the room Kai watched Rayna. Her aura remained bright. She was still surrounded by the ladies in green and politely listened to their chatter. He desperately wanted to interrupt and sweep her away into the dancing crowd. She winked at him, and he grinned back.

Before he could take a step, three young ladies blocked his view of Rayna. They advanced in his direction. Their statuesque figures were wrapped in various layers of green silk. The girl in the middle locked eyes with Kai. Baby blue eyes fluttered at him. Her graceful stride exuded confidence. Her long legs crossed over each other; her sway and poise could have balanced on a tight rope. Kai had never seen a woman walk this way.

All three girls closed in around him. Each had porcelain white skin. The middle girl took his empty hand in hers. Her silky black hair flowed down to her waist. "My name is Senina."

The redheaded girl circled around behind him. Her finger traced the measure of his shoulders. "I am Ciera, and this is Linnea." She gestured to the third girl, a brunette.

"We are the oak sisters," Linnea added.

"We want to welcome you," Senina finished.

Senina continued to hold his hand while the other two pawed his muscular arms. He pulled at his hand gently. Her grip tightened, and she stepped closer. "You will need a teacher."

"We are willing..." Linnea added.

"...willing to guide you." Ciera finished.

The three ladies shared a connection, their speech woven together, each one beautiful and elegant. Yet Kai could tell by Senina's grip that they were no wallflowers. Their muscle tone told him they could put up a good fight. Katori people were known for their exceptional strength and speed. He was sure they were not to be underestimated.

The lighting in the room softened. Gingerly, Kai tugged on his hand and Senina let go. With the most elegant bow he could muster, he placed his hand on his chest and bent graciously. "I am Kai Galloway. It is my pleasure..."

A warm hand wrapped around his arm and pulled. Rayna was suddenly by his side. She curtsied. "Excuse us, ladies. I believe Kai promised me this dance." She escorted him away. Slow, delicate music replaced the boisterous beats of the earlier tunes.

Kai downed the strange substance in his glass and handed it to a woman with a tray. Suddenly, Kai felt like he'd had too much to drink. The feeling warmed his insides and melted his mood. Each care flitted away like dandelion spores on the wind.

Moved by the slow, delicate melody, Kai swept Rayna into his arms. Around her neck, her emerald teardrop crystal hung on a silver chain. "How did you get the chain already?" he asked.

"Orin brought it to me," she responded softly. "He can fashion one for you as well."

Lost in her deep brown eyes, Kai guided her around the floor. This was their first real dance. For the first time in their relationship, they were free to be open with their affection. There was no class divide, no betrothal to separate them.

The melody folded around them. In his mind, nobody else existed but them. Kai felt his heart swell with passion, and his eyes turned green. Rayna's brown eyes sparkled in the golden light. Without asking, he lowered his face to hers and kissed her. They had only kissed a few times over the years, yet none compared to this.

When he opened his eyes. Rayna gazed at him. He was sure if the lights were brighter, she would be blushing. "This is our first dance, you know."

"Do we not count the dances in front of my house?" she asked.

"You mean with your parents watching and a two-foot space between us? No, I cannot say that counts. Plus, that was not romantic."

"True," she agreed.

One tune blended into the next, and they continued to dance, their conversation light and happy. When Kai and Rayna tired, they stopped for water and food, both of which helped clear his intoxicated mind.

While they ate, Kai felt a presence. Someone was watching him. Around the edge of the room, he caught a hint of a man. One moment the stranger was there; the next, he was gone. Dim lighting made it difficult to know if the man was real or imaginary. It made Kai wonder if he were more than a little drunk.

Diverting Kai's attention, Rayna pulled him back to the dance floor. Sweet music lulled him into her arms. Then he felt it again. A presence was calling to him. He scanned the room as best he could. Each time Kai swirled around, he thought he saw someone, but then they were not really there. He squinted towards a decorative pillar. Again, he saw a man leaning against the column, dressed in dark blue with long sandy blond hair and a sharp goatee.

This time Kai stopped their spin and swayed in place. He stared at the man. The stranger had a maturity in his eyes. Upon closer inspection, Kai noticed a few gray hairs. Then the man slowly blended into the stone and disappeared.

Shocked by what he saw, Kai focused. Even with gleaning, the man was not there. *How is that possible?* Kai wondered. Then the man was back. The stranger pressed his hands together and bowed to Kai. With a coy smile, he vanished from sight.

Kai combed the room, both with his eyes and his mind. Determined, he focused and pushed a pulse to find the face he saw. As he searched the crowd, people turned and looked around. They had felt his energy wash over them.

Determined to find the invisible man, Kai continued to search. In the archway, Kai saw the faint outline of a man—a splash of light illuminated his face. A smirk tugged at the corner of the man's mouth. Again, he gave Kai a bow. The stranger reached out with his hand, pulled and twisted, drawing his fist in toward his stomach. The stranger absorbed the energy into himself and disappeared.

A grin formed on Kai's mouth. *To become invisible, you absorb light, draw it into your core. Thanks for the hint.* Not that it told him how, but it was a start. Kai was unsure, but he wanted to believe the man might be his grandfather, Benmar. The features and coloring were indeed a match for his own—and for the vile marauder Keegan.

Kai resumed his spin around the room, Rayna nestled against his shoulder. Fewer and fewer people danced. Seated groups began to collect their belongings and depart. Many were gathering around the arches.

"I think the party is winding down," he said. "I have no idea where we will be staying while we are here." They stopped dancing, and Kai gestured toward the arch they had entered. "We should wait there for Haygan. We also need to find our clothes."

Under the archway, Kai leaned against the stone wall. Rayna mingled with people saying goodnight. From a distance, Kai enjoyed watching her. Her tan skin was a sharp contrast to the white dress she wore under the green silks the women had given her. Even in the moonlight, he could see her soft aura still in bloom without gleaning.

As a face crossed in front of Kai's view of Rayna, he beheld Lucca. His grandfather looked young, thirty-five or forty tops. Not a strand of gray hair. The years did not add up. There was too much wisdom in the man's eyes. "Lucca." Kai acknowledged his mother's father with a polite nod.

"Kai," Lucca nodded, his expression neutral.

Although the man tried to appear relaxed, he stood with his hands in his pockets. Kai had the impression the man was avoiding their history. Their real connection. It was difficult not to notice Lucca's dark brown eyes; they reminded him of Mariana.

Unsure how to feel, Kai held his breath. He did not know this man. Not to mention he could only assume that Lucca stood against him and pushed the Guardians to fight to keep him and Rayna out. As one of the few Lumens, he himself could have helped block Kai's ability to glean. Now he was trying to play nice. No. Lucca was a stranger. "Can I help you, Lucca?"

Lucca raised an eyebrow. "I wanted to see how you are doing."

"Do you really care?" The hostility in Kai's heart vomited out his mouth without thought.

Lucca seemed taken back. "Of course, I care. You may not understand my choices as a chief or as a father, but..."

Aggression boiled inside Kai. "Choices? You judged me without meeting me. Just because I am Keegan's son, I am destined to be bad?"

"You are destined to bring war to our people," Lucca countered.

"And you know this how?" Kai could not hold back. "In all of my seventeen years, this is the first time you've spoken to me. You know nothing, short of hiding behind your precious mountains. So, what, is my name carved in stone beneath this legend everyone is so afraid of?"

Lucca stepped into the space between them. Kai felt immense power radiate out of his grandfather. In fact, the man's aura spiked, and Kai's still-sensitive eyes blinked at the brightness. "Watch your tone. I am your chief. Do not challenge me."

Saving them from an escalating discussion, Haygan placed a hand on Kai's shoulder. "Father," Haygan addressed Lucca. "Pardon the intrusion, it is rather late. Kai, we should find Simone. You and Rayna will be staying with us."

"As you wish, son. Good evening." Lucca nodded graciously and backed away.

Kai was relieved. "Thank you, uncle. I don't like or trust the man. Sorry, I mean no offense. I know he is your father."

"No offense taken. I understand. Half of the heartache in your life could have been spared if he'd have only listened to Kendra and me."

"What do you mean?"

"Well, instead of waiting to see if you would bloom into full Katori, we should have been teaching you and telling you our secrets. Helped you remember earlier. But he insisted you were a Half-Light, unworthy of our time."

"So, when I started to show abilities, Lucca must have decided I was Keegan's son."

"Exactly. The older you get, the more you look like the man."

"And now my white crystal..." Kai continued Haygan's train of thought.

"If only he had listened to Mariana back when he had the chance," Haygan sighed. "Anyway, let's get you two settled."

If it were not so late, Kai would have pressed for more details, but he'd not slept well in days—and even with the power from Alenga coursing through his veins, he felt tired.

Haygan and Simone walked hand-in-hand down the serpentine path that led away from the Agora, Kai, and Rayna following behind. Along the way, Kai tried to observe as much as he could about the new place. In many ways, the city was more advanced than Diu, yet somehow it seemed held back. Nature ruled nearly everything here. Even the man-made structures seemed to resemble plants and vines. Not that there appeared to be anything man-made in the sense he was used to seeing. Even their windmills were different, with vertical curled sails spinning carousel-like around a central shaft.

Everything was a living garden. Liam had talked about the integration of stone around the trees, and Kai noticed that to be true. The main path branched off in many directions. Finally, Haygan turned down a route towards a towering tree. Off in the grass, Kai saw a dark form. "Shiva!" Kai called to her.

Bent on one knee, he greeted the great black wolf. It was so good to see her. It had been months. Seeing her brought it home for him that Smoke was not with him. He was probably still on the other side of the Katori Mountain range. At least he was with Ryker.

Haygan gestured toward a man-sized arch at the base of the tree. "This is the entrance to our home. Above is a network of pods or nests. This is where you will be staying until you choose to live elsewhere."

The tree and its bark were unlike anything Kai had seen before. Thin, smooth pieces of bark lay on the surface. The trunk itself was a weave of thick individual stalks, each twice the size of his body. Around the outside of the central trunk grew a honeycomb of two different vines; one a pale cream color and the other a dark red. Along the ground, exposed roots snaked through a patch of wildflowers and variegated grasses.

Haygan stepped into the network of outer vines. As he walked, tiny white and blue flowers sprang to life, luminescent. Even the vines began to glow. Together they climbed in a spiral, higher and higher up the tree. Rayna ran her hand over the vines, and they beamed brighter. She giggled with delight at the magic of the plants. Her happiness warmed his heart. The more they moved; the more flowers illuminated the staircase.

High in the tree hung several egg-like nests. Each had a different room connected and supported by living vines. The home was different than anything Kai had ever known. There were curved growths in several places on the walls, like shelves that held a few various items.

Along one wall, a stone hearth arch sat waiting for winter. Below his feet, tightly woven vines created a nearly smooth surface. In the corner of the main room, a low table had been coaxed out of the floor. Kai was surprised by how comfortable the texture was on his bare feet. Flowering vines trailed around the ceiling, illuminating the space with a warm glow. Red clay filled the cracks between the vines, making the house feel private.

The next pod was a bedroom. Limbs grown into enclosed baskets created a nest with more flowering vines and red clay. Again, the furniture grew out of the walls and floor. The living branches had been trained to create a harmonious living space built for comfort and security.

There was a narrow ledge for sitting, a round bed, hooks for hanging clothing, and shelves with folded linens and extra pillows, all illuminated by white and blue flowers.

Curious, Kai asked. "How was all this made? Why do the flowers glow?"

Simone plopped a few blankets and pillows on the round bed cushion. "The Bodhima trees are robust once they are full-size; however, when they are small, they need the Cosmos vines to support them. The trees grow as a series of tiny individual trunks that thicken over time, and the vines help hold them together while they mature. Without the trees, the flowers that grow along the vines would wilt in the sun. Even the young vines can burn in the sun until they turn woody. The dense shady canopy benefits the climbing plants. The two species need each other to reach their potential."

Skeptical, Kai questioned, "How do the branches form into pods?"

Simone chuckled. "It is a mystery to me how it is done, but the Kodama actually guides the tree and vines into the shapes they want. A group of Kodama can grow a tree to full size in a day. They work long hours, rotating off and on. Once the process starts, the tree must be completed, or you'll end up with a shorter, lopsided specimen. Although some people like the squattier versions. Closer to the coast, shorter is better because of the high winds."

"Fascinating," Rayna interjected. "How do we get the flowers to turn off?" She reached her hand to trace the vine above her head. It beamed brighter with her touch.

Simone giggled. "The flowers glow because they are attracted to your movement and touch. Once you settle into bed, their light will fade and then go out for the night. The vines bloom at dusk and will be closed by morning."

Simone hugged Rayna. "This will be your room. Kai, you will be in the next pod. Haygan I have the larger one, nestled near the top." She offered the couple a slight nod and left with Haygan.

Nervous, Kai put his hands in his pockets. He clinked his nails against his crystal. "I guess this is where we say good night."

A pink blush colored Rayna's cheeks. "Yes, I suppose it is." She stepped closer and nestled against his chest. "See you in the morning." She kissed him lightly and turned him toward the stairs.

"Goodnight, Rayna," he grinned, glancing backward as he continued up the spiral stairwell to the next pod.

As promised, there was another bed in a nest similar to Rayna's. Simone had left additional bedding and a few pillows on the sizeable round bed. Once Kai slipped under the covers, he thought of Smoke. He hoped all was well with him and Ryker. If what Ryker told him was true, they would be reunited in a day or so. Exhausted, he let sleep take him.

CHAPTER 10

Pineapple Sage

Lost in a dream, Kai watched dawn's rays dance across the white snow. The bitter cold wind burned his face. Squinting into a blinding snowstorm, he held his white crystal. It offered no warmth, but it reminded him why he was there. He searched for a man named Benmar, his grandfather. The snow-covered peaks of the Katori Mountains scraped at the sky. The shadow of a man preceded him in the storm.

Kai tripped over a rock and fell into the snow. When he stood up, he was alone. Through a cluster of ice-covered trees, he found a large cave opening. Inside the nothingness, something waited. Heat pulsed within the walls. Hot breath blew into his face. The walls came alive with ambient blue light, and he came face to face with two enormous amber eyes.

Startled awake, he sat up in his pod. His motion woke the flowers above his head and they bloomed with a faint glow. He looked near the doorway, searching for Smoke, but his wolf was not with him. Awake and restless he took a walk.

Up before dawn, Kai walked through the sprawling gardens deeper into the city. Crickets sang in the night. The occasional owl hoot echoed in the trees. While he meandered, he gleaned Haygan's tree. Everyone was fast asleep. Across the way, he saw a figure.

She waved.

"Senina. You're up early." Kai clutched his hands behind his back.

He caught the scent of pineapple. The full moon shone down from above, its ambient blue light caressing her face. Her bent frame hovered over a bush. Again, the breeze carried the smell of pineapple. He sniffed the air. The aroma was undeniable. Senina's long delicate fingers stroked the plant.

"Glean," she instructed. "See its growth."

Kai watched streams of energy pour into a small but growing bush. Dust particles of power fell from her hand. Light from the soil infused the plants roots. Only the tiniest bits of energy trickled from stones around the plant. Her green heart-shaped crystal glowed as it dangled from her neck.

Amazed, Kai watched. Stems lengthened. New leaves unfurled. Around the tips of the tallest stalks, tubular scarlet-red flowers bloomed. Captivated by the smell and the mystical growth, he found himself crouched beside Senina. He blinked away the magic of gleaning. His eyes beheld the new plant.

Senina curved her graceful neck around to address Kai. "Smells wonderful, don't you think?" She stood and leaned into his shoulder.

"Smells like pineapple. Doesn't look like a pineapple, but the scent..." He paused to stroke the leaves as she had done. The aroma bloomed anew.

"It is a very versatile herb, but its fragrance is the most surprising. The vibrant red flowers attract hummingbirds and butterflies. They grow all summer long and bloom come fall. We cannot always wait for the plant to be ready. I need to collect some for my mother. Can you help me?" she asked.

"I suppose I can help for a moment," Kai said, feeling uncomfortable with her closeness.

Senina opened a green velvet pouch. "Pinch off the flowers and a few of the top leaves like this." She demonstrated.

He plucked the flowers and dropped them into her bag. The pineapple smell drifted around them. After picking a few leaves, he took one and waved it under his nose. "I can't get over the scent. Pineapple, from this little plant."

"Here, take some with you." She plucked a cluster of leaves near the end of a stem.

He gladly accepted the offered leaves and tucked them into his pocket. Over his shoulder, he caught beams of sunlight crawling across the land. The sun's earliest rays pushed against the black night sky. Reds and oranges burned away the purple. Yellow light announced the impending arch of the sun.

"Beautiful, isn't it?" Senina wrapped her arm around Kai's elbow. Standing, she turned them toward the sunrise.

"It is indeed." Kai agreed. "This open landscape allows you to see so much more. At home in Diu, there are buildings, walls, and trees. I never see a wide view of the horizon."

Captivated by the view, he leaned into Senina. She smiled up at him. "From this hill, you can almost see the entire Hiowind city."

"I studied geography, and I know Katori is extensive. But there is no information about your cities or villages. I find it difficult to believe there are only four tribal cities."

Senina curved around to face Kai. "Oh no, there are many cities. The Hiowind city stretches along the mountain foothills. There are even a few Hiowind villages near the white cliffs. Like Diu, there are many settlements. Port Anahita is part of Diu as is Chenowith and Albey. They are individual towns, but they are still citizens of Diu."

"True, I see your point. What makes one tribe different from the next?"

She paused to consider his question. "You know, I've never thought about it. At one point, it was where you lived. And there is a bit of inflection in how we speak from one region to the next. Centuries ago, each tribe claimed a region, but as we grew, the different groups overlapped, and we comingled.

"We all live in trees or caves. I would say the Gemidi are a little different; they are more carefree and tend to wander. I guess that is why they have no Agora. There are three Agoras...well, two. Centuries ago, an earthquake destroyed the Matoku's Agora. It was built on a rocky cliff near a small waterfall, and the Agora collapsed into the ground. Not sure why they never repaired the old one. They built a replacement, but it is half the size of ours. And since their sacred pool was never blessed by Alenga's creation, their young people come here or go to the coast. Most young people do not put off completing their Conhaspriga to the last moment, as you did." She grinned.

This surprised Kai. "So, there is more than one Agora. But only one crystal mountain, right?"

Senina nodded. "Correct. There is only one crystal mountain. Every young person comes here for their stone but can choose to return to their home Agora for Alenga's blessing. The other working Agora is near the center of the Kahoma tribal cities, near the shore."

All their history fascinated Kai—the richness of their culture, and the freedom to comingle regardless of their origins.

Out of the corner of his eye, Kai caught Simone's silhouette in a gazebo. Haygan faced her. They were too far away for Kai to know what they were saying, but he could tell by their posture it was serious. As Simone talked, his uncle cupped his face and fell to his knees in front of her. Kai wanted to go to them but he held back, watching. To his delight, Haygan leaned forward and kissed her stomach.

A sense of joy washed over Kai. He could only assume it meant Simone was pregnant. Feeling embarrassed he had intruded on their special moment, he backed away. "Senina, I really need to go. Thank you for the history lesson."

He darted back toward Haygan and Simone's home. Shiva prowled around their vegetable patch. Rayna collected blackberries and apples in her basket. Kai stopped to help her carry her baskets. "Have you seen Simone and Haygan this morning?" Kai asked.

"I have not," Rayna responded. "They left on a walk around dawn. Oh, there they are. I see them coming down the path."

Kai turned to see Simone in her flowy blue dress holding hands with Haygan. The expression on their faces was pure joy. When they got close,

Haygan put his arms around Simone. "We have an announcement to make. Tell them, Simone."

Simone rubbed her belly. "We are pregnant," she beamed from ear to ear. "I am due in late autumn or early winter."

Rayna ran to Simone and wrapped her in a hug. "Congratulations!"

While the two women whispered and giggled, Kai shook Haygan's hand. "Congratulations, uncle. Does this mean you are finished in Diu? Home in Katori for good?"

The expression on Haygan's face was not what Kai expected. Even Simone stopped her chatter to wait for his response. "I wish I was finished. But I made promises I must keep. I have sent for new horses, three young foals and three stallions from Bangloo. They will arrive early autumn, and I must see them to Diu."

Kai bit the side of his lip. "You will be cutting it kind of close—don't you think?"

Simone pursed her lips, but then rubbed Haygan's arm. "I would not ask him to break his word. But he promised to put in word he would not be returning." She raised an eyebrow as if to confirm this was still true.

"Yes, dear. I will put in notice. I am done splitting my life between Katori and Diu. You are my life."

CHAPTER 11

The Hiowind Tribe

The following afternoon, Kai hoisted a newly repaired windmill blade up a ladder. Rayna covered her eyes to shield them from the bright sunshine. A chord within Kai hummed. The sensation curled the corner of his mouth. He knew Smoke was near. He arched his back to watch Smoke exit the tree line on the distant hillside. The awareness between them was something Kai had learned to cherish.

The wind blade secure, Kai slid down the outer ladder rails and took Rayna's hand. "Smoke is here!"

They crossed the vegetable patch and went into the tall grasses. The wind playfully swirled the stalks. Wildflowers lifted their heads to the sunshine. Kai pointed as Smoke circled the lake, his black fur gleaming in the midday sun. For a moment, Smoke stopped. He turned and looked back.

A dark figure stepped through the trees into the sun. Ryker. Kai shook his head. Did the man own anything besides black? He reminded Kai of Riome with their wardrobe choices. Two loners, hiding in the shadows, trying to go unnoticed.

Rayna brought him back with the squeeze of her hand. Kai felt the powerful connection between him and Smoke. His wolf cleared the far corner of the lake and hopped into the meadow. The grass and flowers tickled his belly. Smoke bounced kangaroo-like around Kai and Rayna. He could not restrain his excitement.

Kai patted the air with his hand, and Smoke calmed. Kai knelt on one knee and rubbed Smoke's neck and head. Smoke greeted him with several licks across the face. For a wolf, Smoke was quite affectionate. Their bond was strong. It felt good to be reunited with his companion.

Ryker made the long walk around the lake. Kai offered his hand. "Thank you for bringing Smoke here to Katori. I can't tell you how much it means to me."

Ryker nodded. "He's is a good companion. Smart. Now that Smoke knows the way, he can show you the entrances on both sides. Mind you, the maze changes, so you will need your wits and sight to glean the path. A person could easily get lost in the ever-changing twists and turns between here and Diu. Best to travel at night, when the Stoneking Guardians make fewer changes."

"What do you mean, changes?" Kai asked. "Like what we saw before?"

"The path is a series of corridors through the mountain. Farther south than the path you take to the waterfalls and through Alenga's Mountain. This route was created for Guardians and other Katori people to come and go as needed. Take the wrong one, and you're lost for days. Small quakes tell you the Stonekings are making changes. I find it best to run. That way I never have to double back should their changes close my selected route."

"When is the best time of year to make the crossing?" Kai asked.

"Each winter, the pass fills with snow," Ryker explained. "Come early spring, it is a raging river, which feeds many of the lakes around Katori. After the big melt, the water subsides to a trickle. Then it is safe to travel."

"It means a lot to know there is another way to come and go. I appreciate the information." Kai shook Ryker's hand.

Haygan approached them from the lake, fishing gear in hand. "Ryker, you're back." The two men clasped arms. "Thank you, by the way, for defending my nephew. Means more than you know."

Ryker nodded, and Haygan took the hint. They walked a good distance away. Kai wondered what they spoke about, but quickly let it go in exchange for Smoke's pestering. Although it had only been two days, Smoke acted like it had been a lifetime.

Shiva bounded from the tree line, running in their direction. Rayna joined in the fun, laughing at Smoke's antics. She rubbed his shiny coat. "Someone is happy that we are all back together."

Tall grass swayed in the breeze. Kai nodded and lay down in the meadow, and Rayna rested her head on his stomach. Together they watched the white-willowy clouds drift across the sky. Smoke tramped around the area with Shiva. For the first time since they'd arrived, Kai felt a sense of home.

◆ ◆ ◆

They quickly eased into Katori life. Rayna often attended the botany lectures, while Kai tended towards the mind and body movement classes. Their centuries-old techniques were very similar to the ones Riome had taught him, although occasionally, he learned something new. While the movements appeared to be slow, gentle postures, he knew that with study and practice, they could quickly become a form of combat. It was these lessons Kai found most useful.

This evening, Kai joined Ryker and Haygan in one corner of the Agora. They practiced moving meditation with a group of young boys and a few other men. Their instructor was an older man named Basil. Streaks of gray littered his black hair. Yet his skin remained youthful. His mannerisms and tone demonstrated wisdom. He was muscular and broad in the shoulders. Kai studied the man's eyes. Windows to the soul.

To the young ones, Basil offered instruction. "We begin tonight with soft movement." Basil began moving his arms, his fluid movements controlled and precise. The group stood in five rows and repeated the same actions. Older men who knew the routine moved in unison with Basil. The younger boys were a step or two behind.

"Focus. Your movements should be controlled. Each motion should flow into the next. They are not rigid, quick moves."

Basil continued to stretch and twist. His muscular hands cupped the air as they rose, then folded together, pressed in prayer, and came to his core. Palm up, he guided one hand out to his side. He followed the same action with the opposite hand.

In a low tone, Basil spoke. "Quiet your mind. Let go of the distractions that pull at you. Listen. Alenga speaks in whispers."

There were too many worries that pulled on Kai. He knew it. His brother Seth's sad boyish face weighed heavy on his heart. Kai had left with little explanation, only a promise to return. A commitment he hoped to honor. Still, Seth was broken-hearted by the departure.

He also worried about Riome sailing the open seas with his father. Disguised as a cabin boy, he knew she would do everything she could to protect King Iver. Before leaving Diu, she told him she intended to learn Nola's true intentions, counter any poisonous potions, and undo Nola's hypnotic spell.

Yes, his mind was loud. He took a deep breath with the next movement, then released it slow and even. Focused on the moment, he felt his mind let the troubles fade. His body moved in harmony with Basil. Again, this new place felt like home. Peaceful.

Everyone followed Basil's beginner moves. Most of the group moved in unison, and Basil repeated the base moves. Then Kai spotted a change. The moves increased in complexity. Balance-challenging poses worked Kai's core. Basil shifted his posture. A grin curled the corner of his mouth as he lowered into a deep squat.

Basil shifted one leg out straight, his toe pointed away, his body perched over the bent knee. Arms outstretched for balance, Basil held his pose. His grin was rewarded with the toppling of three young boys.

"Balance and control. Use your core muscles. Find your center." Basil held his pose while the boys regained their posture. "Don't forget to breathe." He moved into the next position. Again, they fell to the side. "Try a simpler pose, boys."

Basil altered his stance. The boys found that easier. "Next time, pull up into the more challenging pose. Ease back if you must, but always push forward to strengthen your body and mind."

Each pose flowed into the next, meant to work the core. High leg lifts, sweeping arm movements, and warrior poses worked the extremities. Pose combinations slowly flowed one into another, first increasing in complexity then melding into simplicity. Riome had worked many of these same movements into their rotation.

Her methods taught him balance. She insisted on precise yet fluid movements. Focused on the flow, you freed the mind. Many of those same movements were applied in the art of defensive fighting. Riome's lessons served him well in following Basil.

The practice reminded him of home. Kai wondered about his friends. They each risked their families and their reputations to help him across Baden Lake, then returned against their better judgment. Their sacrifice made it possible for him to pursue his desires; a choice, he hoped, would lead him to his mother. It plagued him not knowing their fates.

Kai would need to speak with Haygan. He wanted to find a way to get news to Dresnor that he and Rayna were safe and healthy. His father would want to hear something before summer ended. Plus, it would be good to know if there was any fallout from his departure.

Dante might be livid they borrowed his ship, but Kai was sure the Grand Duke would be more concerned he left Diu and his men abandoned their posts. All things considered, Kai was thankful the vessel had not been severely damaged in the crossing. At least Cazier was aware of where they had gone. Hopefully, his cousin could soften the tension Kai's unapproved absence would create.

Again, his mind took over his focus. Fortunately, Basil took them through a series of cool-down moves, similar to the beginning. A delicate night breeze brought the scent of honeysuckle. Kai's mind returned to his meditation movements. Basil concluded his body, mind, and spirit workout with a bow to the group. The group returned the sentiment, bowing to their teacher. Finished, the young boys ran to Basil, happy they were old enough to attend his nightly practice.

Watching Basil, Kai sensed a humble man. If Kai were to find a teacher, he could not go wrong with Basil. The blue crystal around his neck said he was a Beastmaster. Surely, he would be a good fit. There was no way to know if Benmar would take him.

Unsure about his own gift, Kai fingered the white crystal that hung around his neck. Although he had a knack with animals, there was no guarantee that would be his gift. Kai needed to select a mentor. He shook his head as he left the Agora. Soon. Soon he would select someone. He felt called to Benmar, but was unsure given he was Keegan's father. Would he be a good fit?

Kai walked home in the darkness. The occasional blue and white crystals provided ambient lighting along the path. The white marble was still warm under his feet. The sounds of crickets and frogs hypnotized him with their charm. Ahead he saw Smoke cut through the grass towards Haygan's treehouse.

Behind him, he heard the pitter-patter of bare feet rushing to catch up with him. "Beautiful night," Senina whispered on the wind.

"You are out late," Ciera added.

"Can we walk with you?" Linnea asked.

"Certainly, ladies, though I don't have far to go. I believe you live back near the Agora. What brings you down this way?" he asked, already knowing the answer.

Linnea bowed respectfully. "We came to extend an offer."

Ciera leaned into his arm. "Ask you, if you have selected..."

"...a teacher," Senina concluded, grabbing his other arm.

He shook his head at the round-robin way they spoke. It was as if they shared one mind with three voices. "I have received many offers these past few days. Thank you for yours, but I am not sure who I will choose. Basil is a possibility."

Linnea stepped ahead of them. "Well, there is no rush."

"We are patient and understanding." Senina circled in front of him, pushing her sister out of the way.

Kai stopped to keep from bumping into Senina. Ciera poked her finger into his chest. "You could do worse in selecting your first mentor."

Senina stepped forward inches from his face. "We've had three teachers."

Annoyed, Kai stepped around Senina. "I hate to rush off, but it is late. Thank you again. I will certainly consider your offer." He wanted distance. Room to breathe.

Senina reached for his shoulder. "We leave tomorrow for the coast."

"Come with us," Ciera begged.

"There is much more to see in Katori," Linnea assured him.

Kai hesitated. He wanted to see the shore, maybe even travel to the Mystic Islands, but he had to stay focused. He needed to find a teacher so he could hone his powers and save his mother. "Sounds lovely, but I have much to do here before I begin to explore Katori. Thank you, ladies. Goodnight." He dashed off before they could say more.

When Kai reached Haygan's home, the stairwell was just starting to dim after his uncle's ascent. Quickly he climbed the spiral vine-covered tunnel. Flowers and vines bloomed around him. At the top, he found everyone perched on cushions around a central illuminated blue crystal. The main pod was aglow with white and blue flowers.

Rayna motioned him over. "Kai, your uncle was just saying he and Simone are traveling higher into the mountains for some alone time."

Simone placed her hands over Rayna's shoulders. "I know you two have only been here a short while, and we hate to leave you, but we could use some time to ourselves."

"When do you leave?" Kai asked.

Rayna blushed. "First light, after meditation and breakfast. They are all packed."

Their sudden plans shook Kai. He looked to Haygan. "How long will you be gone?"

His aunt and uncle glanced at each other as if they had not even thought about how long. "Till the end of summer?" Simone answered, but sounded unsure.

"I am sorry," Haygan tilted his head, "time is less important here. But both of you should focus on finding teachers. Kai, as I mentioned the other day again, you should seek out Benmar. I told you he lives near the top of the Katori Mountains. Ryker will be happy to lead you."

It was difficult to argue with his uncle. Kai had dreamed of a snowy climb several times in the past week. He knew it was where he would find Benmar. He folded his arms around his chest. "I know..."

"It's settled then," Haygan said with a chuckle. "Simone and I will leave after morning meditation. You both will be fine. Get to bed, you two." Haygan escorted Simone up the stairwell.

Swiftly, Rayna tugged Kai by the hand. Outside her pod, she stopped to watch Simone and Haygan continue up the spiral staircase. Kai craned his neck to see them disappear out of sight. Patiently he waited for the motion-sensitive flowers to dim in the wake of their departure.

Alone in the ambient flower light, they waited for the house to grow silent. Rayna stifled a giggle welling in her stomach. Kai grinned and brushed the side of her arm. With each move, the flowers around them bloomed with renewed light. How he wished they would stay out.

Excited to finally be alone, Kai stepped toward Rayna. His hand cupped the side of her face. She stretched upwards and tilted her head. He leaned to kiss her. As their lips neared, Shiva and Smoke burst between them, separating their closeness. "Smoke. Shiva. Really?" Kai scolded.

Rayna laughed. She shoved him in the stomach and turned to go to bed. Kai grabbed her by the arm and pulled her back. "Not so fast." He gave her a tender kiss and spun her back on her way.

Content, Kai went to his pod and fell into bed, staring at the fading flowers. His insides brimmed with excitement.

CHAPTER 12

Deception

I t had been weeks since Kai's aunt and uncle left, and still, he had not made a decision about Benmar. He honestly could not fathom what was holding him back. Moonlight splashed over the meadow. Smoke ran through the wildflowers; his black fur showed a hint of blue in the glimmer. Leaves fluttered on the wind. Kai gazed at the star-filled sky, enjoying his quiet stroll. The early hours before dawn were peaceful and quiet, a time he relished exploring the community with his wolf companion.

Along the rolling valley, homes tucked up in the canopies of the Bodhima trees began to glow. People were waking to gather in the Agora for meditation. Dawn would be upon them soon. It was the start of a new day.

From his viewpoint, another cluster of lights in the eastern foothills began to glow. Dim, barely noticeable lights. It was the Matoku city highland tribe; a group he wanted to meet once he learned they were Ryker's people. Knowing what he knew of Ryker, they could not be the simple backwoods people the Hiowind tribe depicted.

Not wanting to be late, Kai whistled for Smoke. Out of the corner of his eye, he caught the silhouette of a woman—Senina. She was alone. He was surprised to see her without her sisters.

She approached and looped her hand around the crux of his arm. Nervous about the closeness, Kai tried to step away and put some distance between them. He looked around the gardens. Senina's grip tightened, and she stepped closer. "Are you enjoying the fresh air?" she asked coyly.

"Where are your sisters?" Kai asked, avoiding her question. "Linnea and Ciera will be missing you in the Agora." He started to walk back through the meadow, eager to find Rayna.

"They will save me a spot. I wanted to be alone with you. This seems to be the only time to find you by yourself."

"Please, Senina." He found himself at a loss for words that would not offend her. "We have to stop meeting like this."

"I simply want to know you. I mean no harm." Her tone was seductive. "I want to know more about your life in Diu. We never left Katori, my sisters and I, before the Conhaspriga. I have studied geography like you, but I have never left Katori."

"You were never curious about the outside world?" he asked as they continued.

"I was curious, but there is so much to love about our world, our simple way of life. We are about community, not about personal possessions and advancements. Here we have no clocks—I believe you call them. Timekeepers. We have no need. The sun tells us when to rise and when to sleep."

Kai shook his head in agreement. "I have to admit your way of life is inviting. There is harmony here, that is true. Although, given the guardian training I have attended, it makes me wonder what they are preparing for."

She gently patted his arm. "There is wisdom in being vigilant. We are not alone in the world. Not everyone believes in living off the land, living in harmony. Greed can consume even the most faithful."

Kai wondered how his uncle managed to live in two worlds. "It is difficult to reconcile the two different ways of living. They both have value, and given the time, you would get used to both."

"Tell me of Diu," Senina crooned. "Or Port Anahita. I have heard of those places. What are they like? Which is your favorite?"

"While I love my home in Diu, Port Anahita's beaches are stunning. There is a town near Diu, Henley, which I enjoy visiting. Although if I had to pick a favorite, Chenowith is a very picturesque city nestled in the foothills."

Senina curled in close as they walked, ever-attentive to his every word. Her hand gently rubbed his arm. "What do you think of the Hiowind Tribe?"

Kai thought of the welcome he'd received so far. "People are people. They are the same everywhere."

"What do you think of me?" she interrupted him.

Caught off guard by the question, Kai hesitated in his response. "Senina, you are very sweet, but I am..." He stumbled through his answer.

A few yards from the main walkway, Senina stopped. Kai watched the stragglers slip into the dimly illuminated Agora. A tightness clutched at Kai's stomach. Senina stepped in front of him, her face close to his.

"Kai, I am interested in you. Let me be honest, I wish you to be mine."

Senina leaned in close, her head tilted to kiss him. Kai placed his hand over her lips. "You cannot own a person. You cannot make me yours because you wish it so. I am with Rayna, she is my future. I knew you were pursuing me. I had hoped you would see I was with her and let it go."

Calm and collected, Senina pulled Kai's hand away from her mouth. She held his hand against her chest. "I appreciate you being honest. Kind, even. But I am still interested, should you change your mind." She graced the side of Kai's face with her other hand. "I will be waiting."

Confident and proud, she took his arm and they continued to the Agora. Everyone was inside, quietly meditating. Through the din, Senina found her sisters and took her place. Kai looked for Rayna in their usual spot. Third row from the back.

She sat straight and tall, eyes closed. He quietly approached. Legs crossed, he lowered himself onto a cushion beside her. He exhaled slowly, centering himself into his meditation. Before he closed his eyes, he heard Rayna sniff. He glanced over as she wiped the corner of her eye. Kai saw the moist streak on her cheek.

A lump formed in his throat. They had been so happy these many months. What could possibly bring a tear to Rayna's eye? *No, no, no!* he clenched his jaw in frustration. Rayna had seen him with Senina, he was sure of it. He could only imagine how they must have looked. Alone in the dark, her face near his, her hand on his face.

There was no way he could explain. Now they had to sit there for over an hour before he could possibly speak with her. All the while, Rayna would imagine the worst. He wiggled on his cushion. His mind raced with how to calm her worries. He thought to touch her arm, but that would bring unwanted attention.

If they left, they would be noticed. Being respectful of Katori practices was essential to their way of life. Although he wanted to go, he held his place. It was the most challenging sit of his life. The minutes crawled and his bottom ached. He shifted again on his cushion, anxious for the time to end, but there was no way to make it go faster.

Restless, he opened his eyes. Sunlight streamed into the Agora. Kai glanced towards the chiefs and the unie. They remained steady and silent. Everyone would wait on their cue to depart. Every second pounded on Kai's heart. He looked to Rayna. She still sat straight and tall, her legs crossed in front of her, palms resting on her knees.

The eldest chief stood, then the unie. One by one they rose, oldest to youngest. Hands pressed together in prayer, they bowed to each other, then they nodded to the group. From a seated position, the people bowed back. After the chiefs and unie walked to the entrance, they turned and bowed to the room, to the spirit of Alenga.

The crowd rose, collected their cushions, and secured them over one shoulder with a long strap. Like their leaders, they bowed to the Agora before they departed. Kai followed suit, attempting to keep up with Rayna. Her smaller frame allowed her to slip through the crowd. She instantly put distance between them.

Dawn splashed over the gardens, and he caught sight of her scurrying between the windmills. She was not headed home. Not wanting to draw attention to himself, Kai quickened his pace. He darted down the first path to step out of the crowd. He made his way through the gardens. Hidden in the cherry blossom trees, he found her.

"Rayna, please let me explain." He reached for her arm, but she backed away.

Tears streamed down her face. "How could you? Especially with her. I didn't believe you were courting her. Ciera and Linnea, they showed me. I saw her in your arms. Her hand on your face. I couldn't bear to watch anything more." She slapped his hand away.

Kai took a breath. "I love you, Rayna, no one else. Period. Those are the only words that matter to me in this world. Senina tried to kiss me. That is true. I stopped her. She wants to come between us."

"You *let* her come between us. You're too nice to her. Her sisters said you take morning strolls in the garden. Now I see you together myself." She turned away.

"I was clear with her today. I told her I am with you. Please believe me, nothing happened." Kai brushed the back of her shoulder.

Rayna held firm, then turned on her heels to look at him. Kai took her hand. "Nothing happened, I speak the truth. If she had kissed me, unwarranted or not, I would be honest. It seems to me those three planned this. They wanted you to see us together, though I am sure she had hoped for more than my hand covering her mouth. Her goal was to plant doubt in your mind."

Tearful, Rayna tilted her head. "When they said you two were meeting in secret, that you did not have the heart to tell me it was over, I scoffed at the idea. But when I saw her wrap her arms around you, it looked like she kissed you. I didn't want to believe it. Senina's gleeful smile walking into the Agora broke my heart. I knew she had been chasing you." She wrapped her arms around him.

Relieved, Kai held her close. "It is not you who should apologize. Senina owes you an explanation. If I could marry you here and now I would, but we are not eighteen yet. My heart is yours, it always has been, since the day we met."

"Oh, Kai." Rayna pulled her head off his shoulder. His blue eyes blended into a dark green. "I believe you. Your eyes always reveal the truth." She kissed him, and he held her in a tight embrace.

CHAPTER 13

Rayna's Awakening

The house felt empty without Simone and Haygan, gone almost a month now, but the pleasure of daily tasks filled Rayna with joy. A delicate breeze blew through the large window and caressed her cheek. Preparing their morning meal, she cut up red peppers, apple slices, and cheese and placed everything on the table.

Across from her, she watched Kai poke at his plate. It wasn't difficult to see he was contemplating something. Finished with her bite, she placed her hand on his. "You know, if you talk about what is bothering you, I might be able to help... Or at least it will no longer be a burden you carry alone."

Kai held his breath and pushed his plate away. "I have been searching for the way to ask you." He held his breath, then blurted it out. "I need to search for Benmar. I have made up my mind, or rather my dreams continue to show me climbing a mountain. I must go. I would also like to go to Albey. I need to ensure everything is well and get any letters from Shane."

This was news to Rayna—she was sure he had selected Basil as his teacher. Kai had spent nearly every evening with the man. "Really? I thought you picked Basil."

"He is a wise man, and he answered many questions about being a Beastmaster. Mostly about how one goes about selecting an animal to emulate. He said I should feel a kinship with my choice. He also told me that I may not have the ability to change, only bond with animals as I do with Smoke. He said that the more I practice, the easier and quicker it happens. Kind of how Ryker and Smoke seemed to take to one another instantly. He also has taught me several peaceful fighting techniques."

Listening to Kai talk made it hard to understand why he wanted to search for Benmar. Basil was knowledgeable, and the man had offered to mentor Kai. Rayna could not imagine a better teacher. And if she were honest, she couldn't help but wonder what Keegan's father might be like. "What can Benmar offer that Basil cannot?"

The heavy sigh that came out of Kai startled her.

"You've made up your mind. Haven't you?"

"I am sorry, Rayna, I have." His expression was determined. "I know this is sudden, and I know I thought Basil would make a great teacher, but my dreams pound on me each night. I must do this. It is Alenga's will, and I am tired of trying to deny what I know I need to do. I think I am meant to find him now."

Unsure what this meant for her, Rayna nodded. "Don't be sorry. When do we leave?"

"Well, you see, that is my dilemma. I need to go alone. My dreams urge me to climb the Katori Mountains, south of the falls, but I think I need to go alone." He waited for Rayna to respond.

The idea of staying behind caught in Rayna's throat, and she stepped away from the table. "What am I to do here without you? Haygan and Simone left, now you are leaving me?" Rayna pouted.

Kai came to her side and lifted her face to look at him. She could see the look of guilt on his face. She could not fight what she felt. In a sense, he was abandoning her in a strange land. While she had made friends, she would still be alone. Kai reached for her hand. "I know leaving you here is a lot to ask."

The pressure in her chest made it difficult to breathe. Two opposing voices rattled her soul. *You've never been alone. Don't be afraid, this will give you the chance to grow. Find your own purpose.*

She continued to stare out the window as if the answer to her situation would fly in through the window. In all of this, she had never really asked herself what she wanted beyond finding her family.

Her contemplation must have taken too long because Kai interrupted her internal conversation. "Maybe you could stay with one of your friends from the garden—Jayla, maybe. Have you thought of finding Imani?"

The mention of Jayla gave Rayna some confidence. She had spent nearly every day with Jayla, and they had become rather close. She reminded her of Julia, her best friend from Diu, now Shane's wife. "Jayla may be willing to let me stay with her and her mother. She is to marry soon and could use help making her dress."

The name Imani swelled her heart. The thought of this girl being her sister battled within her soul. "I don't know if I am ready to see my sister. Finding out why my parents, *our* parents, abandoned me hurts too much to face. What if they are here? Living with her...no, I am not ready to learn why they did not want me."

Kai touched her cheek and pulled her close. "I did not mean to bring her up again to hurt you. When you are ready, I will go with you. You don't have to face them alone."

His arms gave her comfort. "So, when do you leave?"

When Kai didn't answer, Rayna pushed back from him. His hesitation made her wonder how long he had been putting off the discussion. Rayna squinted at him. "You're leaving tomorrow, aren't you?"

He pursed his lips and looked down.

Her eyes went wide. "You plan to leave today?" she huffed.

"Again, I'm sorry. I have been putting this off. I meant to tell you weeks ago, but I've been distracted, and now Ryker is tired of waiting. He told me last night he was leaving this morning."

"So, he is waiting for you now? Right now?" She stormed towards the window. "What, is he waiting downstairs?"

There was no denying her words. He went to her and wrapped his arms around her from behind. "I love you. Please, tell me you're alright with this. You are safe here, in this home, in this community. Jayla is a good woman. As are many others. Even Lucca seems to be trying to mend the gap between us."

She relaxed in his arms. "I know I will be fine, and I know you will return. But I have never been on my own. Sleeping out under the stars did not frighten me because you were there." She turned to face him, her expression a mix of emotion.

"Have confidence, my love. You are stronger than you know." He kissed her forehead and hugged her tight. "I never considered the thought of being alone would be your concern. Or how hard it would be going straight from your parent's house to here. Haygan and Simone have been like surrogate parents, but I know it's not the same."

"How long?" she asked.

"A month, maybe two."

A faraway thought consumed Rayna's expression. She gazed through the crescent moon window. Below she could see a man dressed in black approaching. "You are right." She glanced over her shoulder at Kai. "I cannot hold you back. If Alenga wants you to go, you must go. I will be honest, I am nervous. This will be strange at first, but maybe this is what I need." She spun on her heels. "Ryker is coming down the path. You need to pack. I will be fine. What supplies do you need to take with you?" She approached the shelves with their provisions.

A small grin curled Kai's cheek, "I suppose bread, cheese, dried fish. Any vegetables you can spare."

"I will make you a satchel, go collect your things. You should be ready before he decides to leave without you." She scurried about, placing items on the table. "Go, go," she waved.

While he ran to his pod and collected a few belongings, she packed food and a water sack into a bag. The idea of spending the two months without him jumbled her insides. This would be good for her and her studies.

Moments later, Kai bounded up behind her, all smiles. "Thank you. I will be back as soon as I can. With good news, I am sure. I love you." He pulled her into a kiss.

When he stepped back, she found it difficult to let him go. "Travel safe. You will be back before you know it." She assured herself more than him.

"Smoke, come." Kai tapped his leg.

Rayna heard Smoke run down the spiral stairwell. Kai thundered down behind him, and she watched him dash down the trail. Sunlight seeped through the trees. Much to her surprise, Ryker was gone. Kai turned back and gave her a wave and dashed down the path toward the central part of the city.

Rayna felt surprised at how excited she was to be on her own. This was her time to decide who she wanted to be. Create the person she was meant to become. Deep within her soul, she knew she was more than Kai's girlfriend, more than a baker's daughter, and more than a Kodama from Katori.

The path she chose brought her to this point, and it would determine the course of her future. She would need to listen to the call from Alenga and discover the depth of her power. Her sudden awakening made the essence of her soul feel more connected to the world and the life around her.

Filled with confidence and determination, she bounded down the spiral staircase into the Hiowind city to find Jayla.

CHAPTER 14

Ryker's Truth

People gawked at Kai as he navigated around them. He had to admit he had no idea where to find Ryker, so he walked towards the lake. Then he had an idea. Smoke had spent time with the man, so why should he vex himself searching? With a deep breath, he connected to Smoke, asking for him to find Ryker.

Smoke sniffed the ground and took off through the gardens, headed for the edge of town. They ran around the lake and up the hillside. They entered the woods and veered south. Kai dodged down trees and scaled a steep slope to keep pace. They ran for hours over the sloping terrain. The grass was high against his legs. Sparse trees provided little shade, but the trees grew thicker as they went deeper into the foothills. Tall pine and mighty oak swayed in the breeze. It was a beautiful country.

Smoke darted over a small creek, and Kai stopped. "Hold up, Smoke. Let's stop for a moment." He turned around, getting his bearings on where they were in relation to his Katori home. After running for almost an hour, he was thirsty. He sipped water from his pouch. High in the cliffs, Kai could tell there were more trees and Katori homes. Old large Bodhima trees wrapped in Cosmos vines.

Satisfied, Kai stood up. Beams of sunshine trickled through the branches. He and Smoke stood in a large wildflower meadow within the forest. Kai spun around. "Rayna would love this spot."

Smoke danced on the edge of the meadow, begging Kai to move forward. "Alright, I'm coming." He dashed into the trees, and they were off and running once more.

It wasn't long before Smoke stopped. He sniffed the ground, then the air. Then he doubled back and zipped through the forest. Again, Kai did what he could to keep up with all the detours. "Looks like Ryker is playing a trick on us. Or at least on me. He knew I would use you to search for him." He scratched his chin.

"So, what do we know about Ryker? One, he lives somewhere up here in the high country." Kai ducked under a low branch. "His scent must be everywhere. Not to mention, I am sure he did some fresh passes to confuse you."

Kai tapped his chin. "Second, he is extremely competitive. Loves to win. So, we are playing a game. Time for a new approach."

Focused on the surrounding hillside, he opened his mind. The trees, animals, and landscape bloomed to life. Energy illuminated the countryside. In his mind, he panned outward, sweeping each tree, rock, and river. Nestled in a pile of rocks, a black satchel of supplies sat hidden under dried branches.

They had to be Ryker's. *Now, where is the man*, Kai wondered. Two miles up the hillside, there was a quiet little village nestled into the cliffs. Their gardens bustled with people, but no Ryker. Concerned he'd overlooked the animals, Kai quickly scanned for any shuk in the area. No luck there either. Where was he? Frustrated, Kai ventured through the woods to the black satchel hidden in the rocks. "He was here."

They crossed a nearby stream, and Smoke stopped. Kai looked upstream. "There is a waterfall up ahead. Could he be hiding there? You've lost the scent because of the water. Good boy, Smoke."

The waterfall was short compared to the ones he'd climbed on his journey into Katori. Behind the falls, he found a round stone door with the remnants of a carving, nearly worn away—the triquetra. Curious, he pushed the stone. It did not budge. He put his shoulder into it and shoved harder. The stone shifted.

The door rolled slowly. Sunlight and water poured across the ground in the wake of the open entry. Smoke darted inside, and Kai ran after him. Once he let go of the stone, it started to roll back into place.

"Shoot." Kai darted to the entrance, but it was too late. The door was shut. He studied the stone. There was no way to get hold of the stone, no way to open it from this side. "Great, now I am trapped."

"I'm not trapped," Ryker's voice called out from the dim.

A quick pivot revealed Ryker leaning against a stone archway. "Took you long enough."

Confused, Kai squinted at the man in black. "I gleaned the countryside. I did not see this cave. How?"

"Alenga doesn't wish it. Her magic hides this place. Most have forgotten it even exists. Part of this collapsed centuries ago, but this section is intact. These hills emanate with power, but then much of Katori swells with the power of Alenga. I thought you should see it." Ryker motioned and walked deeper into the cavern. "Even my tribe, that lives on the ridge above, has forgotten its existence. We built a new Agora deeper in our city. I found it because Alenga revealed the entrance. The stone rolled open on its own."

To Kai's wonderment, millions of crystals illuminated the cavern. Decorative white stone columns towered up to the ceiling. Etched black and gray stone adorned the cave floor. At the center, a bright blue light lit up a tiny pool. A round stone covered the hole where the skylight should be.

"We will camp here for the night. This place is very powerful. I have been told you share your mother's gift for visions."

"I do. Though that is not always a good thing. And I most certainly cannot control the gift. The visions of the future happen on their own."

"I stay here often. It is peaceful. Empty. This place gave me a vision. It told me to help you find your way here. I have fulfilled her request."

Ryker motioned to the statue of Alenga carved into the stone wall. Her body half emerged from the rock face, and tiny blue stones bedazzled the thin band around her head. Her outstretched hand looked ready to greet him. Kai could tell this was once a beautiful place.

"It is still early, but I want to travel the maze at night. Less movement by the Stonekings makes travel faster. Plus, if we can get to the backside and go north, we are a day's run from your friends. I thought you should know, most of them stayed behind after you left. They wait for you near Shane's cabin."

"I am not surprised. They are a loyal yet stubborn bunch." Kai touched the stone that blocked the entrance. "If we're not trapped, how do we leave?"

"Since you did not bring my pack, I must retrieve it myself. I left it for you to find. Did you not see it?"

"Oh, I saw it. Didn't even think to pick it up. Thought you were playing a trick on me."

"Fair enough. This way." Ryker moved around the back wall, behind Alenga.

The exit area was darker. Another stone circle pressed against the wall. This time Kai noticed the angle of the design. This stone was also meant to reseal itself. Ryker put his shoulder into the side, and the sound of stone rolling over stone echoed in the space. Kai slipped through the opening behind Smoke. Ryker released the stone and joined them.

Outside, there was a narrow path between giant boulders. Pine trees blocked the opening, and vines covered the ground. Ryker led the way out and found his pack. "We should check my fish traps. We can conserve any dried food you brought for the hike."

Through the trees, Ryker retraced their original path. They checked two traps and found three river bass. On their walk back to the cave, Kai felt a strange barrier around the waterfall. Delicate, but there. "The barrier, who created it? Who maintains it?"

"Alenga. This is her, or rather was, her place. When she walked among us, her home was there. You see the tree? How it is splayed open?"

He studied the split tree. It had a thick trunk and was overgrown with new life, but it was not near as tall as the trees people used today. "I see it. What happened?"

"Before my time. I only know it was hers. As was the cave next to our Agora. She created all the sacred pools. We built great structures to celebrate Alenga. The Katori people started here in the highlands. The barrier ebbs and flows to hide its location from any that come near. Can't say I understand, I am just thankful the place goes unnoticed."

"Have you ever brought anyone else here?"

A smile pulled at Ryker's eyes. "You mean besides your mother?"

Kai gulped. What was their story? "You cared for her."

Ryker grunted as he shouldered open the stone entrance. "I did. But then your father, Keegan, came and took her away. She was missing for over five years before we had news that she had married the Diu King. Your stepfather, Iver, stole her a second time. When I lost her a third time to the sea, I wanted to die, but Simone would not let me. I came back here hoping for a vision of how to find her."

Speechless, Kai helped Ryker clean and cook their fish. He watched smoke trail up from their small fire. It weaved upward to the ceiling and slipped through a crack as if sucked out. What could he say? This man was in love with his mother. Could he use him to help find her? Would that be wrong?

"What do you now about Keegan?"

A snarl curled Ryker's mouth. "I never liked the man. He's an arrogant, power-hungry bully, but many found him charming. His ideas about more freedom for our people challenged the wrong people. While he came from a prominent family, his ideas went against tradition." Ryker paused, his face darkening. "And I hate him for taking Mariana away."

"My father, Iver, told me he found my mother washed up on a beach after her ship crashed. I always wondered how true that was. I cannot imagine what it would have been like to have someone hunt you, or to fear someone so much you were afraid to return home."

The contemplation on Ryker's face and his clenched jaw made Kai feel bad. Hearing about his mother had to be difficult. It was certainly hard to talk about her. "I want to find my mother. If you and Haygan are right, she is in the ocean as a manta ray. I can only hope it is not too late to turn her back."

"Manta rays migrate near the Mystic Islands each autumn. They feed and mate before they migrate back south. I am not sure of the exact location, but someone knows." Jubilation tickled the corners of Ryker's eyes. He tossed Kai a hunk of fish. With renewed spirit, they ate and pondered their next move.

"I want to come with you," Kai interrupted Ryker's thoughts.

Unfazed, he swallowed. "Certainly. I will make the arrangements. We will need a ship. Not a skimmer. I hate those shallow bottom boats. They are great for navigating between the Mystic Islands, but they are terrible on the open sea. We should take Yulia. She is the best Weathervane I know—someone I trust. We will bring Mariana here after."

"What about Lucca?"

"No." Ryker's clipped tone startled Kai.

"You are not fond of Lucca, I take it."

"I am not. I blame your grandfather. Blame him for all of this. He favored Keegan over me. Keegan came from a Hiowind family, but I was Matoku-born. He judged me unworthy—a highlander. Lucca made the wrong choice. Though Mariana cared for me, she obliged her father. He sent me to find Haygan in Milnos. While I was away, Keegan pursued her. When I returned, a year later, they were both gone."

The pressure of the past pushed a sigh from Ryker. Kai felt sad for him. His mother's life was so complicated. How could one person have so many secrets?

"I didn't realize there was any social structure here. Why should it matter what tribe you are from?"

"Normally it doesn't, but parents think they know what is best. Lucca certainly thought Keegan was the better choice."

Tired of talking about Lucca, Kai shifted things. "How can we help my mother?" he finally asked.

"She has been a beast for years." Ryker rubbed his stubbly chin. "She won't be thinking clearly. This place," he motioned to the pool, "it can restore her mind. I know it."

Kai nodded, hoping Ryker was right. He didn't know what else to say.

Ryker put out the fire and cleaned up the stone fireplace. "Get some sleep. I will wake you in a few hours. I want to be through the maze before dawn."

Still overwhelmed by this new information, Kai unfolded his bedroll. Smoke lay near the wall behind him. Somewhere between excited and exhausted, he closed his eyes. He struggled to quiet his mind. The stone floor pressed on his shoulder, and he felt the room swell with power. In a haze, he saw Ryker's sleeping form. He reclosed his eyes.

◆ ◆ ◆

His mind slipped into a wild sleep. Crackles popped in his mind. Snaps of images struck his subconscious. The wind blew against his face. High above Baden Lake, he soared. His vision became clear, and a silver dragon flew in front of him, its massive wings gliding on the wind.

Snap—pop. Alenga's cavern burst with energy and light. His mother's frail body lay floating in the pool. Her cuts and wounds beamed with light. Her muscle mass returned. Her thin, patchy hair regrew across her scalp.

A whirlwind of light flashed. Kai felt pulled through time. His father's bedchamber morphed into being. He sat beside his father, Iver spoke, but the words were lost to his ears. Blood leaked from his father's ribcage. A silver-and-gold-handled blade with blue gems glinted in his eyes—his recent birthday gift, covered in blood. Queen Nola screamed. Bells rang. The word *traitor* echoed in his ears. He had killed Iver with his own hands.

Crack, pop. Kai sobbed, clutching clumps of dirt. He screamed, "Rayna."

Shake. Shake. Something tussled him.

"Kai, wake up," Ryker prodded.

"Dang it, man! Why did you wake me?" Kai's voice thundered louder than he'd intended.

"It is time to go." Ryker's tone was firm, but then he softened. "Did you have a vision?"

Frustrated, Kai sat up. Visions can be a good thing when they show you happiness or offer the solution to a problem, but more often than not, they never reveal what you really want to know. He hated how they came in jumbles or snips, more riddle than truth.

"I had the worst possible vision." He knew it came from this place; this cavern rich with Alenga's power. But the scenes were sharp. They came quick like a punch to the face. He packed quietly while he gathered the threads of his vision. He needed to remember every fragment, no matter how small.

There was no way to know in what order they would happen. Or how long he had. The only thing he knew —he would find his mother. Months from now, the manta rays would migrate around the Mystic Islands. After all, he was meant to bring her here.

He grabbed his blade, the one he had plunged into Iver's chest in the vision. An ache welled in his heart. He felt the weight of it in his hand. He pulled the knife from its jeweled sheath, studying the ornate design. Devastated, he turned away, unwilling to face the idea. "No, I'd never..." He shook his head.

Ryker grabbed Kai's shoulder. "We need to move."

Kai gathered the rest of his things, and they departed out the back of Alenga's cavern. They ran through the trees fast and hard, Smoke at their side. It felt good to run, to pound through his frustration. His vision had to be wrong. He would never kill his own father.

Still, the vision was clear: his blade, covered in his father's blood. How could he possibly stop it from happening? Distracted, he stumbled and crashed in a heap of ferns. Ryker plucked him from the vegetation and continued. "No time to waste. Keep up."

All the landscape looked the same. Greenery, rocks, and rivers. Kai did his best to take note of where the cavern was in relation to where they were going now. The power of that place was important. The magic behind his vision swirled in his head. There had to be a reason Alenga would show him these things. The vivid nature of this vision enhanced by the location caught in his chest. *Focus. I must remember.*

CHAPTER 15

The Maze

"Here, this is the entrance to the maze." Ryker motioned to a set of thick pine trees blocking a pile of boulders.

The staggering rock face towered overhead. In the distance, Kai felt a rumble in the mountain. "Stay close and glean the path. They are making changes now. During the day, they make changes every few hours. At night, there are fewer changes. Search the path. Find your way. If we hurry, we will be through before they change it again."

"Why so elaborate?"

Ryker pushed through the pines, and his chuckle echoed off the rocks. "Because they can. They train to shape the mountains. Where do you think the Katori mountain range came from? Alenga did not make it. Her original mountain hides inside—the place where you claimed your crystal. The Katori of old made the expanse. They covered her original place with their own."

He knew that. Davi and his group had told him as much. "I've heard the story."

"Well, the next generation of Stonekings is always stronger than the last. They practice in these hills. They practice along our coast. The Mystic Islands exist because we made them. Land plucked from the sea. Towers of land pushed up into the sky shrouded in mist."

"But why change the path? Why have one to begin with?"

"We need to maintain a route to Diu without taking a ship around, and not all of us can fly. But even though we need easy access to Diu, we do not want to allow strangers to find their way here. The quakes help keep people away, but make no mistake, they are keen to find a way to Katori. Imagine a trade route with Katori that did not involve the sea? Thankfully, a foolish few search for a way through the Zabranen Forest."

Water trickled through pebbled soil. Kai hopped across, keeping pace with Ryker. "I've met your Guardians. There is no doubt they could stop anyone."

"They are not as heartless as they once were, killing all who enter. Beastmasters must be careful. If we are killed in beast form, we return to our physical body. That is a secret we don't want out."

"What do you mean they change back?"

"You saw for yourself when you cut the wing of the eagle—the man's arm fell to the ground. We believe our last thoughts are of our true form, which results in transforming out of our beastly bodies."

Kai had forgotten that part.

"Better to use Weathervanes, Kodama, and Stonekings to make the route impossible to navigate." Ryker continued. "With a Weathervane creating fog or harsh weather, most turn back."

"Yes, I've witnessed their handiwork." Kai wondered if they genuinely wanted to stop him, would they have crossed a line to kill him?

"Over the years, a few outsiders have found the corridors. There is another pass far to the north, but the Stonekings sealed it. Once two travelers from Diu were caught up there for days, but they finally found their way back out. Both men nearly died of starvation."

Kai contemplated the choices the Katori had to make to keep their home safe from the outside world. In his mind, he could see the passage Ryker took toward the exit. They were close. They had made great time. When they switch-backed through the last turn, Kai heard the stone shift and the ground shake. The wall behind them closed.

They were a few miles above Albey. "We should stay away from the city. It would not be good if anyone saw you. Let's move north before we continue west."

It was a sound plan, and Kai grunted in agreement. Their pace slowed to a brisk walk. For hours they moved in silence. Thankful for the peace and quiet, Kai thought about his vision. What could possibly be changed? Now he would carry the burden of his father's life. He also thought about Ryker's secret love for his mother. How different things might have been if Lucca had not interfered.

Disrupting his thoughts, Ryker stopped. "We should make camp here. No fire. Eat the dried meat and cheese from your pack. We will sleep a few hours. It is best if we travel at night. While we eat, you can tell me about your vision."

Hesitant, Kai lowered his pack. "Maybe you can help me understand what I should do?" Digging for his food, he began to tell Ryker the flashes in his dream, each one vague enough to frustrate even the keenest mind. He noticed Ryker seemed pleased to hear that Mariana would return—it was Iver's fate that Ryker stewed over.

Ryker rubbed his jaw. "All any of us can do is live our lives and see where it takes us. Trust that Alenga has shown you these images for a reason. You will experience each one. I doubt you will have to choose the order. That is already predetermined."

"Should I go back for Rayna? Should I stay away from my father? I don't know what to do. You say I should get on with my life, but how? How can I proceed knowing that I am destined to kill the man who raised me?"

"One day at a time. Tomorrow, we see your men. See where that takes us. Focus on what you know. Then I will take you to Benmar. Your previous vision leads you into the mountain snow following a man. I'd say that is me. You said yourself the dreams will not let up—well, there you go. Easy. Rayna—you can address that when you have real information. Next clue: your mother. I believe Alenga helped me find her cave. She also sent me to help you. Alenga wants us together to find your mother. We are meant to take Mariana to the cave."

Ryker paused, and Kai let his words settle. The weight of it all lifted. "What of Iver?"

"Well, that is delicate. Did you see yourself stab him? With your own hand?"

Kai was about to nod, but then he remembered the vision. It was his blade in Iver's chest, but he didn't see the stabbing itself.

Ryker listened as Kai explained. "See? All you know is that your father gets stabbed by your blade. You only know that you will be there, but not who wields the blade. But either way, the bell may toll for you. When you return to Diu, and you will, you must be ready."

Ryker's words were not reassuring. Kai wanted—no, needed—more answers. Hoping he got it right was not enough. Laying on the ground, Kai prayed for a sign, another vision to tell him more. *Visions are fickle. When you want one, they won't come. If they do, they never show you enough.* He learned nothing new that night.

◆ ◆ ◆

Kai and Ryker strode right into Dresnor's camp, snuck right by the guards, and plopped down by the campfire. Drew came outside to stir the fire. Their eyes met, and he smiled. "Prince Kai." Drew hopped over a stump to take Kai's hand. "Good to see you."

The enthusiasm in Drew's tone made him wonder if his friends thought he was never coming back. "Good to see you too." Kai let go of his friend and looked around. "I see you didn't return to Diu as I instructed."

Drew rolled his eyes. "Did you honestly think we would?"

"I guess not," Kai sighed. "Where is Dresnor?"

"Where is Rayna?" Drew ignored Kai's question. "She is well, I hope."

"Rayna is doing better. I came to see Dresnor. I sent you all home to Diu. Did any of you go home?" Kai motioned to the tiny huts.

Before Drew could respond, Dresnor approached. He nodded to Kai. "Prince Kai." His Kempery-man tapped him on the back and grabbed his arm. "So good to see you well. Redmon went home to send back real news. The rest of us stayed. Tell me, how do you feel? You look great."

"I feel great. The Katori people are taking good care of us. They are rather quiet but pleasant." Kai shook his head.

Dresnor leered at Ryker. "I know you. I've seen you before. Years ago. You were in Diu with Haygan. I never forget a face. You were also at the battle for Town Hope years ago. Are you taking care of my Prince with these mountain people?"

Ryker nodded. "Yes, he stays with my people. Rayna and Kai are both safe with us. They are responding very well to the treatment. Rayna searches for her parents, who we hope to find living among the Gemidi tribe living on the Mystic Islands. It will take time for the letters we've sent to circulate around all the islands. I advised Rayna to let the news settle on them. If they are willing, we will get word back. I will accompany them on their trip to ensure these people will speak with her. You understand."

The tale slid off Ryker's tongue as if they'd rehearsed the story. Kai was amazed at how he wove in the details that aligned with their need to travel. His explanation of Rayna's absence was believable. Although Kai was not sure, he liked to idea of returning home to Diu. But with his father's life in the balance, maybe he should stay away.

Dresnor looked between the two men. "Well, I have news from home. I have a letter for you, Kai, from Cazier—unopened. The letter from Dante I read. Not all good news. Your father made it back from his trip last week, but it was not as successful as in years past. To make matters worse, Landon Penier has escaped a few days after King Iver's return. I do not know how. Guard change or something."

Keeping his emotions calm, Kai listened, but he had his own ideas. Landon's escape had to be Nola's doing, but he wondered how she could have managed it. Keegan's ability to change his face to match anyone he touched gave him pause. Could Keegan have rescued Landon after all this time?

"Your father has been unwell since his return. Bedridden."

"Sick? Again?" Perplexed Kai crossed his arms over his chest. He needed to read his cousin's letter. "May I see Cazier's letter?"

Dresnor retrieved the letter. "It came a few weeks ago. It was marked private on the back, so I did not open it."

Worried, Kai flipped to the letter in his hands. He noticed the symbol on the back, the three letters of his name overlapping to make one sign. His symbol. He broke the seal and began to read. Mostly miscellanea. News of his father's trip and health concerns. A mishap at sea near Bangloo. Two men lost overboard. Kai scanned the letter to decipher the hidden message. *Riome lost. Stay away.* Her letters, R—T, for Riome Tamika in the corner. Then there were other symbols meant to convey a quick message mixed with letters slanted and plucked out of the message to supply information. His heart sank. He held his expression close. He had learned years ago never to reveal what you don't want others to know.

"Same news you shared." Kai chucked his note in the fire, as was their practice to destroy messages. "My father's health and a scuffle at sea. It seems two men went overboard south of Bangloo. A cabin boy and a stowaway. He wants to know when I plan to come home. I will compose a letter to address his concerns, but I cannot come home today. We must continue our treatment, and I will not leave Rayna behind. She would want to see her adoptive parents at the palace. It is only fair that I go back for her first."

Uneasy Dresnor nodded. "Seems I am to trust you with my prince a little longer." He glared at Ryker, clearly uncomfortable with the news.

Ryker interjected. "The boy is like family. I knew his mother years ago, when she was young. It is on this outing I hope to introduce him to his grandfather. He lives on the mountain." Ryker pointed northeast. "I believe it will be a real treat for them to meet. Mariana was well-loved among our people."

Listening to Ryker's half-truths was astonishing. He was a real professional.

Dresnor stood and motioned for Kai to follow. "If I may, I would like to speak with Prince Kai alone. I am sure you don't mind."

Alone, Dresnor leaned in and whispered, as if the distance they had was not enough. "This man. Do you trust him? He weaves a good story, but it's not all truth. Partly, yes. He is good with words, but I can spot a half-truth as easy as a lie. Question is, Kai, will *you* tell me the truth? Like this trip, you did not tell me everything."

"Philip, I told you what I could about these people," Kai insisted. "They are indeed my mother's people. That is true. Rayna has found people with news of her parents. And yes, I would like to meet my grandfather. That would mean the world to me. Spending time with Ryker, a man who knew my mother, I cannot possibly explain what that means."

Sympathetic, Dresnor relaxed.

Kai patted his friend on the shoulder. "Thank you, Philip, for waiting a little longer. I hope to go north to see my grandfather before I collect Rayna. I will be home in Diu for the Winter Festival. That is the honest truth as I know it right now."

Again, his friend nodded with understanding. "A little more truth in your version, but still, you are not telling me everything. For now, I will not push. If I sense trouble, that may change. Remember, I pledged to protect you at all costs. You are our future king now that you are not bound to Amelia and Milnos."

"I understand. Now, I need to write a few letters."

Dresnor extended the use of his hut for Kai to compose his letters. He wrote one to his father, one to Cazier, and one to Seth. Once finished, he and Ryker departed north.

CHAPTER 16

Snowy Climb

Smoke ran ahead through the pine trees. They had walked several miles before Kai spoke. "Seems you have decided my direction."

"It makes the most sense," Ryker replied. "Find Benmar first. Is that not why we came out here?"

It was true that Kai wanted to meet his grandfather, but now that it was time, he was nervous. He did not know this man. "What if he won't teach me?"

"You already know he will. Alenga told you to go and showed you flying with him. He is a Beastmaster, a silver dragon."

"Can I trust Keegan's father?"

Ryker huffed. "Remember Alenga's vision. This will happen. You will ride the wind. We just don't know when. Either way, you must meet Benmar. I know where he lives."

Along their walk, Kai recalled his vision:

Snow littered the sky. Bitter cold ripped through his clothes. Alone he climbed. Fatigued and half-frozen he found himself holding a white crystal. The snow-covered peaks of the Katori Mountains rose in the distance.

A flash of white brought him to a cluster of ice-covered trees. Carved into the mountain, a dark cave opening loomed against the white snow. Inside the nothingness, something waited. He braced himself against the howling winds. He squinted, blinded by the snow.

Inside the cave, heat pulsed within the walls. Hot air blew into his face. The walls came alive with ambient blue light, and Kai came face to face with the silver beast. The dragon's amber eyes glowed.

Kai shook his head at the memory. "How will I know where to go?"

Ryker hopped over a felled tree. "I will take you as far as the snow. You must find your way after that. I have business to attend to for the Kahoma—coastal tribe. Smoke will need to come back with me. You will need to focus on your training."

No questions asked, Kai continued. The sun's rays pierced the treetops. Together they made their way through the woods. Thousands of pine trees littered the forest floor with pine needles. Ryker led him through the trees, moving deeper into the thick forest. The smell of pine tickled his senses with each step. Kai felt at home in the forest. With his new connection to Alenga and the power flowing through his veins, he sensed so much more.

After a few hours of walking, the dense pines gave way to tall redwoods. Bits of blue sky poked through the canopy. Out of habit Kai gleaned the area. He searched for wild animals that might cross their path. They traversed the river to venture northeast into new territory.

Ryker glanced over his shoulder. "Do you see the bear up on that ridge? And the lone wolf on the outcropping?"

"I gleaned them both," Kai responded.

"I figured. You're using your sight to search the forest. Stop it." Ryker's voice was firm but kind.

"Why? I thought that is what we do."

"True. You are Katori, but you are a Beastmaster. I am sure of it. Develop your senses like the animals of the forest. Listen. Look. Smell. Marduk cannot glean. Shane doesn't either. They are hunters: hunter and the hunted. Going against the Lumens should have taught you that. Gleaning isn't your only natural gift. As a Beastmaster, you are so much more. Feel the magic around you."

"But my crystal is white. How do you know?" Kai insisted that mattered.

Ryker turned to glance back at Kai. "Alenga saw fit to give that gift to you, a white crystal, but you have a way with animals. Focus on what you know. As a Beastmaster, you can sense animals. Feel their intent. You will know which ones to run from and which can be approached. It works the same way with people. If you pay attention, you'll sense their true nature. This is your first lesson. Feel the connections around you. Don't take it for granted, develop it."

Kai listened to Ryker's advice. For a man of few words, he had much to say these past few days. Now was the time to absorb every bit of knowledge that anyone was willing to share. While most of Katori had opened their hearts to him, he wasn't sure how long that would last if he chose to return to Diu so soon, even if it were only for a short time.

"Push out with your own aura; the sensitivity you feel on the surface of your skin," Ryker continued. "The soul opens the mind and expands your sight. Do more than see them. Feel them." Ryker hopped across a stream. "The aura you saw around people after your dip in Alenga's waters. You saw that, right?

Kai followed him across the stream. "I did, but that has faded now."

"Life's energy never fades. It changes, but never fades. You were taught to glean with your mind. Now you need to learn to do it with every part of you."

"Can every Beastmaster do this?" Kai asked.

"The short answer is no. They could if they tried, but it is a lost art. People are lazy. They rely on their ability to glean. Everyone likes seeing. Feeling takes effort."

In the renewed silence, Kai let his body sense the surrounding world. He smelled the damp earth, decayed leaves, and cold air. There was power in the ground. He listened to the scamper of animals, the bird's chirps, and the sway of the trees in the wind. Life teemed around him. Ryker's footfalls were hardly noticeable on the trail ahead, but Kai felt the man's physicality.

Around the next tree, Kai let his hand brush the rugged bark. The trunk bloomed with power. Some of the magic seeped into Kai's hand. He felt the energy charge his muscles. It was easy to see how one could sustain themselves or even increase their abilities by borrowing from nature.

The smell of snow filled Kai's lungs. Through the trees, there was a hint of white snow on the ground. Thick flakes began to fall from the sky. The dark form of Ryker against the white reminded him of his dream. He ignored the signs of snow and continued to follow his guide, his new friend.

It saddened him to know Ryker would turn back soon, yet it thrilled him to know he was close. Today, he would meet the silver dragon. The invisible man. His grandfather.

Ryker's demeanor changed. His expression seemed solemn. "You are so much like your mother. You have her spirit." He let go the breath he'd been holding. "I've enjoyed our time together. How I wish I were your father."

At a loss for words, Kai bobbed his head.

"I am sorry you had to wait so long to know what you know now." Ryker stopped in the snow, and turned to look into Kai's eyes. "If you ever need anything, I will help you. I will take good care of Smoke. When you return, look for me around Alenga's hidden cave. I will help you search for your mother."

Kai offered his hand. "Thank you, Ryker. That means a lot to me. Look in on Rayna. She is alone now."

"Consider it done." Ryker let go of Kai's hand.

Their goodbyes were short, and they parted. Ryker walked back down the mountain, and Kai stepped through the snowdrift. The climb became difficult, but he continued. Each step, the snow got deeper. At first, it hardly covered the tops of his boots. Within a few feet, he was knee-deep. Snowflakes collected on his shoulders.

Each gust was colder. The higher he climbed, the fewer trees there were to block the wind. He planted his foot, and it sank thigh-deep into the wet snow. Some steps sank, others did not. The frigid wind froze his soaked pants. More snow fell. It became harder and harder to see where he was going.

Snow whipped around Kai's shoulders. The bitter cold slipped through the threads of his coat. His jacket was soaked through and half-frozen. The icy rocks made it difficult to keep his footing. Every other step he struggled to keep from falling. The steep incline had him zigzagging instead of walking in a straight line.

The air was cold and dry. The wind burned his cheeks. He pressed on. His unusually warm core was almost not enough to keep him from freezing, but there was no turning back now. He peered through the snow. Its whiteness blinded him. He squinted through the storm and braced himself against the howling winds.

A cluster of ice-covered trees came into view. The snow was now hip-deep, and he stepped around the trees. Relieved to see the dark cave opening, he hopped through the snow. Inside the nothingness, he felt it. Something waited.

Kai lowered his arm. Inside the cave, he felt warmth. Heat pulsed within the walls. Hot air blew into his face. A shadowy mass shuddered in front of him. The walls came alive with ambient blue light, and he came face-to-face with the silver-scaled beast. The dragon's amber eyes glowed. Smoke trickled out of its nostrils.

Kai froze. The scale of the beast took up the entire cave, its imposing body size doubled by its massive wingspan. There were so many details to consider. A series of horns protruded from its massive skull, and many spikes trickled down the spine. The wings were a lighter shade of gray, while its stomach was darker than its back. Sharpe talons scraped stone and the barbed tail hovered slightly above the floor.

The beast rustled its wings then unfurled them slightly. Kai stepped back. The dragon cupped its wings inward, concealing its body. Kai felt an increase of heat emanating from the already warm beast. Air puffed around the dragon, and with a white spark, the beast collapsed inward, leaving behind the man from the Agora all those weeks ago.

His white crystal glowed briefly. He was still dressed in dark blue with long sandy blond hair wild about his shoulders. His sharp goatee was grayer than Kai had noticed before. Upon closer inspection, Kai noticed the man's blue-green eyes. The shape of his face looked familiar. A memory flashed in his mind. This face had hovered over his bassinet. A wide smile beamed as the man lifted Kai into his arms.

The realization of his old memory startled Kai. "You knew my mother. We've met before, when I was a baby. How could I possibly remember that?"

"My name is Benmar. Pleasure to meet you, my grandson. Follow me." He strode deeper into the cave, down a well-lit tunnel into a vast living space. "Have a seat." Benmar motioned to a twisted vine wicker chair with a red cushion beside a stone hearth.

"Our memory is a tricky thing. I visited you many times, until you learned to speak. I feared you mentioning my visits to King Iver."

Feeling warmer, Kai took off his heavy coat. "Then you must have known that Keegan was my real father?"

"Mariana told me what happened. Keegan abducted her. She felt it was safer for you if everyone believed Iver was your father. Had she returned to Katori, news would have reached Keegan of your birth. He would have come for you and her, I am sure of that. She would not risk losing you. Iver is a good man and she loved him. Mariana was happy in her chosen life."

"Why did she confide in you, Keegan's own father? Was that not a risk?"

"I don't follow the rules and I go where I please—my book should have told you as much." Benmar smirked.

Kai chuckled. "The Invisible Thief. I remember it."

"I know my own blood when I see it. At first, I only wanted to see if she was happy, maybe apologize for my son's misguidance. When I saw you—I just knew, and she did not deny the truth. I promised to keep her secret and let all Katori believe she had a new life. As you can imagine, Lucca was displeased, but the man's pride kept him from visiting. He turned his back on her and never considered you to be family. I think a small part of him always knew Keegan was your father."

Kai's heart hardened against Lucca. The more he knew about the man, the less he liked. How could anyone abandon their own flesh and blood? His brooding silence was interrupted by his grandfather pouring hot water into a teacup. "Let's not stew about the past or another man's choice. Rest assured, Lucca is suffering for his decisions. His loneliness consumes him. Pity, he has no idea how to remedy his mistake."

Kai pulled his crystal from inside his shirt. "Benmar, is your crystal white, like mine? What does it mean?"

Benmar pulled his chain out for Kai to see. "Yes, Kai, mine is still white. What do you want it to mean?"

He didn't know what he wanted. "I thought I would get a color—blue, actually."

"Do you need to be told who you are? Are you a prince? A Beastmaster? You need to be yourself. What do you want?"

"If I could choose, I would be a Beastmaster. I feel most like myself around animals," Kai admitted.

"Then be that. Alenga is not here to tell us. The white crystal, to me, means freedom to evolve. It seems to come with more than one single gift. Your mother's crystal had a white vein down the center. She could become multiple animals. You have choices."

Kai had never thought about having the freedom to choose. He had so many more questions. He went to ask another, but it came out in a yawn.

"Bring your tea. I will show you to your room. Cave living is different—it takes a little getting used to the lack of sunlight in the morning. These crystals work the same as the Cosmos vine flowers." Benmar motioned to the various crystals embedded into the wall. "Once you settle, their ambient light will fade. Good night, grandson. Get some rest. We have much to accomplish in the coming weeks."

Kai glanced around the hollowed-out space. Like the beds in the tree pods, his bed was a twist of thick vines with a thick pad of cotton covered in linen. He had a table and chair in one corner and shelves in the other. Everything was made from twisted vines.

"Good night, grandfather." The word felt good rolling off his tongue. Kai liked this man.

CHAPTER 17

The Black Soul

Kai awoke. The darkness of his room surprised him, then he remembered where he was. The moment he moved, the Lumen-empowered crystals brightened the windowless cave. He dressed in the ambient blue light. From memory, he retraced his steps back to the main living space. A black pot of porridge dangled on a wrought-iron arm. Water bubbled in the kettle dangling over the fire.

"Good morning, Kai. I hope you slept well." Benmar dropped his armful of split wood into a copper bin.

"Good morning, grandfather. I slept well, thank you." Kai sniffed at the warm meal.

"Breakfast is ready. Grab our bowls and cups."

On the modest shelf, Kai found what they needed. Together they enjoyed a pleasant meal. "Do you live here alone?" Kai asked, looking around for signs of others.

"When Liam, my other student, is not here, it is just me. There are a few others that live within the mountain. Old-timers like me. People who fought in the war. Many find it difficult to be around others after all the violence. That or they simply won't follow the rules of others."

"You fought in the great war?"

"I did."

Kai leaned forward. His eyes locked with his grandfather's. "So, if I may ask, how old are you?"

Benmar chuckled, hearty and deep. "Mind you, age is only a number, but by today's calendar, one hundred and seventy-five. But who's counting."

"You don't look a day over fifty!" Kai stammered. "How is that possible?"

"Questions, questions. Let go of your traditional sense of time." Benmar poured them both another cup of tea. "Why are you here, grandson?" He raised one eyebrow.

Kai thought about his answer. "A vision directed me here. Everyone told me to seek you out, but if I am honest, I came seeking answers. I think you are the person capable of giving them to me. Not to mention my crystal is white, and nobody knows what to do with it."

His grandfather patiently waited.

Kai tapped at the table, collecting his thoughts, his mind a jumble of questions. "I have too many questions, I am not sure where to start. I read your book, but that was all made up, right?"

"There was more truth than fiction in my book. My life was a great adventure. It was a different time, but I don't think that is the right question. What do you really want to know?"

Silence fell between them. Kai pursed his lips. "Tell me about Keegan, my so-called father. How could he turn against this way of life? Why did he kidnap my mother? Why did he turn...?" Kai let his voice trail off.

"Bad? My poor lost son..." Benmar took a deep breath and stood. "Keegan, your father, has a black soul. If you've seen his crystal, you know it's true. It was once white as snow like ours, now it is black as coal." Benmar moved to a more comfortable chair near the fire, offering the adjacent seat to Kai.

"Long story short, Keegan was unable to learn my power to become invisible. He begged to know my secret. It wasn't like I hid the technique, I showed it to you the night of your blessing. Keegan was simply unable to convert the light." Benmar shook his head in sorrow.

"I've not tried yet," Kai admitted. "What you showed me. Not sure I am ready. I was unsure how to reverse the effects."

Benmar snickered. "Good. A healthy dose of humility and fear. Your father was not a humble man—he lashed out. The more he tried, the angrier he became. He assumed his white stone would give him the same abilities. You cannot be who you're not, and he was not me. His arrogance was his downfall. In his fury, he touched the person closest to him, his own mother. His blood boiled with rage. Out of control, he unwittingly pulled on her soul. Nobody understands how, but he shifted. His bone structure, his skin, his hair, all changed. Outwardly, he became his mother. His voice even had her gentle lilt."

Sadness washed over Benmar's expression. "My wife dropped to the ground. Your father just stood there. He shook his head disoriented, his mother lay helpless. For three days he was trapped in her skin. I kept him hidden. Sadly, my wife never recovered. She sat and stared, lost, disconnected from life. She died a few years back. My son did that. Took her from me." Benmar's words held anger.

"I am sorry for your loss." Kai didn't know what else to say.

Benmar continued. "Keegan went on to do it again. This time to his Kodama teacher, then his best friend. Each time, he became more fluid in his change. Fortunately for his victims, they were only paralyzed for a few hours. Their minds return in time; although, they are never exactly the same. My son's gift shatters the mind-soul connection. If you can call it a gift. He was meant to be a healer."

Kai thought of the effects on Kempery-man Marcone. He had lost his memory, but even when some of his thoughts returned, he never again had the sharp mind he was known for. "How could someone knowingly cripple another?" Kai clenched his fists.

His grandfather grabbed at the clear crystal around his own neck. "Keegan's own stone became blacker with each turn, and people began to call him the soul stealer. He was convinced he was the most powerful Katori who'd ever lived. He was sure Alenga had granted him unique gifts for a reason. In his mind, he was superior. To him, there was nothing wrong with his actions."

Kai listened intently. "How did he raise a following after doing these things? Why would anyone believe in him or his cause? For that matter, how did my mother get involved with a man like him? Ryker claims Lucca pushed them together."

"My family was a well-respected family in the Hiowind tribe. Lucca had every intention your mother and Keegan would be together. Ryker is correct, Lucca pushed them together. Mind you, Keegan was a handsome young man, and Mariana enjoyed his company. They were friends. When he became aggressive, she pulled away, but Keegan had his mind set. My son had a silver tongue. He convinced many that the Katori should rule the world. He was exceedingly arrogant." Benmar paused to drain his cup.

Kai tilted his head, wondering. "I hate to ask, but could Alenga not heal your wife? The waters of the sacred pool healed me when I entered."

"Believe me, we tried. Later, my son challenged your grandfather Lucca to the rite of Chief. Keegan attacked Lucca, tried to take his soul. Foolish boy. He had no idea the power the Lumens possessed. There are only three that I know of, and they are all elders. Not to mention when the chiefs and unie fight as one, well, let's just say your father was put down. They cast him out. Banished him from all of Katori."

This confused Kai. "And people still followed him?"

"Keegan convinced people they were trapped in Katori. He told them that even a gilded cage is still a cage. He said the world was ready to know we existed. Not that my son wanted people to choose their own leaders—he felt people should not be controlled. He persuaded them to rise up because they had no choice, given that the elders serve for life, and we can live three hundred years."

Kai nodded with understanding. "Old minds are difficult to change. Fear of trying anything new keeps you from advancing."

"Funny, that is what your father believed. The world outside was changing, and we were behind the times."

Benmar poured another cup of tea and continued. "Your father, however, plays a very long game. Over a year later he returned, only his face was that of a child. Poor thing. Keegan stole his essence. My son walked into the Agora and convinced your mother to go with him. Mariana thought she was helping a student. We never saw her again. The boy was too young to handle the experience, his heart gave out several days later."

Remorse resonated in Benmar's words. Kai knew these choices were Keegan's, yet his grandfather felt responsible. "Years later, we received word Mariana had married the young Diu King, Iver Galloway, and had born him a son. Lucca was bitter. He announced Mariana had made her choice. 'Let her stay in the world of modern man,' he said. Her brother, your uncle Haygan, was denied the rights to visit. Not that it stopped him, but by the time he found a way, she had supposedly died. Haygan delivered the news, then left in search of his sister. We all knew no dragon would harm a Katori without due cause."

"But you came," Kai interjected. "You visited."

"I did, but then I had very little to lose. And I hate rules...maybe Keegan gets that from me. Anyway, the Diu palace was not a challenge. The Mryken, they sensed me, but as a Beastmaster, they calmed in my presence. Over time, they learned to recognize my scent and ignore my visits."

The idea that this man walked the halls of the Diu palace undetected astonished Kai. It also pleased him to know his mother still had connections to her home.

A log shifted, and sparks flitted above the fire. Benmar poked and tossed on a new piece of wood. "Haygan, like many, refused to believe that she was dead. That is how he met Simone, on his search for Mariana. She convinced him to come home. To find you. The horse farm in Chenowith hired him; a young man with a talent for taming, training, and breeding wild horses. It didn't take long for his reputation to grow."

Kai nodded. "He told me about traveling through Nebea. Where he met Dante Carmello. Dante convinced him to train horses for the Cazier family. Then he was offered the position in Diu."

"Enough talk of the past," Benmar announced. "You came here to learn. Grab a coat."

Benmar led Kai through a series of tunnels. Along the way, Kai heard voices echo from the various shafts they passed. In his mind, he saw the network of chambers branch off from the main passage. He was surprised that so many lived within the mountain.

Nearly an hour later, they emerged outside in a snow-covered glade. The sun beamed high overhead. They traveled down the mountain. Confused, he tried to get his bearings. "Are we on the eastern side of the mountain now?" he asked.

"Excellent, Kai. We walked through the mountain. A well-guarded Katori secret. The peaks are narrow and it does not take long to go from one side to the other."

They traveled down the mountain until the snow faded, and the grasses grew tall. Through the trees, Kai caught sight of something large. Strange noises struck his ears: shrieks, coos, and warbles. The ground rumbled slightly. Benmar slipped through the thicket, and Kai followed until the trees parted. His grandfather found a spot on a stone perch. Mouth agape, Kai watched in awe.

Dragons of all sizes covered the mountainside. Many turned to gawk back at him. Nervous, Kai sat on the rock beside his grandfather. Speechless, he watched the dragons mingle, old and young, large and small. They eyed him at first. Some came close and cocked their eyes at him, then at Benmar, only to bound away after a few good sniffs of Kai's head.

"Where do dragons come from?" Kai asked softly.

"The first dragons came from the imagination of two lovers," Benmar answered. "It is said that creating the new creatures took all their energy, and they were lost in the change. From them, baby dragons were born into this world. With their offspring, other Katori shifted into their form. More and more people chose to remain dragons. Over the centuries, their numbers grew."

Listening to his grandfather, Kai watched their nature. Dragons coiled on rocks to bathe in the sunshine. Young dragons popped their heads out of dens within the rocks. Others took flight and disappeared over the trees. He wanted to get closer, but he dared not move from his grandfather's side. "Why do Beastmasters no longer become dragons?"

"The dragons fought for our desire to be free from the rest of the world. They died for us. In retaliation, men everywhere hunted them until we Katori intervened."

"How could anyone get the upper hand over a dragon?"

"Like any creature, they have weaknesses, points where they can be killed with the right weapon—giant spears catapulted into the air. Their young were hunted most aggressively. Men entered dens and slaughtered babies in the hundreds. Dragons everywhere retreated to Katori, begging for our help. Four of the fourteen Mystic Islands solely belong to them."

"What did the Katori do to stop them? And who is them?"

"They—were warriors from Bangloo. They took Milnos first and aimed to take over the world. We crafted the Zabranen Forest into a wild and unsafe border. Our guardians dominated the grounds. The hunters became the hunted. I hate to say we killed all who entered. But in the end, we created our mountains. The earthquake that shook the world created the Katori Mountains, which suited both our desire for seclusion and the dragons' desire for safety. It also cut us off from the world."

"But the dragons fought for Diu in the next war against Milnos. Why?"

"Because Gianfranca Galloway asked for our help to save Diu. She was Katori. At the time, Milnos was getting too strong. All of Katori felt it worth the risk to push them back. The elders felt we would be next, and it would start the great war all over again. But after, the dragon's retreated even more."

With one eye on their surroundings, Kai followed his grandfather. "That still doesn't explain why Beastmasters don't select dragons. Simone is a dragon."

"She is a brave woman. Her parents made the trip to Alenga's crystal mountain. She saw me fly away one night. It took her several months to find me, but she kept stalking me until I agreed to teach her. Then she begged to see the dragons for herself. So, I brought her here. She was captivated. I introduced her to the dragons. The rest was up to her."

"If I were here alone, would I be safe?" Kai's voice wavered in the asking.

"Without our constant interactions, dragons became aggressive. Honestly, they fear being manipulated for a cause that's not their own, and most Katori now fear them. To answer your question, I believe you would be fine. Your humble nature and respectful posture are the only things keeping you alive now. It is not out of respect for me."

Kai started to ask another question, but Benmar stood. "Enough questions for today. We can come back tomorrow."

CHAPTER 18

Fighting Dragons

Over the following weeks, they continued to visit the dragon's meadow. Kai studied their habits, watched them nurture and play with their young. He noticed their individual personalities. Today he and his grandfather walked through the center of their lair. Young dragons hid within their dens, while the adults were curious yet hesitant. They ranged in shades of black and red, some dark and intense while others were more vibrant and bright.

Following his grandfather's lead, he strolled through their rocky warren.

"Why would Liam, a Stoneking, choose to learn from a Beastmaster?" Kai wondered as they walked. "How could you possibly help him learn his gifts?"

"The lessons are the same, Kai. All young Katori must learn to access their gift. The only difference is the manipulation of power into the desired outcome. That, each person must discover for themselves."

"But why you? It can't just be a coincidence you became Liam's teacher."

His grandfather contemplated his response. Kai could see him struggling as he decided how to respond. "I am Liam's teacher because I needed him here. In truth, I needed someone willing to break the rules. Or at least bend them. Liam was that young man. I heard about a young

Stoneking meeting a boy who traveled with wolves. When I asked him about meeting you, I felt it gave him insight into the person you were. I knew a day would come when you would try to come for your Conhaspriga. I needed a Stoneking for that day and I hoped Liam would be willing to help you when all the older elders refused."

"But Stonekings and Weathervanes are so different than Beastmasters," Kai insisted.

Benmar chuckled. "Stop trying to force logic into every situation. Stonekings are more than brute force or physical strength. They see the finished product in their mind, feel it in their bones, then move it out through their hands. Weathervanes are the same. As I understand it, they feel a current running through their veins as they draw in energy. Their magic turns what they've created to alter elements of weather. At least that is what I've been told. Yulia told me how you helped her on the ship. You and Rayna pulled energy from the sky."

Kai knit his brow together. "How did we do that, anyway? Help Yulia, I mean."

"A small part of your gift is accessible once you open your mind to Alenga. The moment you glean, or bond with a companion, you are open to her. Touch a tree or a blade of grass, the energy is there. Now with your crystal and her blessing, you feel it more."

His grandfather's explanation sounded reasonable. "So, the two black dragons you fly with, are they real dragons or Katori people?" Kai asked, focused on one particular dragon that had meandered behind them. Its spiny head bumped into Kai's back. "What the...'

"Ignore him. He's trying to pick a fight." Benmar kept his eyes front. "And yes. They are Katori friends."

"What? Pick a fight?" Kai took a deep breath and was struck again, but this time he fell to the ground with a thud.

Benmar kept walking. "Good luck. See you at home."

Kai sat in the tall grass as Benmar walked away. He had his back to the beast that provoked him, and the creature laid its head a foot behind Kai. The dragon warbled. Kai glanced over his shoulder. Amber eyes blinked at him. The beast's head was the size of a large boulder. His scaly body was a dark metallic gray. Giant horns forked out of the back of its skull. Slowly Kai swiveled around to face the dragon. He slid back a few feet to give the beast space.

The pair stared at each other. Hands on his knees, Kai tried to look approachable, friendly even. He pushed his nature to the dragon, just like he did with Smoke and Ember. Within moments, the dragon began to emanate heat. Smoke rolled out his nose. A snarl revealed sharp teeth. A lump formed in Kai's throat.

With little to lose, Kai pushed his thoughts. *Would you like me to leave? Or can we talk?*

The dragon reared its body back. Head cocked to one side, the beast belched fire into the sky. Heat rained down on Kai.

Mistrustful creature you are. Kai heard the dragon speak inside his mind.

Kai stood to put distance between them. He studied the dragon's eyes and thought about his words. Real words came into his mind from the dragon. The concept was astounding. *We are not for you, little creature. Go back down our mountain, pick another beast. You are not worthy of us.* The dragon continued to murmur words in Kai's mind.

Without provocation, it lunged at Kai. Its nose popped him in the jaw, and Kai fell to the ground. Blood spilled from his lip. "I will not fight you," Kai said aloud, "but I cannot let you continue to hurt me either. I want you to trust me." Kai stood and bowed respectfully.

They stared at each other.

You seek power. Do you not? I see you and your pathetic courage. Go, if you think you can, weak one.

Certain the dragon was done talking and might get more aggressive, Kai wiped his mouth and turned to leave. Four other dragons closed around him. They all bumped him with their mighty heads, tossing him about in their little circle. Kai dusted the dirt from his hands. "If you mean to test my courage or my wrath, I will offer you neither. You have me afraid—I would be foolish not to fear you, but I will not draw my weapon on you. I want to know your ways. I want to become a dragon, but only to search for my mother."

Kai thought about what he'd just said. That was not entirely truthful. "Actually, besides having always wanted to be able to fly, I may need to fight a man who is pursuing me, but that is not what I mean to do with the gift of your connection. I hope to save my mother."

The dragon snorted smoke. *We are not weapons or playthings.* The voice again echoed in his head.

The idea that he was using them for one thing or another struck Kai, and he stepped back. He was drawn to their majestic nature, but it was not right to use them. "You are right. I came here for power, not for the joy of being a dragon. Let me leave, and I will not return."

Two dragons moved to open a path. Kai crossed the meadow, and he climbed the rocks and did not look back. Sliding down the backside, his heart pounded in his chest. Inside the tree line, he sensed his grandfather.

"That did not go well," Kai admitted.

Benmar stepped beside his grandson. "Couldn't have gone any better, if you ask me," he beamed.

"That was the most terrifying moment of my life. Their general distrust of people keeps them from giving me a chance. And they believe I am only after power. But you know, if I am being honest, I was not looking to bond as friends. I need them, and that makes this wrong."

"I wouldn't be so sure they are done with you." Benmar gestured behind Kai.

Kai turned to see three dragon heads peer over the rocks. Two others came from either side. "Fight or flight. Those were your two choices. You did not fight him, nor did you cower in fear. By speaking, you stayed neutral. You gave him the power to choose. The others tried to provoke you, and still you remained calm. Most importantly, you were honest about what is in your heart. Kai, what do you think makes a good Beastmaster?"

"Up until now, I would have said fearlessness. Control? Bonding?" Kai had no idea how to answer.

"Becoming an animal, any animal, takes equal measures of courage and fear. Balance. Too much arrogance and the beast will recoil; too little, and the beast will dominate you. Respect them. You don't bond with a beast, you *become* the beast. Bonds are for companions, but true emulating requires you to embrace their nature. Feel what they feel. They want the same as you, to live free." Benmar circled back to the dragon's meadow.

"When the change happens, will it hurt?" Kai felt the tremor in his legs with each step.

"Only if you fight against it," Benmar responded. "You must believe for it to happen, and if it doesn't happen, then it is not your gift. You may still have a way with creatures, but you may not be able to become one. But know this—you get one animal form. If you have the gift, one golden thread exists inside of you. Once you use it to create the beast, it will only become a dragon. You cannot change your mind."

Even though he knew his mother could become multiple animals, he knew that did not apply to him. Then he thought of witnessing his mother's change. She had screamed in pain, and fear had consumed her face. She had been fighting the change. "Will I look exactly like the one I choose?"

"You are not making a copy of them. You are changing your own elemental structure into a dragon. Your physical chemistry will design the creature you become. Spines, horns, and color." Benmar looked over the dragons. "Do you see the dragon you wish to fly with?"

"Yes. There is something about the one who shoved me."

"Walk with him, understand him. Understand who he is. Develop trust and he will consider your request. He will let you know when he is ready to accept you and if he will let you fly with him. When you do, lay across his back as he flies. Search for the golden thread of creation and let it happen."

"What should I say?"

"He knows full well why you are here." Benmar stopped walking. "You must walk alone from here."

"The golden thread, what is it? How do I find it?" Kai felt both excited and nervous. He held back from the dragon, not wanting to make a mistake.

"Each Beastmaster holds within their soul a golden thread. Two strands twisted together, or rather bonded by many strands. Only if you can find it within yourself can you transform. The change is personal— I think. I cannot know what you or any other Beastmaster feels. There's no place for thinking. If you focus on how, nothing will happen. Hold your crystal, reach inside your soul and open your mind."

His grandfather's words instilled confidence. Kai approached the dragon, the very one that had only moments ago tried to provoke him into a fight. His spiny head lowered to glare at Kai. Its amber eyes blinked, and the beast turned away.

"What changed your mind?" Kai asked the dragon.

Who says I've changed my mind? The dragon's deep-penetrating voice once again echoed inside his mind.

"Why let me come back?"

Not every human is sincere, even with themselves. It was refreshing to get the truth from you.

"How can I hear you inside my head?"

Because you are a Beastmaster. Only another dragon can understand the shrieks and warbles that is our language.

"My name is Kai, by the way. Do you have a name? I cannot very well just call you Dragon."

I am Raijin.

Kai continued to talk with Raijin, searching to understand him. "What are you most afraid of?" Kai half-whispered, worried he was too intrusive.

I fear dragons will disappear from this world and be forgotten. Become creatures of myth. While we live for hundreds of years, our eggs take two years to incubate. Many things can happen, and the egg might not hatch.

They walked and talked for nearly an hour. When Kai tripped over a stone, he learned they also have a sense of humor. Raijin's laughter sounded like a collage of warbles and hiccups.

Hopeful of their growing ease, Kai dared to wonder if his new friend might help him. "Raijin, thank you for today. It is getting late in the day.

I can only hope to ask, as I know I may not be worthy, but I would like to become a dragon. May I fly with you?"

Kai waited in a few moments of silence. The possibility of rejection tightened his chest. Raijin bowed his head. *You have great honor for a young spirit. May you always remember you are not alone in this world. Call on friends when you need them and trust in Alenga. I will help you, you may fly with me.*

In one hand, Kai held his crystal, while the other touched the dragon's body. Electricity surged through Kai's fingers. The thick, scaly skin felt hard like armor. He climbed onto its back, and sat between two large spines. The sense of something cosmic ebbed between them.

The dragon took flight. The wind pressed into Kai's face. The sky opened wide before them. Exhilaration swelled in his stomach. He was flying. The dragon dove, skimming above the treetops, then it climbed high into the sky. They flew higher, and Kai saw the horizon curve. The air became thin.

Kai gripped his crystal tighter. White light beamed brightly within his fist. Power surged up his arm. The expanse of the universe burst into Kai's mind, stardust coiled together into a golden strand. He reached for the rotating coil. A spark bloomed within the thread. The imprint of the dragon's essence mingled with his own.

Within his body, he felt the cord snap inside his chest. He lay against the massive beast as the dragon rolled upside down. Kai plummeted freely through the air. He felt a pulse ripple through his body, and Kai relaxed and accepted the change. His shoulders curled inward, and he felt his bone structure expand. His torso enlarged, skin stretched and thickened, and his complexion turned a dark silver.

Kai's hands curled into talons. He felt every muscle change. The wind blew around him as he hurled toward the ground. He flexed outward; his wings unfurled. His eyelids blinked over amber orbs. Spikes and horns covered his face, back, and tail. Transformation complete, Kai was a silver dragon.

Wings spread wide, he glided over the advancing landscape. The urge to screech overwhelmed him, and he belched out several odd sounds before he got it right. His stomach swelled with heat. He coughed, if one could call it a cough, and fire billowed out his mouth. His enhanced vision had a sharpness beyond anything he had ever experienced.

He soared back towards the Katori mountain range and flew over the summits. The setting sun turned the sky a deep orange to dark purple. When it finally sank from view, the stars twinkled above him. From his left, a silver dragon joined him: Benmar. Kai followed his grandfather down the mountain, and they soared above the treetops.

Baden Lake came into view. They hovered over the water's surface, and his dragon reflection rippled across the lazy waves. With his newfound freedom, he rolled and twisted, spun and flipped through the air. He felt his new body flex, and his mind turned wild.

Lost in the chase, he stayed close behind the other dragon. The lead dragon swooped skyward. Kai followed. Higher and higher they flew. The moon shone above. Kai felt his core temperature rise, and he belched fire. He warbled and screeched with delight at the other dragon. The other dragon answered back.

Kai relished the freedom and flew in front of the lead dragon. They played in the sky. Each roll of their flight thrilled him to his core. They banked hard left and curved around the lake. Their erratic pattern became a game, one trying to outmaneuver the other.

When the lead dragon landed on a flat mountain ridge, Kai followed. The peaceful night washed over him, and he wanted to fly more. A tiny light caught his attention. The lead dragon changed into a man. Kai lowered his beastly head. He knew this man. He felt the warmth of the man's hand press into his scale-covered cheek. "Remember who you are, Kai. Let the golden thread go. Reach for the white light."

Kai felt the urges of the wild beast within his heart. The joy of flight and freedom. He wanted to fly. "Remember those you love. Rayna, Haygan, and Simone. Let's go home, Kai," the man called.

Rayna's laughter echoed in his ears. Kai released the golden thread and clung to the white light. He felt edges of his crystal warm his hand. He felt his body slough off the massive beast. His natural body returned. The unused energy floated back into nature. His knees felt weak. He stepped forward and everything went black.

♦ ♦ ♦

Hours later, he awoke. His grandfather had carried him back to their hidden cave on the mountain. "You will be alright," he said softly. "Changing takes practice, but you must not lose yourself to the nature of the beast. Always cling to a memory or a person here in this life. If you embrace the creature—you could be lost forever. Do you understand?"

The thought of his mother panged in his heart. Had she lost her way in her own dragon? Trapped for ten years, she kept their secret, but would her memories be enough to save her mind? He had to keep faith in Alenga.

His personal experience filled his senses. "While we were flying, I felt free. Wild. In those moments, I was a dragon, through and through. If you had not landed, I would still be circling the skies. Every sensation felt new and powerful." Kai sighed heavily at the idea.

Benmar nodded with understanding. "I am fortunate to be your guide. Alenga has blessed us both with this time together. Now I will make us a pot of tea."

They sat by the fire, resting and reminiscing about the evening. Their late-night talks had become a highlight at the end of each day, an opportunity for Kai to learn more about his family history and connect with his grandfather.

"You know, the first time I saw a dragon up close, I was fourteen. I was traveling to Town Hope—well, at the time, it was called Hamrin. In fact, I saw a silver dragon that night. Was that you?"

"It was me," Benmar admitted. "The look on your face as we swept over the trees overwhelmed me. I belched fire, laughing at your expression."

"So, it is your fault I fell that night?" Kai snapped.

"Hardly, your fear made you step back. Carelessness let you fall."

"I could have died from that fall."

Benmar shook his head. "No, I knew you would not die."

Kai eyed his grandfather. "How did you know some other creature would not devour me as I searched for a way back—or while I slept?"

"Grandson, I was never more than a breath away from your side. Your focus was on the cliff wall and your wolf. And in case you've forgotten, I can turn invisible. You weren't looking for me. But I was there with you."

Benmar paused and Kai let the concept settle.

"Kai, you needed that moment. That night changed you fundamentally. At your core, you began to grow. Iver sent you out, the little prince out to prove himself. You went because you wanted an adventure. The palace, the city, they were confines." He shook his head. "No. You needed to be more. Stronger. Alone in the forest, were you afraid?"

"No, not really. Smoke was with me, and I did what was needed."

"When you stepped into the cave and found a pack of wolves, were you afraid?"

For the first time in years, he really thought about that night and the three wolves that kept him warm when he intruded on their den. After walking for hours trying to find his way back to his campsite, he had collapsed and the alpha and his pack protected him while he slept. They sacrificed their own lives to come to his aid during the fight with the Guardians.

"I should have been very afraid, but no. I knew what to do. Instinct told me to stay calm. Not to mention, I was exhausted by the time I came across the alpha. I pushed my thoughts to him."

"Control is an illusion." Benmar handed Kai a cup of hot tea. "Everyone wants it. Keegan wanted it. Lucca wanted it. But you cannot control much in this life. It is better to bend rather than break. Flow with the current, grandson, but remember you are not alone."

"The dragon told me the same thing today. I wish I would have grown up here, with you."

"Never wish your life away. Our trials shape us. Life's mysteries define our character and surround you with the people you need most. You were meant to live this life. Enjoy the adventure."

"So, speaking of adventure, your book, *The Invisible Thief*... Did you really do all those things? Travel to all those places? Sail the Caprizian Sea? Steal the crown jewels of Bangloo, then return them as a wedding gift to his daughter? I have studied many history books, but that story is not among them."

"It wouldn't be. Theft of those jewels would have been an embarrassment to a very proud nation." Benmar smirked, "But it happened. Now off to bed with you. It's been a long day. No more talking tonight."

Exhausted from becoming a dragon, Kai collapsed on the bed in his alcove. He stared at the starry crystals embedded in the ceiling. His life had changed drastically over these many months. He'd gone from living in a palace to living in trees and caves. And if he was honest with himself, he was happier.

If only he could blend his old life with his new one. But they were two separate worlds unwilling to live together. Duty commanded he become king—like it or not, he was next in line, now that he was no longer betrothed to Amelia of Milnos.

All his life he thought he wanted adventure. Now, all he wanted was peace and quiet. The opportunity to live a tranquil life with Rayna. He thought of her face, her sweeping brown hair, and her soft eyes. Around him he felt the pulse of energy that typically preceded a vision. Quietly, he let go of the day and slipped off into a dream.

Darkness expanded into a sunshine-filled glade. Wildflowers swayed in the breeze. Rayna stepped through the flowers. Her delicate fingers tickled the flower petals. New blooms popped at her touch. She smiled, pleased with her work.

Three girls approached. Senina, Ciera, and Linnea. They encircled Rayna. Kai watched, but he could not hear their words. They each spoke in turn. Rayna's expression changed. Hands on her hips, her posture showed determination. The girls stepped back and laughed. Still, Kai could not hear their words. He couldn't hear anything.

Rayna shook her head at the girls. Her fingers stretched outward. She pulled at the ground, coaxing the earth up around her feet. Roots burst across the glade. Startled, the sisters stepped away. Shock contorted their faces and Senina covered her mouth. Fear washed over her expression. Senina waved at Rayna to stop; her mouth was wide with screams.

Bark crept up Rayna's legs. Craggy gray bark swelled around her and pushed her skyward. The trunk thickened. Rayna lifted her hands, and branches sprouted from her arms and fingers. As the tree engulfed her body, the look in Rayna's eyes turned to fear. Her hair turned woody. Her mouth curled into a scream.

The advancing bark did not stop. What remained of Rayna struggled. Tears ran down her face. She was afraid. The final bit of her face swelled into woody bark and disappeared. Kai gasped for air and burst from his dream. Anger pierced his heart. The love of his life was in trouble.

Kai didn't bother to wake Benmar, he stomped around the cavern, collecting his belongings. His lack of subtlety woke his grandfather. "Kai. Where are you off to in such a rage?"

"Rayna is in trouble. I need to help her. Those stupid girls. They tricked her into turning herself into a tree."

"Hold on. How do you know this? Did you have a vision of her as a tree?"

"Visions, I've learned, come in one of two ways. Sometimes they come in flashes that lack detail, but they show glimpses into the future. Or they come in slow, detail-filled scenes, which usually means I have little time, if any. The vision I just had seemed to be of the past." Kai shook his head, trying to pinpoint how the vision made him feel. "I need to find Rayna." Kai seethed. "Those sisters need to pay for tricking her."

"Grandson, please..." Benmar tried to calm Kai.

Kai ignored his grandfather. "When did Rayna learn how to become a tree?" He stumbled out of the cave. "She looked terrified."

"Be careful, Kai. Half-knowledge is dangerous. You may not yet know the full truth."

"Dangerous? They have no idea. I will show the sisters dangerous."

Benmar placed his hand on Kai's shoulder. "Breathe. You are angry. Anger is our enemy. To find Rayna, you must be your best self. Anger will not help her; it may even prevent you from finding her."

Kai wrestled with his thoughts. "What would you have me do?"

"Revenge only leads to disaster. It will not mend your heart or Rayna's. Before you speak, let your emotions settle. Keep a watch over your words—words can mold others. Rayna must forgive. If she is a tree, it can be reversed. Use your relationship with Rayna to call her back. Just as I called to you, ask her to remember who she was. You will need to find a strong Kodama. Someone Rayna knows. You said Imani claims to be her sister in blood. Find her."

"I don't know if that will work. When I left, I suggested that Rayna meet with Imani, but she was not ready to confront her family."

Benmar rushed to follow Kai. "Trust me, Kai. Her sister will be the best person to help. She is from the Matoku tribe, if memory serves me." Benmar took Kai's bag. "You won't need any of this where you're going."

CHAPTER 19

The Oak Sisters

The morning dew covered the grasses. Tiny beads of water glistened in the sunshine. Rayna followed her friend Jayla to a small flowerbed, one they had planted a few days earlier as seeds. Being a Kodama for Rayna felt very natural. Her powerful connection to plants called to her soul. She loved pushing her hands into the soil. To her, it seemed like being able to touch the sun.

The memory of pushing tiny seeds into the ground and coaxing them to grow brimmed with delight inside Rayna. The morning sunshine felt warm on her face. "Jayla," she said as she stopped to kneel next to a young sapling. "The more I work with the plants, the more I see the magic they hold. Helping them grow seems second nature. I feel and see the sun's power inside the plants."

Jayla knelt at her side. Her short blonde hair fluttered around her head. "Working with the plants teaches you how to harness power from your surroundings. Magic exists in every living thing. We only move it about, never taking too much. The soil has much to give with its depth and variety of minerals. It is best to take from the dirt, but you must be sure you don't harm the other plants."

Rayna swept her long brown hair to one shoulder. "What are we learning today?"

"Today, you will coax the sapling to grow. Restore the apple orchard with a new tree. Make it grow and produce blossoms. We talked about using sunlight and soil last night. Let's see what you remember."

The tiny tree was only three feet high. It had taken a great deal of energy to create the tiny thing, now she would turn it into a full-grown tree with fruit. "It was all I could do to make this little spindly thing. How can I make a tree large enough to bloom?"

"You know what a full-grown tree looks like," Jayla said, "and how the fruit tastes. Start there. Close your eyes and picture the finished tree."

The idea of getting a seed to grow into a plant within seconds would have seemed impossible until a few days ago. But planting an entire garden in a day gave Rayna confidence. Now she was going to encourage her first tree. Digging her hands into the soil, she could feel the bits of old bark from the tree struck by lightning a month earlier.

Deeper into the soil, she sensed worms and bugs. Deeper still, a layer of rocks and moisture. Around them, Rayna felt the other plants and became aware of their needs on the land. She narrowed her connection to the earth to ensure she did not pull from the other flora. "I am ready," she said, accessing the magic within her and her green crystal.

"Close your eyes, Rayna. Think about every detail of your tree. The curve of its trunk, its bark, and the color of the leaves. Let the sweetness of an apple refresh your tongue."

The apple orchard in Diu sprang to life in Rayna's mind. She had spent many hours walking with Kai and eating apples over the years. The smell of their blossoms and the taste of their fruit lit up her senses. Now she pulled the energy from the soil, and it started to pour into her. Sunshine warmed her cheeks, and its power flowed through her veins. With the power instilled within her crystal, she blended the two forms of energy.

Feeding the sapling, she sensed the roots spreading underground. The trunk expanded, and new branches and leaves unfurled. Not wanting to take too much from the soil, she pushed back against the flow to restore the land beneath the developing apple tree.

"Ease back a little, Rayna," she heard Jayla recommend. "The tree will split if it grows too fast, and you will lose valuable sap for the apples."

Heeding her teacher, Rayna held back the flow of magic.

"Don't forget to breathe, young Kodama," she whispered.

Rayna eased and let a breath seep from her lungs. Jayla's warm hand touched her arm, lifted her hand out of the soil, and slid it up the tree. "Now, use the sap and your remaining strength to create the blossoms."

The golden sap within the tree trickled through the trunk. Infusing sap with her magic, Rayna thought of the sweet apple blossoms. She opened her eyes and the tree was filled with white and pink flowers. Delighted, she hugged herself.

"Well done." Jayla stood and pulled Rayna to her feet. "How do you feel?"

"I feel good! Not lightheaded at all this time."

Pleased with her tree, she stepped back to look at the restored apple orchard. Each tree was filled with blossoms of their own. Bees buzzed around her and flitted around her new creation. She was happy.

◆ ◆ ◆

On her own, Rayna ventured outside of Hiowind. The hillside rolled outward, and she imagined Kai taking this route to follow Ryker. An afternoon breeze tugged at her green dress and played with her hair. In the distance, she gazed at the foothills and the Matoku city where her sister Imani lived. She wanted to see her, but the fear of rejection held her back.

Tall willow trees swayed around her. The smells of the forest welcomed her, and she continued. Birds sang from branches. This was the farthest she'd ever gone on her own, and her newfound independence grew with each step. Katori was beginning to feel like home.

The farther Rayna walked, the thicker the trees became, until black rock formations changed the landscape, pushing back the fatter specimens in exchange for shorter, spindly varieties. Spotting a large arch cut in the rocks, she ventured inside to find a tunnel.

Curious, she stepped through and found herself in a beautiful clearing. Sunshine kissed her face. Wildflowers swayed in the breeze. Pleased with her surroundings, she let her delicate fingers tickle a few flower buds. New blooms popped at her touch. She smiled, pleased with her work.

Behind her, she heard giggles. Before she knew it, the oak sisters had encircled her. Senina, Ciera, and Linnea flitted around the wildflowers and glared at her.

Senina took hold of her hand. "Dear Kodama, sister. How did you discover this meadow?"

Ciera pushed at a branch near her head, commanding it to move away. "This is a sacred Kodama place."

Rayna did not like the looks on their faces, nor how they had appeared so suddenly. She tried to leave, but Linnea blocked her path. "Don't go, not yet."

"Were you following me?" Rayna asked.

"Do you want to know why this place is so special?" Senina ignored her question. "We Kodama come here to practice becoming trees. The earth here is very rich, and the rivers from the Katori Mountains flow beneath this place. Our ancestors had the Stonekings create this sanctuary for us. Mighty women, in their old age, became the three oak trees that welcome each Katori into Zabranen Forest. As their descendants, it is our duty to protect this place."

"Do you wish to learn?" Linnea asked.

Ciera laughed. "Her? Become a mighty oak?"

"I don't know..." Senina paused and scanned the length of Rayna. "She is rather small to consider becoming an oak. Maybe she'll be a lavender twistwood."

All three girls laughed at the idea. "Come on, my sisters, she is not brave enough to even try," Senina mocked.

In her studies, Rayna had seen sketches of a lavender twistwood tree. While extremely pretty, the tree remained small, no more than four feet tall at best. Their bark was dark, nearly black, and they often grew twisted, but their pale lavender flowers were said to be honey-sweet.

The comparison to this inferior plant made Rayna's blood boil. She could do this. If they could become a mighty oak, she certainly could too. Glaring at the sisters with her hands on her hips, she was determined to prove them wrong. "I can too," she shook her finger at them.

The girls turned around and laughed. A faint breeze whipped through the trees. "Well?" Ciera crossed back to stand near Rayna.

"What are you waiting for?" Linnea looked around the glade.

"Show us what you can do, little Kodama sister," Senina mocked.

Rayna shook her head at the girls. Her fingers stretched outward. "You just watch what I can do." She slipped out of her shoes to let the earth squish under her feet.

Connected to her magic, her green crystal began to shine. Within the ground, she felt great power. The soil welcomed her touch. Without thinking, she pulled at the ground, coaxing the earth up around her feet. Her toes sank into the soil and roots burst across the glade. Startled, the sisters stepped away.

"Rayna, are you sure you want to do this?" Senina asked, suddenly wary.

Ignoring the sister, Rayna took in a deep breath. The sun baked her scalp. Its power infused her and mixed with the energy from the ground. A mighty oak tree came to mind, and she used her newly created magic to change her form.

Raised off the ground by her expanding roots, Rayna gawked at her situation. One look at the sisters, and she pushed harder at the idea of becoming a tree. Their contorted faces concerned her. Senina covered her mouth. Fear washed over their expressions.

Senina waved at Rayna. "No. Please stop this. You really should not continue!"

Bark crept up Rayna's legs. Craggy roots swelled around her and pushed her skyward. Her trunk thickened. Rayna lifted her hands, and branches sprouted from her arms and fingers. As the tree engulfed her body, Rayna suddenly felt afraid. What had she done? She had no idea how to change back or how to stop what was happening. She felt her skin change and harden. Her hair became heavy and woody. Her mouth curled into a scream. "Please help me!"

The advancing bark did not stop. Rayna struggled but could not reverse the effects. Warm tears ran down her face. She was afraid. The final bit of her face swelled into woody bark and disappeared.

Two of the oak sisters panicked and darted out of the glade. Only Senina remained. Her trembling hand touched the tree. To Rayna's surprise, she felt the girl's fingers caress her bark.

The desire to breathe came over her, but instead of lungs within her chest, her entire body felt the intake of air. Her leaves fluttered in the wind, and it trickled down her trunk. The sun bathed her in light, and it felt wonderful. Deep within the ground, her roots sucked at water and nourished her. Birds landed on her branches and sang to her. Their delightfulness pleased her. Happy, she swayed in the breeze and looked around her glade.

Below, on the ground, a girl slumped. Wet tears ran down her sad face, and she leaned against the tree trunk. The weight of her felt nice, and the mighty oak listened to the sobbing stranger.

"Please come out, Rayna. I am so sorry we tricked you." Senina wiped the tears from her face and reached up at the tree. "I don't know how to help you."

The mighty oak stiffened and searched the cloudy sky. Peaceful and happy, it leaned toward the shifting sunlight. Content to watch the setting sun, the tree ignored the wet creature at her base.

CHAPTER 20

The Kodama

Winter snow filled the skies. There was no time to tramp through the forest. Kai needed speed. In his dragon form, he took flight. He had no idea how to find Rayna's tree or how to find Imani. Katori was a vast country, the woman could be anywhere. His only hope was to follow his grandfather's advice, fly toward Ryker, and search for Imani among the Matoku tribe.

Through the snowy weather, Kai flew higher and higher. Up into the snow-filled clouds, everything turned white. Through the vapors, the early dawn sky emerged. The Katori's peaks came into view, their snow-covered summits clawing at the pink morning sky.

Over the mountain crest, Kai dove back through the clouds. There was no snow yet on this side of the mountain range, but he could smell that the crisp air was ripe for a storm.

He banked a hard right towards the southeast side of Katori. The rolling foothills. Home to Ryker's Matoku highland tribe.

Thick fluffy clouds gave way to thin wispy ones. He crashed through their feathery vapors, his outstretched wings sailed on a cushion of air. The wind rolled over his thick dragon scales. His heart pounded inside his massive chest. Gigantic lungs sucked in the fresh air. Even though his flight had an urgent purpose, it still thrilled Kai to his core. Deep down he held onto the memory of Rayna's face.

Fields of grass unfolded below. His amber eyes scanned the ground. Quickly the details came into view. Treetops. Streams. Rock formations. Each elegantly decorated the land. His shadow floated over the landscape. Alenga's cave was a good indicator he was getting close.

Over the next hill, the main part of the Matoku village came into view. Around and around he circled. His shadow fluttered over the village. People stopped their work and pointed at his looming presence. The people seemed to be afraid. They scurried under trees and near stone structures.

He felt drawn to this place as he circled. Imani had to be here. But how would he find her? He had only met her once, months ago. Imani had been drawn to Rayna, although her companion had acted reclusive and disinterested. Imani claimed to be Rayna's sister, and according to Benmar, she was the person he needed. Would she really help? Could she help? Kai shook the worry from his mind.

Kai's dragon eyes enabled him to see great distances. Just beyond Alenga's hidden cave, he spotted Ryker and Smoke running across the hillside in the direction of the Matoku tribal city. Still, Kai did not land. He collected his thoughts. Benmar's words rang in his ears. Kai knew his grandfather was right. To help Rayna, he needed to be peaceful at heart. He would need to encourage her to be forgiving.

On the ground, one woman stepped away from the group. She strolled into the clearing. Her eyes fixed on the sky. She sat in the tall wildflowers and her hands swept over the ground in tiny circles. Wildflowers and tall grasses bent to her will. A large circle of flowers and grasses fell flat in front of her.

Kai circled low and dropped to the ground into the spot Imani made for him. He shuddered and shook off his dragon form, his true body restored. Once again, blackness took him, and he collapsed into the grass.

Warm hands rubbed small circles on his chest. The woman's face was blurry but familiar. When his eyes focused, he beheld Rayna's older sister. "Imani?" He steadied his racing heart. "I am humbled to ask for your help."

"Kai. You are most welcome here." She patted his arm. "You should be good to sit up now," she urged him upright.

"Are you sure I am welcome?" Kai scanned the villagers. "How long was I out?"

Imani looked around, her smile reassuring. "Only a few minutes. I healed your weary body. Transforming takes time to learn. You must balance the energy you burn in the change. Let the air and sunlight ease your burden. And remember not to force it."

Everyone else remained a good distance away, their expressions a mix of surprise and disbelief. "It has been a while since a dragon has flown into Matoku that was not Simone. Her black dragon form is well known in these parts, but your silver body surprised everyone. Dragons keep to the snowy peaks or to the Mystic Islands. They avoid us, and we give them space. You surprised us, is all."

"Imani, I wish I had time to be cordial, but I need your help. Or rather, Rayna needs you."

Imani nodded heavily. "I heard the cries of my sister last night. One Kodama to another, I felt Rayna's fear. She was afraid when she made her transformation. We need to go to her quickly. Her mind is fragile. Confused. If she has nothing to cling to on this side, she will get lost in being a tree. The life of a tree is most enjoyable."

"I do not know where to look" Kai panned around at the onlookers, "but I do know whom to ask. The oak sisters were with her. They tricked her into changing, at least that is what my vision implied." Kai's tone soured. "I blame Senina."

"Let us find Rayna first. Worry about how she came to be a tree after." Imani stood. "There is a meadow where many Kodama go to practice their techniques. We should start there. While we go, you should cleanse your heart and mind. It will be the bridge Rayna will cross to return."

With an open mind, Kai followed Imani.

Ryker and Smoke darted through the tall grass to catch up with them. "I did not expect you back so quickly. What brings you to Matoku? Has something happened?"

"I had a vision of Rayna transforming into a tree. The look on her face told me she was terrified. Benmar suggested finding another Kodama to help her." Kai glanced at Imani. "My grandfather said that you were best suited to help."

"I can help her," Imani reassured him. "I had hoped my sister would have come to see me sooner."

The curve of her mouth, the small nose, and the shape of her eyes were so like Rayna, it was almost shocking. "She wanted to come, but I leave the reasons why she didn't for her to explain," Kai responded.

Ryker interrupted the moment. "I hate to push, but maybe we could pick up the pace."

Their quick marched turned into a run. Down the hillside they went, Imani in the lead, Kai and Ryker behind. With each step, his anger subsided. Benmar was right; he did not have the entire story. Why would Rayna try something so advanced without proper guidance? Why was she with the oak sisters in the first place? They were hardly friends.

Imani led them through the forest. Her pace was quick despite her small frame. They went over rocks and through a narrow rock tunnel, and then they popped out into a large meadow. Sunlight beamed through the treetops. Squirrels chirped at them from on high. Birds sang and swooned from tree to tree.

The glade was particularly warm, especially since it was snowing higher up in the mountains. Sun-warmed stone curled around the meadow, warming the already pleasant Katori climate. Imani searched the area. "Look for signs of disrupted dirt. Her roots should be fresh. She would have turned up the soil greatly."

All three searched the large meadow. Smoke sniffed the ground, and he was the first to beeline away from the group. His loud, deep bark drew everyone to his side. Freshly turned soil and roots ran across the ground. Kai marveled at the size of the oak tree. Hopeful, he touched the dark ridged bark. "Good boy, Smoke. You've found her."

Smoke worriedly scratched at the tree. Imani ran her hands up and down the trunk. "There is definitely a Kodama in this tree. I can feel her spirit. Given the newly turned soil, I am guessing Rayna lives within. Now we need to coax her out."

"Why could I not force her out?" Kai asked anxiously. "I have done that before. Force people back to their true form."

Imani took Kai's hand. "Yes, I have seen your work. That would be alright for an experienced Kodama or Beastmaster, one that knew their way in and out. Changing one's form requires an anchor. You must know yourself while you explore the possibilities of embracing another form."

It was not easy to be patient. "I thought time was important. We need to free her immediately!"

She shook her head. "You could free her, but then she will not learn. It might damage her mind to break the thread that binds her. When you change, there is a golden thread you envision. That design sequence is real and, in her state, fragile."

Kai stepped around the tall oak. "So, you're sure it is better to leave her this way. I am not sure I can wait for her to come out on her own — if she ever does."

"No, she must free herself," Senina said, entering the meadow.

"You cannot..." Ciera started.

"...intervene," Linnea finished.

Senina held up her hand to her sisters. "Imani is right. You must not free her. She must want to come out. Have you ever seen a felled tree — a hollow, empty shell? That was a Kodama's tree. Her spirit made the center of the tree. When she dies, all that is left is an empty trunk. We reclaim her body and return her to Alenga. The tree depends on Rayna for life, and her on it—they are connected. While she is the core, they breathe and live as one." Her words were solemn.

Heat rolled up Kai's neck. He spun on his heels to face the sisters. "This is your fault! If you were not always chasing me and pushing her, we would not be here right now." Kai heard the velocity and thunder behind his voice.

Linnea and Ciera kept their distance. They too seemed remorseful about the situation.

Senina nodded her head. "You are not wrong. This is my fault. I thought I could win you if I could prove her inferior as a Kodama. I have not mastered the change. But I was wrong. Your love for her runs deep to your core. She is a lucky girl. The fear in her eyes broke my heart. I did this, and I want to make it right."

The word *forgiveness* echoed in his mind. Benmar was right. Kai let his heart soften, and his shoulders relax. "How can you help?"

Senina continued. "As I said, the tree and Rayna are one, connected. We sisters, together with Imani, can appeal to the tree, but you must awaken Rayna's spirit. Without pushing too hard, call to her in your mind. Touch the tree with your hand, speak to her and give her a reason to reach out. I tried to call her, but she did not respond."

Humbled, the three sisters gathered at Rayna's roots. Imani found her own spot, and all four knelt before the tree. Face first they bent over their torsos flat against the ground. They mumbled inaudible words. Their fingers curled into the soil.

Their words soon changed to a harmonic hum. Their bodies rose and fell to the rhythm of their tune. Kai knelt close to the tree, his hands pressed into the bark. He called out to Rayna. Images of their lives together flashed through his mind. Her laugh on the beach the day they met. Her smile picking wildflowers with the basket he'd given her. Them splashing in Baden Lake on a hot summer's day. Holding her hand as they walked through the gardens. Kissing her in the apple orchard.

Each moment filled his heart. He pushed those emotions to her. Focused on Rayna and their connection, Kai spoke. "Come back to me, Rayna. Walk with me once more." To his relief, he heard leaves rustle. Above in her canopy, branches swayed in the wind.

Kai scooted back. The bark creaked and groaned. Dirt and roots wiggled. Branches and leaves receded. The size of the trunk shrank. Roots curled back into the base of the tree. Imani and the sisters hopped back. Slowly the tree's cylinder shape morphed into womanly curves.

The base of the tree shrank, lowering Rayna to the ground. Her bark-covered hair thinned into brunette strands. Her craggy wooden exterior softened into cream-colored skin. The rest of the trunk curved back into

Rayna's true form. Rayna sucked in a deep breath and fell to her knees. She grabbed at her body, arms, and face. Tears streamed down her face.

Thankful, Kai ran to her and pulled her into his arms. "I am sorry I was not here for you. I should have been here." He smoothed her hair as she wept.

Her tears flowed fiercely down her cheeks. Sobs shook her body. Rayna collapsed into Kai and wrapped her arms around him.

"You're alright now. Shhh. I've got you," Kai whispered into her ear.

Wet wild eyes lifted to meet his. Rayna stared at him. "You came. I knew you would." Her breath stuttered. Anxious, she gasped for air. "How did you find me?"

He glanced over his shoulder. "Imani. She brought me here. It was her idea you might be in this meadow."

Rayna glanced around Kai. Her eyes locked with Imani. "It's you. I wanted to find you." She wiped the tears from her face and tried to stand.

Kai steadied her and stood. Rayna panned the meadow and noticed Senina. "You. You did this. It was your foolish idea." Rage consumed Rayna's face. "You will pay for this." She stormed towards Senina.

Worried, Kai grabbed at Rayna's arm. Her arm hardened in fury, and solid wood pushed against Kai, tossing him to the side. Rayna charged at Senina. Senina tried to scream, but Rayna pressed her hand over the girl's mouth. Moss bloomed under her hand. Tears flowed down Senina's face as she grabbed at her mouth.

Smoke barked in confusion. Dizziness made Kai's hand swim. He felt Rayna's wild emotions. Ryker pulled the other two crying sisters back. Rayna seethed with anger. "You did this to me." Rayna continued. "It wasn't a ritual to join you and your sisters. You wanted me out of the way because you want Kai!"

Unsure what else to do, Kai grabbed his crystal and turned into a dragon. His massive form blocked out the sun. He loomed over the girls. Senina's eyes bulged. Her trembling finger pointed at Kai. Kai roared and screeched. Flames billowed out his mouth. Smoke curled out his nostrils.

◆ ◆ ◆

Rayna turned and sank to the ground at the sight of him. The massive silver dragon towered over her, and her heart raced. She wasn't sure if she should be afraid or astonished. Never in her life had she seen a dragon outside of a storybook or a distant blur in the sky over Baden Lake. With shaking hands, she reached out. "Kai? Is that you?"

When Kai shrank back into his natural form, his body wobbled and collapsed in a heap. Rayna watched Imani run to his side. "He should not be rushing his change like this. His mind could get damaged."

Imani took Rayna's hands. "Help me wake him. Sense his dehydration and weakened state. Dig your fingers into the soil. Pull only a little from the ground. Use your magic to convert the energy into power for him."

Rayna did as Imani instructed. Her hand plunged into the ground up to her wrist. The rich soil felt warm to her hand. Harnessing the power within the ground, she pulled it through her heart to bloom with the light her magic possessed. Her green crystal came to life and warmed her chest. Gently she let the energy flow through her other hand into Kai's chest.

Kai blinked and looked up at her. She smiled. "There you are."

"Transforming so swiftly multiple times in one day is unwise," Imani scolded. "I would advise not changing form again for a day or two. And you need to practice more. You let go of your magic instead of pulling it back inside your core."

"Rayna, I hope I did not frighten you." Kai looked to Senina, her mouth still covered in moss, her eyes wide with fear and filled with tears. "Senina knows what she did was wrong. If you want her apology, you will have to give her back her mouth. Revenge will not change what happened, nor will it bring you peace. Forgiveness is your only way forward."

Rayna turned to face her Kodama sister. The remorse in the girl's face panged at her heart. Mortified at what she had done, Rayna ran her fingers over Senina's mouth. The moss faded. Senina wrapped her arms around Rayna's neck. "I am truly sorry. I had no idea what it was like to turn into a tree. I have never tried it. I never wanted to hurt you, not really. Please forgive me."

Stunned, Rayna hugged her back. "My own pride got the better of me. I wanted so desperately to show you I could do it. To be like you... No, I wanted to be better than you and your sisters. I was jealous."

The two girls sat in a tangled heap. Senina fiddled with her fingers. "I have never seen anyone do what you did. Turn your arm into a block of wood. Swing it like a weapon. Turn another's flesh into moss without their approval."

The realization that Rayna had struck Kai caught up to her. "Kai. I am so sorry." She scrambled to reach him. "I hope I did not hurt you. I was so angry. I couldn't see clearly." Her hands patted him to search for damage.

"I am fine, really," Kai assured her.

"Wait. You were a dragon. I saw you transform." She muttered with the excitement of a little girl.

Imani interrupted. "We should all get back before it gets late. Sisters, I am sure you know the way home. Make haste. And take note, I must speak to the elders—all four of you broke Katori law, working against a fellow sister. There must be consequences, I will leave it to them to decide." She shooed the sisters away.

All three girls scurried out of the meadow. Imani looped her arm with Rayna's. "They needed to be humbled," Imani stated. "Those three have been high and mighty since they were toddlers. I am sorry you had to pay such a price. I hope it will not frighten you away from trying again."

"I heard the chanting and the humming. It was very soothing." Rayna reached back to Kai and pulled him forward. "Walk with me. I saw flashes of our time together. They were such happy moments. I am guessing that came from you. Tell me where you've been all this time."

Rayna spent the walk to Imani's home listening to Kai. He told her the news from Diu. Of his trek up the mountain to find Benmar, his grandfather. Riding a dragon. Becoming a dragon for the first time. His first flight. And finally, his vision of her.

Imani led them toward her home with the Matoku Katori. "I will ask, but I am sure you can stay with us tonight."

Ryker stopped. "I have my own place in the hills. You need not worry about me. Spend time with your family, Rayna. I am happy that you are alright. Kai, congratulations on becoming a dragon. If you want help practicing, let me know."

The two men shook hands. Smoke hopped between them, eager to get Kai's attention. "Smoke, I've missed you." Kai knelt and let his wolf come in close. Then he stood to catch up with Rayna.

Imani led them up into her tree home. "Aunt Mina, Uncle Taner. I have someone I would like you to meet."

The couple stood to greet Rayna. Her Aunt Mina had long brown hair braided down her back. Her soft expression verged on tears. Uncle Taner towered over Mina. With one hand on her shoulder, he stroked his auburn beard with the other. Rayna felt their eyes on her. "They are your aunt and uncle? These are not..." She stopped and took a breath.

Imani didn't seem to hear. "Can they stay with us, Aunt Mina?" Imani's eyes dance with anticipation.

Mina approached Rayna. "You look so much like your mother, Rayna."

Rayna looked between Imani and Mina, confused. "So you are not my mother, not Imani's mother?"

"No, honey, I wish I were. I am sorry my sister is not a better person." Mina stepped out of their hug to look at Rayna. "When I received word she'd dumped you on a ship, I wanted to kill my sister. Her letter said her travels with Keegan were not conducive for a baby. You were meant to end up here. When you did not arrive, I am sorry to say, we did not search for you. We had no idea where to look. A baby lost at sea. I figured you..." Tears ran down Mina's already damp face. Again, she wrapped her arms around Rayna. "Dear Rayna, you are always welcome in this home."

Kai saw fresh tears spill down Rayna's cheeks. She returned the hug. Imani joined them and squeezed Rayna tight. "I always wanted a sister," Imani whispered.

Kai was happy to see the three women bond, and he was glad that Rayna had found family. People who wanted her even if her parents did not.

"I was four when my parents left," Imani shared. "Our parents decided to join Keegan, chase after him, and his 'rule the world' cause. Our parents are from the Gemidi Tribe, and we hail from the Mystic Islands."

"How did you come to live here?" Rayna interrupted.

Imani's lips quivered. "They did not bring me here. After about six months, aunt Mina received word I was alone and came for me. I've not the heart to go back, to claim our home as my own." She paused to swallow the pain welling into her eyes.

"When I was seven, my...our parents," Imani corrected herself, "returned but did not stay more than a day. I have lived among the Matoku tribe ever since. This is uncle Taner's tribe. That was twenty years ago." Saddened, Imani fell silent.

Mina smoothed Imani's long hair. "Your parents wanted adventure, and Keegan was inspiring at first. But like I said, my sister was not a good parent. She was selfish, as was your father. They had no business having children. If they dumped you on a ship, without the care to know if you made it safely here, means they are no different than when they abandoned Imani."

Taner leaned into the conversation. "We are sorry, Rayna. Enough talk of the past. We have two beautiful girls now," he beamed. "And if I am not mistaken, a soon to be son-in-law."

A warm hand sank onto Kai's shoulder. He looked at Taner. The man eyed his white crystal and leaned a little closer. "The rumors are true. You are Keegan's son?"

With a bit of pride, Kai puffed up his chest. "I am Iver and Mariana's son."

"Mariana, I have heard the name. Iver? King of Diu?"

Kai nodded. "King Iver raised me as his own. It is with him I learned honor, respect, and accountability. My mother, as you may know, loved all life. She was a good woman."

197

Taner glared at Kai and furrowed his brow. "Still, you are Keegan's son."

"If I am unwelcome, I will leave," Kai said, "but do not judge me for a man I have never met. His blood may run through my veins, but my heart is my own. I am my own man, and I love Rayna very much."

The tension mounted, and Kai felt compelled to leave. Rayna wrapped her hand around his. "Please," she begged. "Do not make me choose. Like Kai, my parents did not raise me, so I am not them, but I love Kai and I will stand with him. Consider getting to know him before you decide what makes a man."

Everyone looked at Rayna. Kai felt the passion in her words and a smile lit up his face. Taner leaned back and looked to his wife, Mina. "It is up to you. She was your sister. I never cared for Keegan, and it is hard to separate the pain he has caused my heart."

Kai nodded. "I do not mean to spoil your reunion."

Taner seemed like a man who was slow to trust, but he no longer seemed inclined to throw Kai out of the house. "It is late," Rayna's uncle said curtly. "We should turn in for the night. Morning meditation will be here before we know it. Kai, we have an extra pod where you can sleep. Rayna, you can sleep with your sister." He led everyone up the winding staircase of their tree.

Kai watched the word *sister* brighten Rayna's eyes. She had a family. "Goodnight...Aunt Mina, Uncle Taner."

Like all the other homes, this one was nested high inside the canopy of a Bodhima tree strengthened by the Cosmos vine. Kai ran his fingers over the vine tendrils. All the flowers along the vine bloomed brighter.

"Goodnight, dear." Mina stopped and kissed Rayna on the cheek.

◆ ◆ ◆

Sunshine danced through the dew-covered trees. From a distance, Kai watched the newly reunited sisters. Imani closed her eyes and took several slow breaths. Her face began to change colors; green and yellow on one side and brown, and gray on the other. The texture also evolved.

The green and yellow became soft moss. The brown and gray turned rough and craggy like bark.

Rayna followed her sister's example. Kai looked on with amazement as the bark and moss flowed down their clothes. "How is this possible?" Kai asked.

Imani opened her eyes. "We become nature itself. Our power starts as a golden thread, same as you. Only we are connected with the plants, where you embrace the nature of animals. What is important for all of us is to know how to let go and embrace the light. The light of our crystal is our touchstone. Without it, we are lost." She shuttered her shoulders and shook her face. The plant growth stopped and receded.

Imani coaxed vines out of the ground. Each one wrapped around Rayna, pulling her downward. Interested in seeing the use of energy, Kai gleaned their interaction. The magic flowing around the two girls was mesmerizing. It seeped out of the soil, plants, and air to mingle with the power radiating from their skin.

Rayna emanated a small surge of light, and the vines released her. With a wave of Rayna's hand, the tall grasses picked up Imani and passed her around the glade. Kai had never seen anything like it, and his imagination burst with the possibilities. All day the two girls giggled and played. Imani delighted in Rayna's development, teaching her how to borrow energy to run faster, create structures out of nature, and blend into the environment.

When Mina approached, Kai eased closer. He knew what they planned to try today. After weeks of learning the basics, Rayna's aunt hoped to teach Rayna how to become a tree without fear. The pressure on Kai's heartfelt unbearable. He wanted to watch, but he feared losing her again. For days, Mina spoke of the risks. There was no way to know if Rayna was ready for this transformation.

Clear of the others, Mina stood firm on a small knoll. "Each of you take a spot on one of the other mounds. It takes a gentle spirit to guide someone and not lose them. Focus on my voice, glean to see the flow of magic. We Kodama have the advantage of drawing power from the ground and from plant life. Our anchor to the earth strengthens us in a different way. The very sun on your face gives you energy. Young Beastmasters pull from their internal core, and for one like Kai, it often results in passing out when he transforms back. Learn to let the sun and nature empower your shift, and you too will get a better result."

Kai shook his head. "Thank you for the advice."

Imani took her place and spoke to Rayna. "Now that you can understand your connection, and know how to reverse it, you can become one with nature. Remember to maintain the border between yourself and nature. Or, like weeds, they will take over. Plants do not have minds like animals; they are more free-spirited life elements."

"Let's begin." Mina waved her arms around her body, and roots began to snake through the green grass. Her once green dress morphed into craggy brown bark, climbing halfway up her body, and stopped.

"Rayna, my dear, this is just like transforming your skin, only you must go deeper. In your mind, see the golden thread of creation. Wrap your mind around it while keeping a grasp on the light of your crystal. Push your roots deep into the ground and pull energy from the soil, not too fast. Borrow—don't steal. Remember, you are in control. Do not let the magic overwhelm you."

Both Imani and Rayna mimicked Mina. Kai wondered what it felt like to be a plant. He knew he enjoyed being a dragon. The thought of his mother all these years without her crystal worried him. He knew well enough the light grounded his mind. It was essential in letting go of the dragon form. Without her crystal, how would she ever be able to return to her human form? Would she stay a manta ray forever?

He sighed. There was nothing he could do until the manta rays migrated closer to the Mystic Isles. For now, he tried to put the thoughts out of his mind. All afternoon he watched them. He was most amazed when the branches of Mina's tree moved without wind. Her limbs creaked and groaned. Just as quickly as she became a tree, her branches receded, her trunk shrank, and her roots curled back into the ground. Mina dropped to the ground and walked around Rayna's tree.

"Very good, my dear. Hear my voice. See the glade in your mind. Feel the life here. Use it to sense Kai's location." Mina glanced over her shoulder.

Without warning, roots burst from the dirt beneath Kai and propelled him upward. The root basket cupped around him, and the exhilaration thrilled him. Rayna was getting stronger.

"Well done, Rayna. Now come back to us, nice and slow. Ease out of the change. The more you practice, the quicker you will become."

The root-basket holding Kai dropped downward in a staccato motion. Jolted, Kai hopped to the ground and stepped away. Ever so slowly, Rayna's wooden exterior softened into cream-colored skin. Transforming back into her true form, she ran her hands over her body, arms, and face.

"That was a much better experience." Rayna moved to Kai's side. "Sorry, Kai, still getting a handle on my magic. Seeing the world as a tree is nothing like seeing as a person. Every part of me was able to see, from the tips of my leaves to bark on my back. But it was more shades of light. Not sure I can put it into words."

Happy to be part of her experience, Kai pulled her in close. "Mina, I want to thank you for taking Rayna into your family. I know it means a great deal to her. I should also thank you for allowing me to stay with you these many weeks."

Imani edged around her aunt. "You're not leaving already, are you?"

"Within a day or two." Rayna nodded. "Kai wants to be near the coast to travel to the Mystic Islands to find his mother."

Kai pulled his mother's necklace from his pocket. "I believe her crystal will help me find her, and from what I've learned, she will need it to transform and remain a human."

The expression on Mina's face was not hopeful. "I don't know if that will be enough, Kai. She has spent too long intertwined with her animal spirits. I fear she has lost her mind."

"I will not give up trying," Kai insisted. "After I save my mother, I need to return to Diu. I promised to attend the winter festival, and I worry about my father's health." Looking to Rayna, "I assume you will want to visit your parents in Diu."

Rayna shook her head in agreement. "I miss them, and I owe them for the love they gave me."

CHAPTER 21

Lucca's Betrayal

Returning to Haygan's home felt comforting. After weeks on the mountain with Benmar and then weeks with Rayna's new family, Kai was anxious for autumn. He knew it would soon be time to search for his mother. The anticipation kept him up most nights. But when they arrived, they found more than his aunt and uncle.

Simone's parents, Freia and Pedmar had come for a visit. They were pleasant polite people: cheerful, sun-soaked Weathervanes who loved their daughter. Freia doted over Simone and her pregnancy. Her hands rubbed Simone's tiny bulge. Her skin tone was more of a reddish-brown hue, but her eyes were dark like Simone's. "We should have come earlier, my dear. I have missed you so much. But we hate to intrude."

Simone rolled her eyes back at Haygan. "You are always welcome at my house in Hiowind, mother," she said with the tone a little heavy on the word *mother*.

"Well, my dear, we are here now. Come. Let's get you out of the sun." Freia motioned to the Bodhima tree-home.

"Simone, Kai and I should pack for my trip to the coast. We leave within a few days."

Pedmar was a rather tall man with strong features. His complexion matched Simone's caramel hue to perfection, though his eyes were a brilliant blue. He swept his arm around Simone. "Still helping the outsiders. Hmmm. He should be here with you. Will he even be around to raise his own child?" Pedmar scoffed.

"Father. Please. Haygan has dedicated his life to providing the Katori people with knowledge of the outside world. Not to mention he has discovered news that Mariana lives. Her very son stands here with me today. Kai is her son." Simone motioned to Kai behind her on the stone path.

Haygan patted the air in defense. "You need not defend me, Simone. I will be back later tonight. Don't wait up. Kai, you're with me." Haygan stormed off back down the path.

Great, two nights with these people, Kai thought. Leaving was looking better and better.

"Haygan, wait. That went...strangely. What happened back there?"

"You know me well enough. I am not one to explain. I love Simone and would give my life for her. Her parents know that, but it is not enough. I will not defend my choices. Neither should you, by the way. When the time comes."

"You mean when I want to return to Diu?"

Haygan nodded. "Lucca believes you will be torn between Katori and Diu."

Not wanting to talk about Lucca, Kai dropped the subject.

Later that evening Kai walked around the Agora and came upon two men standing in the garden. He knew it was wrong to eavesdrop, but when he discovered his uncle and Lucca speaking privately, he found himself listening.

"Did you know he has Mariana's necklace?" Lucca spoke to Haygan in hushed tones.

"I did, but it is his business to share with you or not. Ask him about it. If you want to go with him in two days—ask. Have you done anything to earn his trust?"

Lucca crossed his arms and clamped his jaw shut. Kai could hardly believe his ears. They were arguing about him. He stuck his hand in his pocket to retrieve his mother's necklace. *I am coming, Mother. Soon, we will be together again.*

Lucca poked at Haygan. "I suppose you also know the boy has been up to train with Benmar? You did know! That man raised Keegan. I doubt he will do much better with Kai than he did his own son. Benmar is a rebel. Why do you think is he an outcast living on the mountain?"

Haygan stepped away from his father. "I thought he loved dragons. He is a bit wild, certainly, and I know he felt bad after what his son did to our family. He could not face us after Mariana's abduction, but Benmar is still a wise man."

It was impossible to see Haygan's expression, but Kai knew all too well that his uncle, like several others, urged him to seek out his other grandfather. Unwilling to listen any further, Kai turned to leave, but he heard Lucca's tone bellow.

"I speak of tradition, Haygan. We must protect our way of life. When you've lived as long as I have, maybe you will understand. As Chief of the Hiowind, it is my duty to protect and lead our people. Wisdom comes from experience. And I have spent decades studying people."

"Father, we cannot live in fear. Keegan is a menace, but you and the elders defeated him before. Why are you afraid now?"

Lucca waved off Haygan. "Don't you see? Kai—he is the piece Keegan was waiting for. Mariana was to be his source of power. She possesses multiple abilities. Kai and his white crystal will draw Keegan like a moth to a flame. The boy is destined to change our world. Need I remind you?"

Kai could hardly believe what he was hearing. Were they still worried about his destiny? He had been here for months; they should know his spirit by now. Had he not proven his ability to keep their secrets even before he came to Katori?

"You don't know the boy," Haygan argued back. "He has grown into a good man."

"Kai will be just like his father. Arrogant and willful. The apple doesn't fall far from the tree. The boy will be our downfall. His father will come for him and bend his ear. Together they will force us into the open. Keegan wanted nothing more than to use his Alenga-given powers to subjugate the entire world. It was Keegan's wish then, and I doubt he has changed. We need to stand united in this, Haygan. Mark my words. Keegan is coming. Kai will either bend willingly or become a weapon. Either way, I will not let Keegan have what he desires."

It was difficult to stomach the conversation between Haygan and Lucca. No matter what, Lucca had made up his mind. He was never being kind to Kai in the hopes of mending the past. His grandfather only wanted to keep a closer eye on him. Unwilling to listen anymore, Kai stormed back to Haygan's home and collapsed onto the bed in his pod.

◆ ◆ ◆

Dawn's early morning rays tiptoed into Kai's pod. The oval-shaped window cast a warm glow over Kai and bathed him in sunshine. Feeling rested, Kai wiped the remainders of sleep from his eyes. He shifted in his bed to gaze out over the Hiowind village below.

The smell of wet earth lingered in the air. Down below, people busily worked the area. Weathervanes whipped up funnel-shaped rotating wind. Their small air collectors scooped up the debris along the path. As it gathered more and more sticks and leaves, the swirling mass grew. Once the mass was a few feet wide, the funnel spiked upward and shot over the massive garden to a composting pile.

In another area, one large limb had struck a small statue, knocking it into another. Both now lay broken in a heap. Kai watched a man transform into a black gorilla and pick up the massive tree limb and carry it away. The next two men, Stonekings with dark red crystals, reset the main section of the two statues upright. To Kai's amazement, both began reassembling the broken pieces. Their hands held the rock in place, and their fingers pressed around the seams. Within minutes they had remolded the pieces like sculpting clay.

Even with scattered tree limbs and vines, the place was magnificent. Kai was amazed at the open display of magic. Through the trees, he could see the top of the Agora, and he felt the thrum of magic pull at him. He closed his eyes and focused on the Agora. Connected to his sight, he drew his mind near the pool. With one hand, he touched his crystal.

Alenga's spirit spoke to him. *There is no time to waste. You must hurry.* A flash of his mother's face broke his connection. Anxious about his experience, he grabbed for his pants, laying across the chair, and shoved his hand into the pocket. His mother's necklace was not there. He tossed the room upside down and found nothing.

When he reached Rayna's pod, he found it empty. Voices echoed up from the main family room, and Kai bounded down the stairs to join everyone. Simone handed Kai a cup of tea and sat down next to Haygan. "Good morning, sleepyhead. We had a terrible storm last night. Would you mind helping Haygan repair our windmill? The storm damaged several of them, and ours helps move water around the community."

"Happy to help, Simone."

Rayna smiled and pulled her hair to one side of her face. Kai bent to whisper in her ear. "Rayna, have you seen my mother's necklace?"

She arched her back to look at him. "I am sorry, Kai, I have not. You usually keep it in your pocket."

"Haygan, by chance, do you know where my mother's necklace is?"

"Hmmm, no." Haygan crinkled his brow. "You always keep it in your pocket, do you not?" Haygan swung around and tugged on his boots.

Fear welled in the pit of Kai's stomach. He darted back upstairs to his pod to look again. No necklace. He had it just a few hours ago. Held it in his hand listening to uncle Haygan and Lucca argue. Kai held his breath, and anger clamped around his heart. Frantic, Kai stuffed his hands inside both his pockets one last time to be sure—the crystal was gone. His one hope of tracking his mother was lost to him. His father Iver had entrusted the valuable possession to Kai, and he'd lost it.

"NO! Not lost—stolen."

Hearing the commotion, Haygan stepped into Kai's pod. "What's wrong?" He surveyed the disarray. "Kai?"

"It's gone. My mother's necklace is gone. I had it with me last night, and now it is gone."

The look on Haygan's face was eye-opening. Before Kai could respond, Haygan motioned for him to hurry. "Get your boots, Kai. We need to see my father."

There was little Kai could do but trust his uncle. This was Haygan's country; these were not Kai's people. Along the way, he glared at each person, wondering who he could trust. Was their day-to-day sincerity real? Kai no longer knew what to believe.

Hot on the heels of his uncle's fast pace, it dawned on Kai. Chief Lucca—only he would care to take the necklace. He knew its value; they had argued over the fact only hours ago. Haygan would never steal from Kai, not even to help Lucca.

"Haygan, do you think Lucca took the necklace?" Kai asked, choosing to keep quiet about the argument he'd witnessed.

His uncle would not look at him. Focused on the way ahead, Haygan marched down the pristine walkway. Kai noticed the clenched jaw, the white-knuckled fists. Haygan was angry. When they turned down the path toward a cluster of four Bodhima trees, they bumped into Basil.

Haygan stepped back. "Basil, my apologies. Can you tell me, is my father around?"

Basil stood before them straight and tall. His chiseled features were that of a statue carved into perfection. Towering over Haygan and Kai, he was dressed in flowing blue linen with a matching blue crystal—Beastmaster. His size made Kai wonder what massive creature he could become.

Basil nodded to Haygan. "I have not seen him this morning. I came to tell him about the storm damage," he motioned to the trees, "but your father was not home." The man's voice had a deep soulful tone. His dark green eyes focused on Kai. "Hello, Kai, how goes your Beastmaster practice?"

"Fine, thank you, Basil."

Haygan's demeanor softened. "Thank you, Basil, I appreciate your kindness." His uncle pivoted back the way they'd come.

Kai noticed that Basil was following them at a distance. "Do you think Lucca took my mother's necklace?" he whispered.

"There is no doubt in my mind where the necklace is or who took it from you. Autumn is fast upon us and my father has different ideas about Mariana."

"I thought we had a few days until we needed to leave."

"No, you leave now. You must chase after Lucca. It is on you to make haste. My group is leaving for the coast soon, but you cannot afford to travel with me by cart. I have one more trip to make to Diu."

Disappointed, Kai asked, "You will not go with me? Can your trip not wait? I don't know where to go or anything about the Mystic Islands." Kai darted ahead and stopped his uncle. Would Haygan not abandon his plans to travel to Diu given the circumstances?

"You know I cannot. I took this time off, but now I must finish this last trip. We need to find Ryker so he can escort you. Liam and Yulia are already on their way. If you move fast enough, you can catch them. They will be useful in navigating the Mystic Islands to the migration waters of the manta rays."

"But uncle, this is for my mother, your sister."

"I have obligations, Kai." Haygan stepped around him. "My word is my bond. I owe Diu horses, and when they arrive from Bangloo, I need to be there to collect them. A trade to make up for the time I was away this summer. With the baby coming, I want to be here. There will be no more trips to foreign shores. Simone and the baby are my priority now. Ryker will guide you."

Kai could not understand how Haygan could choose Diu over family. "But..."

Haygan raised his hand. "Finish the journey to find your mother. Ryker will see you reach Lucca and save Mariana. I love my sister very much, but I do not need to be in the way of your reunion. She will be disoriented enough without another face to remember."

CHAPTER 22

The Rafter

Basil edged up behind Kai. "I couldn't help but overhear you want to travel to the coast. The fastest route is the Makani River. Believe it or not, the river flows faster than traveling by horse. I have a raft if you are interested. You will need an experienced rafter to navigate the rapids and the bidirectional water changes."

Kai raised an eyebrow. "Bidirectional? You mean to suggest the water flows in both directions?"

"In a sense, yes." Basil kept pace as Haygan led them through the city. "Most of the river is divided by rocks, but there are points that open to allow you to cross and change your direction if needed. The churning vortex in the median is very dangerous."

"Thank you, Basil. We would appreciate your help." Kai shook the man's large hand.

When they reached the outskirts of town, Haygan spotted Ryker running in their direction. "Does he ever stay in one place?" Kai asked, watching him approach.

Haygan waved. "He is an unsettled soul."

Ryker came to a stop. "Haygan. Kai. Basil."

"Where are you going?" Kai questioned.

"With you. I believe we are going on a trip."

"But how could you know? We only just decided." Kai knit his brow in confusion.

Ryker curled the corner of his mouth. "Alenga sends me where I need to be, and right now, you need me with you. Do you not?"

Kai remembered the power within Alenga's cavern and how it offered visions to Ryker when he stayed there. "I do. We must chase after Lucca—he stole my mother's necklace. He is bound for the coast and then the Mystic Islands. I am not sure where the manta rays migrate, but first, we need her necklace back."

"One thing at a time." Ryker moved through the group back into the city.

♦ ♦ ♦

Smoke stood proudly on the hillside, Shiva sat behind him. The bright sunlight glinted across his ears and back. Kai wished he could take his wolf. As much as he wanted to, it was better to leave him behind. Their raft was already too crowded. "Sorry, boy, I can't take you with me." Smoke tilted his head, and through their connection, he spoke—*Be strong, Kai.*

Ready to leave, Kai kissed his aunt on the cheek. "Aunt Simone, take care of yourself and my little cousin." He looked to her round baby bump. "I will be back with my mother before the baby arrives, I promise."

Simone handed him the last of his supplies. "I wish I could go with you. You could use dragon on your side. Whatever you do, don't transform over the ocean. If you cannot hold your form, you will crash into the sea and be unable to survive in your weakened state."

Kai nodded, then with a heavy sigh, he shook his uncle's hand. "I still wish you were coming with me."

Haygan patted Kai's shoulder. "Catch up to Lucca, get the necklace back. Find Yulia and Liam—they will help you reach the Mystics in time."

Rayna stepped up to Kai. He couldn't help but notice her heavy pack. Before he could object, she spoke. "Don't even think you're leaving me behind. I am going."

"I wouldn't dream of it." He grabbed her hand, and they waved goodbye.

The warm autumn sun ducked behind a puffy white cloud. As the river came into view, Kai couldn't help but wonder if this was really the fastest route. "Ryker, are you sure we must take the river? Can I not fly us to the coast to catch Lucca?"

"If you were an experienced Beastmaster, maybe. But even dragons must stop for rest and water. You're not ready, and I cannot carry you for a day while you recover. If Rayna had more experience and could bring you out of your weakened state alone—maybe. It is best we take the Makani River with Basil."

When they reached the river, Basil was already tying down supplies. His raft was basic, a flat platform kept afloat by buoyant wooden beams and cross-tied with braided straps. In the center were three crates to hold supplies and four long wooden paddles.

The small cove had a dock long enough for two rafts on each side to keep them out of the rushing water. One raft was missing. The thought of Lucca ahead of them twisted Kai's stomach in knots.

Kai and Rayna found a place to sit near the center on either side of the raft, and Ryker took the front while Basil took the rear.

"Before we hit the open water," Basil instructed, "there are a few rules. If you fall in, try to reach for the raft, but don't panic. Float down river feet first, and do not let go of your paddle. There are points when the rapids settle, and there you should swim to shore. We will catch up to you."

Basil continued to instruct everyone with his paddle. "Even in the rapids, you will need to help us paddle. In fact, you will spend most of the trip paddling. But at times, you must listen for my instructions. This is right forward, and left backward." Basil demonstrated. "At times, I may need to correct our course, and you will need to be ready."

Suddenly, riding the river seemed more dangerous than Kai anticipated. He could see the rippling water outside of the cove moving quickly. Looking into the water near the raft, it only appeared a few feet deep, but he could see rocks below the surface.

"Ryker, I need you to keep us clear of any protruding rocks. I will try to keep us in the center of the river as much as possible, except when the dividing rocks disappear. The current near the opening can suck you in and pull you across. If we are not angled for a crossing, it will flip us over."

Rayna eyed Basil. "Is there anywhere we can stop along the way?"

"There are slow spots and other coves to pull out of the current. I will keep watch for opportunities to rest, please do not worry."

With no more explanation, Basil shoved them away from the dock. The moment they reached the river, Basil and Ryker used their paddles to turn the raft into the flow.

The first part of the river was smooth and slow. They had time to paddle and take in their surroundings. Parallel with the river, Kai watched as they passed travelers along a black dirt road that rolled through the countryside. It didn't take long to see their meandering carts and horses were no match for the pace of the river.

Even moving at this speed felt slow; Kai wanted to fly. As a dragon, he could make faster progress, but when he landed, he would most likely pass out for a day. Even without his Aunt Simone's warning, he knew transformation was too great a risk, given he did not know how far he could fly being a new Beastmaster.

Resigned to the river, Kai gawked in every direction. Except for the tall Bodhima trees around the central part of Katori, the valley opened into vast rolling hills and meadows as far as one could see. Random groves popped up here and there, offering shade for travelers near the river. The occasional trading post town along the route swelled with travelers.

Gauging the sun, he could tell the river they traveled took them as much south as it did east. To the south, the rolling hills bubbled into a bluish-black mountain ridge, its size dwarfed by the snow-topped Katori Mountains.

It didn't take long for their raft to hit faster water. Silently the group continued to paddle down the growing rapids. The speed at which they traveled continued to increase. At times, Kai dared a look to Rayna. She too looked overwhelmed by the constant effort to keep them angled away from dangerous rocks.

Kai paddled, getting splashed with water again and again. The ebb and flow of the river went on this way for hours. It was almost a relief to see the sun begin to set. As the sky turned several shades of red, orange, and yellow, Basil guided them into a sheltered cove. Three docks jetted out into the slow current, all three decorated with blue and yellow crystals set aglow to mark the location of the docks.

Posts with bright lanterns snaked along a path near the shore and disappeared into the woods. Raft upon raft leaned into each other, propped against trees, or scattered along the water. People walked along the shore, venturing into the trading post.

"We must stop for the evening." Basil waved to a man on the dock. "It is unwise to navigate the waters at night. There is a trading post with lodging near the road. They welcome travelers, and there are many pods with three or four racks for sleeping. Ryker, if you could see about making a trade, the rest of us can find a campsite and start a fire."

The man at the dock helped pull their raft into the weeds, and the group followed Basil through the congested trading post. Ryker stepped into a line to barter for a pod while Rayna and Kai followed Basil to a vacant campfire.

The small town boomed with travelers. Men and women and families all huddled around campsites, laughing and telling stories. Kai searched the travelers, hoping to find Yulia and Liam. They were nowhere to be found.

Beyond the squat trees used by the tradesmen, a long line of Bodhima trees dotted the ridge. Each tree held nearly eight pods, many already set aglow by the Cosmos vine flowers. Set off to the far end were two older looking oak trees. They seemed abandoned.

After they made a fire, Kai and Rayna set to explore the mature trees behind their campfire. A set of staggered stone slabs curved around in a semicircle in front of the old trees. There were posts for tying off horses, a few abandoned wagon wheels, and a few cracked wooden barrels.

Growing into the rocks were two massive oaks, each with two separate, upside-down basket-like pods. Curious, Kai climbed up inside. It was clean but well used. No decorative bedding like at Haygan and Simone's home. At the center was a flat woven shelf large enough for two.

With one arm, he heaved Rayna up onto a round ledge. "Seems nice. Better than sleeping outside. Safer too. Your bedroll should help with comfort and warmth." He laid his back down onto the vine bedframe. "At least I hope your bedroll is enough." He wiggled his body on the thatched surface.

Rayna sat beside him. "I wish we could share a pod."

"Someday soon," Kai responded.

She nodded. "How is it Julia and Shane were married so young? We are the same age."

Kai cleared his throat. "Consent. Both of their parents had to give consent. Even if your parents agreed, my father never would. He believes eighteen is the youngest anyone should be married. He was twenty-four when he married my mother. Claims he was too young, though it was the best day of his life."

"Hmmm, I am not so sure my parents would consent. My dad's conservative, too. If we want to be married, we must wait until it is our choice, not theirs."

"We should get outside. They will be serving dinner, and we don't want to be missed. I still have your honor to protect." Kai smiled, kissed her on the cheek, and jumped through the hole in the floor.

From the ground, he offered Rayna help as she dangled her legs over the edge. In a simple hop, she was back on the ground and joined the others around the fire.

After changing into dry clothes, the group enjoyed a warm meal. It had been a long day, and even with his Katori endurance, Kai felt the effects of his rigorous afternoon on the river. Basil poked at the fire.

Kai soaked a piece of bread in his vegetable stew. "You are friends with Lucca, right?"

"I am very close to our chief." Basil sipped his steaming hot tea. "What do you want to know about him?"

"Why is he so angry with me? He doesn't know me, yet I get the feeling he only sees Keegan when he looks at me."

Kai noticed Basil was not good at hiding his emotions. For a brute of a man, he wore his heart on his sleeve. "You do favor your father, but it is what Keegan almost made him do." Basil let out a heavy sigh.

Rayna twisted to listen, her back pressed into Kai. Basil's expression turned remorseful, and he leaned into the fire. "You want to know why Lucca is upset? We all know there is no love between him and Keegan. But Lucca's story goes back much farther. It is about a girl he killed experimenting with his powers—another Lumen. Many believe that to advance your abilities, you must bend the limits of the past. By pushing your mind to see the edges of our magic, new paths can be developed."

The truth behind advancing your magic resonated with Kai. He'd seen as much with Rayna and her manipulation of Senina's face, turning her skin to moss, and with Benmar's ability to turn invisible. And hearing about Keegan's ability to steal souls and become another. These were new and unique abilities.

Basil sipped his tea and continued. "There are so few Lumens ever born. Understanding their magic often comes with a price. Usually, the cost was a burned home or scorched garden. Now and then, some were brave enough to test each other. Lucca and Natali were very advanced. They pushed the limits of their powers. Lucca learned to create a shield of light, and Natali created a blast beam. Teaching each other, they tested their new magic. From there, one can surmise that Lucca was simply too powerful for her. The elders tried to heal her, but it was too late. She was gone."

Kai knit his brow together. "So, what does that have to do with Keegan or me?"

"Keegan and his followers marched around the Agora in protest. But it was not enough. As words and emotions escalated, Keegan challenged Lucca. He and his rebels attacked the Agora. Lucca fought back and Mariana was hurt, caught in the crossfire between Lucca and Keegan. While it took all the other chiefs and the unie to stop the protest, Lucca refused to use his magic ever again. The mere mention of Keegan reminds him of that day."

The news shocked Kai. Hurting your own child must have destroyed Lucca. "I had no idea." Kai was beginning to learn he knew very little about his mother and his grandfather. Their past and their choices remained a mystery. "So why are you helping us?"

Basil chuckled. "What makes you think I am helping *you*? Lucca needs to come to terms with you, and running off won't help either of you mend the past. You two need to try at least to find common ground."

Kai noticed that Ryker remained silent the entire time. Knowing how the man felt about his mother, Mariana, it had to be difficult to relive the past. "Well, whatever your reason, thank you, Basil."

Basil stood and stretched. "If we mean to catch Lucca tomorrow, and I believe we can, we need to be up at dawn. For safety, someone needs to keep the fire going all night. We should take turns keeping watch. Ryker, would you mind going first? I can go second, and Kai can take the last shift."

Ryker nodded and walked off into the shadows.

Kai sighed in relief. "Sounds good to me. Wake me when it is my turn; I will wake everyone at dawn."

He walked Rayna to her pod and then went to bed.

◆ ◆ ◆

When Kai woke, it was Ryker who jostled him. "Wake up. Basil is gone, and so is our raft. I asked around, nobody saw him leave. But we no longer have a raft to ride the river." Dawn peeked through the cracks of Kai's pod.

Rubbing the sleep from his eyes, Kai swung his legs to the floor. His back ached from the lack of padding in his bedroll. "What do you mean, Basil is gone?"

Ryker jumped out of the pod and Kai followed. Sure enough, most of their supplies were gone and the raft was no longer tied down by the shore. After waking Rayna, they surveyed their situation. Ryker poked at the smoldering embers. "Seems like after I woke Basil and went to sleep, he abandoned us. He took most of the supplies and headed downriver in the night."

"Are you sure?" Rayna asked. "Maybe the raft came loose on its own and floated away. Basil could be trying to..."

"No," Ryker snapped. "His bedroll is gone, as is his fishing gear and cooking pan. He left. I ran downriver to see if I could find him, but he is gone."

Kai poured his water over the embers of their fire, his gut in knots. Stranded in the middle of nowhere, they had few choices. If only he could transform and fly them, but it was too risky for a young Beastmaster to carry passengers. "So, what do we do now? We have no raft or horses. I can't see begging another group to help us."

The expression on Ryker's face showed determination. "I am not giving up." He poked at the smoldering ash to be sure their fire was out. "But we can only run for so long. We are less than halfway there. It takes two-and-a-half days by river or five to six days by horse."

Rayna's sighed, braiding her long brown hair. "Basil was so helpful, why would he leave us?"

Ryker shook his head. "Foolish. We all fell for his lies. He is Lucca's closest friend. I should have foreseen this. We never should have trusted him. Now he knows we hope to travel with Liam and Yulia. He will tell Lucca everything."

"It is not your fault, Ryker." Kai tied his bootlaces tight. "We all trusted him. But since we're stuck here, what is the alternative to running?"

"As a shuk, I can cover more ground. You two will need to ride. Leave everything but our remaining food. We must travel as light as possible."

Kai tossed Ryker his bedroll. "I will keep an eye on the road for Liam and Yulia. Besides needing to catch Lucca, we need them to help navigate the Mystic Islands."

"Agreed," Ryker stowed their supplies in one tree pod while Rayna packed all their food into a single bag.

Watching Ryker transform into a black shuk, Kai noticed the ease in his change. He wished he'd had more time to practice. The mighty beast stooped to allow him and Rayna to climb up.

CHAPTER 23

Caught in the Middle

All afternoon Ryker ran. Overhead the glaring sun burned their shoulders. The shuk's black fur felt hot against Kai's hands. The pounding of his paws was barely noticeable across the terrain. As they rode, Kai eased into the rhythm of their stride, finding it rather like riding a horse. Even with the occasional stop to cool off, it was easy to see everyone was feeling the wear of their situation.

There was no sign of Lucca or Basil. Each raft they spotted caused Kai's heart to jump with anticipation, and then fall when the rafter was someone else. After the third group, Kai wondered if he had somehow missed Basil. Doubt crept around the corners of his mind. Thoughts of reaching his mother in time filled him with determination, and he gleaned the river ahead. Still, there was no sign of Basil or Lucca.

The shimmer of the water was blinding, and Kai closed his eyes for a moment. Rayna tapped his shoulder and pointed. "It is another string of wagons. Maybe Liam and Yulia are with them."

Kai counted three wagons with seven individual riders. Ryker slowed. They eyed each passenger and meandered close to each cart, but when they confirmed Liam and Yulia were not among this group either, they plodded onward. Mile after mile, they traveled between the black road and the blue Makani river, snaking through the landscape.

Even though Kai was not doing the work, he was beginning to feel exhausted. They needed to stop again soon, at least for Ryker's sake. When the trees thinned, they were back in the full sun, and everything got hotter by the minute. Sweat dripped off Kai's face. Even with the small breeze, the weather was unusually warm. Concerned for Ryker, he reached out with his mind. *Ryker, we should stop for water. You need a break.*

There was no response. He hated to beg, but they needed to stop. He could feel the sweat on his back where Rayna pressed against him to hold on to his waist. He tried again. *Ryker, you are no use to us dehydrated and weak. Please take a break.*

The beast continued with no response. Reluctant to beg further, Kai continued to watch for Liam and Yulia as they passed travelers on the road. It had been a while since they'd seen anyone on the river, and Kai was beginning to lose hope. Basil was gone, and Lucca was even further out of reach.

It was late in the day when Ryker finally stopped near a grove of trees. The sun's heat had soaked everyone with sweat. Rayna handed Ryker and Kai water, and they drank greedily. "We should eat," she suggested, giving them both a chunk of dried bread and fruit.

The wind blew through the shady trees, drying Kai's shirt. It felt good to sit still. Even though he'd spent days in the saddle traveling around Baden Lake, riding a shuk seemed harder. Ryker ran faster, and it was less than comfortable without a saddle. But he had to be thankful for his friend's fortitude.

Unsure how long the man could continue this pace, Kai wanted to consider walking a bit. Sitting in silence, he studied Ryker. He was a quiet man like his uncle Haygan. "Any chance we could walk for a while? I want to catch Lucca, but not at the price of you giving out."

"I can make it, although we should probably stop more often," Ryker admitted.

Rayna chucked her apple core. "Hand me your water pouch. I can refill all three from the river before we get moving."

Ryker drained his and tossed it to her. "Thank you, Rayna."

Kai watched her head towards the river. Exhausted from the day, he closed his eyes and released the tension from his shoulders. The air smelled of wet earth and decaying leaves. Birds chirped in the trees and flitted about.

"KAI! RYKER!" Rayna shouted. "Come quick!"

They hopped to their feet and darted through the trees toward the river. "What's wrong?" they shouted in unison.

When they reached the water, they saw Rayna pointing downriver. "There, it's Basil's raft! I am sure of it!"

Ryker waded into the slow-moving water and removed the large branches covering the raft. "She's right. It is his raft—this is your bag, Rayna. No more walking. Grab our food, we take the river."

Piling onto Basil's raft, Kai looked to Ryker. "Why would he leave this behind?"

"I don't much care." Ryker pushed them out into the rolling water. "Maybe he caught up with Lucca. But we will make better time, and we will not need to stop until nightfall."

Pleased they would get several hours on the river, Kai angled his paddle to straighten them out. In the center of the river, they moved into the flow. The splash of each wave felt refreshing after the heat they had endured all morning and afternoon. Each stroke of their paddles increased their speed.

The rise and fall of the water made for speedy travel. Each time the rapids eased and the water became smooth, Kai craned his neck to search for travelers on the road. He feared they would sail right by Liam and Yulia without even knowing. Around the next bend, he spotted a few riders. Two men—not them. Feeling brave, he stretched his leg out in front of himself and glanced at Rayna. She smiled and splashed him with her paddle. Before he could retaliate, Ryker poked him with his paddle. "Don't get careless, Kai."

After the stern glare from Ryker, Kai focused dead ahead. His back stiffened, and he paddled hard through the water. When a wave of water splashed him in the back, he turned to see the corner of Ryker's mouth curl into a smirk. "Seriously, Kai, this is no time for fun."

Rayna laughed and splashed Kai again.

"Very funny," Kai said, returning the favor drenching her.

Before he could splash Ryker, the river dipped and the rushing water bounced them along. The surge of water increased their speed, and everyone paddled to avoid a downed tree on their right. Large rocks near the center pushed them farther and farther left. The black rock median came dangerously close. Ryker used his paddle to angle them away.

A man and woman waved to them from the other side. Kai watched their raft sail in the opposite direction. They looked totally at ease on the river. It made him wish Basil was with them. He had been so helpful knowing when and where to traverse the rapids.

As the sun began to sink on the horizon, the river carved deeper into the landscape and the ground rose higher. Barely rested from their last set of rapids, Kai took a breath and paddled. Navigating the cascades, Ryker barked out orders to keep them angled in the right direction.

Kai and Rayna sat on either side, paddling with or against the waves to avoid rocks. "A few yards ahead," Ryker called. "There is a split in the rocks dividing the river and switching the flow, stay to the right!" he yelled.

Kai dug into the water with his paddle. He could already feel the pull of the crossing. "Harder, paddle harder!" he hollered.

Everyone paddled as hard and as fast as they could. As they neared the crossing, the rush threatened to pull them into what was best described as a vortex churning in the center of the roaring rapids. With Basil, crossing these spots seemed simple—now they fought for their lives. The cold water splashed over the sides of their raft and seeped through the timbers.

In the hopes of veering them to the right, Kai leaned away from the curling vortex that begged them to come closer. The speed of the craft slowed, and the whirling water sucked at their raft. They were losing control. No amount of paddling was going to stop them. The churning vortex pulled them into the crossing.

"Paddle!" Ryker ordered.

When they hit the center, Kai expected them to shoot out the other side as he'd seen another rafter do the day before. Instead, they bounced off the rocks and spun back into the churning whirlpool. Their angle was all wrong. As they bounced and turned in the center, water swamped them from all sides. Rayna fell into the center of the raft. Ryker paddled but nothing changed.

Kai looked at the bindings holding their raft together. Two strands broke, then another. "The raft is breaking apart!" He stared at Ryker and then the raging water on both sides.

The sharp, slippery rocks provided no chance to evacuate. There were nearly fifty feet of treacherous rapids between them and the shore on either side. If they were going to survive, he needed to think fast. Taking hold of his crystal, he took a breath and reached for the golden thread within his soul. The magic coursing through his veins felt powerful.

Not wanting the break the raft further, he jumped into the river as the transformation began. The rushing water pushed him under and carried him away. His spine rippled with new vertebrae, and his body expanded. His fingers curled into sharp talons and his arms bulged with muscle mass. As his wings unfurled, Kai became the silver dragon.

Bursting out of the river, his dragon wings stretched wide, lifting him into the air. Circling back to the others, he saw Ryker grab hold of Rayna as the raft broke apart. They fell into the water and disappeared. Fixated on the river, he waited for them to resurface. Rayna popped up first, then Ryker. Kai flew over the rapids after her. Gliding over the water, he grabbed Rayna with his talons, careful not to squeeze too hard. With the next few beats of his wings, he was over Ryker and lifted him from the roaring rapids.

Up into the sky Kai flew, ever mindful of his friends dangling in his talons. Near the riverbank, Kai eased Rayna and Ryker close to the ground and let go. They dropped to the ground and turned to face him. He knew what this meant—if he changed back, he would be of no use to them.

Interrupting his thoughts, he heard Ryker in his head. *You did the right thing, Kai. Saving us.* The man's warm hand touched Kai's scaly dragon face. *Do you feel up to flying? We must continue to search for Liam and Yulia.*

Kai thought about the risks. *I will not endanger you and Rayna for speed.*

You can do this, Kai. Just keep near the ground. If you lose your connection, we won't have far to fall.

He looked to Rayna for her approval. She shook her head and spoke out loud. "I believe in you, Kai."

The pressure of carrying them weighed on his heart, but he lowered his dragon wing to allow them to climb up. Their weight was hardly noticeable. With a few thrusts of his wings, he lifted into the air. Higher and higher he went. Below on the ground, he saw his shadow, the span of his wings and the curve of his long barbed tail. Then he noticed how high he was and swept closer to the road. The wind in his face felt amazing and the pleasure of gliding filled him with excitement and desire.

The dragon within begged to go faster, to belch fire, and warble. He let out a chirp and spat a flame across the sky. In the back of his mind, he heard a voice. *Kai, hold fast to your real life. Find the balance between your two worlds.* Ryker touched his neck.

The reminder shook Kai's core, and he dropped a few feet. Holding his breath, he refocused his mind to keep the connection to his Beastmaster form and his life as a person. He flew straight and steady, alternating his mind between his mission and his dragon form.

To Kai's relief on the road ahead, he spotted a group making camp. On his second pass, he saw Liam and Yulia. He dropped to the ground and let Ryker and Rayna down. Unsure what else to do, he let his mind flood with memories. He released the golden cord and held onto the white light. His hand clutched his white crystal and he transformed back into his natural form. Disoriented and tired, he found it impossible to stand. White stars floated in the periphery and blackness pulled him down.

◆ ◆ ◆

When Kai awoke, he was lying on soft grass. The sun had nearly set and he saw Liam and Yulia gathered near the water's edge. They whispered and walked the riverbank. Liam pointed to the opposite side, a level spot of grass in the curve of the river. Yulia nodded in agreement. Liam stepped forward.

Beside him, Rayna held his hand, Kai watched, curious. "Rayna, what are they doing?"

She leaned over him, "You're awake. I tried to wake you, but the transformation was too much for me to correct without another Kodama."

"How long have I been asleep?" he sat up and looked around.

"Not long, maybe an hour. I guess I helped a little." She motioned to the changing sky.

"What is happening?" he asked again.

"According to Yulia, this is a narrow point in the Makani River. They elders would like a bridge built to connect both sides. Liam asked for the honor of making it."

Liam approached the river. The smooth flow glistened with sunshine. On one knee, Liam pushed his hands into the soil. The ground rumbled. Stone punched up through the ground in front of Liam. Sod burst into the air. Liam's arm muscles flexed as he curled them. Slowly Liam arched his arms upward and joined them together as he stood. On the opposite side of the river, more rock emerged from the soil. From where Kai sat, he smelled dirt and grass.

Thunder shook the ground, and the two structures curved toward one another over the narrow point in the river. As Liam's hands came together, the stone arches merged, forming one solid bridge. Pleased, Liam stepped through the group.

Interested to see what might happen next, Kai stood and joined the gathering. Feeling disoriented, he leaned into Rayna. Standing in a semicircle, the group watched. Everyone waited while Liam studied the ground. Happy with the location, he rubbed the dirt with his hand in an ever-expanding circle. Beneath his friend's touch, the soil turned to solid stone. Even in the fading light, Kai could see the polished sheen Liam created.

Perched on his knees, Liam pulled on the edge of the disk. As if working clay, the stone responded and expanded five feet wide. With no effort at all, he spun the stone slab. Using the palm of his hand, Liam pushed downward creating a rock bowl with a lip.

Pleased with his handiwork, he stepped to the center of the bowl and tapped his fingers over the middle. Over and over, he struck the same area. To Kai's surprise, the hard surface turned to dust beneath his touch. If Kai had not seen it with his own eyes, he would not have believed it possible. "That was spectacular, Liam."

Liam smiled but did not boast. "Good to see you up and about, Kai. Ryker told me you were chasing Lucca and Basil. And that you needed my help through the Mystic Islands."

"That is the long and short of it." Kai bobbed his head. "I mean to save my mother when the manta rays come near the islands. I can only hope we are not too late."

"Well then, it sounds like there's no time to waste. We will leave first thing in the morning."

While a man named Chance built a fire at the center of the stone firepit Liam created, Ryker, Liam and Kai caught fish from the river to provide a bountiful dinner. They were all content despite what was to come once they reached the shore.

Later that evening, Kai found a place to lie on the ground near two trees. Liam took a spot a few feet away.

Kai gazed up at the starlit sky. "Liam, you said Benmar asked you to come to my aid. Why did you?"

Liam stared at the blazing fire. "Benmar, your grandfather, is a good man. Many seek him out as a teacher, but he only accepts a few. Make no mistake, the chiefs and the unie watch him. They are not fond of him or his living with dragons. You must remember, he is Keegan's father in their minds, first and foremost."

"If he is such an outcast, why in the world did you ask him to be your mentor?"

Befuddled, Liam tossed up his hands. "I didn't! He approached me in the Agora on the day of my blessing. He told me we had a friend in common. Benmar follows you very closely. He mentioned your name, and I was hooked. You made such an impression that day near Chenowith—the day in the clearing with your wolf pack. Benmar told me when it was your time to claim your own birthright, the elders might not send a Stoneking to open the way. I was happy to come. I don't believe anyone has the right to decide what should be up to Alenga."

"Thank you again for being a dedicated friend." Kai acknowledged the support. "I know Lucca thinks very little of Benmar. What do you think of him?"

"Strong-willed, wise yet kind. He took me flying once. He climbed so high into the pitch-black sky. I had a strap around his dragon's neck, and I held on tight. Your grandfather rolled into a dive." Liam's expression filled with delight.

Listening to his friend speak of his grandfather reminded him of his own experiences with the man. He had a good soul, and no matter what Lucca thought, Benmar did not make Keegan into the man he'd become. Keegan chose his own path.

"I thought we were going to crash into Baden Lake," Liam continued. "At the last moment, he pulled up and skimmed the surface. The water sprayed up behind us. I have never felt anything like it. He treats me like family."

"Sounds amazing. The flying part." Kai reflected on his own flight as a dragon. Kai brought his eyes down from the night sky. Liam's peaceful nature was still there. He had the same calm demeanor from two years ago. "Can I ask you a question, Liam?"

"You mean, besides that one?" Liam chuckled. "Sure, go ahead."

"Were you angry that I lied to you about who I was when we met?"

"Why would I be angry? If I remember, you didn't really *lie*. You may have omitted your last name and the fact that at the time, you thought you were a Half-Light, but you never lied. You were curious. Who wouldn't be? Your mother told you stories. That's what mothers do. Kendra told you stories to earn your trust. Clearly, you have gifts. A talent like yours would not have stayed hidden. You are no Half-Light. You are a true Katori child, and I believe you had every right to know your heritage."

"Maybe. But not everyone believes I should have been allowed to come here. That I should have been denied my gifts."

"That was for Alenga to decide. And she does choose." Liam scoffed. "Did you know, not everyone has a gift? That not everyone is blessed by Alenga?"

"I'd heard that. Why?"

"You would have to ask Alenga. It is her decision. Often those that don't have a gift admit they never really wanted the responsibility. I think Alenga knows our hearts. Mind you, they still have the speed, the ability to glean, and long life. The few that are disappointed go a little crazy at first. But they accept their fates."

"Sounds like maybe Alenga was right to pass them over. If they go crazy without power, what would they do if they had it?"

Liam laughed. "My thoughts exactly."

"Are you two going to talk all night?" Ryker chided. "Or would one of you like to swap the midnight shift with me?"

"Sorry, Ryker." Kai turned over and closed his eyes.

CHAPTER 24

Within Reach

Once on the road, they ventured due east into the rising sun. High above a flock of birds dotted the sky. This time they rode horses. Kai and Rayna together, Yulia with Ryker and Liam on his own. Grateful Chance was willing to ride double with someone else, Kai and his group rode hard toward their destination. They were only an hour from the coast, and it was hard not to push their mounts.

Over the next hill, the ground spread out into a wide valley. On the horizon, the deep blue water edged against the pale sky. It was a welcome sight. The main Kahoma city clung to the shore all along the coastal cliffs as far as the eye could see. Where the road and the river bisected the city, Kai noticed the largest concentration of structures.

Everything about Kahoma seemed unique. There were many stone structures and music flitted through the town. Before long, the dirt road transformed into a sandy-colored flat stone path with bits of crushed seashells. Coming down the hill, Kai could see the main wide road carved through the center, while smaller roads curved away on either side.

The more he studied the layout, he realized the city was designed like a wagon wheel, with meandering spoke roads connected by other offshoots. Everything encircled the center structure, the Agora, the Kahoma's temple to Alenga. It was another behemoth of a building. All throughout the city, statues of sea creatures popped up out of fountains.

The Bodhima trees here were squatty and stout. Cosmos vines snaked around their trunks adjoining the next tree. Much like the Hiowind village, some homes utilized stone structures to weave additional space and create bridges between dwellings. And like everywhere, the water flowed throughout the city—a blue ribbon of life inside a stone channel.

"Now we have to get to the shore. We may yet catch Lucca," Ryker insisted. "Yulia, can you and Rayna get more supplies? Meet us on the beach when you can."

Yulia nodded, and she and Rayna disappeared into the crowd.

Ryker hustled through the crowds. Liam and Kai kept pace. While they went, Kai tried to look at his surroundings, but the streets were too crowded. Twice he bumped into someone when he gawked at the city.

People offered pleasant bobs and smiles as they passed. Much like the Hiowind tribe, the Kahoma dressed in bright colors, though the style was less flowy and more form-fitting. They wore their hair restrained in braids, beads, and silk strips. That is unless it was cropped short. Another difference was that a few wore sandals or heavy boots.

Kai kept pace behind Ryker and Liam. Their speed continued to accelerate. There was no more time to take in the sights. Focused on their destination, he searched the stretch of land before them. Even at their pace, it would take time to reach the cliffs. A sheer cliff, to be precise.

Ryker arched around the edge of the city before they reached the cliffs. His speed slowed dramatically to weave through the growing crowd. Along the cliff, people gathered, each wearing various shades of purple—Weathervanes. Kai studied their movements and their glowing crystals. The first drops of rain struck Kai's head. Small wet beads. One, two, three. The wind smelled of saltwater and seaweed.

A steady stream of people came from the cliffs. Confused, Kai stepped closer to the edge. Stone stairs on the cliff wall provided access to the beach about forty feet below. "Wow, the cliffs are much higher than I expected," he called out.

More rain fell. Larger drops. One after the other, a steady stream of wet. Ryker wormed through the crowd. He did not wait. Kai slipped between two men and followed. The wide stone stairs were pitch black with a bit of grit embedded in the surface. "There," Ryker pointed to a long pier in the distance. "It's Lucca boarding a boat."

Down below the cliffs, a white sandy beach met the rolling blue waves. Two boats bobbed against a wooden pier. Kai watched three men scurry onto a small cutter. He gleaned the men boarding the ship— Lucca, Basil, and another man, whose purple crystal gleamed bright.

"We have to catch them!" Kai pushed through the crowd, knocking a woman to her knees. "Sorry, ma'am." He helped her stand before continuing down the stairs behind Ryker.

Lucca was within reach. Kai could taste their success. After all their struggles, he had caught Lucca. He would force him to return the necklace. Heart pounding, his feet stepped onto the soft sand. A few drops of rain smacked his cheeks.

A signal light at the dock waved in the air. The blue sky disappeared behind the converging clouds, dark and swollen with rainwater. Ryker's boots dug into the sand, and Kai raced to keep up. The heavens opened and a deluge fell from above. Heavy, blinding rain soaked the beach.

One vessel left the dock and charged into the waves. By the time Ryker and Kai traversed the length of the pier, Lucca's boat was out on the open water. The wind whipped around the beach, and Kai held onto a post. Waves slapped the wood and splashed them both. The water was cold. The sea was angry and dark. Salt accumulated on his lips.

"Why don't the Weathervanes stop the storm?" Kai shouted over the thunder.

Lightning cracked the sky. "Stop it? They are the ones creating it. Take another look. See the sun on the other side of the break? My guess is they are here to help Lucca leave, and keep you from following." Ryker motioned to the cliff top. "This is not natural, but the ocean will be happy to feed their creation and the storm will last for hours."

The darkening sky and black sea made it impossible to see much. But the sun did indeed shine down on Lucca's departing vessel. On their side, rain lashed at their faces. Waves pounded the pier. Lightning and thunder loomed overhead. Kai turned back to the cliff. Tiny purple lights dotted the precipice, crystals worn by the Weathervanes. Yulia stepped up to Kai, a large leather bag slung over her shoulder. "We will be going nowhere until this storm lets up. Come take shelter in the caves in the cliffs."

◆ ◆ ◆

When the storm passed, sunlight poured through the cave entrance, and Kai felt the heat warm his back. "Time to go." Ryker grabbed their food supplies and Liam led the group to the shore.

"According to the boat master," Liam pointed, "my boat should be ready. It should be on the far side of the beach with the other beached vessels."

Liam weaved between two sailboats. He led them to a strange-looking twin-hulled craft bridged by a wide deck with a suspended central cabin. Scanning the repairs made by the boat master, Liam ran his hand down the side and smiled. "The man does great work."

Continuing around the ship, Liam inspected everything. His hands rubbed the dark wood in small circles. "What is this?"

Kai came around the side and caught sight of a scorch mark on the left hull. "Lucca did this." Liam seethed, placing his hand over the odd-shaped hole. "These burn marks are about the size of a man's hand. This entire section is below the waterline and will need to be replaced. It will take days."

Rayna ran her hands around the blackened section. "I could patch this—in a fashion. We cut trees down, but they still carry energy. I'm sure the wooden planks still have some life left in them." She cupped her hands around the cavity. Her green crystal bloomed with light as she pressed at the wood.

Beneath her touch, root tendrils and bark grew together, sealing the void. The spot looked like the core of a tree had grown into the damaged area. "How did you know how to do that?" Ryker asked.

"One of the lessons Imani taught me. Consider everything is possible, and maybe it will be." She smiled and leaned into Yulia, who beamed with pride at the young Kodama.

CHAPTER 25

The Gemidi

Bag in hand, Kai nodded and joined the others on Liam's newly repaired skimmer. His double-hulled craft bobbed on the tiny waves next to the pier. Everyone helped Liam stow their supplies into the various compartments within both hulls. Rayna stretched out on a hard wooden deck in front of the main cabin.

Liam untied his boat and pushed off the pier. With a few minor adjustments to the twin red sails, the ocean breeze set them in motion. Gracefully it sliced through the tiny waves. Yulia perched on her knees in the middle of the rope netting. Her sleight of hand tamped down the waves in front of the boat. Unhappy with her current location, she moved to the solid decking in front of the mainsail beside Rayna.

Excitement stirred Kai's imagination. Salty mist sprayed alongside them. The hull bounced steadily across the water. He had never sailed on the ocean. His most recent trip across Baden Lake against twenty-foot waves made him wonder if the ocean's wild nature would be more than they could handle on such a small ship.

Ahead of them, Kai saw large waves break; they formed a barrier around the mainland. Each one crested over and crashed into a whitewash of power. Towering rocks jutted on either side—the very same rocks Liam claimed to have crashed his boat on months ago. Liam worked the sails, angling the vessel. Yulia's movements intensified.

The first of three waves rolled upwards. Liam's ship climbed up the wall of water. Water splashed the decks. Yulia slammed the heel of her hand down and her magic smacked the crest smooth. Gently they rolled over and down its slinking back. They raced up the second upsurge, and Yulia increased their speed. The skimmer soared up and over the second wave before it could break.

The third and final barrier wave swelled. The top began to spill over in spray of white. Their ship rose with the water. The wind pushed them higher. Yulia spun the wind to give them lift. Even Liam gasped in amazement as his hulls floated a few inches above the sea, the rudder the only part still cutting through the water.

Liam adjusted the sails. The wind propelled them faster. Everyone but Yulia clung to the vessel. They were still not high enough. The crest of the wave threatened to crash over their deck. With both hands, Yulia split the surf apart. Whitewash crashed away from them. Liam's boat slipped through the opening and floated into calmer waters. The ebb and flow of the ocean unfolded into a limitless horizon.

"With the help of a Weathervane, it normally takes two days in open waters to reach the edge of the Mystic Islands. If we stand any chance at catching Lucca and Basil, we need to press harder," Liam instructed. "It will make for a tougher ride, but I don't think we have much choice."

Everyone agreed it was a sound plan. Rayna tossed the remaining bags down the stairs and climbed into the suspended cabin. Kai followed. He dropped his pack in the tiny cramped cabin. It offered a place to sit out of the sun, two long planks on either side for sleeping and storage compartments. Unable to stand upright, he bent his back to keep from knocking his head. "Not much room to relax."

Rayna nodded, stowing the rest of their supplies. "You are going to save your mother, and all this," she motioned to their situation, "will be worth it."

It was good to have her near. He'd known no matter what, she was not about to stay behind while he risked his life chasing after Lucca and the fulfillment of his lifelong dream to find his mother. "I am glad you're with me." He pulled her close and bumped his head. "Ugh, I am going up top. Too cramped down here."

She patted his arm and led the way. Back on top, Kai listened to Liam explain how his quick skimmer was best used for racing. "While they were not really the best on the open sea during a storm, we use these vessels to traverse the distance between the islands and the mainland quickly. With a Weathervane at your side to calm the sea and supply ample wind, it turns a four-day cruise into a two-day race."

It was easy to see Liam loved the thrill of riding the waves, even if his ship was taking a pounding with a faster pace. All around him his friends supported him. He was lucky.

During the first few hours on the open water, Kai saw nothing. Just wave after rolling blue wave. Sunshine burned his shoulders and glared across the water. White puffy clouds drifted in slow motion across the afternoon sky.

Perched on the foredeck behind the rope netting, he watched, his heart pleading to catch Lucca. But no amount of begging gave him what he looked for. They were nearly four hours behind Lucca and Basil. Yulia's wind continued to speed them through the open water and soften the rough sea protecting Liam's craft.

Everyone on board seemed to lean forward with anticipation. Squinting, Kai leaned forward when he noticed a glimmer of white. It was a speck of another ship racing against the waves. Kai and his group were catching up.

Pent-up anger hardened Kai's heart. He wanted the old man to know he was coming. Focused on Lucca's ship, he gleaned the gap. They were just out of reach.

The more Kai focused on Lucca, the angrier he became. The angrier he became, the more energy built within his core. Collecting and suppressing energy only compounded its power. Unable to hold the magic back, he pushed the pulse out with Lucca's betrayal on his mind and one thought attached—*I will save my mother.*

Across the ocean, a spear of light bolted from Kai's mind, headed straight for Lucca. Kai gleaned and he could see his magic sparkle over the water. A ray of energy collided into the mind of Lucca. Kai saw his grandfather step back and turn to face him. One thought returned— *Please don't.*

A pang of sadness in his grandfather's response struck Kai, but his words made no sense. Undeterred, Kai felt compelled to continue. As if he could propel them faster, Kai tapped the ship. New bitterness bubbled as he thought of Basil's betrayal. If Basil had not betrayed them, Kai might have caught Lucca already and recovered his mother's necklace. At the very least, he could have forced his would-be grandfather to take him along to rescue his mother.

Why the man had to be so stubborn, Kai did not know. Did they not want the same thing? To save his mother? Lucca's hatred of Keegan rolled around in Kai's thoughts. What little Kai knew of his father's deeds, he could understand the emotions, but why his grandfather's feelings transferred to him, he did not understand.

Each passing hour they gained on Lucca's ship. Liam was right, his boat was built for speed. Lucca's boat was larger, but it was not nimble. As the two vessels neared, the Weathervane on Lucca's craft switched focus and turned on them. Lucca's boat slowed and the man waved his hands at the sky. Unsure what he was doing, Kai called back. "Lucca's Weathervane is up to something."

But it was too late. Kai felt static raise the hair on his arms and neck only seconds before a lightning bolt struck their sail, ripping it in half. Flames ate away the material. Yulia's wind billowed through an open gash. Liam's skimmer lurched to a stop, dead in the water. When the second bolt streaked across the sky, Yulia raised her hands and deflected the shot into the water.

Helpless to stop them, Kai watch as Lucca's ship resumed speed putting renewed distance between them. Behind him, Yulia dowsed the remaining flames and Liam scurried to a storage compartment. "Help me removed the damaged sail!" he shouted, snapping Kai back to their situation.

Kai pulled the rope to release the sail. They had been so close. Out of the corner of his eye, he watched Lucca and Basil slip away. While removing the old sail only took moments, stringing the new one took longer than Kai hoped. With each passing minute, his grandfather widened the gap between them.

Once they were back underway, Kai searched the open seas for their target. His grandfather's ship was once again hardly a speck on the blue horizon, and the sun was setting fast. When he felt the boat slow, he looked to Yulia. He wanted to beg her to continue, but she had been working all day without so much as a break.

Kai climbed to the back. "Thank you, Yulia. I know it was a lot to make up for the hours Lucca and Basil had ahead of us. We will catch them tomorrow."

"We will, I promise," Yulia assured him. "Even Lucca's Weathervane will need a break at some point."

◆ ◆ ◆

Come dawn, Yulia again resumed their pursuit. The sun rose behind them, casting a yellow streak against the blue sky. Within a few hours, Kai and his group were back in the running. They could see Lucca's boat getting closer.

In the distance ahead of his grandfather, Kai saw a massive gray and white fog hovering along the blue horizon. Ryker called Liam to the helm and Yulia increased their speed. The hulls hydroplaned over the tiny waves. The saltwater sprayed their faces. Lucca's vessel disappeared into the mist ahead of them. Frantic they were losing them, Kai stomped wildly across the rope netting to the front crossbeam.

His white-knuckle grip folded around the beam. "Go faster, Yulia. They're getting away."

"Let me navigate, Kai." Yulia continued her aggressive movements, propelling them forward. "I brought us this far, but I will not break this ship apart for your pursuit."

Faster and faster, they raced. The white haze billowed out over the ocean waves. The mass of nothingness grew closer with every bounce of their vessel. Feeling overwhelmed by the eeriness, Kai climbed to the helm to stand near Liam.

Yulia backed off their speed as they entered the gloom. The sunlight was replaced with dark gray emptiness and the waves subsided into dark ripples. The sounds of splashing echoed around them. The faintest rays of sunlight serpentine above them outlined the towering landmasses on either side.

Kai gleaned the dark void. Trickles of light snaked through the mist, revealing their secrets. Much like the Katori coastline, rocks of all shapes and sizes jutted out of the ocean floor. Within the fog, Kai saw dark towers. Looming spires of rock. The closer they got, the more significant the rock formations became. Above and below the waterline, they threatened to slice any boat that dared to enter.

Liam aptly steered clear of danger. "Here is where my boat really comes in handy. Her shallow bottom allows me to navigate more directly. Lucca's boat will have to make more turns to avoid scraping the jagged rocks below the surface. Glean the way, and you will see what I mean."

Slow and steady, they steered through the fog. Kai continued to gauge their surroundings. Twice the height of the palace, island towers loomed overhead. Rayna gazed up at the towering island beside them and pointed. "The islands are staggering; it appears as though each island is supported by inverted cones. The base must be miles wide."

"You are correct, Rayna." Liam pulled on the sail to angle them around a rock formation, "They are designed to be difficult to climb. The few daring souls who enter the fog find it impossible to navigate, and we must later remove their wrecked ships to keep our paths clear."

They sailed deeper within the shadowy mist, passing the first set of islands. The occasional beam of sunlight cut through the darkness. Jagged rock formations along the surface sank and reemerged with the rolling waters. "There," Ryker pointed. "The light must be Lucca."

A yellow glow bobbed up and down with the rhythm of the waves, then disappeared. Kai gasped, until they weaved around a rocky tower, bringing the light back into view. Cautiously Liam guided their boat around each obstacle. "Can we not go faster?" Kai squinted into the darkness. "They are putting distance between us now."

"We should be careful, even with our shallow bottom skimmer, there are still dangerous spots."

The sounds of splashing echoed off the walls around Liam's boat. Yulia leaned over the side and muttered under her breath. "What are you doing, old man?"

Kai noticed her concern as Yulia climbed to the front rope netting, her hands instantly in motion. Before he had time to ask her what was wrong, he felt the boat raise and lower, raise and lower. "Tidal wave!" she called out.

The rushing water pushed at Liam's ship. Yulia did her best to squelch each growing wave, but then each wave bounced off the protruding rock formations and back again. Waves smacked at them from all directions. They were like a toy boat in a tub. Every move Yulia made caused another set of waves.

In the distance, everyone watched as the light floated skyward. Kai could not believe his own eyes. Ship and all, Lucca disappeared into the air. The dark shadows made it impossible to see how his boat ascended. "Is his ship flying? How is that even possible? Now, what?" Kai glared upward.

"Liam, we need to move out of this spot, get ready." Yulia stirred the wind, and the skimmer lurched forward, scraping the side of the island.

Another wave sloshed them back in the opposite direction. Riding across the waves, Liam turned the ship around the next island base. More waves sloshed and knocked the skimmer into a rock. Liam cringed as his ship groaned. Yulia pressed them faster. Liam twisted and pulled at the sails and rudder, angling them through the treacherous darkness.

The farther they went, the less the waves rolled. When the water settled, Liam angled them through a narrow gap and into a larger channel leading to the center of the Mystics.

Yulia altered her hand gestures. The wind billowed and the mist diminished. The sunshine reached through the towering islands. Liam adjusted the rudder, and they cruised between two islands. Yulia maintained their speed and kept the fog at bay. "Do you know where we are, Liam?" she asked.

"I do, but we are way off course for the island Lucca took. Mine is this way, we should keep going. I can ask my father where the manta rays gather. We will catch Lucca, don't worry, Kai."

Kai craned his neck to survey the distance above them. "Fascinating structures, your islands, but due to the outward angle, there was no way to climb up. How did Lucca get up?"

"Well, unless you can fly, you don't. Like I said before, to come here, you need a Weathervane and a Stoneking."

"Not necessarily," Yulia interrupted. "The wave that washed back on us...I think Lucca's Weathervane created a geyser—a shaft of water to carry them up. When they were up, he let the water collapse, probably in hopes it would wash us away and give them more time."

"There, that one. That is my home island."

"How can you tell?" Rayna asked. "No offense, but even with the fog lifted, they all look the same."

"Do you see those protruding peaks? They are sea stacks—part of the original island before we pushed it into the sky. I simply know by the curves and peaks, and how deep into the Mystics we've traveled."

Yulia slowed their speed. Rayna pointed to the waves. "Don't you have to worry about erosion? The waves are constantly hammering the base."

"That is true. The stone we pushed is extremely durable. Not to say the Stonekings don't inspect the base from time to time, but each section is several miles wide. It would take centuries to erode. The top is not that much wider than the base."

Yulia reversed her movements, and the wind swirled around the sails, forcing them to billow backward. The vessel lurched and slowed to a crawl. Changing her motions again, she calmed the winds, and the waves shrank to a waveless pool.

Kai searched the area. "Where do we put ashore? Or are we riding a geyser like Lucca?"

"Technically, we don't land per se. And we cannot use a geyser because it would damage my suspended cabin." Liam pointed. "We take the ship with us, but I must lift it off the ocean floor. Again, another benefit of the design of our boats—twin hulls supporting a shallow lofted center."

Liam dropped the sails and leaned off the back of his boat. His hand reached into the water. Kai craned to observe his friend's hand movements beneath the surface. Eyes closed, Liam tensed his hand, his fingers angled downward. Below the surface, through the crystal-clear water, Kai saw ripples in the sand. The water appeared to tremor. When he heard thunder rumble below the surface, he looked to Rayna. She peered over the boat's edge beside him.

The sandy ocean floor glistened in the sunshine; it appeared to be only a few feet deep. That is until Yulia stopped her movements, and the eerie fog settled back around them.

Liam leaned into the mast. "Everyone, hold onto something."

Everyone grabbed on tight. Liam strained, and his arm muscles flexed under the exertion. His fingers curled inwards. The ground rumbled as it rose and displaced the water. There was a thud as the sandy soil pressed against the bottom of the boat. The two hulls settled into the wet sand and Liam raised his clenched fist. They began to rise. Higher and higher.

Through the fog they were lifted, the blue sky returned. Etched black stone towered beside them with various ledges covered green foliage. Below them, the fog closed in around the water. The wind pressed down on them as they rose, Liam took them higher still. Above them, Kai saw a green edge protruding out from the black rock. As they came level with the extensive outcropping, four men waited at the entrance to a stone archway.

Liam brought the ship even with them and stopped. The men performed a series of movements extending a platform to Liam's column. Together they tugged at the ground beneath the vessel, sliding it sideways onto the landing. Two men approached Liam's column and shoved downward with one foot each. The tall column collapsed back into the sea.

The Gemidi village was very similar to the mainland. The one thing that became evident, however, was nearly everyone they saw here was a Beastmaster. The Beastmasters switch forms fluidly from human to beast and back again—eagles, wolves, and black leopards. Blue was the predominant crystal color.

Weathervanes were the second most frequent. They worked with the Stonekings on windmills and structural repairs, while the few Kodama tended gardens. Kai and his group kept a quick pace behind Liam, who led the way to his family home. "We will need to resupply and ask around. Someone had to see Lucca. Since we have no idea where he is going, we need to ask questions. We can spend the night with my family before we head out at first light."

Kai hated the delay, but he had to listen to his friend. While he wanted to continue his search for Lucca, they needed information and more food. Not to mention, there was no use trying to glean his grandfather's location—they were chasing a Lumen. Each time Kai tried he saw nothing. The man hid his light very well. On land, Kai hoped they could make better progress. With Ryker's ability to transform into a shuk, they could catch their scent and chase them down.

Liam's family were very welcoming, although Kai got a distinct impression, they were disappointed their youngest was not a Beastmaster. Sonja, Liam's mother, quietly inquired about his progress, "How are your lessons going, my son?"

"Fine, Mother." Liam tucked his hands in his pockets and curved his shoulders inward.

Darden, Liam's father, patted his son on the back. "Don't worry, boy, there is plenty for you to do around here besides protect our lands. Besides, I have your brothers."

All three brothers teased Liam's gift. "Well, he always did enjoy playing in the dirt as a boy," one brother joked.

"Right, I remember that. He'd come back home covered in mud," the second brother mocked.

"Wait, didn't he used to *eat* dirt too?" the third one questioned.

The boys laughed. Each one bumped into Liam as they ran ahead on the path. Their swift change into beast form surprised Kai. Rayna squeezed his hand; her expression portrayed her concern.

"Don't worry," Kai assured her, "they're just having a little fun. Ignore them, Liam. They will get bored eventually."

Three giant pure white wolves trotted ahead of them. Their thick fur bounced as they walked. They were not as large as a shuk, but they were larger than an average wolf. Kai wondered if they were as large as Smoke. He missed his companion.

The boys circled around the small group and came up behind them. Ryker nudged one off the path with his shoulder. The others charged, ramming Liam. They knocked him to the ground. Liam dusted himself off and stood up. Sonja led Kai, Rayna, Yulia, and Ryker up the spiral staircase into their home. When they reached the main pod, Kai noticed a large window overlooking everything. The narrow terrace wrapped around the entire home and connected to the next home over.

Liam stood below, talking with his father. His three brothers stood together in a tight huddle. Their devious expressions made Kai worry about what they were planning. Darden waved his hands as if dismissing Liam. Kai tried not to stare. "Beautiful view," Rayna whispered. "When we have our own home, I want a large window like this. The ones in Matoku are way too small."

Kai smiled at her comment. "As you wish, my dear." Her talk of the future lightened his mood.

Growls from below drew his attention back down to the boisterous nature of the three older brothers. He could tell Liam tried to ignore them until he could take their torments no longer. They had knocked him down one too many times. His brothers roamed around the family tree. Each wolf stood tall blocking the entrance to the home.

Kai watched from the balcony. Rayna gasped as two circled again and charged. Liam dodged the first but was struck by the second. "Stop them, they are going to hurt Liam!" she begged.

"He must stand up for himself or they will never respect him," Ryker interjected.

"Ryker is right, there is nothing I can do," Kai said, watching from above.

Liam patiently waited on the ground where his brothers had put him once again. Knee down, he clenched his fists. The wolves circled and charged. Liam's knuckles turned white under the strain of his grip. His brothers were nearly on top of him. He faced them without hesitation.

At the last second, Liam pounded both fists into the ground. A large rock burst through the dirt. The wolves could not stop in time. They crashed into the stone wall, landing in a heap. Liam pushed his fingers through the soil and curled them upward. Stone claws sprang from the soil. A stone cage surrounded the three helpless wolves.

Surprised by Liam's trap, they dropped their beast forms and begged for release. Liam laughed, "Now play in my dirt, big brothers. I'll think about letting you out."

Astonished, Liam's father emerged from the house. "I am proud of you son. You held your ground. Seems we all misjudged your ability. I am sorry. Let your brothers stew in their stone cage. Serves them right for taunting you." Darden offered Liam the lead. "It is good to have you home, son. Now, introduce me to your friends."

Father and son climbed the spiral staircase around the tree to join the others. Liam motioned to the group. "You know Yulia. This is Rayna and Ryker from the Matoku tribe, and this is Kai, grandson to Chief Lucca of the Hiowind, son of Mariana." Liam sighed. "Long story short, when a storm kicked up off the Kahoma mainland, we were...separated. We would like to catch Lucca, but if we knew where the manta rays migrate, well, we could meet Lucca in the right place."

Liam deftly omitted the facts about Basil abandoning Kai and his group on the river, Weathervanes creating a storm delaying their departure, and Lucca burning a hole in the side of his skimmer. He could only imagine his friend did not want to worry his parents or admit they were really chasing a tribal elder.

"I would greatly appreciate any information you could provide." Kai lowered his head in respect. "It was most unfortunate that we were separated from my grandfather. It is my wish to join him in hopes of saving my mother."

Darden squinted and tapped his chin. "Sorry, son, I don't know much about manta rays. There is a woman on the far side of town, let me see if I can find her." Liam's dad stepped toward the stairs. "She may know something, or know someone who does. I will be back."

CHAPTER 26

Island Hopping

Come morning, Darden had news. "Chief Lucca was seen island hopping this morning. He came through here around dawn. Seems he is bound for the outer rim of our islands. He was inquiring about the migration of manta rays, same as you."

Kai perked up. This was good news. "Where do they migrate?" he asked.

Rayna placed a calming hand on Kai's hand. "Darden, do you know where they migrate?"

"I do not. Nor did the woman I spoke with. She suggested there was a man on Muley Island who might know. She directed your grandfather to seek the same person."

"Muley?" Liam responded with a bit of concern. "An island overrun with dragons. What crazy person lives there?"

A sense of urgency blossomed with Kai. "Time to go. Autumn is upon us and Lucca knows now is the time to find my mother."

Ryker stood and gathered their newly supplied packs. "Thank you for the supplies, Darden. We owe you for your hospitality."

The two men shook hands. Liam kissed his mother goodbye and they departed.

◆ ◆ ◆

What Kai was learning about the Katori was enlightening. The Gemidi were wilder than any tribe he had met. And they were quickly becoming his favorite. Free spirits that loved to take everything to the extreme. Today would involve one such pastime that Kai had to admit sounded fun, if only it were under better circumstances. They were going to hop islands.

The possibility that you could leap into the air and let an updraft sweep you over to the next island was too tempting not to try. Kai figured it might be the closest thing to flying in human form. It was a four-mile hike to the jump point. His stomach churned with anticipation. If Lucca was only a few hours ahead—maybe he still had a chance to catch him.

The path ahead split in two directions: the thick foliage dropped away to reveal the edge of the island. Their panoramic view of blue sky and the neighboring island was breathtaking. From where they stood, they could see two distinct islands. The enormous gap between was a bit unnerving. Kai and Rayna stood near the edge and peered down into the barely visible water below. Liam spoke with a man lying in a hammock. He offered the man a satchel of food and motioned. "This way. We are going to that island." Liam pointed straight ahead.

"Why not there? Let's go to that island." Kai pointed left and Rayna followed him down the path.

"No!" Liam ran over to stop them from walking any further. "See that marker?" Liam pointed to a stone pedestal.

The angled surface bore the mark of a red flame; a crystal inset into the rock. Kai touched the gem, and it shined red. Clearly the Lumens had empowered the stone to glow as some kind of warning. "What does the flame mean?"

"Dragons live there. They prefer to be left alone and we respect their boundaries. Plus, there is no guarantee anyone lives over there to send us to the next island."

Through the island foliage, Rayna saw two yellow eyes staring back at her. "Did you see that? Something was watching me. Big amber eyes."

Everyone looked but did not see anything.

"Well, it's gone now, but it was there. I saw it," she insisted.

Kai squinted at the thick vegetation. "How many islands belong to the dragons?"

"Four of the fourteen islands solely belong to the dragons." Liam responded. "We give them their space and they respect ours. We do not mingle the way we did in the past."

Ryker leaned into the conversation. "But didn't you say Muley Island has dragons?"

Liam rolled his eyes. "It does—but Muley has hornless dragons, they tend to be less aggressive. It would be safer if we travel around this way."

Liam pushed them back up the path. "We hop to that one. There is a day's travel to the next jump point over a wide gorge, a third jump to another island and one final hop to reach Muley Island." Liam pointed in various directions like they should know where he was taking them. "Might take us two or three days, but if we catch a boat, we can raft the river to make up time."

Kai nodded. "I have to trust you know where you're going."

The gap was nearly thirty feet wide. Unsure, Rayna insisted Liam jump first. The tall gangly man swung out of his hammock. His awkwardly large hunched stature towered over Kai. Faster and faster he rubbed his hands in a circle. The man's hands cupped and ballooned outward. His movement resembled someone stretching and kneading dough. He rolled the wad of air around his hands and tossed it over the edge like an unwanted ball.

The man glanced at Rayna while he worked up another air ball with his hands. "Don't worry, I've never dropped anyone. Not yet anyway," he jested.

Wind whipped aggressively around the island's edge. Liam peered close to the edge; his dark hair whipped straight up. He ran back into the trees. "Get ready, Liam. Your ride is coming back up!" the man shouted, scooping down and up.

Kai's stomach felt tight. His eyes drifted from the Weathervane to Liam, who shook his hands and bounced on his toes to pump himself up. He bent slightly and waited.

"GO!" the tall man shouted.

Liam took off running. Faster and faster he went. When he neared the edge, he jumped into the air. The updraft lifted him high into the sky. He sailed over the distance and his feet bounded down on the other island. A small dirt funnel swirled at his feet and blew away.

Exhilarated, Kai got into position. The sound of his own heart pounded in his ears. He looked to Rayna. "You're next," he laughed.

The man repeated his movements, waited, and shouted, "GO!"

Kai sprinted toward the edge at full speed. The wind whipped around him as he neared the edge. He leaped into the air. A sphere of wind engulfed him. He felt the air lift him into the sky. "Woohoo!" he bellowed. His arms and legs remained in the motion of running, like that would somehow help him cross.

When he landed on the other side, the wind balloon dispersed. He turned to see Ryker up next. He landed with ease and Yulia took her place, making the jump like an expert. Rayna paced. She took a few extra steps back into the trees. "Come on!" Liam shouted as if she could even hear his words. "She cannot hesitate when she reaches the edge, she must jump," Liam warned.

"She can do it. I know she can," Kai assured him. "You can do it Rayna!" he shouted, even though there was no way she could hear him.

The gangly man motioned to the edge. His frustration with Rayna was evident by his erratic, insistent gestures. Finally, Rayna took her place. His arms flailed and stirred the air. One foot out in front, she bent over her knee. Kai watched with anticipation. "Come on Rayna, you can do this," he whispered under his breath.

Suddenly Rayna took off running. Her legs went faster and faster. She leaped into the air as she neared the edge. The wind blew her long hair straight up. Her arms and legs continued to try and run. The cushion of air lifted her across the gap, and she landed softly on the other side. "Holy Alenga, that was amazing!" She grabbed at her heart. "I don't know why I was so terrified," she laughed.

Liam laughed. "Now who's the thrill seeker?"

Elated, she offered a wave across the breach. The tall man waved and returned to his hammock. Together they ventured through the woods.

Ryker transformed into a shuk and sniffed the ground. His beastly head shook in Kai's direction. *Lucca and Basil were here.* He spoke to Kai.

"What was that, Kai?" Liam asked, his expression revealing his confusion.

"I can understand animals now," Kai responded. "The ones that try to speak to me, anyway. Katori Beastmasters make the most sense, though, because they tend to speak in clear complete sentences."

"How interesting," he responded.

Everyone followed Ryker in shuk-form through the woods. He kept a fast pace, but with their Katori speed, none struggled to keep up. Through the trees the sounds of rushing river water confirmed their assumptions—Lucca was taking the same path to Muley. Three boats with men lay in wait. Liam paid them with food and wine, and they were underway.

The river moved fast. Short shallow rapids bumped their boat along. Although Yulia aided their vessel with a little wind magic, it still took the better part of a day to reach the next jump. The entire trip Kai was a mix of emotions—bouncing between anger over Lucca's betrayal and his excitement over his mother's recovery. He felt so close to the realization of his dream to save his mother. He would restore the missing part of his heart.

Around the next bend in the river, their raft slowed and ran ashore. Everyone climbed up the embankment and followed Ryker's shuk form through the woods. When he led them to the gorge, he changed back, ready to jump. "We are still on Lucca's trail."

Liam nodded in agreement and approached three women standing near the edge. While he negotiated their transportation, everyone eyed their next jump. To their astonishment, the gorge was more of a canyon to nowhere. Ryker leaned between Kai and Yulia. "Nope. I don't know about you, but this looks like a long drop to the ocean below. There is no way one of their little wind gusts will reach the other side."

Kai couldn't help but agree. Before he could protest, Yulia motioned. "There goes Lucca and Basil. If they can do this, so can you."

Out over the vast hole, two bodies flew on a pocket of air. Halfway across their arch they began to drop, and a second gust pushed them back up. Kai watched them sail out of sight. "How? Not possible." Rayna's mouth fell open.

Four men walked in their direction. The round beefy man asked, "You people ready?" His jovial grin lit up his face. "We are calling it a day after you lot. Too dangerous to fly at night. Can't say we've ever dropped anyone, but I am not about to press my luck."

The skinny man lit a torch set inside a metal box on a stone pillar. Kai watched the man spin the metal box. As it went around, the torchlight flashed again and again. The one open side created a signal. With a few minutes, three checkpoints along the arch of the canyon flashed in return.

"Look," Liam leaned into the group huddle. "I know this bit looks intense, but if we don't go now, we must wait until dawn. We are practically on top of them. I have not paid the men, it is still your call."

"We're going," Yulia blurted out before Kai had the chance. "I've never done anything like this, but if that old man can do it, so can we."

She had echoed Kai's sentiment, but he did not want to push. It looked dangerous, no doubt. "Rayna, are you sure you want to go? I won't think any less if you want to stay behind, or if we must find another way."

The gulp of air she swallowed showed her nervousness, but her actions showed dedication. "I'll go first," Rayna stepped up. "I'm guessing those other signals were from other Weathervanes meant to keep me afloat."

"You are correct. Like I said, we've never dropped anyone, and I've been doing this for over a decade."

Everyone else stepped in line. Liam dropped them his entire pack as payment. This was a costly jump but as far as Kai was concerned, he could spend a lifetime walking back if he needed to. Saving his mother was all that mattered.

Watching the others run and dive over the edge was terrifying. Now he knew why Rayna wanted to get it over with. Waiting was agony. He watched her run and dive. As the wind carried her, he held his breath.

Each bounce along the way kept her afloat until she dropped out of sight onto the other side.

Ryker went next.

Liam nudged Kai. "You're up after Yulia."

When it came to his turn, Kai bounced on his heels to pump up his adrenaline, then as fast as he could, Kai sprinted down the dirt path toward the edge. Arms outstretched, he dove into the emptiness. A rush of air propelled him skyward. He could feel the different gusts lifting and pushing him along. From his viewpoint, he could almost see over the mountains. The sky was turning orange and blood red as the sun sank from view, blocked by the islands.

Thud. Kai landed feet first on the other side and Rayna rushed him with open arms.

"Where's Ryker," Kai asked, scanning the area, "and Yulia?"

Liam folded his arms. "Ryker said he was certain we were hot on their trail. He shifted into a Shuk, Yulia climbed on top and they darted into the woods."

This had to be a mistake. How could they leave him behind? "We were so close. Stupid—stupid—stupid." Kai pounded his fist on a palm tree. Everyone had their own agenda on this trip. He knew Ryker's connection: his love for Mariana. Kai had to imagine Yulia chased Lucca for her own reasons too.

"Since we have been unable to glean Lucca or Basil, maybe we can glean Ryker and Yulia. Follow their path?" Rayna suggested.

The idea gave Kai little solace. He took a breath and gleaned the jungle. Agitation was not the best mindset for gleaning. Eyes closed, he reached out with his mind. The jungle floor unfolded in his mind. Palm trees, river rapids, and rocks. The area teamed with life. No sign of Ryker and Yulia. Concerned, he pushed harder, farther. Other people roamed the distant village, but no sign of his friends.

"Ryker and Yulia are gone. Wiped from the island, or hidden." Kai looked to Liam for answers.

"We know Lucca needs the same information we do." Liam picked up Ryker's abandoned pack. "To know where the manta rays migrate.

Muley Island is still our destination. Lucca is traveling the same route. Let's keep moving. I can get us there."

CHAPTER 27

A Line in the Sand

L ost in his reverie, Kai let his troubles fade from his mind. The new day held promise within the pale-yellow sunshine cast over the landscape. Both delicate and powerful, the light danced on Kai's open palm. The fresh air filled his lungs with peaceful understanding. Birdsong delighted his ears. *Life could be simple and easy if we let it.*

The journey to their last jump was quiet without Ryker and Yulia. Kai kept his thoughts to himself. He could hardly believe his friends had abandoned him last night. They should have stayed together. His only comfort was Liam kept a quick pace and he knew where they needed to go.

Kai glanced at the red flame crystal pressed into a stone pillar on the path to Muley Island which warned all to turn back. Rayna waited near the edge, her beautiful frame bathed in sunlight. The thought of a life with her overwhelmed his heart. She was everything to him. Then the joy of her twisted and something nagged at him to turn back. *Take Rayna by the hand and live.* The feeling thrummed again and again.

The sound of Liam's voice shattered the moment. He spoke to a young woman living within the trees. Her small two-pod home was perched high in a tidy little glade—a white marble spring set perfectly into the grass gurgled with charm. Even the air smelled sweet. *What a way to live,* Kai sighed at the idea of her freedom.

"The Weathervane says a group of four came through in the wee hours. Paid her a hefty sum to fly them over in the dark. My guess is Lucca did not make camp as we did. He is well ahead of us now."

A new feeling pressed on Kai's heart. He wanted to act—this seemed to be the time to move and move fast, but something nagged at him to wait. He needed to trust his gut. Wind rustled the palms. The flutter of fabric caught his attention. He studied the various purple shades stitched together among the foliage.

Interrupting his thoughts, Rayna motioned to the Weathervane. "Kai, we need to keep moving."

Liam nodded in agreement. "We will only fall farther behind. Kai, are you listening?"

"We wait." Kai approached the cloth billowing in the breeze. "We are meant to take a different path." His hand brushed away the vegetation.

The others looked at him, confusion on their brows. Hidden in a cluster of tall grasses, Kai found a small skimmer with a billowy purple sail. "How much to borrow your boat?" Kai asked the woman.

"More than you've got," she chuckled.

Liam looked at Kai and the boat. "We don't know where to go. What is the point of a boat if we don't know where we are sailing?"

Wind whipped through the trees. A thud spun Kai on his heels, and his hand fell to his dagger on his hip. Yulia walked into the clearing. "You made it." Her expression was resolute. "Lucca already has a boat and is lowering to the surface. Hurry."

Stunned, Kai's mouth gaped open. Words lost between his mind and heart. Yulia betrayed him. "You and Ryker left me behind. Why should I trust..."

"The answers you seek are a waste of time. Trust us—act now. Ask questions later." Yulia moved around the group and handed the woman a bundle of rolled leather, a hunting knife, and a chunk of flint stone. "We need your boat to sail to Dragon Spine."

The woman agreed. "I'll take his offering too. I don't get much wine these days."

Liam, Yulia, and Kai pulled the boat from its hiding place. "She is not as big as mine, but she will do." Liam marveled over the lines of the vessel.

Kai peered over the edge of the island. "How exactly do we get down? There is no pillar to lower the boat."

"Well, if you thought island hopping was fun, you should try freefalling." Liam pointed to the edge. "Whenever you're ready, Yulia."

She gave him a nod and rolled her hands, then Liam fell backward off the edge. Rayna screamed. Kai dashed to the rim. A gust of wind blew upward against his face. Through the misty shadows, he saw Liam fall. Sunlight chased after him as Yulia worked her magic. Before he struck the surface, he twisted and dove into the water, with barely a splash. The blast of wind disappeared, and the fog began to collapse once more.

No sooner did Liam sink below the waves than he reemerged along with a sand-covered pillar of stone. Up through the silky fog he rose, higher and higher with a platform for their boat. Kai shook his head. "You are one crazy person, Liam," he said as his friend reached their level.

"We Gemidi are thrill-seekers. The crazier the better." Liam patted Kai on the shoulder, and then pulled the skimmer to the tower of wet earth.

◆ ◆ ◆

They sailed out of the mist. The sunshine and clear sky was a staggering contrast to the thick gray fog surrounding the Mystic Islands. Kai blinked while his eyes adjusted to the brightness. For the first time, they could see more than a few feet in front of the boat.

The pale blue sky and dark blue ocean formed a clean flat line across the horizon. With their unobstructed view, they continued their pursuit. Anticipation bubbled within Kai and he climbed to the front deck near the crossbeam. Water mist sprayed around the bouncing boat. Lucca's boat was within view. They were close.

Three lone figures, Lucca, Basil, and Ryker, hopped out of their boat onto a curved patch of sand. A partly exposed ridge of beach surrounded by jewel tones of blue and green water. The wind-swept edges of the sandbar gave way to nearly a dozen protruding rocks, which shrank in size as it trailed the rim of the island. Kai could see why they called it Dragon Spine Island.

Angry with Ryker, Kai glared at Yulia. "Tell me why Ryker stands with Lucca?"

Yulia shook her head. "We were close, and Ryker could smell Basil and Lucca. He did not want to lose their trail. We both felt if we could get to Muley first we could get the answers you needed and get back. Only… Lucca did not stop last night. He found us on Muley this morning—they argued, and I ran. I had the information about Dragon Spine Island. As for anything else, you will have to ask Ryker."

Rayna called back to Liam and Yulia. "We are almost there. I see the sandbar beyond the waves."

Their vessel fought the waves to make the turn. Yulia shifted the wind and Liam angled the sails to force them across the water. All Kai could do was watch. Lucca perched himself on top of a stone slab. Basil stood looking out over the sea. Ryker blocked the sun from his eyes with his hand, scanning the water.

Kai knew full well they were searching for his mother. Anger stirred in the pit of his stomach. *How dare they come and do this without me? Steal her away. She is my mother.* Kai's fury focused on Lucca and he leaned forward as the boat dipped down the next wave. Extended over the front of the vessel, a wave punched Kai in the face.

Washed over the edge, Kai plunged into the cold ocean. Down under the dark waves, he sank, and the curved bottom of the boat sailed on. Desperate to reach the surface and not be left behind, Kai kicked. His head popped up above the waves, and he wiped the water from his eyes. The saltwater made him cough. Tossed about in the waves, he heard Rayna shout. "Come about, Kai is overboard!"

As quick as anything, Liam's spun the boat around to fetch him. Yulia's arm movements changed and the purple sails sagged from lack of wind. Her hand movements changed and, to Kai's surprise, he felt the water swirl around his body. The water gripped around his midsection and thrust him skyward.

Arching over the waves, he glided in a funnel of swirling wind and water. When he reached the deck, the shaft dispersed and dropped him. He landed on his feet. Yulia rolled her eyes. "We don't have time for foolishness. Focus, Kai."

Their boat circled back toward the sandbar. The skimmer cut into the shallow waters. Yulia dropped her hands and the residual thrust propelled them onto the beach. The others scrambled from the boat behind Kai. His rage-fueled movements were focused on the unsuspecting Lucca. He saw his mother's necklace resting in Lucca's open palm. The crystal glowed bright.

Kai ran. Fifteen feet, ten feet, he was nearly there. He refused to be excluded. Five feet, a blast of energy emitted from Lucca, thrusting Kai backward. The wet sand caught him.

Lucca turned on his perch and focused on Kai. "You think I didn't know you were coming? Ryker did not fool me with his lies about doing what was best for Mariana. I knew Yulia would help you. Go, home boy, you are of no use here."

The thought of being cast off provoked Kai. "She is my mother," he seethed.

Ryker grappled with Lucca's white-knuckled fist and he thrust the chief's hand downward. "Let the boy stay. He deserves this more than any of us."

Brought to his feet, Lucca puffed up his chest. Wind tussled his black hair. "NO," he thundered, turning his wrath on Ryker. White light illuminated around his fist and a blast of energy thrust Ryker into the air. He splashed down in the water twenty feet away.

Mariana's necklace dropped into the sand at Lucca's feet. Kai held his breath, he wanted to reach it. Lucca turned on Kai. "You cannot save her. Nobody can. Her mind is no longer human. She is lost to us and I will ensure she remains free."

Water rolled down Kai's face and the ocean breeze cooled his skin. As he listened, magic poured into him. He felt the surge seep into his back. The added strength surprised him. Out of the corner of his eye he saw Yulia, Rayna, and Liam—their movements were flooding him with power.

"We draw a line in the sand here, Lucca." Kai closed the gap. "I will not give up."

Lucca blasted Kai with his magic. Kai leaned into the pulse and held his ground. The magic from his friends became a shield and the energy bounced back. Lucca grabbed at the power and tossed it towards Kai's friends, flinging them into the water.

"You're not listening, boy. Mariana's mind is lost. She spent over a decade as a dragon until your light forced her back to her true form. Confused, she took the next form she knew and again reverted to a beast. You are not strong enough to guide her back. Nobody is. Plus, I don't trust you. Keegan is pure evil, and you are his son. Let her be free."

Devastated by his grandfather's words, Kai stepped around Lucca into the shallow blue water. Waves licked at his knees. He was nothing like Keegan. His heart ached to see his mother. Tiny white splashes dotted the shallow water around the sandbar. Tears ran down Kai's face. The manta rays were here. His mother was near.

Lucca scooped Mariana's necklace from the sand and placed it on the stone perch. "I give my daughter to the sea."

Kai tilted his head as he watched Lucca grab a large rock. His heart pounded in his ears and he felt the weight of the world fall on his shoulders. It could not end like this; he would not lose her now.

Tears ran down Lucca's face and he lifted the stone over his head. "I love you Mariana, may you find peace."

All the years of sorrow swelled in Kai's chest. In his mind he could see his mother, feel her very soul. He could not let her go. Not wanting the moment to continue, he held his breath and charged at Lucca. His magic gripped time like a vice. Everything around him felt heavy and thick as time slowed down, but Kai pressed forward.

With Lucca's arms slowly falling, Mariana's crystal sparked to life. Blue and white light beamed from the stone. Seconds before he crushed the stone into dust, Kai scooped it away with his hand and dove into the water, putting distance between him and his grandfather.

Rayna and Yulia yelled in their direction. Everyone spun to see a Caroco ship bearing down on them. They had all been so busy arguing amongst themselves they did not see it come around the far side of the mist. Ryker shouted, "Get out of the water, Kai!"

At ramming speed, the ship sailed into the shallow water. Waves of sand and water sprayed as the vessel beached itself. Wind whipped through the air. Keegan and four Weathervanes jumped into the sand. Their purple crystals beamed with magic. Fear gripped at Kai. His friends glanced at him for direction. He had no idea what to do.

More of Keegan's men hopped onto the beach. There were four of them, their crystals shining blue—Beastmasters. They were followed by dozens of soldiers in black with a red star on their chest. They stood behind their leader, poised to strike. Kai held his breath at the sight of them. They were outnumbered.

"My son," Keegan smirked, "we finally meet face to face."

Lucca glared at the sight of Keegan. "Why are you here?"

"I came for my son—he belongs to me."

"I am not your son!" Kai shouted.

Keegan laughed. "You are every bit my son. As we sailed around the Mystics, I felt your fury. Your magic electrified the air. I see your passion even now behind your changing eyes. You are just like me—as is your white crystal."

Kai had noticed the tension in his mind and felt it change the color of his blue eyes to green. "I am nothing like you, Keegan, and your crystal is no longer white. It is black, just like your soul."

Keegan snarled and pointed at Lucca. "This man ruined me, and he will do the same to you. Trust me, son, Lucca took everything from you. Anything bad that has ever happened to you is his fault. Let me guess, he stood against your Conhaspriga. His Guardians tried to keep you out."

Kai twisted his eyes to glare at Lucca, but his grandfather stood resolute. Keegan laughed. "I'm right, he did. Every moment you suffered after the loss of your mother is his doing. The Katori elders were cruel to abandon you."

His father's words stung, but it was all true. Lucca had never believed in him. Hatred filled his heart, and he turned to glare at his grandfather. Before he spoke, Rayna's soft hand clasped with his. "I believe in you."

Lucca clenched his jaw, but his gaze lowered. "Keegan is not wrong, Kai. I made choices. They may have been mistakes, but everything I did was out of love for my daughter—even today."

The thought of his mother reminded Kai why they were all here. He could not risk Keegan discovering the truth about his mother being alive. His only choice, for now, was to align with Lucca. "I stand with my chief—my grandfather. I will never follow you, Keegan. You should leave."

"I was afraid you might choose him." Keegan motioned to his men.

The Weathervanes began to work their magic with deft aggressive strokes. They created a windstorm around the sandbar. Sand swirled, and Kai shielded his eyes. Shafts of ocean water rose overhead. Before anyone could move, they punched down on Kai's group.

Kai fell, pounded into the beach. He gasped for air, and the water poured over him. Dazed, he searched for Rayna. To his surprise, Rayna, Yulia, and Liam remained standing. A cascade of water slid off a dome of air created by Yulia's outstretched hands. Ryker and Basil pulled themselves up from the wet sand. Lucca stood in a dry spot; his fists clenched in fury.

The sneer on Keegan's face filled with pride. "I've had years to think about this day. You bested me with the help of the elders, but you're alone now, old man. It must be my lucky day. I will have my revenge. ATTACK!"

A blue spark announced Ryker's transformation into a Shuk. Basil beat his chest, blue light sparked within his crystal. His muscles rippled and bulged with black fur. Doubling in size, Basil became a gorilla.

Ramps dropped from Keegan's ship, and more men in black flooded the beach. Lucca blasted the first group.

The wind whipped over the sandy beach. One of Keegan's Beastmasters transformed into a grizzly bear. Ryker attacked. They rolled across the sand, all teeth and claws. Fur and blood stained the beach.

Wind and waves struck the beach against Yulia. She battled the Weathervanes, deflecting what she could. She pulled lightning from the clouds. Four against one—they fought back, returning her charge. She was cast into the sea.

Two dark brown eagles took to the air. They swooped downward, claws ready to attack, but Lucca pulled at their forms and men fell from the sky into the surf. More men rushed Lucca, swords drawn. Disarming the first man, Lucca punched him in the chest and kicked the next in the knee. Landing punches and kicks, he took on the onslaught.

Charged by Keegan's men, Kai fought back. He had only his dagger for defense. His Katori speed was his advantage against mere men. The first man jabbed his sword at Kai's ribs. Kai sidestepped and disarmed the man. Using their own weapons against them, he defeated his attackers, but they kept coming.

Seaweed crawled up the beach past Kai's feet. Over his shoulder, he saw Rayna, her hands willing the ocean's bounty against their attackers. Liam punched the next set of men with a blast of sand and rock. Keegan motioned and the Weathervanes assaulted Liam with a barrage of wind and waves. A sand-filled wall of wind formed to protect Liam. Yulia was back in the fight.

A man punched Kai in the jaw. He fell to his knees. A spot of blood dripped from his mouth. The man dropped in the sand beside Kai. Hand out, Lucca urged Kai to his feet.

Kai took his grandfather's hand and stood in time to block a Caroco man about to stab Lucca in the back. More seaweed crept up the beach, dragging men into the water. Rayna was thinning the horde.

Two new people, a man and a woman, emerged from the chaos. Green light bloomed beneath their shirts. They waved their hands and the sea vines receded and turned on Rayna. She fell to her knees and was dragged across the sand to their feet.

The woman kneeled at Rayna's side. Blade drawn, she paused. Kai noticed the bewildered expression as the two women stared at each other. The curve of her face, the shape of her eyes was all too familiar. She had to be Rayna's mother. There was no other explanation for the similarity or her hesitation.

The woman reached out, her brow furrowed in confusion. "Rayna, is it really you? How are you here?" She recoiled and looked at the man behind her.

A punch to the face brought Kai back to his own fight. In several swift strikes, he dispatched half a dozen men. Standing in the center of chaos—Keegan laughed. He pulled at the sea, willing the vegetation to attack Lucca. Each strike brought more joy to his eyes. Even though Lucca held his own, the Keegan seemed happy to have this moment.

When Keegan stopped to shout at his men, Kai turned to see the result. On the ship, Kai noticed a line of men. Their arms were raised, and he spotted the silver weapons in their hands—hand cannons. They took aim. Fear gripped at Kai's heart. They were in trouble. Keegan was besting them by sheer numbers, and now he was using hand cannons. A weapon that could shred any hope they had of surviving.

Kai had to stop this. Heat swelled in his throat. White light sparked within his crystal as his fingers clutched the stone. Within his mind, he grasped the golden thread of creation, embracing the nature of his inner dragon. The speed with which it happened pinched a nerve. Kai had rushed the transformation.

A prick of pain shuttered down his spine, but he kept going. Shoulders curled inward, his bones flexed and expanded. His skin morphed into scales. Wings unfurled, and his fingers curled into razor-sharp talons. Kai transformed into a silver dragon. The heat welling in his throat spat fire across the front of Keegan's ship. Men screamed and burned.

Beside him, Ryker used his knife to free Rayna from her bindings as she lay on the beach. Her mother stepped back and dropped her knife. She was unwilling to kill her own daughter.

"Fly away, Kai!" Lucca called. "Ryker, catch." he tossed his hand in the air.

A curved piece of silver and a blue crystal gleamed in the sunlight. Kai's amber dragon eyes watch his mother's necklace fly through the air. Everyone's eyes focused on the crystal. Even Keegan stopped to follow the crescent moon pass between Lucca and Ryker. "Mariana's necklace? How can this be?" Keegan shouts.

Ryker snatched the crystal and took Rayna by the hand. Kai extended his wing and he flew into the air. Below, faces stare in astonishment. His dragon shadow glided over the white sandbar. A battle frozen by the arrival of a beast few still claimed.

Caught by the idea he cannot leave, Kai circled. In the water to his right, a swarm of dark creatures fly like birds under the sea—manta rays. *My mother must be among them*, Kai thought. There must be a way to save her. He refuses to leave without her. On his left, the battle resumed.

Kai's remaining friends struggled. Liam and Yulia fell to their knees. *I must help them.* He circled, spraying fire across the Caroco men. Yulia shielded herself and Liam with a wave of water. Lucca continued to fight, blocking wind and wave with a shield of light. Basil swatted men into the air with his gorilla strength and Katori speed.

Rayna shouted for him to leave, but Kai ignored her appeal and circled again. Two eagles swooped to attack his riders. Kai banked hard and smacked them with his wing. On his next pass, an iron bolt grazed his neck. The pain trickled down his spine.

Rayna screamed.

Ryker pounded on Kai's hard scaly back. "Fly away, Kai!" Ryker shouted.

Unsure where the shot came from, Kai came about. He hated abandoning his friends and leaving his mother behind. There had to be a way to win. He was a dragon, after all.

Blue-green water unfolded beneath his massive wingspan. White sand littered with Caroco fighters and Katori warriors. He dove low. Heat welled in his throat. He opened his mouth to belch fire. Pain pierced his wing. A metal bold struck in the bend of his wing.

Rayna screamed. "We must flee, Kai!"

Below on the ship, Kai saw Keegan reloaded another bolt into his crossbow, the bulky stand secured to the stern of his ship.

Afraid, Kai swooped over the ocean. With a few beats of his wings, he was in the air and angled toward the looming fog of the Mystic Islands. In pain, he looked back at the beach. He saw Keegan drop his weapon and raced to the back of his ship. Focused on Kai, he yelled. "Where is Mariana?"

The sun beat down on Kai's bleeding wing. It hurt to fly. Even the gash in his neck was starting to throb. He felt his grasp on the golden thread weaken. Faster and higher he flew. They were not close enough. The gray haze beckoned him to safety. He wobbled in the air. Panic set in. He was losing control of his form.

CHAPTER 28

The Hunted

Black waves rolled over the ocean below his wings. The white mist lingered around the hidden islands. Each flap of his wing shot crippling pain down Kai's dragon spine. He wobbled again. "You can do this, Kai," Rayna begged.

Warmth ran down his wing. Kai could feel Rayna's hands press into his scales. She was trying to heal his wound. The bolt held fast. It was not enough. Into the mist he flew, engulfed in the nothingness. Black stone appeared before him, and Kai veered, his barbed tail scraped the side of the island in their path.

The more Kai flew, the harder it became. He turned and rolled to avoid the sea stacks. His dragon eyes gleaned through the maze. He needed to fly up out of the darkness. Pulling against the weight of his own body, he flapped his wings. Every movement felt thick and agonizing. The dense fog gave way to sunshine. A tropical field of lush grasses and wild plants unfolded before him.

Exhausted, Kai curled his talons to his chest. Gliding lower and lower, he felt the grass rake his tail and lower legs. He thought of Ryker. *Get ready to jump,* he instructed. The moment before his dragon body struck the ground, Ryker and Rayna jumped clear and he rolled to one side. Unable to stop, he slid across the ground, kicking up dirt and grass. Once he came to a stop in a pile of dirt and sod, Kai grabbed the white light within his soul. His true form returned, and he collapsed in a heap.

A clump of dirt pressed into his face. He tried to sit up. Tiny white stars danced around his vision. His head throbbed. The world blurred in a swirl of green and blue. Up was down and back again. He felt sick. Rayna rushed to his side and pulled at his limp arms. Her words slurred around his head, and blackness took him.

◆ ◆ ◆

Rayna knelt behind Kai's motionless body in the tall grass. She brushed dirt from his sweaty head. The silver bolt stuck out of his upper back near his shoulder. Blood oozed out of the wound. "What can I do for him?" she asked Ryker.

Ryker scanned the skies.

She figured he watched for other Beastmasters who might follow. "Ryker, we have to help Kai. What do I do?"

He did not look at her. "Pull out the bolt and heal the wound. See if you can wake him. I will keep watch."

The task sounded simple, but making a mistake terrified her. Up until now, Jayla or Imani had always guided her on how to wield her magic. *They always do most of the work,* she thought. She held her breath. This was no time to panic or have self-doubt.

"We need to move," Ryker knelt next to Rayna. "Keegan saw us. More importantly, he saw Mariana's necklace. He *will* come for Kai."

The knowledge that they were still in trouble stirred Rayna into action. She wrapped her hand around the silver bolt. The metal was warm with the heat from Kai's body. With the other hand, she pressed against Kai's back. With her eyes closed, she searched her soul for the knowledge and power to heal Kai.

Rayna's breathing slowed. The sun warmed her back, its power filling her body. Beneath her knees, the grass and dirt gave her more energy. Light blossomed within her green teardrop crystal. In one swift motion, she withdrew the bolt and pushed her magic into the wound.

Her hands glowed with power. Kai's puncture wound began to close. Deep within the gash, she sensed the bone fracture seal and the muscle regrow. The use of so much magic weighed on her. She did not have enough energy to heal the injury completely. A tear slid down her cheek. A warm hand pressed down on hers. "You can do this Rayna," Ryker assured her, offering her a bit of his own magic.

The magic from Ryker gave her the strength she needed. Filled with his power, she continued to repair the damage. "Thank you," she said, opening her eyes. "I am afraid I do not have enough magic left to wake him, but at least his neck is no longer bleeding and his shoulder wound is closed. If Keegan is coming, what can we do?"

"We are exposed here in the open. We need to hide, but I cannot carry Kai and run very fast—not as a man anyway."

Rayna stood to survey their surroundings. "If we could make it to those mountains, maybe we could hide there." She pointed across the jungle.

"Once I transform into a shuk, you will have to pull him onto my back."

She nodded. "Will I be able to communicate with you?"

"I can understand your spoken words, yes, but I cannot talk back to you as I would with Kai."

Rayna nodded—she would be on her own to provide direction. After Ryker transformed, he laid next to Kai. Even on the ground, he was a massive beast. His thick black fur felt course against her skin. Thankful for her Katori strength, Rayna pulled Kai onto Ryker's back and climbed up behind Kai.

On the move, Ryker eased into a run. Rayna held on with her legs to keep from slipping while putting a hand on Kai to keep him from bouncing off. As before, Ryker's rhythm felt natural, like riding a horse. When they entered the dense jungle, Ryker slowed to sniff the air. His massive head craned right, then left.

From atop Ryker's shuk form, she scanned the area as he did, unsure which way to go. Relieved she did not have to choose, he went left. The ground evened out, and they weaved through the trees. Palm trees and vines gave way to another clearing. Overhead an eagle soared above them. Rayna noticed it circling. Its high-pitched call barely reached her ears, but when a second approached, she knew they were in trouble.

"Ryker, we have to get out of the open! They've spotted us, I am sure of it. Take cover back into the jungle!"

♦ ♦ ♦

Kai's arms dangled next to his head. His upside-down body bounced, making it difficult to breathe. Black fur brushed his face. *Where am I? Ryker?* He wanted to move but could not find the strength. The rhythm of Ryker's shuk form rocked him back and forth. In and out of consciousness, Kai caught flutters of his surroundings. Green ferns and giant red stalky flowers. Rocks. They splashed into a babbling brook and he noticed more leafy plants. Rayna's hands pressed into his back. "Over there," she called. "Go that way. Back through the jungle."

Black paws pounded through the tall grass below his head. The setting sun struck his eyes, and he closed them. The desire to sleep tugged at Kai. Again, he passed out.

♦ ♦ ♦

Rayna slid from Ryker's back and pulled Kai into the grass. His limp body was loose and floppy, making him difficult to move. Behind her, Ryker transformed back into his usual self. To the west, the setting sun cast looming long shadows across the land. "Why are there no Katori on this island?" she tilted her head to glance around Ryker.

"Not all islands have people," Ryker responded. "Any that live here are most likely hermits. People who don't want to live near others. They will not help us—just the opposite, they will avoid interaction and hide like a wild animal might."

This was not good news. She and Ryker could not even rely on other Katori to help them. Her arms and legs ached from the riding and holding on to Kai. "What do we do now? Everywhere we turn, there are Beastmasters stalking us. Keegan is sure to find us."

Ryker stretched his back. "I need to lead them away from you. Confuse them with new cross-tracks to hide our true trail."

She breathed heavy. "What can I do?" She glanced down, noticing Kai stir. She knelt to touch his head and side. "Kai," she jostled him, but he did not wake. "I cannot just sit here."

"Keep him safe. With the sunlight fading, we will be difficult to spot from the sky. But those leopards you spotted will be coming. It will not take them long to discover our trail. I will double back the way we came, lead them away. Hide in these trees." He stepped into the thicket with Kai.

Rayna's stomach tightened as she watched Ryker transform and disappear into the night. Alone, she listened to the creatures of the night. Strange jungle bugs chirped, and other animals squeaked. A rustling noise sent her into the underbrush. On her knees, she hid and held her breath. Connecting to nature, she encouraged the vines to conceal her location. The smell of freshly stirred dirt mixed with a sweet fragrant flower. The vinea around her bloomed with bright white moonflowers.

Reaching to touch one, she heard another noise and lay on her belly beside Kai. Through the filtered moonlight, she spotted a strange creature scurry around the ground. It sniffed the air and weaved through the grass in her direction.

Their eyes met, and the animal froze. Sniffing the air, it ventured closer to her and her sleeping companion. It's long, sleek, fur-covered body was milky-white with a black mask, black feet, and a black-tipped tail. It had short legs and a round head with pointy ears on either side. Curious, it climbed into the vine-covered undergrowth.

The animal's pungent smell reached her nose, and she scrunched up her face. Its beady black eyes blinked. It sniffed her and nosed closer to Kai. Rayna kept silent—she could not risk revealing her location to anyone nearby.

Up close, she decided it looked like a cat. Or a cross between a weasel and a cat, given its long body and fluffy tail. "Are you a daakoo, little bandit?" She had seen a sketch of one in a book, but in the low light, she could not be sure. She had no idea what they were capable of or if they were a threat.

When it let out a trill, followed by a few low whistles, Rayna smiled. It did not appear to be threatening. On the contrary, it was friendly. Then four more daakoo leaped through the vines. Each one circled closer. Three hopped on Kai and snuggled into his back, and the other two curled up around his neck. Kai groaned under the weight but did not wake.

She was about to shew them away when the daakoo began to purr and rub all over Kai. "Do you know he is a Beastmaster?" she whispered. Unsure what else to do, she kept quiet and held her nose. "You smell awful." She waved her hand in front of her face to clear the stink.

Another louder noise caught her attention. The daakoo lowered their heads and hissed. "Shhh," Rayna whispered.

Frightened, Rayna peered through the vines into the darkness. A rustling disturbed the vegetation. When the leopard stepped into the moonlight, she held her breath. The leopard sniffed the ground and walked in their direction. Unafraid, the daakoo slipped through the vines.

Angry barks and screams echoed into the night as the daakoo approached the leopard. Rayna watched the encounter. The leopard moved to avoid the daakoo stepping around it in the tall grass while keeping eye contact. A foul smell bloomed in the air and Rayna covered her face with her shirt collar.

The daakoo pack darted off the way Ryker had gone. Rayna lay holding her breath, partly out of fear, but mostly because of the smell. The leopard sniffed the air in every direction, but it was easy to tell he had lost the trail due to the daakoo scent. Unhappy with the situation, the leopard left the way it had come.

Rayna's heart thumped in her throat. Thankful, the smell of the daakoo masked their scent and covered their trail. Fairly certain the leopard had been a Beastmaster, she could only hope it would not return. For now, she remained hidden–and grateful the smell had improved with the departure of the daakoo.

Beside her, Kai stirred and grabbed his head wincing in pain. Bleary-eyed, he stared at her. She was relieved to see him awake. Her face was near his, she could see the relief that she was with him. Moving onto his side, he massaged his ribs. A vine scratched his cheek as he tried to sit up. The action made his head swim and he fell back down.

Rayna whispered. "Keep still, Kai."

"Where is Ryker?" he murmured, but before she could respond, he passed out once more.

Through the trees, a man darted into the clearing. "Rayna," he called.

"This way Ryker. Over here." Rayna answered, stepping out of the vines. "You were gone for hours, where did you go?"

"Beastmasters are everywhere. Keegan is here too. They have found the point where Kai crashed into the island as a dragon. Even with all my deception hunting tricks along our trail, they could still find us. We need to move into the mountains."

"I saw a long dark ridge," Rayna pointed, "back that way. Maybe there is a place to climb up or a cave to hide in."

Ryker nodded. "Either way, we should get going."

She wrapped her hand around the moonflower vine to create an opening. Kai moaned. "What is happening?" he asked.

"I am glad you are awake, Kai." Ryker offered a hand up. "Can you move on your own?"

Kai rolled his head around to see Ryker. "I think so," he stood and stumbled.

Ryker put his arm around Kai's waist and his other under his armpit. Crossing through the jungle was slow, but Ryker found a gap in the rocky cliffs. The tunnel was dark at first, so Rayna gleaned the maze until moonlight revealed the exit.

Black cliffs loom overhead as they passed through, then they found themselves in a narrow canyon. Bathed by the moon, Ryker, Kai and Rayna stumbled over the rocky terrain. A mile into the canyon the walls opened into a clearing, and towering palm trees decorated the landscape. The moonlight illuminated the curve of the stone walls. Around the next bend, Ryker stopped.

"It is a dead-end," he growled.

Overhead two eagles circled and screeched before disappearing back toward the entrance they had just walked through. Fear swirled in Rayna's stomach, and her heart began to race. "They've spotted us and there is no way out." She eased around Kai. "You must go up." She touched his face then looked skyward. "Keegan is hunting us. In Kai's weakened state, he is unable to help fight."

Ryker eased Kai to the ground and grabbed Rayna's shoulders. "There must be another way. We cannot give up. Maybe I can lure them away again," he insisted.

"You tried, but there are simply too many of them." Rayna looked forlorn. "Even my own parents still help Keegan. Just because she did not kill me when she had the chance, does not mean my mother will not kill you or Kai."

"You are right. We've nowhere to run." Ryker shook his head. "I should have seen its end before we entered."

Holding his head, Kai tried to stand but collapsed. "What are you considering, Rayna?"

She did not answer—she couldn't. If she tried to speak, she might change her mind. There was no other choice. This was up to her now. She might be able to save them, or at least by them time.

"There's no use." Rayna kissed his cheek. "I must hide you, high on the ledge above. You should be able to climb around the canyon and get away." Her tone was resolute.

"Are you sure about this, Rayna?" Ryker begged.

There was no hesitation in her response. "You know the answer. We must save Kai. Hold him tight." Her heart ached, but she knew this was right.

Ryker grabbed Kai around the waist. Standing next to them, Rayna closed her eyes and summoned nature. The wind stirred and kissed her cheeks. Stars and moonlight danced on her shoulders. Even the ground accepted her call for power. Her green teardrop crystal glowed, and she grabbed for the golden thread of creation.

◆ ◆ ◆

Kai reached for her. His heart swelled with emotion. He did not understand what was about to happen. *Is she staying behind?* "Please, Rayna, don't do this." The pain in Kai's head persisted. He wanted to stop Rayna, but the lack of strength eluded him. His legs felt shaky. No matter how much he wanted to, he could not stand on his own. He was helpless. All he could do was watch.

He watched Rayna's slender form transformed into craggy bark. Her arm stretched outward. Kai felt Ryker's grip tighten. Even with his blurry vision, and throbbing head, he knew what was happening. A branch scooped them off the ground and lifted them skyward. Higher and higher they went. He watched as her face disappeared into the folds of the trunk.

Looking skyward Kai watched the cliff walls pass by. Pinpricks of light sharpened into individual stars overhead. To his relief his vision started to clear, but his arms felt heavy and his legs would not hold him.

"Higher, Rayna, higher!" Ryker shouted.

Below, Kai saw the dirt under Rayna's might oak tree heave. The extra earth propped her higher. Roots bulged, her trunk expanded, and up they went. Green moss hung over the black lip. Ryker jumped, taking Kai with him. Unable to make his legs support him, they stumbled.

Kai's throat was dry. "What of Rayna?" his voice rasped. "We cannot leave her behind."

"She will hide in her tree and follow when they've gone," Ryker tried to assure him.

Guilt welled in the pit of Kai's stomach. Why were they sacrificing for him? "What is happening?"

Kai stepped along the wide canyon's ledge with one arm around his friend's waist. Still weak, Kai relied on his friend's strength to hold him upright. That's when he noticed his hand felt wet. No. Ryker's shirt was wet. There was a gash in Ryker's side. Looking back, he could now see the full breadth of Rayna's beautiful tree. "Ryker, please. You're bleeding." He tried to dig in his heels to stop them. "Why are we running? We cannot leave her."

"We are being hunted," Ryker responded but did not stop. "Keegan and his men followed us here. After you crashed landed, we removed the bolt. Rayna healed your wound. Besides being weak from your transformation, you lost a lot of blood. We could not wait for you to wake up. We were exposed in the clearing, and we had no choice but to move. Rayna spotted eagles following us. I found a place to hide you and I tried to lure them away. I heard them—Caroco men. Katori warriors. I saw Keegan here on the island."

Kai rubbed his sore ribs. "You were a shuk carrying Rayna and me."

"We needed go fast. She is a very brave woman." Ryker finally stopped.

Tall palm trees now blocked their view of Rayna's tree. Kai stepped to the left to bring her back in view. From this distance, she seemed small against the black stone backdrop. He pushed his foot down and took a step then a second step back in her direction. On his fourth step he collapsed. "We must not leave her behind." He craned his neck to see around another treetop.

"We cannot go back," Ryker responded, although he followed Kai without resistance.

This didn't feel right to Kai. She should not sacrifice herself for him. More than ever he wanted to go back. This was all his fault. If only he'd stayed in the glade this morning. He felt sad seeing her standing all alone.

There was a whisper on the wind. *Come back.* Kai felt Rayna's plea. Empathic to her plight, he edged closer. Moonlight bathed her tree embodied tower of strength. A statue of life in a barky tomb. He wanted to run to her, but he lacked to muscle control to do so.

Down in the valley below, Keegan and his men wormed through the canyon. It was too late. Trapped, Rayna would stand alone. From this distance, all Kai could do was watch in fear. What would Keegan do against one lone Kodama?

Unable to stand on his own, Kai crawled on his hands and knees back in her direction. Ryker grabbed his shoulder. "Stop, Kai. There is nothing we can do."

There was something he could do—go back. He watched Keegan study Rayna's tree, but he could not hear the man's words. The men with him searched the bushes and rocks. A tightness clamped around Kai's chest. He pulled free and scrambled around the ledge. He had to get closer. He had to save her.

Then Kai heard him.

"Oh, my dear Kodama sister." Keegan's words echoed through the canyon. "How foolish of you. A lone oak in the middle of a palm tree jungle. Where is my son?"

Kai wanted to vomit when Keegan ran his hands up her trunk. He tried to stand, but Ryker's hand pushed him to the ground and held him fast.

"Where is the trickster Ryker? Does he lay in wait?" Keegan stepped back and whispered to his men.

Kai edged closer, pulling Ryker with him. "Come out, dear girl, there is no need to hide in your tree. I will find Kai. Then you will all explain to me what you were doing on that sandbar."

The hair on the back of Kai's neck stood on end. Magic filled the air. Black clouds blocked out the moon and stars. Wind stirred the air and Kai tensed. Thunder rumbled in the sky. White lightning streaked across the darkness. "What are they doing?" Kai whispered.

"I don't know," Ryker answered, crawling along the edge to get a closer look himself.

"If you will not come out willingly," Keegan seethed, "I will drive you out." He motioned to his men—Weathervanes wielding their power to create the brooding storm.

One man flicked his wrist and bolt of lightning zapped the top branches of Rayna's tree. Sparks popped and she caught fire. The oil within her leaves bloomed into a pale-pink glow, before turning ash-white, and blowing away in the wind. Her upper branches burned. Rayna's tree swayed. The strike flashed in Kai's eyes and his heart wrenched with pain. His soul heard her screams. He had to help her. "NO!" he shouted, but his voice was lost in the storm.

Kai crawled closer. Tears ran down his cheeks as he watched a second bolt of lightning strike Rayna's trunk and lower branches. The tree burst into flames. Keegan laughed. "Stubborn girl. Hit her again and again."

The sight of her burning made Kai wretch. Her screams intensified within Kai's soul. A third and fourth bolt struck Rayna and the tree split, collapsing to the ground. Flames ate her bark. Smoke curled high into the air. The smell burned his throat. Agony shot through his heart. She was dying, and he could not save her.

Adrenaline coursed through Kai's veins. He curled his fingers in the moss and pulled at the lifeforce around him. The vegetation beneath his hands withered and turned black. Some of his strength return to him, and he hobbled around the edge. One hand traced the rock face wall, and with it, he took more power. His might returned with each step.

Her screams subsided, and silence engulfed Kai's mind. Loss and rage battled within him, and he dove headfirst off the cliff, barreling into three of the Weathervanes, breaking his fall. They did not get up.

Ryker landed as a shuk, taking out five Caroco soldiers. One man tried to get up, and Ryker's beastly paw punched him back to the ground. His silver eyes zeroed in on Keegan before he transformed back into his natural body.

Surveying the new players on the field, Keegan spun on his heels. "There you are, my son. And you brought your dog with you. Ryker—still chasing what is not yours, I see."

Hatred bubbled inside Kai as he listened to the pop and crackle of the fire consume Rayna's tree. The faint smell of burning flesh caught his attention. He could not believe it was true, the love of his life was gone. But, he could not feel her presence. Her screams were gone—their connect was gone. His heart felt hollow and empty and his insides screamed in pain. Rayna was dead.

Kai had no idea confronting Keegan, would cost him Rayna's life. His father was a man more determined than ever to get what he wanted regardless of the outcome. Keegan murdered Rayna to get at him and now all he wanted was revenge. Spiteful angry thoughts consumed his heart.

There was no time for tears. Kai clenched his fist and scowled at Keegan. "You will pay for her loss, Keegan."

"My dear boy. You cared for her." Keegan smirked. "What a mistake. I must harden your heart. We are gods. There is no room for emotion or love in this life."

Tempted by his father's words, Kai lunged, but Ryker stepped in his path and grabbed Keegan. Before he could punch the man, Keegan grabbed Ryker's neck. "You and I have been at odds for far too long. Shall I strip you of your youth, suck the life from your bones?"

Kai watched in horror as gray hair streaked Ryker's temples. Lines formed on his face. His bone structure became more pronounced as his muscles withered. Yet he did not fight back. He dangled like a fish on a hook.

"No. I would hate for you to miss my rise to power," Keegan proclaimed, pushing life back into Ryker. "You will see this world bend to my will."

Finished, Keegan dropped Ryker to the ground and turned his eyes on Kai. Blue turned to green, an ability Kai knew all too well. Quick as lightning, his fierce grip took hold of Kai's neck. The magic emanating from his father's touch paralyzed Kai. Unable to lift his arms in defense, he regretted getting so close.

This had been a mistake, attacking a man he did not know how to fight. Kai swallowed the lump in his throat as he watched his father's hand curl around his mother's necklace daggling beside his own. Sorrow for all his mistakes stabbed at his soul as he felt the chain snap. His so-called father beamed with pleasure.

"My dear boy. Tell me what on earth were you doing in the middle of the ocean with this? Why were you and Lucca fighting over...?" Keegan's words trailed off, and his eyes danced with delight. "She is alive, isn't she? The rumors of her death were lies meant to deceive me. Tell me what I want to know, boy?" Keegan shook Kai.

CHAPTER 29

Promises & Forgiveness

"Let him go!" Lucca's voice bellowed.

A blast of light knocked Keegan the ground; he dropped Kai and the necklace. Able to move, Kai snatched the crystal and shoved it into his pocket. Ryker was still on his hands and knees, holding his chest, each breath an act of labor. Yulia and Basil stepped around Lucca.

"Yulia, please, help Rayna!" Kai pointed to the blazing tree behind them.

Rain fell from the sky, dowsing the flames. The smell of smoke and charred wood filled the air. Lucca approached, hand outstretched, and lifted Ryker to his feet. Their eyes met. Sympathy and compassion welled in his grandfather's eyes. A wave of light poured down Lucca's arm into Ryker.

"This is what you do with your Kodama magic, Keegan." Lucca glared at the man. "You siphon life instead of healing others."

Rejuvenated, Ryker stood on his own. Ready to fight, he glared at Keegan and his remaining men. More Caroco soldiers joined the fight, armed to the teeth, swords and hand cannons at the ready.

"Cheap shot, old man." Keegan dusted the dirt from his hands. "I am done playing games with you. Give me the necklace. I will find Mariana, and she will stand at my side. You too, boy." Keegan glared. "One day, you will see. I was right all along. We Katori are meant to rule this world. Not hide."

"Never," Kai insisted. "I will fight you with my dying breath if I must."

"Fine with me, boy." Keegan brought his hands up from his sides and clasped them together.

Vines from the jungle floor wrapped around everyone. Kai fought to hold his ground; he managed to break the first few, but more took their place. The multitude brought him to his knees. Basil and Ryker struggled and transformed. Their broad beastly bodies ripping the coiled tendrils. Yulia pulled electricity from the air and singed the unwanted shackles.

Lucca stood proud. Light emanated from his core, and the restraints burned away. "I have always tried to be a peaceful man, but you test my limits once again, Keegan. You do not want to see what I am capable of."

Laughter echoed around the canyon. "You are nothing without the other Lumens. What power do you really have? You're weak, we both know it. The combined power of all three of you is something to fear, but you are alone. You have not really used your magic in decades. Even when you burned your own daughter, you had no real power. She stopped you easily. This little display of light, is it for the boy? Are you giving him hope?"

There was a history that Kai did not understand, but it was easy to see these two men hated one another. He tried to free himself—a few vines snapped but were replaced with more. "Stay put, boy," Keegan seethed.

Pulled back down, Kai crumped against the evergreen bindings. Whatever faith Kai had was being tested. He prayed to Alenga for deliverance. Lucca looked down at him. Tears welled in his grandfather's eyes. "I am sorry, Kai. I was wrong. So many times, I was wrong. I never wanted any of this to happen."

The sadness in Lucca's expression wiped away the resentment in Kai's heart. He could feel the torment in his grandfather's soul. The man struggled with a choice. *Life is precious.*

Keegan pulled a hand cannon from his belt. "I am done playing with you. Kill them all." He aimed at Ryker's head.

White light bloomed around Lucca's clenched fists. Kai held his breath, his heart begging for more time. He felt the air thicken with his magic. BANG! White sparks and debris spat from the hand cannons hovered frozen in time. Lucca's eyes bulged at this foreign weapon. Everyone hung suspended. Time inched forward, struggling against Kai's power.

Fighting the green tethers, Kai felt the energy within the vines coiled around him. He thought of all the lessons he'd learned to let nature empower him. For once, he needed to bend with his magic instead of force it. Rayna's aunt Mina's advice rang in his ears—let nature empower your shift.

He gained power, taking it from the very vines imbued with Keegan's magic. Time stopped, yet he was free from the constraints. Connected to his inner dragon, he focused only on changing his hand.

Kai felt the power transform his hand. Claws extended, he sliced through the withering powerless vines, freeing half of his body. He shook off the transformation and reached out and grabbed his grandfather's ankle. The alteration of time shielded them both. Lucca looked down at him with understanding. Time pushed back, eager to creep forward.

A blast of pure energy ripped through the air, aimed at the lead balls fired in their direction. The metal balls glowed red and dropped to the ground. Lucca continued, his pulses melting the weapons. Kai breathed a sigh of relief, letting time resume its natural speed. The Caroco men screamed and fled the canyon, clutching their burned black hands.

In pain, Keegan yelled. His hand smelled of burned flesh. He turned his hand over and gazed at Lucca while his hand began to heal itself. Red, blistered skin turned pink and then healthy. "You'll have to do better than that, old man."

The remaining Weathervane pulled lightning from the sky. Yulia deflected the strike, sending it back at the wielder faster than he could react. The man dropped to the ground; a black mark burned into his chest. Smoke rose in a twist above his prone body.

The remaining Beastmasters transformed. Basil attacked Keegan's Beastmaster. His gorilla grappled with a grizzly bear. Ivory bear claws racked across Basil. Blood poured from the wound, and Basil returned the blow. As a shuk, Ryker attacked the two remaining Beastmasters, two leopards.

Using his dragon claw, Kai ripped through the remaining tethers. Two Kodama rushed him. He recognized them from the beach. The woman who favored Rayna stared at him—her mother. Tears streaked her cheeks, but she fought anyway. Her blade slashed at him while the man, presumably Rayna's father, sent new vines to restrain Kai.

Kai used his own dagger to block her blade. The creeping plant coiled around his leg and climbed to his torso. Sucking power from the vine, he felt the Kodama's magic pour into him. It felt awful to think he was fighting Rayna's parents while she lay dead only a few yards away. Drained of all they had to give, the spent plants fell to the ground.

Out of the corner of his eye, Kai saw Keegan charge Lucca. Kai feared the man's grip; he knew his father's touch could paralyze his grandfather. No sooner did Keegan's fingertips touch Lucca than his grandfather's arms went limp. Kai had to save him. Instead of using his own energy, Kai used the power he'd collected and transformed into a dragon.

Unable to spray fire for fear he'd hurt Lucca, Kai struck them both with his wing. Both men flew into the air in opposite directions. Lucca hopped to his feet first, hands at the ready, bloomed with light.

Keegan pulled the crossbow from his back and aimed it at Kai. A blinding light exploded from Lucca. The heat was palpable to Kai even in his dragon form. Screams rang in Kai's ears. Helpless, Keegan recoiled several feet back, shielding his face. Again, Kai smelled burning flesh.

Magic poured from Lucca. Bright white light consumed his grandfather's body. Kai watched in awe at his grandfather's might. The sound of his magic hummed and began to expand. Everyone stopped to behold the sight. It was like looking at the sun. Lucca's power thrust Keegan across the ground.

Behind the raw display of power, Kai could actually feel Lucca's rage. A wave of light poured over Keegan, burning away his clothes and hair. Keegan's skin tried to heal but the new flesh burned away. Curled into a ball, Keegan tried to shield his face and core.

Kai couldn't help to feel sorry for his father. He shook off his dragon transformation. "Lucca, stop, that's enough," he shouted over and over.

Lucca dropped his arms and the light sucked back into his body. In shock, his grandfather dropped to his knees. Kai looked at what was left of his father. He lay barely breathing, his charred form gasping in agony. The red and black burned flesh left little of Keegan. Smoke rose from the ground around him and glowed red hot. It was astonishing that his father survived. Kai wondered if Keegan's Kodama powers could reverse so much damage.

Haunted by what he'd done, Lucca wept. "I promised never to use my powers to hurt another." Unable to look Kai in the eyes, he covered his horrified face. "I am so sorry. I never wanted this."

They all gazed at the ground. Kai almost felt bad, but then two eagles swopped in and carried Keegan's body away. Basil and Ryker released their enemies, and they too fled into the night. Rayna's parents darted into the jungle.

A renewed sadness washed over Kai as he beheld Rayna's split tree. The realization of what he'd lost crippled him. Rayna was gone, and it was his fault. He should not have circled back to attack Keegan and his men. They could have flown to freedom. His arrogance put her in harm's way.

Kai wept at the scorched remains of her hollow tree. Smoke twirled over her charred remains. The loss of Rayna was more than he could bear. Their time together had been too short. He screamed at the sky and grabbed the broken earth, his tears melted into the soil. He wanted her back. "Why is there no body?" Kai wept. "I thought Katori return to our true form when they die?"

Yulia came to his side. "We do." She crawled up the dirt mound to gaze inside the hollow tree trunk.

Lucca joined them. "Kai, I am so sorry for your loss. Let me help you recover, Rayna." He reached the base of the split tree, but he too found it empty.

Kai grabbed at the dirt, begging it to return Rayna to him. "Where can she be?' He connected to his sight and gleaned the area. Hoping maybe she had crawled away during the fight. She was nowhere. Then he looked down at the knoll on which he knelt. Below the dirt, he saw her body curled in a ball cocooned by twisted roots and vines. "Hurry everyone. DIG!" he shouted.

Unsure why, everyone began to dig away the earth below Rayna's tree. Lucca ripped roots from the ground. Kai clawed like his life depended on it. Basil pulled dirt away and snapped several large roots. Ryker dug and then stopped. "I feel her," he announced.

Together they removed the dirt from Rayna's burned body. Her shirt and pants scorched black, the entire right side of her body was seared black. Kai pulled her from the shallow grave and held her to his chest. Tears streamed down his face. The smell of her burned flesh made him feel sick

Lucca reached for Kai. "I am so sorry for your loss, grandson."

Then Rayna inhaled a tiny breath. Kai lowered her fragile frame and looked at the crumpled form. "She is alive!" he gasped.

Lucca tugged at Kai. "Bring her over to fresh soil. Hurry, Kai. There is no life to give in this burned ground."

Unable to comprehend, Kai looked from Rayna to Lucca. Ryker lifted Kai to his feet, and they carried Rayna to the spot where Lucca pointed. "How can I save her, none of us are Kodama?" Kai watched her lungs lift in her chest once more, and he looked to Lucca for his wisdom.

"She is still alive. We can save her. Glean, Kai, and know my purpose." Lucca knelt at her side, his hands pressed into her burnt skin. Kai gleaned and saw the truth of his grandfather's words. Magic began to flow through Lucca. He could see the power his grandfather pulled from the ground.

Yulia and Basil joined them, both touching Rayna's body. Yulia pulled from the sky, and Basil grabbed a nearby tree. Kai did the same taking from the earth beneath his knees.

"She is Kodama," Lucca whispered. "Give her life. Push your energy and the lifeforce within the world into her. Pray to Alenga to save her life."

The power flowed through Kai's hands. In the far reaches of his soul, he spoke to Alenga. "Please save my love. Give her my life and all that I am so she may live."

"Dearest Rayna," Lucca whispered. "Hear us now. We call to you. Use the magic from each of us. Heal thyself. Pull from nature herself."

A tinge of green light bloomed within Rayna's crystal. Then it beamed, bright and magnificent. Rayna's body glowed. The burned skin began to turn pink and healthy. Her shallow breathing improved. Tears fell from Lucca. White light sparked within and sank into the remaining holes in her skin, healing almost completely. To Kai's relief, she opened her eyes. He scooped her into his arms and kissed her dirty face. "Promise me, we will never separate again. Never one without the other."

She wept in his arms. "I promise."

Caught between joy and agony, Kai shuttered to think of a life without her. He thanked Alenga for her gift and squeezed Rayna. She held on tight weeping. Everyone stepped away to give them space.

When she was able, Rayna looked at her hollow tree and the earthy grave she'd survived in. "Keegan's touch was powerful, he tried to make me turn back, but I held firm." Through wet tears, Rayna spoke. "The first lightning strike hurt, but the leaves and branches took the blow. The second strike hit my trunk, and I felt my skin burn. There was nothing I could do. Keegan's eyes pierced through the heart of my tree. He is Kodama, his whispers trilled down my spine—commanding me to come out. Keegan wanted to kill me." Her eyes welled with new tears. She curled into Kai's arms.

"I saw the lightning strike you again and again," he held her tight. "I am sorry I could not stop him. How did you survive?" Kai wiped mud and tears from her face.

"When I heaved to raise you to the ledge, my roots created a ball within the ground to push me up. The only thing I could think to do was hide in the cavity below my trunk. My burns were severe, and I felt the final strike split my tree as I slid into the knoll of dirt and roots. They kept me hidden as I passed out. All the pain was too much and I don't remember anything until now."

She wrapped her arms around Kai and sobbed anew.

Holding her close, Kai watched Lucca, his expression that of a broken man. Uncomfortable with asking his grandfather, he turned to Yulia. "Why is Lucca upset about stopping Keegan?" he whispered. "Basil told me about what happened when he was young, and the girl who died, and how he hurt my mother, but Keegan deserved what he got."

Yulia knelt next to the couple and stroked Rayna's hair. "All life is precious, Kai. Even Keegan's. There is always another way."

With new eyes, Kai looked to his grandfather. He remembered Dresnor's words about the burdens of war and the invisible scars they leave behind. Kai knew all too well the faces he carried around in his heart of the men he'd dispatched.

Ryker stepped into his view. "Where is Liam?" Ryker asked Lucca.

Lucca's gaze recalled the moment. "We separated after finding the spot where Kai crashed into the island. After hours of tracking the Beastmasters, I came upon the black ridge, and I found Yulia, then Basil found us. When we saw the blaze..." he swallowed hard, looking at Rayna.

"We ran to the fire," Yulia continued for him. "I have no idea what happened to Liam."

Ryker stepped forward. "Take me to the place you last saw him. I will find him."

Basil and Ryker disappeared into the forest.

The sorrow in Lucca's expression weighed heavy on Kai's soul. No words passed between them. Yulia took Rayna by the hand and covered the girl's bare shoulder. "Let us find you some clothes and water, my dear."

Lucca and Kai sat in silence, left with years of bitterness to unravel. The weeds of unresolved anger caught in Kai's throat. What could he say to this man? He wanted to forgive and let go of the emotional pain. There were no words he could utter to start the conversation.

Lucca went first. "I am sorry I hurt your mother, Kai. I forced her into a relationship she did not want, and Keegan turned on us all. When I learned of her choice to live in Diu, I didn't even visit, not even when I heard of your birth. My pride kept me away. Her death shocked us all, and I tried to discover the truth. Honestly, I blamed Iver for being away. I blamed you for being born. I was foolish."

Lucca hunched with guilt. His shoulders curved inward, and he wrapped his arms around himself. "When you displayed magic, I shunned you. Fear of what you might become kept me locked in battle with you all these years. The more I gave into my fear and anger, the more it took over. There was no room in my life for anything else."

Listening to his grandfather, Kai watched the man change. His demeanor softened; his shoulders relaxed. He released a deep breath and his burden with it. "When I learned you plan to recover Mariana, I knew I had to stop you. When she was forced out of her dragon form when you lit up the world, her first instinct was to select another creature, the manta ray. Her connection to life as a person was gone."

The road to forgiveness went both ways. For years Kai wrestled with angry emotions, but this new clarity helped Kai see he had been just as stubborn. "Forgiveness will heal us both. My own pride kept me from seeking you out when I reached Katori. I am sorry, grandfather." Kai extended his hand.

Lucca pulled them together. "Grandson."

"What about my mother?" Kai asked, stepping back.

"There is no use now." Lucca shook his head low. "The manta rays are gone. Mariana is gone. I am sorry, but that is how it must be."

Something nagged at Kai. He did not come all this way to give up. He was meant to save her; he knew it with all his heart.

Over Lucca's shoulder, Kai saw Liam and the others return. "Liam, you made it." He shouted. Their reunion brought them closer. In Kai's mind, they were forever friends. This man had risked his life twice for someone he hardly knew. That said a lot about Liam's character.

Liam looked relieved. "They had no Stonekings." A smirk tugged at his lip. "And—I can walk through mountains and leave no way to follow. The only thing is, I could not find the others after I managed to lose the Caroco warriors. I did, however, manage to trap a fair amount of them in stone." He motioned to an unknown prison.

The rest of his friend's story faded into the background as Kai thought of his mother. Although Lucca wanted to give up, Kai refused to let his mother go. He knew Keegan was still out there. The man would never give up. And now he also knew Mariana was alive. Kai pulled the necklace from his pocket and secured it around his neck beside his own chain.

Lucca looked at Kai. "You must destroy her crystal to prevent Keegan from finding her."

"I am going to save my mother," Kai countered. "You can either come with me or be left behind." Kai approached the others. "I mean to save my mother tonight. I feel Alenga in the air, she pulls at my soul. The sea calls my name. Who is with me?"

The white crystal around Kai's neck bloomed bright enough to cause the others to shield their eyes. Confidence filled his soul and he took hold of his stone. The golden thread of creation floated in his mind and he felt his Beastmaster magic flow through his veins. With ease, he transformed into his silver dragon.

Ryker and Rayna stepped up first, climbing his wing. Lucca stepped forward but paused. "I disagree with this, but I do not want to be left behind."

He can come. Kai spoke to Ryker.

"Kai said you can come. But know this, chief or not, I will not allow you to stop him."

Lucca nodded in agreement.

Yulia waved them on. "You cannot carry all of us, and you will need a ship to get Mariana home. We will bring Lucca's boat to Dragon Spine Island."

In agreement, Basil and Liam stepped next to her.

Kai flew into the starry night.

CHAPTER 30

Mariana

awn's early rays burned across the horizon. The majestic red and yellow pushed back the night and filled the sky with promise. Ripples of light floated over the ocean. Dragon Spine Island curved out before Kai, beckoning him. Gliding over the sea, he sailed lower and skimmed the water with his claws before landing in the wet sand.

Ryker, Rayna, and Lucca slipped from his back. The thought of changing did not worry Kai; he felt a peace in the balance between his Beastmaster form and his natural body. Letting go of the golden thread, he reached for the light and eased out of his dragon. The change felt natural and did not drain him of his strength. Instead, he let the energy around him feed his change.

Nobody said a word as they peered over shallow waters. Dark forms fluttered in the shallow water around the beach. The manta rays were still here. Kai touched his mother's stone hanging from his neck. The blue crystal glowed in his hand. He called to her with his soul. It warmed in his palm. Again, he reached out to his mother. The gem glowed through his fingers.

Ryker shouted. "I thought they would be gone already."

Thankful, Kai clenched the crystal tighter and begged. *Mother come back to me. I need you.* The school of manta rays turned away from the

291

rocks. Ryker's finger followed them around the shallow water. "They are coming. Are you ready?"

"Please, Kai," Lucca shouted. "Don't do this. Consider what she might want. Her mind is gone. You will only bring back a hollow shell."

Kai squeezed his crystal against his mothers. The ocean called to him. His heart swelled with magic and he dove into the sea. Below the surface, he swam into the deeper water. He stretched out his hand and touched the wing of one of the passing manta rays. Peace and intelligence reverberated through his arm. In his mind, he searched for the golden braid that would allow him to change his form. A spark illuminated his soul. The sequence coalesced into a chain. He understood their structure—he felt their grace.

Arms outstretched, he stopped kicking his legs. Light burst from both crystals around his neck. Enveloped in the glow, his body morphed. His skin darkened. Wing-like fins developed from his shoulders to his feet. His face changed. A tail grew.

Wings stretched out wide, he flapped them up and down. His body moved through the water. He opened his wide mouth, and a gulp of water passed through. He closed his mouth and felt the water wash over his new gills. Exhilarated by his new form, he felt the urge to swim faster.

The more he moved, the more euphoric he felt. Faster and faster he went. He caught up with the school of manta rays. Kai surged into the group. Harmony emanated within the cluster. The group turned, and he followed. In the dark water, he saw the giant manta ray leading them. He rushed forward to hover beside her. His right eye looked at her graceful movements. He called to her in his mind—*Mother.* His wing dipped down and brushed her back.

Their touch was electric. He saw her face. Her trapped life as the dragon. Years of torment at the hands of her captors. Freedom in the arms of the sea. He swam with her. He knew how easy one could get lost in the desires of a wild animal. The power behind the transformation and enjoyment in the sensation of his new body. He had always loved the ocean. It called to him.

Drawn into the mesmerizing rhythms of the group, Kai lost himself. The majestic nature of their swim lulled his heart. The wild rhythmic feelings flooded his mind. The dark blue waters of the open sea surrounded him. Consumed by the peace, he followed. Thoughts of his mother faded. He felt at peace here. He could disappear into the deep. Quiet and free.

The giant manta ray surged forward. Kai pursued. It advanced ahead of the group and turned. He regained his place with her. Their eyes met. Elated, he angled upward. The manta matched his movements. Thrilled by the exhilarating freedom, he went faster. Angled toward the surface, he flapped his massive wings harder. His speed increased. The giant manta kept pace. They burst above the surface of the water. Caught by the flash of sunlight, one eye saw the flying manta ray, his other eye beheld Rayna standing in the distance. *RAYNA.* His mind slapped back at him, and he remembered why he was here. *I must save Mariana...my mother.*

They dove back below the surface. He chased after his mother. He had to focus on why he was here, lest he get lost in the ocean. She darted through the water. He followed and pushed his intentions to his mother. *Remember*, he begged with his mind. *Come back to me.* The more he chased, the more she darted away. She left the others and swam alone.

Frustrated, he darted ahead of her. *Find me, mother,* he called to her. *Find me in the maze.* He thought of Diu and the garden maze. The pink and white flowers she sprinkled down on him. The sunshine on his face and the wind in her hair. He turned and darted around her, bumping her with his wing. She darted after him.

He angled to the surface and burst into the air. Dragon Spine Island was a speck in the distance. She was right behind him in the air. He dove back down. Back and forth they swam. He bumped her, she tapped him. He laughed in his mind and thought of her face. *Come find me, mother,* he called once more.

He looped around his mother's manta ray form and tapped her again. Her smile beamed in his mind. She flew out of the water over him. Chasing after her, he soared out of the sea. They were on target; the island was dead ahead. Darting around her into the darkness, he took a chance.

He coiled inward and let go of the thread that created his manta ray form. His body shrank. The wings and tail disappeared; his head, arms, legs, and torso reformed. The two glowing necklaces dangled about his neck. Deep below the surface, he floated. Holding his breath, he waited for her. His legs kicked slowly to keep him in place.

She charged through the fathoms. He saw the speck of white from the underside of her wings. She zipped right and left. He called again. *Mother, come back to me.* She slowed. Her massive form got larger as she neared. Eyes on him, she circled. Kai held out his hand. She swam closer. He waited. Once around, she tapped him on the head. The second time around, she brushed his hand with her wing. He called again. *Remember me.*

The massive manta ray stopped in front of him. Its one beady black eye sparkled with recognition. Her wing touched her glowing crystal, which hung around his neck. A burst of light emanated around her. The manta ray's body shrank. The tail receded. Mariana's form returned. They floated below the surface, face to face. They were together again. He held out his hand. He was close enough to touch her, but he waited.

Mariana looked at him, at his hand. Her hand drifted up next to his. She tilted her head. Their fingers touched. Sadness consumed her expression, and she pulled him into her arms. He grabbed her with all his might and squeezed tight for fear she might disappear. Her body went limp. Kai kicked for the surface. He held his mother in his arms.

Their faces broke through the surface. He gasped for air. Dark waves rolled. He shouted, "Ryker, help us!"

All he saw was water. Desperate, he tried to keep his mother's face above the waves. He kicked his legs and paddled with his free arm to keep them afloat. The circular motion was daunting. Saltwater splashed at his face.

Behind him, he heard a return call. Over his shoulder, he saw Lucca and Ryker running through knee-deep water around the sandbar. A white sail billowed behind them in the wind. Liam, Yulia, and Basil hopped from their boat. Kai kicked hard to reach the shallows. Ryker pulled Mariana from Kai's grasp and heaved her to shore. She coughed out water and slumped into the sand.

Liam pulled Kai to his feet and helped him to shore. Exhausted, he fell beside his mother. He pulled her close, her frail body lay motionless in his arms. His entire life changed the day she left. Her return would alter it again, of that he was sure.

Lucca knelt beside them. Sand clung to Mariana's pale face and long brown hair. Gently his grandfather tried to wipe it away. "You should not have brought her back, Kai. She may never wake up. I pray I am wrong."

Lucca's words bounced off Kai's heart. He refused to accept that rescuing his mother was not part of Alenga's plan. He even pushed away any worry about Keegan and if he might return. For now, he had everything he ever wanted, and that was enough.

The rising sun washed over them all. Dragon Spine Island cradled them on its sandy shores, and the ocean licked at their heels. Kai lay in the wet sand, embracing his mother. He felt the culmination of a lifetime of struggle wash away in the waves.

Next to him, Ryker held Mariana's hand. It wasn't hard to recognize the years of anguish on the man's face. There was a never-ending love he carried and lifted Kai's spirit. Rayna leaned into his side and let her head rest on his shoulder. Kai had so much to be thankful for, and he promised to hang onto it all.

Lucca took a knee and touched his daughter's hand as a tear slid down his cheek. "Alenga, I pray you can protect them all from what is coming next. Keegan is not finished."

CHAPTER 31

Let There Be Light

The boat ride was somber. There were few words to capture the emotions swarming around Kai. Staying by his mother's side, he refused to let go of her. As the wind tousled his hair and waves bumped their vessel, his heart pounded with delight and sorrow. He felt the need to keep squeezing her hand, reaffirming his new reality. The fear she might disappear, or he might wake from a dream, made it difficult to look away.

He wished she would wake up, but she lay silent, like a sleeping princess from a fairytale. A small part of him wondered if his grandfather was right. Had he made a mistake bringing her back? No matter how much he wanted to believe he was meant to save her, he had never seen her wake in his dreams.

Rayna sat with Kai, her hand on his leg. Thankful for her support, he wrapped his arm around her and pulled her close. Kai wanted to ask her to heal the cuts on his mother, but she still bore a few pale pink scars from being burned alive in her tree. Marks, he hoped, could be treated by another Kodama.

For now, he held on to them both. The memory of his dreams told him his mother should be healed in the sacred waters of Alenga's cavern. He had to have faith and see this through.

Across from him, Ryker also kept close to Mariana, occasionally stroking her hand. Ryker's love for Mariana made Kai think of his father, Iver. Would his father ever be allowed to know his mother was alive? He shook away the answer he knew was true; they would never meet again.

Basil kept watch over the dark waves behind their vessel. Lucca, however, hovered at a distance. His gaze drifted over Mariana and Kai, then around the horizon. He searched for lurking foes over every wave, and Kai felt the anxiety building in his grandfather. If he didn't know better, he'd swear it looked like the man was holding his breath the entire trip.

Yulia mastered the wind and waves to speed their journey around the Mystic Islands. Kai was thankful when her tireless efforts brought them within view of the Katori mainland. Liam stood steadfast at the helm, guiding them to the pier on the pristine white beaches below the Kahoma city.

Being a tribal chief gave Lucca little anonymity. His presence in Kahoma brought unwanted attention to their precious cargo. People flocked to the shore and whispered amongst themselves about the sleeping woman they carried across the sand. One word from Lucca and a man darted across the beach toward the white cliffs towering overhead.

Ryker carried Mariana; his boots punched into the soft white sand. He stopped at the bottom of the stone staircase along the white cliffs, the crowd parted. When their group reached the top, a carriage was waiting for them.

Wrapped in purple silks, Kai noticed a woman, a Weathervane, waiting for them near the carriage. She had short black hair, decorated with strands of white and purple crystals that trickled down to her exposed dark brown shoulders. Her regal appearance and wise expression were familiar to Kai, but he could not place her. She approached Lucca, and they whispered a few words.

With the wave of her hand, a young girl at her side disappeared into the crowd. When she pressed her hands together and bowed to Mariana's sleeping form, Kai knew where he'd met her—she was at his blessing. She was one of the unie—Wilda, he believed was her name.

"Kai, good to see you again," Wilda said as she approached. "Welcome to Kahoma City. Lucca informs me you plan to take your mother to the highlands. He says you found the lost Agora. Is it true?"

What could he say? He knew what his dreams had told him. "Good to see you as well, Wilda. It is true—I have found Alenga's Agora. Alenga directs me to reopen her cavern. I will follow her vision as I did in bringing my mother home."

The young woman returned with a bundle of white silks. Wilda nodded to Lucca and Kai. "May we care for her? We have silks to protect her on your travels back to Matoku. May we come with you?" she asked.

The thought of an entourage did not set well with Kai. "Thank you, Wilda, for the silks, but I am not sure..."

Lucca pressed a firm hand over Kai's shoulder. "Wilda, we are honored by your request. If you could gather the elders from every tribe, I would appreciate them coming to Matoku. Give us time with Mariana alone, but we may need your strength if we hope to wake my daughter. I will come to the city when we need you."

Wilda gracefully bowed to Lucca. "As you wish, Chief Lucca. I will bring everyone together."

◆ ◆ ◆

Days of agonizingly slow travel along the road to Matoku had Kai bubbling with anticipation. He so desperately wanted to speak with his mother. He couldn't decide what he would ask her first. Tears of sorrow and joy brimmed in his eyes, blurring his view of the landscape. He wiped his tears away before they could fall. Holding his chin high, he took a deep breath to cleanse his emotions from his throat.

The fulfillment of Kai's dream took them to Alenga's cavern, tucked in the hills near the Matoku's tribal city. Mariana's motionless form lay wrapped in white silk in the back of a padded open carriage, drawn by two white horses. Off the main road, Ryker led them into the rolling hills. A babbling stream burbled along its bed, bubbling over rocks and branches. The sunlight danced on the ripples and beamed into Kai's eyes. His hand rested on his mother, unwilling to leave her side.

Everything in Katori had a delicate rhythm—Alenga's presence flowed over the land. You only needed to be open to her energy. The closer they came to the barrier, the greater the power thrummed inside his soul. He looked to the others to see if they, too, felt her magic. A smile bloomed around Ryker's lips—Kai knew that his friend felt at home here near Alenga's cavern. Yulia and Liam focused ahead with no sign of recognition. Lucca's head rose, and he turned to look at Kai.

Lucca's brown eyes narrowed on the waterfall in the distance. "Grandson, do you feel this place? You were right. There is great power here."

Kai sighed heavily. "Yes, grandfather, it is Alenga's lost Agora."

"Have you been here before?" Lucca asked Kai.

"I have." Kai shook his head. "I dreamed of my mother in this place. Alenga bid me bring her here."

"This place is proof Alenga walked among us thousands of years ago." Lucca glanced at Mariana and then to Kai. "I never thought I would see it with my own eyes. I can feel Alenga here like no other place in Katori. Our history says Alenga opened a portal to this world. It must have happened here on this hill—she walked our shores. Her love for this world created life itself."

In a soft tone, softened Basil asked. "How could we have let this place fade from our lives?"

Lucca shook his head. "I don't know."

Eavesdropping on their conversation, Yulia twisted around to face Kai; her knees pulled to her chest. "If that is true, there would be a great deal of power here. The chance of restoring Mariana might be possible."

"The cavern is rather amazing." Kai shifted to extend his bent leg out straight beside his mother. "Damaged, but still impressive. The dome is no longer open to the sky. Maybe Liam can reopen it?" he suggested.

Liam sat beside of Yulia, his legs dangling off the back of the carriage. "I would be honored to try." He glanced back at Kai. "Knowing Alenga walked here, I am surprised there are no pilgrimages to this place."

Lucca's wrinkled nose and creased brow conveyed a sense of confusion. "I really cannot say how we forgot this place." He shook his head as if the truth would come to the surface if he could rattle it free. "There are stories about her time among our people, and legends of our future, but the location was all but forgotten. I know I have walked these hills, yet I never felt her power before. We have many tomes and maps of our civilization, and I know them all. There is no mention of this place. It is almost as though it was erased from our history."

The group fell silent. Each seemed to ponder the mystery around their discovery. The very possibility Alenga had erased her time among the Katori puzzled Kai. When their carriage pulled around the hillside, he took a breath and lightened his heart. They had made it.

Water cascaded over the rocks above them. Alenga's broken tree peeked through the green undergrowth on the hill. Ryker stopped their carriage and hopped from the seat to the ground, then approached the back. "Kai, I will stay with Mariana. Show Liam the Agora."

Behind the falls, Kai found the round stone door with the worn triquetra. Liam ran his fingers over the faded symbol, then let his hand sweep wide over the surface in a circling motion. Kai put his shoulder into it and shoved the stone. It started to shift, and Liam rested his hand on the door. "Allow me, Kai," he patted Kai's arm.

Kai let the stone roll back into place. Liam touched the surface of the stone. Under his touch, it rolled open with ease and held its position. "It will remain open until I close it," Liam assured Kai.

Sunlight and water splashed into the opening. Yulia, Rayna, and Kai entered ahead of Basil, followed by Lucca and Liam. Once inside, Lucca illuminated the embedded crystals lodged into the walls. The room bloomed with a warm amber glow. Kai felt the power level rise, but it still felt stifled. There had to be more to give. The sealed dome above the pool blocked the sun that typically bathed an Agora.

Liam circled the room, touching the walls, pillars, and ground. "It seems as though this structure sank into the ground." He stopped at one wall and pressed both hands into the stone. "No—the ground washed over the land and covered it. There are many other structures buried in this direction—tree homes, windmills, gazebos, and remnants of a greenhouse. If I didn't know better, I'd swear half a city rests within this hillside."

Yulia stepped up to the wall next to Liam. "Can you clear it away?" She asked.

"Given enough time, certainly, but with more Stonekings, we could restore the hillside within a matter of days."

The vision from Alenga was specific; the Agora should be filled with light. "Liam, I must ask you to try and find a way to open the dome— without the river pouring inside." He knew it was a lot to ask for his friend to move a river, but they needed sunlight. "Can you do it?" Kai pleaded.

Liam narrowed his eyes. "Water from the river will need to be diverted, or it will rush into this room. I will clear most of the earth around the front and redirect the waterfall before I open the dome."

Basil stepped toward the pool and looked up. "Liam, is it safe for us to stay inside while you make these changes?"

"The structure is sound, but it would be wise to come outside until I am finished." Liam darted outside ahead of the others.

Ryker waited near Mariana; her pale complexion was as white as the silk that cocooned her delicate frame. Waiting felt like an eternity to Kai. Each minute they stood in silence made him doubt his choices. Had he done the right thing, saving his mother and coming to this place? Only time would tell if she would ever wake or if his selfish act was for nothing.

When the ground began to rumble, Kai watched dirt and pebbles flow down the hillside into an empty ravine. Each movement of Liam's hands revealed new remnants of the ancient Agora's pink stone structure. Its elaborate carvings peeked through various clumps of dirt and thick vines. The hillside fell away, revealing several marble statues, petrified dwarf trees, and the curvature of a decorative water fountain.

Next, Liam directed the waterfall to flow into an exposed channel beside the Agora's dirty-white pathways. The clean water washed away the debris and trickled through the winding canal.

When Liam opened three of the five large stone archways leading into the Agora, Kai felt the barrier fall. Moments later, the center of the stone dome peeled open like an onion. As the hole grew, fresh air and dust illuminated sunlight poured flooded the space. Liam smiled at his handy work and motioned to the others to approach.

Kai felt the Agora thrum with magic. Peering down into the sacred pool, he noticed a blue triquetra inlaid within the bottom began to glow. The air became thick with power. Ryker eased Mariana's body into Kai's arms—his mother felt frail and empty. The time had come to restore his mother. He sensed Alenga's presence even before he stepped into the water. The lukewarm water felt silky against his skin. Minor scrapes and cuts healed as the water crept up his legs and torso.

Mariana lay floating in the pool; Kai held her lightly above the surface. Her wounds beamed with light, muscle mass returned, and her thin, patchy hair regrew across her scalp. Kai watched his mother's white skin regain its youthful pink glow.

Alenga's face bloomed beneath the water, and her hand wrapped around his leg. She tugged at his soul, and his spirit sank beneath the surface. "Kai, my Katori child. You have great courage and faith in the face of doubt. Hold onto your trust in me. You will need it a while longer. There are many trials ahead for you. I cannot reveal everything to you as the future is not set."

Amazed by the power bolstering his spirit form, he looked to see his mother's spirit standing beside him in the water. Her soft smile and kind eyes plucked at his heart. "Mother."

She did not speak.

Kai studied his mother's gaze and noticed the thousand-yard stare behind his mother's eyes. He turned to Alenga. "Can you not restore my mother?"

"Her spirit is still tangled with the Beastmaster coils in her soul. It will take time for her mind to return. I cannot fix this with the snap of my fingers—nature has a balance even I must heed. Know that she may not return to you in the way you hope. Be strong, my Katori child. Even in your darkest hour, I am with you."

The sacred earth mother's words rang in his head. It was hard to hear her tell him to wait, but he was happy to hear there was hope. Kai nodded with understanding. "I will protect my mother until she returns," he promised.

Alenga touched his forehead. "Remember what I asked you to do, Kai. I bid you, bring my children home—Davi and his family, and any Katori outcast who wish to return. Lead them through my crystal mountain and bring them here. You will need them for what is to come. I will grant Liam the power to restore the tunnels of my crystal mountain."

With the wave of her hand, Kai's spirit rose back into his body. He was once again standing in the sunbathed sacred water of Alenga's lost Agora, holding his mother. He lifted his healed mother from the waters and placed her on the stone floor. Everyone anxiously looked at him as his aura bloomed with power. As on the day of his blessing, he could see his friends' aura glow.

Kai took Liam's hand. "Alenga bids you to repair the tunnels in her crystal mountain." Light flowed down Kai's arm into his friend, Liam nodded with understanding.

Then Kai told them Alenga bid him bring home the lost children of Katori. He touched his grandfather's arm, and the power flowed between them. "You must help me bring them home, grandfather. Alenga also told me it would take time for my mother to return, and she may not return the way we hope."

Lucca nodded with understanding. "I will help you in any way I can, grandson."

Ryker ran his hand over Mariana's head. "I will protect your mother, Kai."

Outside, Kai sensed the arrival of others. "The elders are here, Lucca. I am sure many will wish to see this place, Alenga's Agora, and proof that my mother lives."

"Let them wait." Lucca knelt next to his daughter and Ryker. "Come sit with your mother."

The words of Alenga weighed on Kai's heart. He did not want to leave his mother, not after he just brought her home. He let his hand rest on her hand, and he watched her steady breath raise and lower her chest. Thoughts of his father Iver crossed his mind. "I wish I could bring Iver here to see my mother."

Ryker glanced at Kai. "You know that can never happen. Mariana is lost to her old life. But you have another parent who needs you. Iver needs you."

Lucca leaned into Kai's ear. "Keegan will return, and you must be ready. Gather your Katori friends before your return to Diu. They, too, will need time to prepare for the future."

Somehow, Kai knew Lucca and Ryker were right. He had to return to Diu; he had promised to be there for the winter festival. Iver was unwell, and Kai needed to know if Riome had returned after being lost at sea. He knelt, and he held his mother's hand. Rayna leaned into his side. For one brief moment, they could all be together, before their world turned upside down again.

The End